"...very well written and [he] paints a wonderful picture."
Tracie Hogeboom, *Avid Reader*

"...the words and the descriptions actually jumped off the page at me...I was reading a book but it felt like watching a movie."
Wild Bill Snyder, *Retired Business Owner*

"*Whispers of The Greybull* defies categorization. From suspense and intrigue, to romance and cowboy charisma, *Whispers* will capture the imagination of all readers."
Rock Ray, *Former McDonald's Franchise Owner*

"It was a great read...an attention grabber to the point where you can't put it down."
Tony Wilson, *Big R General Manager*

"*Whispers of The Greybull* is as well written and compelling as any novel by the famous Louis L'Amour, or any other western wordsmiths."
Bob Graham, *Cowboy Poet/North Idaho Mule Club*

Whispers of
The Greybull

Stephen B. Smart

High Mule Publishing

ISBN: 978-1-4507-6642-5

High Mule Publishing
www.highmulepublishing.com

First Edition – Trade Paperback

Printed in the United States of America

Dedication

This book is dedicated to the late Dr. William Stifter, a loving family man, successful doctor and a true hero. On a short vacation, sixty-four-year-old Bill Stifter took off on a charter flight up Lake Chelan. The plane carried an experienced pilot, along with Bill, his wife, and two other passengers. After liftoff the float plane's landing gear was never retracted and when the plane touched the water on landing, it flipped and began to sink.

The pilot escaped out the door leaving Bill in the front seat and the other three passengers in the back. Water began to fill the cockpit while Bill climbed into the back and undid the seat belt of his wife and helped her out the door. Next he helped a dazed sixteen-year-old girl and steered her through the water to the opening.

He then began helping an elderly woman, but there was trouble and the two never made it to the surface as the plane sank in the cold dark waters of the lake.

Dr. William Stifter was an extraordinary man made from very special leather and will be missed by many.

Whispers of
The Greybull

Prelude

1868—Canvas Creek, Wyoming

Vern Creager rode into a stand of aspen, leaves fluttering in the light breeze. The scent of leather and sweat mingled with fresh alpine air as he surveyed the secluded meadow nestled high on the steep side of an isolated ridge. He tied his horse and pack mule to separate trees and walked to the mule's side to loosen the ropes securing the left pack. He removed a small hammer and a long narrow object tightly wrapped and tied in thick canvas and he laid it several yards from the stock at the edge of the trees. Still wary, he glanced across the meadow where a massive Limber Pine stood alone then he bent to unfold the canvas package exposing a rusty, fourteen-inch-long bayonet.

He slid the bayonet and a small hammer into his belt and started across the meadow to the tree. He knew once in place, only a keen eye would notice it, and even less likely would anyone understand its significance—the marker that would guide one from Creager's hidden trail to the ancient Indian path that existed further up the ridge. Through the years, Vern and his brother had taken great care never to leave even the slightest trace of a connection between the two, and they intended to keep it that way.

For over a year, the two brothers had meticulously planned every detail to transfer the gold from their isolated mine down to their cabin and then to Oregon Trail and back to Iowa. Now, just as they intended to begin their plan, Vern had been alarmed to find fresh horse tracks on the lower trail just off the valley floor. After a heated discussion with his brother, Virgil, they agreed the risk was too much and they decided to take only half the gold from the mine and return the following year for the rest.

They reminded one another they hadn't gotten this far by being careless. They were smart, cautious men, having avoided detection by traveling only at night, with one brother always staying close to the small ranch cabin while the other worked the mine. By plan, the two brothers even looked and dressed alike and grew identical beards.

Vern took a moment to plan his ascent through the gnarled, thick Limber Pine. While other trees of its generation had died in the decades of droughts and forest fires, this tree had stood strong and survived. He moved to the base of the tree, and after several minutes of laboring up the branches, he finally reached the limb above which he intended to place his marker. He removed the bayonet from his belt and drove the blade into the tree between several small branches, where it was mostly hidden by pine needles. He removed the small hammer from his belt and pounded the bayonet several more inches into the thick bark.

After climbing down, he stepped away and studied his work, pleased that the bayonet was visible only with the most careful scrutiny. Shirt damp from sweat, he could feel the early evening temperatures setting in. He knew that even with some cross-country shortcuts, it would be well into the night before he would make it to the homestead. He would take every precaution, not even lighting a match for a much-needed cigarette, careful of anything that would give away his presence.

It was only a few hours before first light when a tired Vern finally saw the silhouette of the log cabin in the dim light of the moon. The saddle creaked as he swung down from his buckskin and tied the horse and mule to the slumping hitching rail in front.

He knocked softly on the thick plank door with callused knuckles, using the signal he and his brother had agreed on. He waited for the response. A chair scraped against the cabin floor, and a few seconds later Virgil unbolted and opened the door. They quietly exchanged greetings at the doorway, and then unloaded the mule, bringing the two seventy-pound packs into the cabin and placing them in front of the large, carbon-stained stone fireplace where a small fire crackled. Vern breathed deeply, and then sighed. "Those loads were sure heavy for one man. I wish old Jasper was a might shorter. Leastwise, he stood still the whole time I was loading, and the packs rode good."

With only the fire's glow for light, they unloaded each pack as their shadows flickered on the walls. There were eight small bags of gold dust, a couple bags of small gold nuggets, and a dozen large, heavy bags of high-grade ore. Virgil reached for one of the four custom-built oak boxes stacked neatly in the corner and began packing each box, distributing the weight as evenly as possible. Several minutes later, and without saying a word, the two were finished.

Virgil studied Vern for a moment and then pushed back his dirty black hat and wiped his brow with the sleeve of his shirt. "You absolutely sure no one saw you?"

"I'm sure. It was just like always, a few coyotes howling and nothing more. I did bring you something, though. You know the old Indian tunnel opposite our diggings? Well, a couple of days ago I was up there picking around and durn if I didn't find this nugget. Biggest damn lump of gold I've ever seen." Vern removed the heavy rock from his shirt pocket and gently tossed it to his brother.

"Well, that's some nugget," Virgil responded with a chuckle.

"I don't know how many times I walked down that way—probably right past it—and never thought to dig there," Vern said as he watched Virgil examine the round chunk of gold.

"This may come in handy," Virgil said. "I'll keep it in my coat 'til we get on the main trail. I have the other boxes and furniture stacked out back beside the wagon and the horses are all harnessed and ready in the barn. I can start moving the stuff if you need a break. I ain't done much but sit here drinking coffee for the last couple hours. I'll sure as shootin' be glad when we have her loaded and are across that son of bitch McCabe's land and his Greybull Ranch."

Vern nodded. "I could use a minute to sit and drink a cup; then I'll be fine. Go ahead and start loading. I'll help you in a couple of minutes with the heavier stuff."

Virgil headed toward the back door, stopped and turned, "I'll put the scatter gun just outside the door by the boxes, so don't accidentally bump it while we're working." Vern looked up and nodded.

Virgil walked to the back of the wagon and removed several boards from the wagon's bed, exposing a metal door. The wagon's hidden compartment was of cunning design and well planned, like everything the Creagers did, and each box fit perfectly into the space. When Virgil had finished, he shut the metal door and carefully fitted the wagon's wooden floor planks back in place. He would need Vern's help to load the rest. Their plan was simple: make the heavy wagon appear as inconspicuous as possible, just like any other hard-luck rancher moving on. They would have to leave the cabin unoccupied for at least a year, but they would send a letter to a friend in town saying they were just visiting family back East.

Virgil returned to the cabin and opened the door, and Vern looked up from the fire. "Ready for a little help?" he asked as he set down the almost empty cup.

"Take your time. I think I'm worrying about nothing. Finish your coffee," Virgil said. He pulled a wooden chair away from the table and sat down beside his brother.

"I'm going to tell you something that you might need to remember," Vern said in a quiet voice. "You know Grandpa's bayonet? Well, I took it with me last trip and hid it about fourteen feet up in that old monarch of a Limber Pine at the edge of the meadow, the great, big one with the stumpy limbs. I figured if anything happens to us, then at least the family would have some landmark." He raised his cup and drained the dregs and stood up.

"Good idea, as long as you hid it good," Virgil said, and the two men walked out to the old freight wagon.

"As soon as everything is loaded, we'll hitch up the team and head out. With any luck, we'll reach Meeteetse Creek by first light and then head for the main trail," Vern said.

"Do you think we brought enough out to pay off all our debts on the farm?" Virgil asked.

"Hell yes I did, don't worry. When we get back to Iowa we'll have enough gold to buy any ranch in the country."

A half moon honeyed the sky, dimly illuminating the ranch yard. The brothers began loading the largest, heaviest boxes on the top of the planks, thus hiding the compartment, and then they stacked the rest around it.

They were almost done when the sound of a gunshot broke the stillness of the night and the brothers scrambled for the cover of the heavy wagon. A storm of flashes and shots erupted. The two brothers pressed their bodies against the wagon. Vern grabbed for the Colt tucked in his belt, pulled back the hammer and fired in the direction of the muzzle flashes. The wagon and its load provided some protection from the hail of bullets, but it was obvious to both brothers that they needed to act fast. Virgil had needed both hands to carry the boxes and had left his scattergun leaning against the wall just outside the door and getting it would be next to impossible across open ground.

"We got to get out of here!" Vern bellowed.

At that moment, Virgil felt the hot pain of a bullet as it ripped through the lower right side of his chest. He covered the wound with his hand. "Run for it, Vern. I'll catch up with you later!" Several more bullets sent chunks of wood flying off the wagon, into the air.

Trying to keep the wagon between him and the gun flashes, Vern dashed for the protection of the cabin's log corner. If he could make it to the horse, he might be able to make an escape with the cabin as a shield. He broke for the corner and was almost there when the searing impact of a bullet ripped into his side and another nicked his forearm. The impact momentarily knocked him to the ground. He staggered to his feet and struggled to make it around the building's corner, collapsing on the hitching rail in front of his horse. He ducked under the hitching log and with great effort, untied his horse. He swung himself up into the saddle and drove his heels into the gelding's side, slapped the long reins against its neck. The horse wheeled backwards and then leapt forward and disappeared into the night. Moments later, the mule yanked its head back, breaking its worn leather halter, and it followed the horse kicking and braying along the trail.

At the wagon, heavy sweat beaded on Virgil's forehead, and he knew he had to act immediately or die. He slid to the ground on his hands and knees and began crawling toward the high grass and sagebrush. Bullets sliced through the air above his head and he could hear the sound of men yelling close by, but he fought the urge to stand up and run. Moving through the thick sage was slow and he could hear people searching for him, yelling back and forth. Somehow he had managed to avoid their detection and several minutes later the sound of voices and gunshots finally faded.

Several hours later as the first gray light of morning hit the mountaintops Virgil bloody and weak, rose to his knees and scanned the area for movement. His side wound bled profusely, and the continuous crawling had bloodied his hands and knees. He studied the landscape for a few minutes, looking again for movement, before slowly standing erect and walking toward town, feeling the pain riddling his body.

Part I

The Greybull

Chapter 1

February 1937—Nine Mile, Montana

Cole Morgan stood alone in four inches of snow and stared at the fresh dirt atop his parents' graves. Large snowflakes had begun to fall and the wind of late winter blew snow through the trees and across the headstones. He remained stoic, standing quietly saying his goodbyes, for he was an only child and they were the only family he had.

Behind him, a man cleared his throat and Cole swung around to find a man with trusting eyes. He hadn't heard any footsteps. Cole studied the man for a moment, guessing him to be in his fifties—leather skin and hints of gray inching into his sun-bleached hair.

"Cole," the man said, holding out his hand. "I was a friend of your dad, name's Allen Skimming."

Cole nodded and shook the man's hand, noticing the strength of his calloused grip.

"I'm very sorry, son," Skimming said. "I know this don't seem real to you." He put his hand on Cole's shoulder. "Let's head back to the house and out of this snow," he said. He walked like an athlete long past his prime, and his barrel chest merged with a belly that fell slightly over his belt buckle.

"How did you know my father?" Cole asked.

"Rode with him in every rodeo from Cheyenne to Pendleton, your dad was one special man and made from the type of leather you could rely on. He saved my bacon more than a few times. We spent a lot of nights in cheap hotels and barns before he met your ma," he said. "What are your plans now?"

Cole shrugged and looked down

"I know about your knee injury," Skimming said. "I'm sorry your football days are over."

"I really don't know."

Skimming handed Cole a small piece of paper. "Well, this may or may not interest you, but I manage a large ranch in Meeteetse, Wyoming. We could use somebody like you, college trained with a degree in range management."

"I'm really not interested," Cole said as he shook his head slowly.

"Maybe you'll change your—"

"I don't see that happening. Nice to meet you, but I need to go." Cole turned to walk away when Skimming grabbed his elbow.

"You read that letter and call me when some of the dust settles. I got a challenge that may interest you."

"I appreciate it, but I'm really not interested. I'll keep the note. Thanks for coming. My folks would have appreciated it." Cole tucked the note into his inside vest pocket.

Two weeks later, he was going through his parents' closet when he found the jacket he had worn at the funeral and remembered Skimming. He unfolded the small tightly folded paper and read:

Your dad and I were once very close friends and we wrote each other about twice a year since you were born. Your father shared a lot about you, your sports and schooling. He was very proud of you. When he told me about you studying range management and how good you were at it, I took the liberty to write some of your professors at the beginning of your junior year, and to say the least, I was impressed with what they had to say.

Your father was pretty sure that you would either sign a football deal or you would try and start a ranch in Montana, but with all that happened, I wondered if you might be interested in another opportunity.

I work on a large ranch in Wyoming called The Greybull, and it could use someone like you, someone with skills and knowledge of proper range management and introduction of the latest hybrid grasses and the like. I would like to talk to you about coming to work with me for the McCabe family, the owners of the ranch.

Unfortunately, the last five years have been hard with the drought and all, but I believe if you are anything like your dad, you could be just what the doctor ordered.

Cole was flattered by the note, but the larger appeal for him was simply the chance to leave Montana and old memories behind.

Three weeks later, Cole finished packing the last of his belongings into the bed of his pickup. It was a typical Montana spring morning, cold and windy with broken skies of white clouds. For several minutes, he stood looking at the freshly painted "For

Sale" sign that stood prominently in front of his family's home. He turned to his 1935 International pickup, opened the door, and slid behind the steering wheel. He sat for several minutes before he started the truck and headed down the gravel road that led toward town.

Chapter 2

April 1937—Meeteetse, Wyoming

The cloud of dust that had followed him all morning finally overtook Cole as he slowed the truck at the outskirts of town. It had taken thirty hours and change, three flat tires, and an overheated radiator to get him from Nine Mile, Montana, to the middle of nowhere. Downtown Meeteetse was three blocks of brick and wood buildings, with rows of plank boardwalks on either side of the street. A number of pickups and cars sat parked on Main Street, and several horses slept at hitching rails. Other than the Greybull River he had crossed coming into town, Meeteetse looked like a dozen other lazy towns he had passed through in the last three days.

Most of the buildings looked like they were built before the turn of the century, flat-fronted and in need of repair. Advertisements covered the building fronts and some of the shed roofs over the boardwalk drooped from neglect. He noticed several saloons and a café that, at least from the outside, looked liked it was the best prospect for a decent meal.

Cole's truck door squeaked as he got out and stretched and headed toward the boardwalk in front of the Red Rooster Café.

He walked through the door of the café and felt a familiar dull pain in his left knee. Cole chose one of the far tables and sat down facing the front door with his back to the wall. His father, a naturally wary man, had always taught him to be alert to his surroundings, especially in new places. Within a couple of minutes, a waitress pushed through the swinging doors in the corner, order pad in hand and a smile on her face. A tall, slender girl, she looked to be about nineteen with long, brown hair, a narrow face and green eyes.

"I just made a fresh pot of coffee," she said. "And we have some soup left over from lunch."

Cole looked at his watch and realized that it was already mid-afternoon. His stomach growled, a reminder that he had skipped breakfast.

"I'll have the coffee and a large bowl of soup. Take a roast beef sandwich too, if you got any."

"Sure thing, I'll get the soup out to you in just a minute."

The walls of the café were dirty stucco, and black-stained wood beams hid several small spider webs on the ceiling. Soon she was back with the soup.

"Here you go. This should start to fill you up."

"So Butch Cassidy was through here?" Cole grinned and pointed to the picture.

"So they say."

They talked about the spring weather, and then she returned to the kitchen.

Cole was enjoying the soup when the screen door slammed open and two men entered the café. Rough and unshaven, they had the look of trouble. The bigger of the two was an inch over six feet and heavy set with a wide face and square jaw. He took the last puff on his cigarette and dropped it to the wood floor, crushed the butt with his boot and sat down at a table near the front.

"Get me some coffee and soup, Suzie," he hollered back into the kitchen. "I'm starving"

The waitress came through the small kitchen doors and placed Cole's sandwich on his table. Scowling, she shuffled over to the men's table. "Jake, I got coffee and sandwiches, but I just sold the last of the soup."

Jake glared at Cole's soup bowl from across the room, then at Cole himself. Jake rose from his chair and lumbered to the front of Cole's table.

"And who might you be, stranger?"

"Someone hungry who got here first"

Jake stood silent for a minute in front of Cole. Without saying another word, Jake turned and headed back to his table. The waitress set down his coffee, and as she started to turn back to the kitchen, Jake reached out and put his arm around her waist.

"Let's cuddle, honey," he said, laughing as he yanked her onto his lap.

"Take your filthy hands off me, you bastard," the waitress hissed, bright red in the face.

"Now, that's no way to talk to your new boyfriend," Jake said, and the other man at his table whistled and laughed. Jake pinned her arms to her sides as she tried to squirm away.

Cole slid back his chair and stood up, feeling adrenaline tighten in his arms. From his pocket he palmed a silver dollar into his left hand. He knew he needed an edge. Cole slowly and purposely walked across the room until he stood face to face with Jake Prentice. "Let the lady go now, and apologize to her."

Jake smirked, amused. He let go of Suzie's waist, stood up and slowly moved toward Cole, raising his arms in mock surrender. Their eyes met and from his palm Cole flicked the shiny silver dollar at Jake's right boot. In the fraction of the second, as Jake's attention was drawn to the coin, Cole stomped on Jake's boot and hurled a right cross to his chin, burying knuckles into bone and skin, and with contact a crack rang out in the diner. Jake was sent tumbling backwards into the oak table where he tripped and fell, hitting his head on the thick edge. He lay still as a trickle of blood oozed from the corner of his mouth.

Cole, breathing heavily, turned to the other man. "Are we done here?"

The other man stood up and slowly shook his head. "Mister, you don't know what you've started, but you can bet we'll finish this later."

Cole nodded to the man. "You be sure and tell your friend that I expect him to come back and apologize when he feels better."

The other man began dragging Jake out the door. Suzie turned, a little shaken up, and slowly made her way over to Cole, who introduced himself while picking up a chair. "I apologize for the mess. Hope I didn't cause you problems."

She smiled. "No, he's been asking for it for some time. Jake is a drunk, a brawler, and a real troublemaker. It's about time someone put him in his place. So tell me, what brings you to Meeteetse? We don't get many strangers."

"I took a job on The Greybull Ranch," Cole said as he bent down to pick up some of the scattered silverware.

"Just so you know, you just whipped one of the Prentices," Suzie said. "That family leaves a whole lot to be desired. The only one worth a damn is their cousin, John Prentice, the banker. Good-looking feller that one but a mite full of himself, in my opinion. I personally never cared for him much. He's been courting Julie McCabe. Her daddy, Wes, owns the ranch you're gonna be working on."

"Great, can't wait to meet him," Cole said hesitantly.

"Well, I hope the job lasts, honey. My Jay works out there, and his last paycheck was two weeks late and that isn't the first time that's happened. He only gets to town once every two weeks, but he's sure worth the wait. He's probably the best-looking cowboy in three counties."

Cole smiled and knew he should get going. As he turned to leave, Suzie flashed a big smile, "You sure and tell Jay 'hi' from me, you hear."

Chapter 3

After stocking up on eggs, bacon, coffee, and beer at the general store, Cole drove to a secluded spot along the Greybull River. He wasn't due at the ranch until the following day, and he wanted a chance to enjoy the spring weather. With a warm sun above, he unloaded his gear and removed his shirt to wash off three days of dust and sweat in the river water. He had a stitch in his side that had been bothering him, and he hoped a good stretch in the cold river would take care of it. As the sun nestled into the black rock peaks to the west, he built a fire and cleared twigs and debris from a small grassy area for his bedroll. That evening, with the dim glow of the town lights several miles away, he gazed up at the clear night sky, where thousands of stars shown like tiny candles.

He felt empty and alone, and he missed school, his friends, but mostly his family. A coyote howled on a distant ridge and Cole tensed at the thought of the nightmares he had come to expect every night since his parents' death. A couple of beers relaxed him, and his mind wandered to the Greybull Ranch. He lay down on his cloth bedroll and watched the fire flicker, and listened to the embers crackling. Shadows danced on the sagebrush, and he thought of his father, and the many fond memories of pack trips they had together.

Under the Wyoming stars he found himself exhausted from his trip and anxious to begin work on The Greybull. A dull stomachache that had dogged him for the past couple of days kept him awake tossing and turning throughout the night.

Chapter 4

Cole awoke to the loud snort of a mule deer doe drinking at the river's edge. Seeing Cole move, she bounded across the wide, shallow water in two quick vaults and disappeared into the brush. He rolled out of his bedroll, stretched, and looked toward his truck, his pride and joy. When clean, it was a shiny dark gray and his only possession of any real value. He had rebuilt the side racks to hold more gear, and it now held not only his clothes and tools, but everything he could salvage from his parents' home.

A canvas manty, tightly attached with several ropes, protected the majority of his worldly goods: four large, old, wooden boxes containing everything from pictures to his dad's guns. It had torn him up to sell his folks' bed, kitchen table, and the chairs that his dad had made by hand during Montana's hard winters. The only furniture he took from the homestead was his grandmother's rocking chair that had been crafted by her father in England before coming to America in the early 1800s.

Cole gathered some dry grass and twigs to kindle a new fire. The valleys here were vast, dry, and mostly treeless, until they merged into the timbered foothills of the mountains. It was a place a man could travel for miles and miles without seeing much sign of humanity. He found that he was comfortable with himself and the solitude that came with the vast and roaming skies of Montana and Wyoming.

The area around his campsite was speckled with the bright magenta of pincushion cacti in full bloom. Within yards of where he camped, a spring bubbled out of the ground and meandered into the Greybull River. Cole filled his coffee pot with fresh cold water, set it over the fire using a tripod of metal rods. He used a cast iron skillet between two rocks for frying eggs and bacon, which he hoped would take the edge off his stomachache.

When finished, he cleaned his cook gear and packed it away in a metal box that had belonged to his father. After a few minutes, he took a deep breath, collected his thoughts and headed for The Greybull.

The graveled clay road that led to the ranch was rough and rutted, so the little truck rocked back and forth, almost uncontrollably at times. The road's shoulders were covered with bluish-white sagebrush and sprinkled with clump fescue. Scattered groups of mule deer and antelope grazed near where the river met grassy fields and every once in awhile Cole braked hard for the large jackrabbits as they dashed across the road. In the distance, a pinnacle of rock at least a quarter mile wide towered several hundred feet over the valley floor. The road swept wide around it before resuming its westerly course. The pinnacle was almost solid mud shale with little vegetation and looked totally out of place in the otherwise rolling landscape. Far ahead on the horizon, Cole noticed a log and stone entrance rising from the sagebrush.

After another ten minutes or so, Cole finally drove under the towering arch entrance of the ranch. The huge log, easily three feet in diameter, sagged slightly in the middle and spanned two eight-by-eight columns of river rock. A heavy, weathered beam hung from the log on two large, rusty chains, spelling out "Greybull Ranch" in faded white letters, with a lazy circle "G" beside it. Several hundred yards past the entrance sagebrush gave way to green valley grass that rolled as far as the eye could see. Being late spring, the grass was already tanning brown.

The road continued its rough route before turning south along a ten-acre lake full from the spring runoff. Cole eased over an old planked bridge above the small creek that fed the lake. The distant outline of a large house, flanked by cottonwood trees, began to take shape on a large plateau overlooking the valley. Even from a distance, the elegant white house was an imposing structure, as big as any house he had ever seen. The home rose at least three stories into the sky, with a steep roof divided by a massive red brick chimney.

Architecturally, it was not much more than an incredibly large saltbox design, but the beautiful porch—with six large white columns and wide front steps stretching out to meet the gravel road—made it imposing. Two large gables covered with heavy shake roofing rose ten feet above the roof. The top two floors of the house had white shiplap siding, but the first floor consisted of red brick accented with black shutters.

As Cole drove closer, he saw that despite its grandeur, the mansion had clearly seen better days. The siding was in need of paint, and weeds had crept far closer to the house than should have ever been allowed.

On his left were four barns, a number of corrals, and a large bunkhouse. A dozen smaller cabins lay scattered further to the east of the house and behind the barns. All were in equally poor repair. Up close, it was hard to imagine the beauty of the place in its prime.

Large cottonwood trees dotted the dry short grass of the yard, and others shaded numerous smaller buildings behind the main house. As he pulled his truck to a stop at the wide steps of the home's porch, a young boy with shaggy hair took off toward the main house. The trip had been bumpy, and Cole took a minute to check his boxes in the back of the truck before turning to see Allen Skimming walk up from the barn with a large smile on his face.

"Found your way out here, did ya? Good trip?"

Cole smiled and wiped his brow. "Quite the journey, but I enjoyed seeing new country."

"Let's walk over to the bunkhouse. I'll introduce you to some of the boys after you get settled, though some of 'em are up west gathering strays on the Frank Fork. The McCabes are sure excited to meet you. We all wanna hear what you think about improving the pasture. That professor of yours sure talked you up." Allen grinned as he turned and pointed toward the bunkhouse. "The showers are in the end of that building. Take an open bunk. Breakfast is served at six sharp in the cookhouse yonder. The McCabes want you to have dinner with them tonight at the big house. I'll send the butler, Tyler Raines, over to get you in an hour or so."

Cole walked into the bunkhouse and threw his worn leather suitcase down on the open lower bunk next to a cracked window. He brushed away several cobwebs and sat down on the rough wooden bunk. The bed was about a third of the way down the narrow bunkhouse, in an area with several windows facing the large front yard of the McCabe's home.

It wasn't long before hot water was pouring over Cole's tired body. The trip had been hard. His neck and shoulders ached, and there was a knot the size of a small chestnut in his lower back. He walked from the shower to his bunk bed where a lone light bulb dangled over the two-by-eight headboard. Both the lower and upper bunks were vacant, and Cole took the better pillow from above and hit it several times, creating a small cloud of dust. He used one of his undershirts to pull over the pillow as a substitute case.

He dressed in his best flannel shirt, a newer pair of jeans, and boots that had been his father's. He had only been dressed for a few minutes when a short, slightly overweight man walked into the bunkhouse. "Welcome to The Greybull, Mr. Morgan. We will serve dinner in about an hour. Are you ready to join us at the house?"

Cole was surprised with the man's manners and the dignity with which he spoke, not often found in these parts. "You bet. I'm Cole Morgan, nice to meet you." Cole shook Tyler's soft hand. From Tyler's physique, Cole assumed he probably worked strictly in the house doing the cooking, cleaning, and general house management. He certainly wasn't a cowboy.

A pleasant breeze stirred through the willow in the front yard as the two headed up the front stairs to the house. Tyler opened the hand-carved front door and showed Cole into an expansive formal room where a massive chimney stood centered at the far end. Above the fireplace hung a life-sized portrait of a formidable looking man dressed in a tailored black suit with high riding boots and a black derby. His pose was almost challenging, with one hand holding a riding whip tucked up against his suit and the other arm extended out, holding a decorative cane, the head of which appeared to be a cougar.

"Who's that in the painting?" Cole asked.

"That, sir, is Mr. Gillis McCabe, the ranch's founder," Tyler answered. "It was painted shortly after a remodel of this house about seventy years ago."

They walked further into the huge foyer, took a right down a wide hallway and entered an ornate dining room. The inside of the house was carefully detailed, like pictures Cole had seen of the great homes in the East, and a person could not miss the masterful craftsmanship that had gone into its construction. In college, Cole had taken several courses in architecture, and, though he knew that would not be his major field of study, he enjoyed the thought and engineering required to create a building of this caliber. Throughout the house Cole noticed the beautiful furniture, ornate ceiling moldings, and old but expensive rugs. All the intricately carved trim and floor-to-ceiling wallpaper was impressive, but slightly yellowed with age. Though old, it was certainly impressive to Cole who, until college, lived in a three-room cabin.

Allen saw him enter the room and headed over to greet him. "Let me introduce you to everyone. This is Wes McCabe, the owner of The Greybull Ranch, and this is his wife, Sally."

Wes looked to be in his late forties or early fifties, with a fair amount of gray in his thinning hair, and thick mustache. He was just short of six foot with a lean build, a gentle smile, and an intelligent presence. Sally, on the other hand, was truly statuesque, standing nearly the same height as her husband. She was in her late forties, and must have, at one time, truly been a beauty. Fine tan lines etched her face, but her high cheekbones, well-developed body and her thick brown hair still made her a very attractive woman.

"Allen says you were the top of your class at Washington State College," Wes said.

"Well, that might be a stretch," Cole said. "I always wanted to ranch—maybe have a nice place somewhere in Montana so I studied extra hard, but things just haven't turned out exactly like I planned."

"They seldom do," Wes replied.

Sally and Wes both told Cole how sorry everyone was to hear about his folks. Cole quickly found himself uncomfortable with the conversation, and the pain in his side was getting worse. He tried to seem interested, but was distracted, when the most beautiful girl he had ever seen strolled through the doorway and walked up to him.

"Julie McCabe," she said. "Are you the Mr. Morgan that I've heard so much about?"

Julie McCabe had long, glossy black hair and piercing dark brown eyes. Her face was narrow, and her low-cut, tight, dark-blue dress revealed just enough of her full breasts that Cole had to concentrate to keep his eyes off them.

"Yes ma'am, I'm Cole Morgan. This sure is a beautiful home you and your folks have here."

"Well, Mr. Morgan, I hear you were a real star football player at Washington State College—quarterback, if I remember what Allen said. I can't say that I have ever seen a real football game, just some of the men playing around in the park."

"I hurt my knee, and I'm not sure it will ever be good enough to play again, but things happen. I feel fortunate that I got a good education as well as the opportunity to play. I have a lot of great memories. And please, call me Cole. "

"You sound pretty humble." She looked straight into his eyes. Her confidence caught Cole off guard. There was no back-up in this woman and he knew it.

"That seems like a while back now and probably means nothing to anyone here, leastwise, it isn't important now. Life has a way of showing you what's important."

Cole was about to say something to Julie when Wes McCabe tapped him on the arm. "Cole, I would like you to meet Bob Ballard. He has worked for the ranch for the last twenty years and done a fine job doing it." Ballard was broad shouldered, big but not sculptured, a man that gave a sense of power in his mere presence.

Cole stuck out his hand and noticed Ballard was just a hair slow doing the same. "Nice to meet you Bob."

"I go by Ballard, and nice to meet you, too." His handshake was more like a vice grip. Ballard was stocky, taller than Wes, and dressed in a bright red shirt with yellow trim on the shoulders. He seemed intelligent, but reserved, with not much warmth coming from his crooked smile. His face showed wear, with a thick growth of stubble, though Cole was sure the man must have shaved that morning.

"Allen runs the ranch, but Ballard keeps the ranch hands in line," Wes said.

A well-dressed, elderly couple walked up to the group, and Wes took a step back to allow them to meet Cole. "Cole, this is Russ and June Jones. They live in Meeteetse, and their family has been living here for close to a hundred years," Wes said with a smile.

Everyone was enjoying the get-together when Tyler walked into the room and whispered something to Wes, who then said to Tyler, "Show him in, show him in." Tyler was gone only a moment. He came back into the room with a short, heavy man in a worn leather coat and large, dark brown hat. The man appeared to be in his sixties and had a strong purpose to his walk. The man removed his hat.

"Dutch Brown, how are you? Welcome! Can I get you a drink?"

"Thanks, I wouldn't mind a whisky. There's a nip to the air." Tyler poured him a drink.

"What brings you out at night this far from home?" Wes asked.

Dutch took a sip of the whisky and then looked up at Wes. "We're missing a man."

"You're missing a man, how long as he been gone?"

"His horse showed up two days ago at the bottom of Noon Peak. You know the mountain that borders our property on the far south end?"

"Yeah, I know the place. I've ridden it a couple of times over the last twenty years, but I'm not real familiar with it."

"Well, one of our hands named Lippy Moore was out checking cattle on the southern exposure of that mountain, and he never showed back up at the ranch. We sent men out and all we found was his horse, and since you're without phone service, I thought I'd stop just in case."

"I haven't heard anything, but we'd like to help with the search, if you need any more men," Wes said with a grave face.

"I appreciate the offer, but I'm not sure I'd be able to tell them where to start. Hell, we've gone over the ground he should've been on at least a half a dozen times, and we haven't found squat. It rained hard the day Lippy rode out, and unfortunately there isn't much for tracks, leastwise any my men have been able to follow. It's like he disappeared off the face of the earth. Lippy was a good man and a good cowboy—he wouldn't just fall off his horse and disappear. Well, thanks for the drink and the offer of help. I need to keep checking with people, and, hopefully, someone will know something, but I'm plum buffaloed as to what happened."

Dutch turned and started out the doorway when he stopped and slowly turned back toward Wes and Allen. "One more thing I didn't want to say in front of the ladies. There was some blood on one of the stirrups. I'll keep in touch if we find him or need any help." With that, he turned and walked out the door.

Chapter 5

Wes turned to Allen. "In a couple of days I want you and one of the men to go over to Dutch's and see if they have found Lippy and if there's anything we can do for them. This'll be hard on everyone." He furrowed his eyebrows. "I wonder what happened."

Allen looked back at him and slowly shook his head, and then the two rejoined the group.

During dinner, Cole visited with everyone and tried to answer some of their ranching questions about irrigation and hybrid grasses before he excused himself. It bothered him that a man was missing and possibly still alive.

As he started walking out, Julie joined him and laid her hand on his arm. "Leaving so soon? I didn't get a chance to visit with you much."

Cole smiled, trying not to wince from the increasing pain in his stomach. "Maybe you can show me around later, and I can get a rain check on that visit."

She cocked her head. "I'm not used to being turned down; I'll have to think about the rain check." She turned and returned to the group.

Cole headed across the large, grassy, open area to the bunkhouse. Inside, two cowboys sat around a roughly built table playing cards. The men looked salty, weathered and tired, but they jumped to their feet when they noticed the pain etched on Cole's face and saw the difficulty he was having just trying to stand.

"Grab his arm and let's get this guy in his bunk. What's going on with you?" said a man with a salted beard.

"I've just got a whale of a stomachache. I'll be fine in the morning." Cole strained as each man grabbed an arm and helped him lie down on his bunk.

* * *

After Cole left, Julie walked up to Allen. "Is there something about Cole's family I should know?"

Allen sighed and shook his head sadly. "It was the end of February, and the Morgans had gone to Missoula to shop. They were headed home late up a windy road when a logging truck going down the mountain lost control. The truck jackknifed, and the load of logs landed on the Morgan's sedan. They were killed instantly."

Julie's hand covered her mouth. "That's horrible. And he had that knee injury, too?"

"Yeah, Cole had just begun to walk without crutches from his football accident when his folks died. He was quite the legend in the Bitterroot Valley. Many say he was by far the best athlete to ever come out of that area. His senior year at college, he was team captain and an all-American candidate. If his personality and work ethic are anything like his dad's, then we're real lucky. God knows we could use some luck."

* * *

Cole dozed between sharp stomach cramps. At four in the morning, he awoke to one of the wranglers shaking him at his shoulder.

"Partner, are you ok?"

"I'll be fine," answered Cole in a weak voice. "I just got a bad stomachache."

"Partner, with all that moaning you've been doing in your sleep, that's a far sight more than a sour stomach. I'm getting the boss." The wrangler ran out the door toward Allen Skimming's cabin.

When Allen got to the bunkhouse, large beads of sweat hung on Cole's pale forehead. "It's my stomach," Cole groaned, "Feels like someone is cutting me up from the inside out."

Allen turned to the wrangler that had fetched him. "Jay, I need you to drive over to the Schmitz ranch and use their phone to call the doctor. Tell him to hurry—we got a problem."

A little over two hours later, the doctor walked through the bunkhouse door. He examined Cole for a couple of minutes, then turned and faced Allen. "His appendix may be about to rupture. He needs immediate surgery. He's running a high fever, probably ignored the pain for few days and now he's in bad shape. We need to move him to the house. Have Sally boil some water and hurry!"

A spare guest room on the main floor was quickly converted for the surgery.

* * *

Cole struggled to open his eyes and found himself in a strange room with a large black cat sleeping at the foot of the bed. The room was spacious, almost totally white including the furniture. He could feel the bandages around his tender stomach and at first, he wasn't sure if he was dreaming. He didn't remember the room or how he had gotten there, but he heard something and realized that someone was sitting at the far end of the room at an old roll top desk. His back was to Cole, and it appeared he was searching through papers.

"Good morning," Cole whispered.

The figure stiffened for a moment, then shut the oak roll top and turned to Cole.

"Well. Good morning to you, too," Tyler said, smiling. "Thought you would sleep a lot longer, hope I didn't bother you. Can I get you anything?"

"Water . . ."

Bile rose in Cole's throat, and his whole lower abdomen felt like he had been flattened by a truck. With even the slightest movement, throbbing pain pulsed throughout his gut. Faint voices drifted up from the hallway, and Julie McCabe walked through the door. She smiled when she saw that Cole was awake.

"Mr. Morgan, we were worried sick about you!"

"What happened?"

"It was your appendix. You're lucky you didn't die. If it wasn't for the doctor, I think you would have."

Cole relaxed a little. She looked so beautiful with her soft white skin, black hair draping her face, and the contrast of her tight yellow dress. He thought to himself, if the angels in heaven were this pretty, then dying wouldn't have been too bad a deal.

Cole pointed to the cat sleeping on the bed and asked, "So, who's my friend?"

Julie laughed. "That's Smokie. He's pretty much allowed the run of the house. He's been keeping you company since we put you here."

Cole looked at the room and the pressed linen. "This is the fanciest bed I've ever been in."

Julie smiled. "Grandpa brought it from Virginia after the Civil War. A lot of the furniture in the house is from the south."

Suddenly, Cole felt faint and couldn't keep his eyes open. As he fell back to sleep, Sally McCabe walked into the room. "Julie, why don't you watch him for the next hour or so and then I'll take over for a while. He had a mighty rough night. He lost a lot of blood, but he's one tough young man. That's the third bad thing that has happened to him in six months. Trouble seems to follow that man like stink on a skunk."

For the next few days, Cole awoke just long enough to eat a little, before his body demanded more sleep. On the fifth day, he woke to see the doctor, Julie, Tyler, and Sally standing beside his bed. "Son," the doctor said, seeing Cole had opened his eyes. "You are one lucky cowboy who pushed me to my limit and almost to yours. If you weren't in such good condition, I don't think you'd still be here. I need to take a look at those stitches." The doctor carefully moved Cole and removed the bandages to look at the surgical wound. "Looks good healing faster than I would have guessed, I'll come back in a few days to check on your progress, but I think you'll be just fine."

Moving around and redoing the bandages had taken its toll, but Cole felt reassured by the doctor's comments. "Thanks, Doc. Hopefully some day I can return the favor."

"All I want from you now is to rest," the doctor said, with a slight smile of reassurance.

Cole closed his eyes and relaxed as Julie fetched a bowl of warm water, soap and a washrag. Turning back the quilts, she carefully washed Cole's face, chest and underarms, as she had done for the last two days. "I'll be back later to see how you're doing. Right now I have to help Mom." And with that, she kissed him on the cheek and left the room.

A few minutes later, Tyler entered and started cleaning up. "I'm glad we didn't lose you," he said. "You were one mighty sick fellow."

Chin, the cook, entered the room and, with Tyler's help, took Cole into the bathroom down the hall. When he was done, Chin and Tyler placed Cole back into his bed and pulled up the bedspread decorated with lace and small frilly violets.

Several days later, Cole awoke and struggled to the large dresser containing his clothes. With great effort, he dressed himself. He didn't feel comfortable in the fancy white bed, and he knew that the other hands would be talking about the new guy and his special treatment. His legs were wobbly, and beads of sweat formed on his forehead while he walked down the steps and toward the bunkhouse. Julie was passing by the window when she noticed Cole struggling across the yard. With her teeth clenched, she stormed out of the house and flew down the steps. "What in the blue blazes do you think you're doing? The doctor said you weren't to move for another couple of days!"

Cole leveled his eyes at her. "Listen, I really appreciate what you and the others have done for me, but it's time I get out from under your hair and back to the bunkhouse."

Julie uttered a few choice words under her breath and glared while Cole turned and headed toward the bunkhouse. With the pain starting to resurface, Cole carefully lowered himself into his bunk. He was exhausted from the short walk and found sleep in seconds.

Later he heard one of the roosters crow just as a young cowboy shook him awake. "You want some breakfast?"

Cole sat up and struggled to his feet. He realized that his legs were far shakier than the previous afternoon, and he appreciated the help.

"I'm Jay Taylor. A couple of the men said you stumbled in here last night in bad shape, said it was your appendix."

"I'm feeling a little rough, but I'm doing fine. Couple of days and I'll be working again."

"Like hell you will," Jay replied. He laughed and carefully helped Cole to his feet. Leaning on Jay, the two slowly headed toward the cookhouse. "I heard about you being a big college guy and all, and your string of bad luck. Hopefully, that's done with. I think you'll like The Greybull—it's a mighty fine ranch."

Cole responded with a little bit of pain on his face, "So far, I've liked everyone I've met." Cole noticed Jay's large silver belt buckle and made the mistake of asking about its background.

"I won it over at the Cody rodeo for bull riding on a bull named Ball Breaker, first cowboy to ride that bull for more than eight seconds. Mean son of a bitch. I met my girlfriend that day, and she's the sweetest, prettiest thing you ever saw."

Cole looked at him and smiled. "Her name wouldn't be Suzie, would it?"

"Now, how in the heck did you know that?"

"The Prentice brothers introduced themselves to me in town while I was talking to Suzie, and we had a disagreement on manners."

"Those brothers are two of the meanest boys in town," Jay said. "Last year, they put one of my friends in the hospital over nothing, dang near killed him." Jay was only medium height and had a thin build, and Cole didn't want to start anything between Jay and the Prentices over the meeting with his girl.

When they entered the cookhouse, Cole noticed that they were the only ones there. "Where is everyone?" he asked.

"Hell, we missed the rush. If this wasn't my day off, I probably wouldn't have noticed you still sleeping in the shadows. I'm getting a late start, and then I'm headed for town. Chin gets a little upset when people are late, or for that matter early, but he usually leaves out something for the stragglers." While they ate, Jay continued his steady flow of information about the ranch, his girlfriend, how much fence he built last week and his life, seldom giving Cole even a chance at a question. When they were done, Jay helped Cole to his feet and they headed back to the bunkhouse where Cole took a seat on the bench on the porch, looking toward the big house. He had just planted himself when he heard his name.

"Howdy Cole, how you feeling?"

Cole could only remember the cowboy's first name and hollered back, "Great, Elmer! I'll be up to snuff in no time." Elmer was leading a sorrel pack mule with several wide rolls of barbed wire sticking out the top of the pack.

He stopped for a second, like he had more to say, when the mule reached up and ripped his hat from his head and dropped it to the ground. "Doggone it, Otto, knock that crap off," he yelled as he retrieved the hat. With a disgusted look, he waved and continued to the barn.

"That's some mule," Cole laughed.

"Yeah, that old pack mule has been around at least twenty years, and he has more personality than most humans I know. Everyone likes Otto. He's level headed and smart, a bit of a legend on the ranch," Jay said.

"A legend a mule legend?"

"Pretty much. About ten years ago, he made a name for himself by saving a calf by running off a lone wolf that had attacked a cow-calf pair. One of the cowboys saw it from a ridge overlooking a small basin. I guess this wolf grabbed the calf, and it let out a loud bawl and both the cow and old Otto came a running. Otto catches up to this wolf, spins and lays both barrels to that wolf's side and dislodges the calf. The wolf was hurt bad and tucked its tail between its legs and disappeared into the sagebrush. Old Otto, he's quite the mule," Jay said as he turned to leave. "Will you be all right here?"

"Yeah, I'll be fine, thanks for the help." Cole smiled at Jay. For the rest of the day, Cole rested, ate, then went to bed early.

He felt better the next day and was up early, walking around to explore the immediate grounds surrounding the bunkhouse and big house. He was walking just south and west of the big house when he heard a low whine. A small stone building several hundred yards from the others seemed to be its source. On the south side of the one room building was a thick wooden door framed in stone with a high, small window just above it. It took some effort in his weakened state, but Cole pushed opened the squeaky door to find a water-powered turbine with numerous pipes filling the room. On closer examination, the pipes appeared to be well maintained, and the gate valves were obviously being checked and oiled on a regular basis.

He concluded that this turbine produced the power and water for the ranch, something he thought was amazing for an isolated ranch. From some of his engineering classes, he knew that when water dropped a vertical foot, it picked up approximately a half a pound of pressure. So, he thought, the whole house had to be on some type of gravity feed system. Cole was fascinated by the design and could see where pipes led up the hill and decided if he felt well enough he would try to hike to the source the next day. Cole opened the door to leave and was surprised to see Julie leading a large, black Quarter Horse on a trail about ten yards above the old stone building.

"You must be feeling stronger. You sure are moving a whole lot better."

"Yeah, I was going stir crazy on my bunk and decided to stretch my legs."

Julie laughed, smiled, and continued leading her horse up and over the small ridge where the mechanical building sat. "See you later," she hollered over her shoulder.

The next morning, Cole awoke at dawn to the crow of a rooster, got dressed, and headed toward the trail he believed headed up the mountain to the water source. He didn't figure that he would be gone all that long, but he decided to slip on his heavy coat because of the brisk morning breeze. A couple of minutes past the stone mechanical building, he found what appeared to be a seldom-used trail, the entrance marked by a rusty wagon wheel partially buried in dried mud.

The trail rose gradually, and he believed it had been used in the past by cattle. The track seemed gentle enough as it meandered up the hill, but it wasn't long before he realized the hike was going to take far longer than he had hoped. The heat of the rising sun on his forehead brought on a full sweat, and he knew he was pushing his limits.

After hiking almost forty-five minutes, Cole came to a high, jagged rock outcropping that he climbed, allowing him to view north, back to the ranch houses far below. He continued up and around the rock and over a small rise, where he looked west, down into the small canyon toward the sound of falling water. Walking to the edge, he was impressed by a waterfall tumbling into a large manmade pond with a small earthen dam at one end. The pond collected the water and allowed it to enter a screening pipe that headed through the dam and down the mountain. The crust of rust that had accumulated on the old pipe told Cole the system had been in place for years.

Exhausted, Cole sat on a small boulder to take a rest. The small beach and wet rocks glistened as the sun rose over the pristine landscape. It felt good to just sit after the hard hike. He sat on the rock for half an hour while the sun continued its ascent, exposing more details that had been hidden by shadows just minutes before.

Cole was studying the dam's design when he saw a set of fresh wolf tracks in the mud, only a few feet from where he sat. He had seen many fresh wolf tracks and knew the wolf that had made them was only hours away. He had not meant to get so far away from the house, and he had told no one that he was walking up the canyon. How could he have been so stupid as to not even carry at least a knife? Cole stood and studied the area and on closer examination, he identified at least five additional sets of tracks. This was a fair-sized pack, and Cole had no idea how close they were.

A cold chill went up his back. Would they sense his injury? Why hadn't he been more careful? In his current physical condition, he was no match for any predator, and he knew it. He considered wolves to be a master predator, and he had experienced their brutality firsthand.

Years ago, several of the more isolated families around the Nine Mile had lost livestock to the wolves, but his worst memory was of a five-year-old neighbor boy who had been killed less than a hundred yards from his cabin. The boy's mother heard screams and ran to the front door to see a large gray wolf dragging her son into the woods. She screamed at the wolf and ran into the woods. The two vanished into the forest. A large search party with dogs tried to catch up with the wolf, but what they found wasn't pretty.

Cole knew he had to focus as he headed back down the trail to the house. He carried a large stick in his hand, and it served as both a makeshift cane and a club. He realized how isolated The Greybull was, tucked up against a huge tract of harsh, rugged federal land. With as much speed as he could comfortably muster, he made his way down the trail. After twenty minutes, he made it back to the safety of the ranch and collapsed onto his bunk.

Later that afternoon, he got up and told Bob Ballard about the tracks.

"Yeah, there's a renegade wolf pack we been hunting for about two years. Never seen wolves that close to the ranch before—you sure they weren't coyote tracks?"

"I know the difference between a coyote and a wolf," Cole said.

"We did lose two good riding horses a year ago," Ballard continued, not noticing Cole's scowl. "Some of the boys tied up their horses by Anderson Creek and went to work on a drift fence. When they got back, the wolves had killed one of the animals, and the other one was so tore up they had to shoot it. They got at least ten head of cattle over the last year that we know of. The McCabes even offered a hundred dollar a hide bounty. We haven't got a single one of them yet, so you better keep your eyes open and your head down, college boy."

Cole gritted his teeth and held back a choice comeback as he walked away from Ballard.

Over the next week, Cole met most of the other hands while he did light-weight duty, from working on the equipment to helping with building repairs. He hadn't met all the men, but he was developing a relationship with the majority of them during meals and after work in the bunkhouse. One member of the McCabe family checked in on him at least once a day, then reported his progress to the doctor when they traveled to town. Cole especially cherished the visits from Julie and sometimes made a point of trying to accidentally run into her. For exercise, Cole would walk down the road a little over a mile several times a day and then head back to the barn and sit on an old wood bench outside the bunkhouse where she kept her horse.

Several weeks later, Cole awoke early to a Saturday morning filled birds' song and sunshine, along with several of the guys snoring loudly in the back of the bunkhouse. He got up, showered, and put on some clean jeans and a red plaid shirt. Originally, he had thought he would ask Allen Skimming for a quick tour of the ranch but later decided that he would much prefer the company of Julie.

Outside, Dodge Start came walking up from the barn and met Cole on the porch. "You're looking better, Cole. What are you up to today?"

"I think I'm going to try and see if I can get a tour out of Julie McCabe."

Dodge laughed. "Good luck," he said as he turned and entered the bunkhouse.

Cole decided to wait until ten o'clock to go up to the house and ask Julie for a tour. At about nine-thirty, he was sitting mending a harness, working up the courage to talk to Julie, when he heard the sound of a car motoring up the gravel road. It was a mint 1937 Chevrolet Master Deluxe Touring Sedan, the same car Bette Davis drove according to an article in *Life* magazine he had read.

The car was a thing of beauty. It rolled to a stop in front of the house and out stepped a dark-haired man dressed in a blue suit and a white hat with a bright blue band. He moved purposefully and quickly, like an athlete, and was as big as most of the linemen on Cole's old football team. The gentleman headed to the front door, knocked, and was let in. After a few minutes, he came out with Julie, opened the door of the car for her, and they sped down the road, leaving a small cloud of dust that drifted toward Cole and the bunkhouse.

"Who the hell was that?" Cole mumbled under his breath.

To his surprise, Allen Skimming answered a couple feet behind him. "That, sir, is John Prentice, the banker, one of the wealthiest men in Wyoming."

Cole shrugged. "How about showing me some of the ranch today?"

"You bet. I had a couple of other things I needed to do, but they can wait," Allen said. "Let me show you something first."

The two walked about a quarter of a mile south of the house to a large weathered barn. Behind the barn were at least four corrals, several herds of horses, and a small group of mules.

"When you're feeling better, you need to come over here and pick you a horse. We like everyone to take a two- to three-year-old and work on breaking them into a good mount. Then we sell them to eastern dudes that need good riding stock. The market is still halfway solid for high quality horses, and it's another way for the ranch to make a buck. You put a solid year of good ranch work on a young one, and with a good teacher and rider, you can usually create a damn good horse."

Cole opened the first gate and went into the herd, quietly talking to and examining each animal. The first thing he looked at was their build. Could they carry a large man all day? He looked into each horse's eyes to see if it seemed scared or nervous. He watched for a settled and trusting eye. Straight legs and good composition were also important. He didn't care much about looks, as he knew often the best looking horses didn't have the other parts, the heart for endurance and intelligence for bad situations.

For the next twenty minutes, Cole walked through and viewed both pens of horses. When he was done, he went down the hill to the smaller corral that contained the mules.

"You don't want to look at them," Allen hollered from a distance. "They're all just mules. No self-respecting cowboy would ride one of them on this ranch."

"I just want to see what's available," Cole hollered back. "Can I take a couple days to decide?"

"Take your time. We best be heading up to the house and tell Chin to get the lunches ready."

Chapter 6

Allen Skimming's International pickup was two years older than Cole's, white with the ranch's circle lazy G logo painted on its door. The truck showed battle scars from too many off-road trips and too many days in the sun.

Allen put two tin lunch pails in the back, along with a thermos of coffee and a large canteen of water. The truck had a slight tick, but seemed to purr while they headed down the road from the ranch. They took a left turn and headed west up the valley.

The road was new territory to Cole, dried hardpan with sparse gravel that would have been nearly impossible to drive on wet. From the piles of loose dirt on the shoulders, Cole could tell that a blade had recently worked on it.

Allen looked at Cole. "Pretty smooth huh? We had a mule team pull a scraper down this road about a week ago. We need to do that several times a year to keep it drivable. This section of road was rougher than the entrance road, if you can believe that."

"It took a tough man to put this ranch together," Allen continued. "Gillis McCabe, Wes's grandfather, wasn't someone people messed with. I think he was in his twenties when Gillis made his fortune in the shipyards of Norfolk, Virginia. Just before the Civil War, he sold out and made a huge profit, and then for some reason he headed out west. He fell in love with the wide-open spaces, and spent the next ten years buying up ranches in the area. Gillis built the original ranch house in 1870, but it was damaged by a wildfire around '72. A forty-mile-an-hour wind had shot flames across the fire line, burning some of the main house and half of the other buildings. Gillis rebuilt the home in the original location, larger and with far more quality, around 1873."

"Didn't Wes say his grandpa died reasonably young?"

"Yeah, he died in a robbery outside a small store about forty miles north and east of here in '77, at the age of fifty-nine. They think someone tried to rob him; however, the police found Gillis' unfired gun in his pocket, as if he had expected trouble. His wallet was still in his coat with over two hundred dollars."

"Strange he didn't get a shot off and they left his money," Cole reasoned.

"Yeah, it was," Allen continued. "They buried Gillis on an isolated ridge about fifteen miles west of here, overlooking the valley. Except for a narrow trail to the top, there's not much access anymore to the grave. The hill is known to the locals as Whisky Ridge after a trader that used to sell moonshine to the Indians there, but that was long before Gillis bought it. The family marked the grave with an eight-foot-tall cross made of heavy timbers and a rock base. On a clear day, you can see it from the valley. The country around the grave is so rough and steep that even the cattle seldom find their way up there. In my opinion, Gillis was smart, but kind of a weird duck."

"What happened to the McCabes after Gillis died?"

"Jake, Gillis' son, had a knack for engineering and was responsible for the power plant that set up electricity and a reliable water source to the house. He had a brilliant mind, but he wasn't much of a businessman. Unfortunately, since Gillis died the ranch has never achieved the same financial success. Jake died in his late twenties, leaving Wes to run the place. Gillis' money had long since run out. Rumors were had of a missing safe, bonds, and other valuables, but none of it was ever found."

Allen cleared his throat and continued, "The ranch isn't making money, and with your knowledge of range management, Wes decided to hire you and take a new look at some old problems. When he told me he was willing to give you a shot, I decided I would see if you had any interest in coming out here. The death of your folks just accelerated the process. I had written to your range management professor, Kneeland if I remember right, about a year before your folk's accident, and he said you were almost as good a student as you were an athlete. Said you were one quick study. I know you're no savior, but we are hoping that with your experience with new irrigation techniques and all the new varieties of grasses, you might bring some fresh air and a fresh look to an old business."

Taken aback by Allen's flattery, Cole shook his head. "I sure appreciate all of the confidence everyone seems to have in me, but it's mostly book smarts and working in the summer. I haven't done much more than test a lot of pasture bunchgrass in the greenhouse and study hard in my classes."

"I understand. But all that education can't hurt and we have to try something different."

The dirt road took a sharp right, and in the distance stood the remains of an old cabin and barn edged up against the hillside. "Are there many old homesteads on the ranch?" Cole asked.

"Probably twenty or more that I know of. Every now and then, one of the trail hands finds a new one when he's looking for strays, usually just one room, all by itself deep in some timber. Some of them are built in the strangest places and must have been built by those gold-crazy prospectors. Wanna take a closer look at this one?"

"Sure," Cole said. "This old stuff brings out the detective in me."

"This homestead was built by Virgil and Vern Creager, two brothers that homesteaded in the mid-1800s. Be careful inside. It's not unusual in these old cabins to have trap doors, and occasionally one of the ranch hands takes a fall through them."

Cole looked through the old, dusty glass window, trying to examine the inside. He had heard of trap doors built into cabins to allow the inhabitants to escape in case of Indian attack or wildfires, and he would love to find one first hand. Cole tried to open the door, at least two inches of solid wood, but it stuck solid. The building had settled, and the door no longer hung well on its frame. Cole turned to Allen, "Can you give me a hand with this door? It's real jammed up." With both of them pushing, the door finally swung open to expose a dusty, shadowy room. It was furnished with only a table and two good chairs; a third dusty chair lay broken in the corner. The years of rot, decay, and pack rat scat had given the room an unpleasant musty smell. Cole walked about as Allen stayed outside, pouring himself a cup of coffee out of his thermos.

Some of the walls were covered with old, yellowed newspaper, and he could read a few of the dates from before the Civil War. He had seen several old, abandoned cabins back in Montana that had used newspaper on the wall and knew it was sometimes used as cheap wallpaper to give the home a warmer look. A couple of old rusted cans remained on the shelf, and a few more lay discarded on the floor. In the center of the farthest wall was a large stone fireplace with some recently placed kindling and a neatly stacked pile of logs beside the hearth.

"What's with the wood?" Cole yelled out the door.

Allen walked to the doorway. "These old homesteads may see a person only once in a couple of years. We'll put wood in cabins in key locations and make all the ranch hands aware of them. The cabin has to be good enough to protect a cowboy if he gets caught in a bad storm and needs to hole up for a couple of days. We saved more than a couple of sorry cowpokes over the years that were caught with their pants down during a bad storm. Everyone knows where the main ones are, and that just makes things work a whole lot safer."

"You say the ranch hasn't allowed many people to come on the place?"

"No, not really. The Greybull has always been off limits to visitors as long as I can remember. It started way back when Gillis McCabe bought the place. Someone started a rumor about a gold mine up in these parts. Somehow word spread, and they had a hell of a time keeping prospectors out. From what I been told, some of them even shot at the cow hands, and butchered more than a couple of the ranch beef. It took almost ten years to get all of them squatters out of these hills and off the ranch. They thought for sure they were going to strike it rich, but when it was all said and done no one found nothing."

"I'm going to look around for a couple more minutes," Cole said. He explored the remaining two small rooms and was interested in the different stuff the ranchers left—a small bed frame, a dusty old chest, plates, a desk and another broken chair, until he reminded himself of what little he had taken from his own house when he left. As Cole walked out the back door, he noticed the grass sprouting around an abandoned plow and other old equipment that cluttered the field in the back. On the east side of the cabin was an old, heavy-duty wagon that caught Cole's attention. At first glance something just seemed out of place about it.

Allen walked around the corner and immediately saw what interested Cole. A large piece of the wagon's sideboard had rotted away and exposed a hidden bottom.

"Now, what in the hell do you suppose they used that for?" Cole asked.

"I don't know, but it sure is strange. Never seen that before, maybe gun running or something?"

Cole reached over and pulled out an old lead ball from the rotting sideboard. "Looks like these boys may have run into some kind of trouble."

"Well, the Indians in these parts were pretty much friendly when old Virgil and Vern built this place. I'm not quite sure what that's from," Allen said.

They continued walking around the homestead, looking at the remnants of the old corral and barn. A slight indentation in the ground led to the remains of an old shed where the trail branched and headed up the canyon. "This is a beautiful little valley. I think I'll take a walk up this trail and lighten my load," Cole said.

"Take your time. I'll get the lunches out."

The trail meandered up the valley, and Cole found a secluded spot. On his way back he saw what looked like a rusted chimney sticking above a gangly wild rose bush. With closer examination, Cole determined that he was looking at the remains of an old moonshine still. In those days, a still was worth a lot of money, Cole thought to himself, and no one would have left a perfectly good still without good reason. Maybe this fella hadn't volunteered to sell.

Allen walked over and handed Cole his lunch and canteen and then sat down. "You know that dirt road we came in on is basically the only route in or out of the ranch. This here road dead-ends about eight miles west of here at a small ghost town. There's only a skeleton of one building there now, but at one time I hear there were close to ten buildings in all. It only existed for a few years around '51, and no one I have ever talked to could remember why it started or went bust. Probably it was sheer isolation would be my guess." Allen munched on a handful of dried apple pieces.

"A lot of history around," Cole said.

"Yeah, there is. This is tough land and needs smart, tough men to manage it. It's frustrating at times with the weather and the drought. By the way, I need to warn you, if you're driving out here and it starts to rain, this road becomes impassable in a matter of minutes. There are places where this clay road has no bottom." Allen shifted his sitting position.

"Are there many roads up in these mountains?"

"None that goes any distance, these mountains are difficult to travel through unless you can find cattle or game trails. But hidden among them are hundreds of beautiful lush valleys, something I wish we used more productively. These mountains are rough, so many sheer cliffs, steep hill sides and rockslides, and it's difficult to get around."

Cole shook his head, gazing at the dry grass in the valley. "It's real unfortunate this drought has hit this area so hard. Who would have thought that this weather would plague this region for the five straight years. Are we going to be anywhere near Gillis McCabe's grave site?" Cole asked.

"Nah, it's about five miles back down the road, but you can probably see the cross if it stays clear. I'll try and point it out to you and show you where the road takes off on our trip back. You know," Allen continued, "before they put this ranch together and called it The Greybull, the Indians referred to this area as Whispering Hills."

"Why'd they call it that?" Cole asked.

"Well, it started way back with their legends that said the hills would whisper to lone warriors as they made their journeys through it. Even now, people talk about strange things they see, like lights up on the hills where no one should or probably could be. I can't speak for back then, but I have sure heard and seen some mighty hard to explain stuff in the twenty years I've worked here."

"Like what?"

"Well, like what just happened to that cowboy named Lippy over on Dutch's ranch. About every five years, something like that happens, and no one can figure it out. One that got a lot of talk that I can remember happened about fifteen years ago. A guy named Pete Wilson, who worked for the Forest Service, disappeared. He worked by himself and was an experienced woodsman, building bridges and mountain cabins, repairing and developing trail systems and the like. He worked mainly in the undeveloped parts of the forest to help with wildfires and such in late spring through early fall. Pete built a real sturdy small cabin in a high valley about forty miles north of here. The cabin sat real close to the Yellowstone boundary, in a valley known as Dead Indian Meadows."

"That's a strange name. Why'd they call it that?"

"They named the valley after some cowboys found a skeleton in a small cave at the base of a large rock with a lot of those Indian petroglyphs on it. No one knew if the skeleton was Indian or not, but the name stuck. Pete's cabin was tucked real nice into a stand of aspen that looked down on a meadow, a real pretty place. About twice a season, a forest service pack train would deliver him supplies. In the middle of his third year, an old packer named Laxton, if I remember right, rode in and found Pete's mule and horse loose in the meadow about a mile from his cabin. The mule had a couple of nasty cuts on its rump that could have been caused by a bear, but they weren't sure.

"The door to the cabin was torn right off its hinges, but there was no sign of Pete and no clue as to what happened to him. They found blood in the cabin, but after two weeks they gave up, never did find a body. Pete knew the mountains like the back of his hand. He was a survivor."

"So there was no sign at all?"

"None, and that's just one story. You ask Ballard about his experience one night over by Jack Creek. He'll tell you he saw something or somebody moving in the dark for a good part of the night. Spooked him real bad, says whatever it was even stole some of his clothes."

"Funny. He talks like he's the toughest guy around."

"What do you mean by that?"

Cole shrugged. "Nothing, he's just been a little difficult to get to know."

"I know he's a little rough sometimes, but he's always been there when I needed him," Allen said.

"Anything else?" Cole asked as he finished his sandwich.

"Probably the one that would be the most interesting to you would be the experience Julie McCabe had two years ago. She went out for a ride on that big black Quarter Horse of hers named Gun Smoke, and got out into the foothills about five miles from the house, when her horse stumbled and threw her. Her head hit a rock, and she had no idea how long she was unconscious, but when she woke up, she was lying in the shade of a small bush with her head on a wad of grass, and her horse was eating by a nearby tree. She never heard or saw anyone or anything after she woke up; she didn't know what to do, so she just rode home."

"What about you? Ever seen anything?"

"Yeah, a couple of years ago, one of the hands got a message that his ma had passed away. I decided to ride up to the line shack he was working at and relieve him, so he could head for the funeral. I only planned on staying two days, before one of the other hands was supposed to relieve me. That night I had spilled some coffee on my shirt, so I took it off, washed it, and securely hung it on a tree to dry. The next morning, I got up and my shirt was gone. I searched for over an hour just in case the wind had blown it off, but no shirt. And I'm not the only one that has lost clothing up in those hills at night. Whatever it is, it seems to like clothing."

"Sure is an interesting ranch you got here," laughed Cole.

"You'll think that until something weird happens to you," Allen said. "But we had better start heading back."

"By the way, you didn't finish telling me what happened to that cowboy named Lippy on Dutch's ranch," Cole inquired, as he opened the door to the truck.

"They never did find him, but I got a little more of the story. I guess when they found his horse, it had lost its head stall, and Dutch told Wes and me there was a lot of blood on one stirrup as he left. He didn't want to spoil any of the ladies' dinner, talking about blood and all."

Cole looked over at Allen. "I feel bad for that man's family."

"We all do, Cole, we all do."

On the ride back to the ranch, Cole changed the subject.

"So, what's the deal with John Prentice?"

"You've opened a big box." Allen rubbed his forehead. "I've known John since he was about sixteen. First time I met him, well, sort of met him, I was at a grange hall dance, and a friend of mine and I decided to take a smoke break in the parking lot. I was leaning against a wagon having a smoke when I noticed John and his cousin standing around this Model A. From where I could see, the younger boy must have seen a bottle of shine on the seat of this car and started to reach through the open window. Just then, the cowboy who owned the car happened to come out of the grange and caught him red-handed. This cowboy was a solid six-foot. Well he grabbed the boy by the arm and had some words with him, yelling that he caught a thief. John Prentice was only sixteen but already about six two and stocky. He walked over to the cowboy, grabbed his shoulder, spun him around, and laid one hell of a lick to his chin. The cowboy folded like a deck of cards, hitting the dirt like a sack of potatoes, and then John kicked him until he rolled under the car."

"Prentice sounds like a guy you don't mess with," Cole said.

"He was just plain mean as a kid, and I don't think he's changed. When he was about twenty-eight, he and a well-to-do fellow from Cody started some type of loan business with John collecting the late payments. I believe they did real well for about three years, and then his partner died in an accident about ten miles south of Cody. The man didn't have any relatives, at least none that anyone found, so all of a sudden Prentice ended up with the business and most of the guy's money. When he was about thirty-four, he bought a major part in the bank in Meeteetse and in another year was sole owner. He's got a reputation for foreclosing on people. I never had to deal with him until he started seeing Julie, and between me and you, I never cared for him much."

Cole was silent for several minutes, until Allen pointed to a big boulder to the left of the road. "That's the start of the road up to the old grave site, but I ain't been up there for over ten years. Not much up there but the old cross and a good view. It's a dead end trail that ends in some steep cliffs and boulders."

About an hour and a half later, the two rolled into the ranch, just in time for supper. Allen excused himself, and Cole headed to the mess hall. Most of the hands were already planted in their favorite chairs and were waiting for Chin to put out the chow. Cole greeted everyone as he entered. There were several new faces at dinner, and Cole sat down beside a cowboy he hadn't met before. "I'm Cole Morgan." He held out his hand to a clean-shaven, wiry man in his thirties, with a hat that looked like someone had drug it behind his horse for at least a year.

"Nice to meet you, I'm Archie."

Cole smiled. "Know what we're having for dinner?"

"It's steak night and hereagains."

"Hereagains" Cole said, "What are hereagains?"

Archie chuckled, "That's what the boys call leftovers. Anything that doesn't get eaten shows up on the table again, so the boys just call them hereagains."

Across the table from them sat Dodge and Clyde, and Clyde was loudly telling a story. "Well, I was coming down that steep part of Coyote Creek to the west, and I went through this thick patch of old timber, and there it was—a rusty chunk of metal sticking out of this huge rotted stump. Immediately I knew I had struck it rich and found old Creager's bayonet."

"So, you found the bayonet?" Dodge asked, with a look of excitement.

"Hell, no, I didn't find it. It was a rusty old pick head. Some miner must have stuck it in a tree so he wouldn't lose it or something. The handle had long since rotted off, but it sure looked like a bayonet. Closest I've ever got to being rich."

Everyone around the table laughed. A moment later another cowboy entered the room and sat down across from Cole. The man was Cole's size, with a two-day-old beard and a dirty shirt. Cole stuck out his hand. "Cole Morgan."

"Lowell Starr, and yeah, I know who you are." He ignored Cole's hand.

"There a problem?"

"Never did much care for you college boys who play cowboy in the summer. Not worth a damn, in my opinion."

"Well, I didn't see anyone asking you, but I guess you got a right to your opinion."

Chin interrupted them with a large plate of steaks, which he set in the middle of the table. Cole reached with his fork to spear a large rare one when Lowell, who was reaching for a steak at the same time, stuck his fork firmly into the top of Cole's hand. Lowell pulled back, leaving the fork standing for a moment in the muscle between Cole's thumb and index finger.

"Looks like college boy never learned his manners," laughed Lowell.

In one swift motion Cole stepped up on the four-man bench and jumped over the table, hitting Lowell with all the impact of a middle linebacker. Lowell tried to throw several punches, but they fell harmlessly off Cole's shoulder. The two men fought to their feet, and then Lowell fell backwards from two quick blows to the face. Bloodied, he staggered and fell backwards against the wall and slid to the floor. Cole took off his handkerchief, wrapped his hand, and returned to the table and sat down. A couple of the men went to help Lowell, who was knocked out cold and bleeding from several spots on his face.

"I can't believe what I just saw. That man is one quick cowboy," Clyde said to the man helping Lowell. "Did you see that speed?"

Dodge and Jay got up and went over to Cole. "You all right, how's your hand" Dodge asked?

Cole looked at his hand and then Lowell's face, "Seems to me it's going to be a mite better than his face."

Jay looked at Cole. "You're not much on starting a fight, but you're hell at finishing them." One of the men had gone out and now returned with Allen, as Cole dished himself out a large helping of mashed potatoes.

Allen stood and took a long look at Lowell's still body and his bloody face, while two cowboys tended to him.

"May I have a word with you outside?" Allen said, with a frown on his face. The room had been silent, but now Cole could hear the whispering as he left.

"When I asked folks about you no one said you had a temper. Don't make me regret hiring you. Now, what the hell happened in there?"

"He seemed to really want a piece of me and quite frankly, I was happy to oblige."

"I hung my reputation on you. I hope you know times are tough. I know twenty other cowboys who'd love to have your job, even with the trouble The Greybull's been having. There'll be no more fighting. Understood?"

Cole nodded.

The next morning, Cole walked to the horse corrals below the barn and for over an hour studied all the horses and their movement, attitudes and physiques. Finally, he moved to the mule corral. It didn't take Cole long to focus on a tall sorrel john mule with four white socks and a white spot that looked a lot like a teepee on its rump. The mule had good muscle structure, alert ears, and calm eyes. Cole was no greenhorn when it came to sizing up horses or mules, and he knew he had a good one in this animal. He knew a well-trained mule could out-walk, out-climb, and out-jump most any horse, while eating and drinking about half as much. He respected the way a good mule picked his way through even the worst country, and he particularly liked the way they were always aware of their surroundings.

The mule's ears turned toward the house, and Cole looked to see Allen heading his way, so he turned and walked back over to the pole fence.

"How's the hand?" Allen asked.

Cole looked down at his hand. "I want to say I'll try to stay out of trouble from now on. But that fellow came lookin' for it. If I put you in a bad place, I'm sure sorry."

"I don't think it'll happen again, at least with him. I just fired him. We don't need that kind of crap around here. To be honest, I never cared much for that guy, but he left me no choice with that fork crap."

"I'm sorry it happened. Probably shouldn't have hit him."

"Hell, I would have," Allen said, with a grin on his face. "Now, which horse have you picked?"

"If it's all right with you, I'd like to have the sorrel mule over there in the corner."

"Mule!" barked Allen. "Is this some Montana thing?"

"I just really like that mule."

Cole and Allen both laughed, and the two headed back up the hill to the house.

"Hell of a story behind that mule," Allen said. "We had penned up one of our best Morgan mares to breed in the morning to one of our Morgan studs. Sometime in the night the mammoth Jack we call Dexter, jumped the fence and then jumped into her corral and bred her. Mr. McCabe was one pissed fella when he found out—almost fired the hand in charge of the breeding. When the mule turned two, the guy we had breaking most of the horses took a liking to him and spent a little extra time with him. That mule is probably the first animal out of the whole crop that you could ride. Tim Doud was great with animals, so good that a ranch over near Cody hired him out from under us for almost twice the money."

As they approached the bunkhouse, Cole noticed Julie by the barn, saddling her horse for her morning ride. "Boy that girl sure rides a lot."

Allen smiled. "How would you like to come to dinner at the house tonight and tell the McCabes what you come up with so far for changes around here?"

"Best offer I've had all day," Cole laughed, red-faced that Allen had seen him watching Julie. He looked forward to seeing her at dinner, but, for now, he needed to get back to work.

Cole had been using one of the ranch's older horses to survey the closer parts of the ranch. Today he'd take the mule that he'd decided to name Patch, for the white teepee-shaped spot on its rump. Cole knew that Patch was green broke and just needed miles to develop confidence. He loaded his saddle and tack in the back of his truck, attached the horse trailer, and brought Patch over to load. When Cole opened the trailer door the young mule just stopped, and no amount of pulling, pushing, or shouting was going to do anything to get him into that trailer.

"Need some help?" asked Elmer, a crooked smile appearing under his handlebar mustache as he watched Cole's frustration.

"I thought Allen said all the horses had been broke and loaded before."

"He did, I suspect, but that there ain't no horse."

With that, Elmer stepped in the barn and brought out a small bucket of oats. "Let's just see if this doesn't help the situation." Elmer put his can of oats in the trailer, and he couldn't get out of the way fast enough as Patch stepped inside and settled into eating.

Chapter 7

Over the next couple of months, some of Cole's ideas were put into practice at the ranch. Summer set in, and he worked with the crew on developing new stands of fescue grass he planted in test plots around the valleys. He continuously found new parts of the ranch he wanted to explore; including an area about eight miles west of Gillis McCabe's gravesite, east of the old Creager homestead. He had noticed the country appeared greener than on his last outing and was curious to find out more about an area that showed promise above a large bluff. Cole was about to load Patch into the homemade trailer with its weathered sideboards and wood spoke wheels with no brakes when he glanced between the buildings. Someone was in the process of backing the ranch's old Ford flatbed up against the loading ramp. Curious, he watched as the door of the truck opened and Julie slid from behind the steering wheel.

"Good morning," Cole shouted.

For the first time, Julie saw Cole's truck and Patch tied to the side of the trailer.

"Good morning," she answered, barely audible from forty yards away as she lifted her saddle.

Cole walked over to see if she needed help. "Anything I can help with?"

Julie turned with a saddle in her arms, and looked at Cole for a several seconds with a firm look on her face. "No, do I look helpless or something? Maybe you think women can't drive trucks. What is it with you men?"

"Wow," Cole said, "I just was trying to help, I didn't mean anything by that."

Julie looked at Cole with the saddle still in her arms, then she dropped it at her feet. "Sorry Cole, I'm not mad at you. I'm mad at . . . Never mind, it's my problem not yours."

Cole waited a moment and said, "If you're going for a ride, you're welcome to join me."

"I appreciate the offer. It's very nice of you. But I need some space today. I have a beautiful place that I go once in a while to think. I just need some time."

"I understand, maybe next time."

"Maybe," Julie smiled, turned, and put her saddle in the truck.

Cole returned to the truck, finished loading Patch in the trailer, and slowly drove off. Even as light weight as the little trailer was, it was difficult pulling it up the steep hills. After an hour of driving, he pulled the truck and horse trailer over onto a flat spot beside the road and unloaded the mule. Patch stood quietly as he was saddled and bridled. With his four white socks and white rump, he actually looked pretty impressive under saddle. He stood fifteen and a half hands high and weighed around eleven hundred pounds, a good size for a riding mule.

Cole tied on a set of saddlebags, a small axe, a scabbard with his father's bolt action 30.06, and a large canteen. He figured he wouldn't be back for at least five hours and wanted to be as prepared as possible. He had no more than gotten into the saddle when a large jackrabbit ran between the legs of the mule. Patch's large ears came to attention and though he never flinched, his eyes followed the rabbit across the road and into the sagebrush. This is going to be one great mule, Cole thought, as he pulled on the reins and headed south toward the base of the ridge.

He hoped to find an old game trail or natural ledge in the terrain that would allow him to wind through the rock outcroppings and cliffs to the upper benches he had seen from the truck. Patch's gait was smooth, quickly covering several hundred yards through the sagebrush to the foothills that led to the ridge. The brush slowly turned to forest and grass, and eventually thickened to dark timber. Over the years, the cattle had used the trees for shade and a maze of worn trails crisscrossed throughout the timber.

As they gained altitude, the terrain steepened and the few remaining trails were more visible and well worn. They picked their way around deadfalls and rocky patches as they worked themselves toward the thicker timber. The forest floor was brown with rotting pine and spruce needles and soon their trail petered out at a large deadfall. Long ago, there had been a trail here, but it had been lost to a huge rotting log that now blocked the path. Cole dismounted and began to scan the ground for traces of animal tracks, as he moved laterally along the ridge. Several minutes later, he noticed some pine needles were disturbed on the other side of a large, mossy stump. After carefully examining the marks, he determined an animal coming down the hill must have made them. For the next five minutes, he back tracked the animal's trail. The rough, barely visible track soon turned into a well-used game path that meandered up through the rocks. It headed up the hill at a steep grade. The trail seemed to end where a large log had fallen across it, and there appeared to be no way around due to the steep rock face and large boulders on each side. The way the log laid over the trail made it a good three feet high at its lowest point. It would take him a while to chop through it with his ax and move a section so that Patch could pass through. Cole began hacking away at dead branches.

There was one last branch on the other side of the log that Cole couldn't reach, so he led Patch to within a foot of the log, then used his ax to climb to the other side. He laid the lead rope down on the log, knowing Patch had been taught to ground tie, and removed the last branch. When he finished, the young mule looked like he might follow, so Cole pulled on the lead rope. Patch paused for a second, then with one bound and saddlebags flying, he cleared the log by over a foot, and they were on their way.

Cole led Patch on foot as they made their way up the ridge and over a small rise. The sun met his face as he emerged from the heavier timber and found himself on top of a steep, two hundred foot cliff that formed a semicircle around a small, picturesque basin below. In the center of the basin was a beautiful one-acre lake with grassy banks. Sweat coursed down Cole's face as he took off his cowboy hat and wiped it with his handkerchief. Cole took a moment to catch his breath and decided to sit down on a large flat boulder while he took in the view. Below him he could clearly see the small lake had a tall, narrow waterfall dropping in from the south. Suddenly he spotted a black horse tied to a tree on the shore— Gun Smoke.

"What the hell?" Cole said, quietly. He walked back to Patch, who was tied to a tree several yards back from the rim, and retrieved a collapsible telescope from his saddlebags. He extended the eyepiece to its full twelve inches and leaned against a boulder to steady his view. It was definitely Julie's horse, he thought as a blur of movement appeared in the water just out from the bank. Cole dialed the scope's focusing lens, until it was clear at four hundred yards. His mouth dropped open as a naked, glistening Julie McCabe walked out of the water toward her horse.

He strained to make out every detail, as she retrieved a towel that lay over a fallen log on the bank. He knew he shouldn't be looking, but Julie, naked and wet in the sunshine, was too much for him. In what seemed like only seconds, she had put on her clothes, mounted her horse, and ridden back into the trees to the east. He could do nothing for a moment, but then he felt guilty that he had watched. He was mad at himself that he hadn't had the strength to turn his head and leave, but the image of her kept running through his mind.

He needed to shake off his daze and decided the best course of action was to ride in the opposite direction, hoping they didn't meet. How she had gotten to the lake, Cole had no idea, but hoped by going west he wouldn't cross her path. He felt guilty enough without accidentally running into her right now and having her put two and two together, that wouldn't be good.

Cole and Patch headed west, up and away from the lake toward the top of the ridge. The higher ground was sparsely treed compared to the dark timber below and there were several game trails to choose from. He followed one of the more well-worn trails for over an hour as it headed up the ridge. The trail leveled out and then dropped into a small valley dotted with meadows. The first meadow was not as open as the rest, with aspen patches and lone pine trees growing every fifty yards, but there was still plenty of tall grass covering the ground. Midway through the meadow, Cole saw several elk skeletons on the ground beside a thicket of trees, probably the work of wolves, he thought. A three-foot wide stream meandered through the meadow's bottom, and Cole let Patch drink. He dismounted and also drank from the cool creek, and then refilled his canteen. Cole remounted and noticed the sun glinting off something metallic about a hundred yards to his left.

Why the hell would someone pack something metal all the way up here, and then leave it? Patch picked his way through the scattered trees until they came into a small grassy opening. Cole's eyes immediately focused on what he believed were the mangled remains of a propeller, half buried in the mud, standing like a lonely grave marker. Tilted and battered, it looked like it had been there for at least a couple of years. Small parts of the plane littered the ground for at least sixty yards in every direction. Several of the pieces were actually stuck in a large tree, while the majority of the badly rotted canvas, wood, and small chunks of metal were scattered everywhere. Cole worked his way up the valley through the crash site, trying to better examine the wreck and determine whether anyone had died. He had one of his questions answered when he walked up a small rise and came upon two burial sites marked with three-foot high wooden crosses. The graves were mounded with rocks and had grass growing up through the gaps between them. Whoever buried these people had taken some time and effort to do a good job. Cole spent the next hour surveying the wreckage, trying to get a feel for what had happened. The wooden crosses, however well built, had no information on them, and whatever other clues that may have once existed appeared to be gone now, with the exception of a chunk of metal that Cole believed to be part of the tail of the plane. A few numbers on the tail section were still visible, even though most were unreadable.

Cole had seen a handful of planes flying, and only a couple up close at an aerial barnstorming show while he was in college. He remembered the plane had numbers about this size on its tail section, and he had asked one of the crew about it. The gentleman had told him that the numbers were a form of identification. As he stood there looking at all the wreckage, he knew for sure he wasn't going to bring up the fact that he had found the old crash site. He couldn't let Julie know he was on the ridge above the lake. He would get a chance to visit with Allen sometime the following week and ask him about the plane and who died there.

Cole was about to turn around and head back to Patch, when he got the sensation he was being watched. In one swift movement, he whirled and looked where he had been walking. Cole stood still for a moment, but nothing seemed out of place. The only thing moving was a small bird jumping from limb to limb several yards away, however, the feeling of being watched continued.

Cole took Patch off the picket rope and got into the saddle. He didn't like this place and was bothered by his uneasiness with the wreck site. For a moment, he thought about trying a new way back to the truck but quickly dismissed the idea due to the many steep cliffs and rocky ground. He was looking forward to dinner, seeing

Julie again, and explaining some of his ideas on ranch management and irrigating using captured, high mountain streams.

Two hours later, he reached the truck, opened the door to the old trailer, and watched Patch walk in like he was an old hand. Cole smiled and rewarded him with half a coffee can of oats. This mule had warm eyes and gained Cole's confidence faster than any animal he had ever ridden.

On the drive back to the ranch, Cole stopped at one of the many tufted fescue grass samples plots he and a couple of the men had planted that summer. In some cases, the test plots were designed to gauge resistance to overgrazing, and in others, to try different varieties. Cole was pretty sure that the grass outside the enclosure would be severely overgrazed, but he was unsure how some of the new seed he had introduced would grow in the alpine meadows.

When they got back to the ranch, Cole took Patch from the horse trailer, rubbed him down, and put him back in the large pasture for the night. He drove the truck and trailer behind the barn and unhitched the rickety trailer, then made his way toward the bunkhouse to shower and change his clothes.

Getting out of the shower, he hurriedly dressed, and met Jay Taylor coming into the bunkhouse.

"You going to the big dance over in Cody tomorrow?" Jay asked.

"I hadn't thought much about it, mainly because I didn't know there was one. But it sounds fun."

"Why don't you ride over with Suzie and me?"

"Two's company and three's a crowd. I'll go, but if it's okay with you, I'll drive myself and see you two there."

Jay had immediately warmed up to Cole after hearing about him coming to Suzie's defense his first day in town.

"You bet it's all right," he said. "We'll look forward to seeing you there."

Cole left Jay in the bunkhouse, and on his way to the McCabe's, he met Tyler Raines sweeping the front stairs.

"Mr. Morgan. How are you this glorious day?"

Cole was always taken back by Tyler's formal language. "Not bad, not bad at all. I am finally feeling like I kind of belong around here. What's new with you, Tyler?"

"I received a letter from my daughter. She and her husband just bought a ranch and she's expecting."

"That's great. Where's their place?"

"It's about thirty miles east of town. It's little, but really a pretty place, even has a stream and a pond. I hadn't thought they would be able to work anything out with the bank, but somehow they did."

Cole congratulated him on his future grandchild and headed to the house. He was sure Prentice had helped in some way. It pissed him off that Prentice had so much power and was after Julie as hard as a mule after a bucket of oats.

Sally McCabe met Cole in the hallway. "Well, good evening, Cole. I trust everything is going well for you. Would you care for a drink?" It had been almost five months now since he had taken the job on the ranch, and he was starting to feel like he found a new home where he really belonged.

"Straight whisky, please," he answered.

"Just like Wes. Never knew how you men could drink that stuff straight."

Julie came down the staircase to the right of the fireplace and headed straight for Cole. "Why, Mr. Morgan, haven't seen much of you for a while."

Cole found her beautiful in her blue dress.

"Sure nice of your folks to invite me to dinner makes a great end to a Friday."

Wes McCabe came into the room with Allen, the two deep in conversation. "I'm not sure how we should handle this with Brooks breaking his leg. I planned on him working the Canvas Creek next week. I guess we'll need to find us another hand," Allen was saying.

"Cole, glad you could make it, come in, come in," he said in a hurried tone. "Have a seat by me." Wes motioned Cole toward the head of the table. The group sat down for dinner at the large oak table that was centered in the room. Tyler carried in a huge ham shank on a silver platter and placed it beside big bowls of mashed potatoes and fresh strawberries.

Wes looked at the food and smiled. "This should keep everyone busy for a while. So, Cole, you've had some time to look at the entire ranch. What do you think?"

"Well sir, there seems to be a ton of potential that isn't being used. I think the secret to this ranch is utilizing the water from the mountains better, the rotation of cattle, and the addition of new grasses."

"Interesting, we need to talk further—"

Julie interrupted. "Do we have to talk business all the time?

Wes turned to Cole. "We'll talk later."

At the end of dinner, Tyler returned with another round of drinks for everyone as they retired to the great room. The finely crafted room was full of very old, hand-carved furniture with soft tasseled cushions, arranged in groups to allow for more comfortable, intimate visiting. "So, Cole, what were you saying about rotating cattle and crops?" Wes asked, taking a puff on his cigar.

"This place is impressive, but there's a lot more that can be done."

"Like what?"

"I have a number of thoughts. First, the field-monitoring plot stations are showing me the growth rates of the new fescue grasses compared very favorably to the native varieties, but I need to have more information before I recommend any changes. I also believe that we aren't utilizing the water from the hills to near its potential."

"Interesting, anything else"

"Yes. I am also looking at a better utilization of the land by moving the cattle up the valley earlier, following the season's new grass closer, and preventing the cattle from grazing too long in the spring and damaging the range for fall."

"Interesting. Don't you think what Cole is saying has merit, Allen?" Wes said.

"Yes, I totally agree. I look forward to looking at all Cole's ideas. After all, that's why we brought him here," Allen responded, taking a large puff from his cigar.

"My greatest challenge is the big picture—mapping, trying to get my mind around the varied topography at The Greybull," Cole said. "I just wish there were some good, accurate maps that I could work with to help me locate all the different pastures and then develop them as to the soil types and moisture requirements. I understood from Allen that the ranch might have been surveyed at one time and I was hoping you knew about the documents."

Wes sat in deep thought. Finally, he spoke. "Yes, I do believe I mentioned that to Allen. Years ago, I remember my dad talking about Gillis hiring engineers to survey the ranch, but I really don't know where a person would even start to look for that stuff. That material might've been lost in the fire we had here in one of our storage sheds years ago. Quite frankly, I don't even know if they completed the work or not, but if they did, it would probably be up in a dusty part of the attic somewhere. I was up there looking for something not a week ago, and I don't remember seeing any maps. I'll tell you what, tomorrow is Saturday, and if Julie has the time in the morning, we'll go up there and see what we can find."

"I appreciate it," Cole said. "It would sure help with my work."

By noon the next day, Cole was knocking on the door of the big house. After several knocks, Tyler answered the door, "Good morning, Mr. Morgan, may I help you?"

"Good morning, Tyler. Is Mr. McCabe available?"

"I'm not sure. Was he expecting you?"

Just then, Cole heard Wes's voice in the hall, "Cole, is that you? Come in, come in, and shut the door, Tyler. You're letting the flies in." Wes looked at Cole, shaking his head. "We didn't find what we were looking for, not a single plan. Only thing we did find was a few dusty old papers from Grandpa's day, where he wrote about pastures on one of the pages. I don't know if there is anything in there that might help you, but why don't you take this and check it out." Wes handed Cole a thick stack of old, dusty papers and a small diary.

"Thanks, I will. I appreciate you looking for me. I'll talk to you later after I spend some time with these."

Cole read through most of the papers and was surprised to find some of Gillis McCabe's ideas on different pastures and how the surveyors had broken down the task of surveying the ranch. He had written down certain sections of land, but there were no maps or clues to where the maps might be. The notes contained very little he could use, so he focused on the diary. It took over an hour to read, and on the last page, he was struck by a passage Gillis had written:

I believe I may have finally found the trail that Mrs. Jones spoke of. It traveled in the toughest of country. I believe that with some work and energy I will find it.

The cryptic passage confused Cole, and he wondered if it had anything to do with that talk of lost gold. The top of the page was dated August 30. Cole turned to the front of the booklet and saw the date 1877 written on the inside cover. The next page said only that he planned to go check on a title. It seemed strange he didn't finish it. Later that day, Cole went over to the big house and Wes asked if he knew why the diary notes weren't complete.

"The reason the diary stops on August 31st, 1877, is because that's the date Gillis died in a robbery. Real bad deal. No one ever caught the guy," Wes said.

"He was murdered?"

"No one really knew the details for sure. But there were lots of rumors."

"Thanks," Cole said. "I still have some chores to do. I'm sure I'll have some more questions for you later."

As Cole walked back to the bunkhouse, he wondered why Gillis McCabe had written he needed to check on a title only to die at a small grocery store. As he opened the door to the bunkhouse, he met Jay Taylor coming out, "Yeah, Cole, how you doing? Still going to the big dance in Cody tonight?"

"I think I am. Will there be lots of people?"

"Heck, with the rodeo and dance, about everyone in these parts will be there. Some mighty pretty ladies show up, if you know what I mean."

Cole grinned. "You know, I could use a little dancing with some beautiful ladies."

By two o'clock that afternoon, the men who didn't have to work headed to the showers to get ready for the dance. Cole had just put on a new shirt, when he heard the sound of a car in the driveway. He peered out a window and was disappointed to see Prentice's car rolling to a stop in front of the house. He should have known that John would be taking Julie to the dance. Prentice opened the door and got out with an air of importance. Cole hadn't noticed Tyler sitting on the bench under the weeping willow, until he got up and headed over to greet Prentice. Several minutes passed as they talked, but they were too far away to hear the conversation. It appeared that Prentice was scolding Tyler, who threw up his hands. The conversation ended when Prentice jabbed Tyler in the chest with his finger and then headed to the house.

Now what in blue blazes was that all about, thought Cole. He finished dressing and walked to his truck. As he opened the door, he heard a voice behind him.

"So, are you going to the dance, Mr. Morgan?" Julie said as she emerged from the barn wearing a beautiful yellow spring dress.

Her presence surprised him. "Yes ma'am. You shouldn't be sneaking up on a man, might give him a heart attack or something."

Cole took a breath and then in a confident voice responded, "I thought there might be a lady or two that I might talk into a dance."

"Well, I'm sure you'll find some that would enjoy a man with two left feet." Julie giggled as she walked back to the house and drove away with John.

"Hey Cole" Jay hollered from outside the bunkhouse. "I got a problem. Can you give me a ride? My car seems to have given up the ghost."

"Sure, but what's wrong with it?"

"I think it's the starter, but I'm no mechanic. All I know is, I'm not missing this dance with my girl for nothing." He hopped into the truck, and Cole started the engine.

Jay directed Cole to Suzie's grandparent's ranch, thirty minutes away on good roads. "You don't know this spread, but this is where I used the phone when you had that thing burst. Woke them up in the middle of the night, lucky for you they were home."

"I've seen the place from a distance, but I didn't know this was their ranch."

"Yeah, it's the closest place with a phone," Jay said.

Suzie met the truck in front of the house with a huge smile, wearing a pretty flower-patterned dress. "Boy am I glad to see you," Suzie said, as she gave Jay a huge hug and planted a kiss on his lips.

"Wow, I guess I am one lucky cowboy," Jay said as he turned toward Cole, blushing.

"Suzie, do you mind if I go in and thank your grandparents personally for their kind help?" Cole asked.

"You bet, come on in."

The inside of the house was clean, but everything looked worn and tattered. Suzie introduced her grandparents. "Cole, this is my grandfather, Phil, and my grandmother, Martha."

Cole walked up to each one, "Thanks, without your help the doctor said I wouldn't have made it. I apologize that Jay had to wake you up in the middle of the night." Cole felt immediately comfortable with them, and they reminded him of how he felt the first time he met Suzie.

They all said goodbye, and the three of them squeezed tightly into the front seat of Cole's truck and headed for Cody. "I sure like your grandparents. Do you live there?"

"Yeah—I lost my job at the Red Rooster, but it didn't pay worth a damn anyway. Now I'm worried I might need to move to Cody to find work."

"I wouldn't worry until you know that's the case. Have your grandparents lived there all their lives?"

"They first moved into an old cabin just south of where the house is today and then built this one, lived here ever since. In fact, Grandma worked on Greybull Ranch when she was in her early teens."

"Mind me asking how old she is now?" Cole asked.

"Late seventies, early eighties, I think"

"So that would have had her working for Gillis McCabe just before he died."

"Uh huh, she told me one time that she worked for him for about two years if I remember right, in the late seventies until he passed away. Liked him, I guess," Suzie said, shrugging her shoulders. The subject changed to the dance, but Cole's mind was racing. Maybe Mrs. Schmitz knew the whereabouts of those maps.

Chapter 8

It took almost two hours to make the trip to Cody on gravel roads, a small price to pay for the year's biggest dance. As they entered the south end of Cody, Jay pointed to a general store. "Cole, would you mind pulling over at that white building."

Cole noticed the liquor sign and smiled. "Get me a small bottle of whisky for later, and I'll pay you when you get back." The wood-framed building was in rough shape, with the roof missing a few shingles and paint peeling off in long strips. Several older men sat on rocking chairs on the front porch, passing the time in conversation.

Jay ran in and returned with two bottles of whisky in a brown paper sack. "I sure need something to take the edge off my dancing," Jay laughed. Suzie smiled and nodded in agreement.

Several blocks into town, they turned west toward a large whitewashed building. The parking lot was filled with people, trucks, and cars, as well as a few horses and carriages. They parked beside an older Model A Sedan. People were clustered everywhere, walking, talking, and laughing, as they saw friends they might only see once or twice a year. Large logs separated the parking area from a wide-open field in front of the grange hall. Logs with flat tops were also used as benches around a wide fire pit with roaring flames, a romantic place to go when the dance ended.

Jay noticed some of the local girls eyeing Cole as he got out of the truck. "Might be a good night for you Cole by the looks of things. I know a couple of them."

"I bet you do, and if I were you, I wouldn't go there," Suzie warned, in an ornery tone.

The shirt Cole chose for the dance was the new one he had bought for the funeral. It wasn't his normal baggy attire, instead much tighter fitting. Cole was encouraged to see that a number of ladies seemed to be without dates. While sizing up the action, Cole noticed Allen Skimming leaning against the front wall of the grange. "Jay, I'll catch you and Suzie a little later. I'm going to talk with

Allen." He walked over to Allen and said, "Allen, glad you could make it, didn't know you were a lady's man."

"Someone from the ranch had to show these fine ladies how to dance," Allen chuckled.

The talk turned to work and how well his mule and the fescue plots were doing. "The McCabes really appreciate the ideas you've brought to the table. God only knows, with their financial issues, they needed something. I think they're actually going to see a slight profit this year. That hasn't happened for some time. You should have heard all the nice things they said about you at dinner Wednesday night, when they had John Prentice over for dinner."

"Prentice was over last week? I didn't see him."

"Oh yeah, they had an early dinner, and I think he was gone before you got back from being out all day, long day for you. Anyway, I wasn't privy to everything, but they needed to talk about the ranch's finances. John runs the bank in town where they get all their loans, and they renew everything about this time every year. It was all business."

Cole remembered the plane wreckage on Decker Mountain and he decided to ask Allen who was in the graves and what happened with the wreck. He felt plenty of time had elapsed since he had been up there, and his curiosity was getting the best of him.

"Plane wreck" Allen said, surprised. "I don't know of any plane wrecks. As far as I know, there's never been an airplane crash on the ranch. Hell, for that matter, I ain't ever even seen one flying over the place."

As soon as Allen spoke, Cole knew he had opened a can of worms and wouldn't hear the end of it. "Oh, I figured you would know all about it. Someone buried the bodies and even put up a cross over each of the graves."

"Graves, well I'll be! That's more than strange. I'll talk to Wes and the sheriff and some other folks and see if anyone knows anything about a wreck or a missing plane. Let's head up there Tuesday and take a look. You say there are two graves? You wouldn't be pulling my leg now, would you?"

"No, not much up there but the graves and pieces of wreckage, but its there"

They moved inside the grange hall, where the band was just starting a new song and couples were beginning to fill the floor.

The building that they used as a grange was huge and as big as most of the buildings back at the university. Whitewash covered the boards, and a large porch surrounded the entrance. The porch was made of rough, pine planks set with spikes to keep them straight. Inside, the lighting was better than he expected, and you could easily see faces across the room.

Cole decided to get a glass of lemonade, before he picked the lucky lady to try his dancing skills. As he headed to a table, he saw Julie and John Prentice pick up some drinks and head to the other side of the dance hall. Cole couldn't help but notice the number of guys looking at Julie and the number of ladies looking at John. He didn't much like it, but they did make a nice-looking couple. Julie's eyes met Cole's, and she smiled and gave Cole a little wave from across the hall. John must have felt the movement of Julie's wave, because he turned and looked. When he saw Cole, he gave him a hard glare, but Cole smiled in return.

A heavy-set, elderly woman in a pink dress poured Cole a glass of lemonade and handed it to him with a smile and a laugh. Cole thanked her and went back to scanning the room for a dancing partner, when he thought he saw a person he recognized out the corner of his eye. For a minute, he couldn't place him—and then he remembered. Cole couldn't recall his name, but he was the brother of the guy he had fought when he first came into town. The man was staring at Cole, and when their eyes met, the man turned and blended back into the crowd. Cole wanted to relax tonight, dance, and enjoy life. He hoped he didn't need to deal with this again. The grange was so crowded that he decided to drink his lemonade outside on the porch, where he could enjoy it without being bumped into.

As soon as he got outside, Jay and Suzie came over. Jay reached into his shirt and pulled out a flask and poured a little whisky in Cole's drink. "Suzie and I decided to use your truck for a few more minutes." Suzie smiled and winked at Cole.

"Hope you two are staying out of trouble," came a voice behind the group. They turned to see Bob Ballard, wearing a neatly pressed bright red shirt and shining hair from a generous amount of setting cream.

"It looks to me like you're having way too much fun," he laughed good-naturedly and smiled as he passed them to enter the hall.

"That's the best mood I've ever seen him in," Cole said.

"It's amazing what a little whisky will do," laughed Suzie.

For the next couple of hours, Cole danced with a number of ladies who caught his eye. He noticed it was a lot easier to talk to women than it had been back in his four years of college. Cole walked across the room toward a young, shapely brunette who was chatting with some friends. When he got closer, he made sure to get her attention.

"Can I help you?" the young lady said with a flippant attitude.

"I was wondering if you dance as good as you look." Cole smiled.

"I'm Marlene, and if you're asking for a dance, let's do it."

"I'm Cole Morgan, nice to meet you. I haven't been to a dance in Cody before, but I'm enjoying the scenery."

They danced the next three dances, laughing and talking. Marlene's blue eyes were beautiful, and Cole was attracted to her devilish smile. It was not hard for Cole to see she was very interested and would be happy to spend the rest of the dance with him. They danced to a few more songs, then Marlene smiled and said, "Let's go out to my brother's car and get a couple of cold beers. We need a break."

"That's the best offer I've had in a long time." Cole took her hand and led her through the crowd to the parking lot. Oddly, he felt a sense of guilt, but he wasn't sure why. He knew in his mind who he really wanted to be with, but he also knew that was not going to happen. He shook his head. It would be stupid to be faithful to someone he had never even kissed, and she being on the arm of someone else. As they walked to her brother's truck, a young girl ran in front of them and stopped. She seemed about sixteen and had to think before each word she said.

"Hey mister, my dad used to know your dad back in his rodeo days. He got a little busted up like your dad. He wants you to come over to his car. He got something for you."

"Let's see what this guy has to say," Marlene said with a smile. "Maybe you'll get lucky and he owes your family money."

She pointed to an older Chevrolet that was parked about twenty yards from the other cars in the shadow of a large cottonwood. Cole saw a person behind the wheel, but couldn't make out any facial features. Cole was about ten feet from the car when he stopped. The person inside slowly opened the door and stood up. Even in the shadows, Cole could tell this was not an old man but a much bigger, more agile person. The man came out from behind the car door, but Cole still couldn't see his face.

"Well, Mr. Cole Morgan! I see you met my younger sister. It was nice of her to go get you and bring you over so we could talk. It's downright considerate of you to finally leave the safety of the ranch."

It was Jake Prentice, the man he had knocked out in the Meeteetse café. Cole sensed movement behind him and felt a heavy sinking in his stomach. His dad had always cautioned him to be aware of his environment and not let his guard down. Carefully and slowly he glanced behind him and faced three more men standing in a perimeter about ten yards away. Cole let go of Marlene's hand and motioned for her to move aside. As she did so, Jake lunged at Cole.

Cole dove under Jake's swinging fist and threw a quick punch to his stomach and then rolled over. When he had regained his feet, he was surrounded by the other three men. In the moonlight, he recognized one of them as Lowell Starr, the man who had put a fork in his hand at dinner a couple of months earlier. He didn't recognize the smallest man, but the third man was Jake's younger brother, who had been watching him earlier inside the grange. Cole moved against the car to protect his back, as the three men moved closer. Cole knew he could only throw so many punches before being overwhelmed.

"I'm really going to enjoy this," Lowell muttered.

Cole braced for the attack, when suddenly, a huge red streak came out of nowhere and tackled two of the three men. It was Ballard, fighting like a mad man. Cole swung at Lowell and connected to the side of his head, then kneed him in the stomach, and he rolled to the ground. All two hundred forty pounds of Ballard condensed into a loud thud, as he threw a bone-crushing blow to Jake's brother's jaw. The second man Ballard hit was probably eighty pounds smaller and four inches shorter, and Ballard's second thunderous blow sent him to his back.

Marlene screamed with a tremendous voice. Cole turned to her but felt a hard blow to the back of his head that sent him to his knees and then to the ground. Even though he was dizzy, he rolled to his back as quickly as he could to see what had hit him. Jake Prentice stood over Cole with a large tree branch and was coming to finish the deal. He swung with all his strength and at the last second, Cole rolled to his right. The branch brushed his face and shoulder and broke on impact as it hit the ground. He jumped to his feet and closed in on Jake, who threw a punch that Cole easily blocked. With football star speed Cole unleashed everything he had. His blows backed Jake up against the car—one punch to the stomach, two to the face, then repeating the sequence until Jake's limp body was leaning against the car. Suddenly, someone grabbed Cole's arm. It was the sheriff, yelling, "Enough, enough!" Jake slowly slid down the car until his bloodied face landed in the dirt. The two men Ballard had beaten looked terrible, with torn clothes and several angry cuts on their swollen, crimson faces.

Cole had absorbed a number of blows with only a half-inch cut under his eye that oozed streaks of blood down his face. Ballard's new red shirt was torn and stained with blood. Ballard was bent over and his breathing was heavy but he still appeared to be full of power and fight.

Cole looked at the Prentice bunch and admired the damage Ballard and he had inflicted. "Thanks for the help." Cole said.

"No problem, I saw you and that girl headed out to who knows where, and I was thinking, that lucky son of a bitchin' cowboy, when I saw these three guys tracking you. It didn't seem fair for you to have all the fun, and us riding for the same brand and all," responded Ballard, with a big grin.

"I owe you," Cole said. As he started back toward the dance floor, he stopped and looked back. The two Prentice brothers and Lowell Starr lay unconscious, and the last member of the group was moaning beside the car. The sizable crowd that had gathered around them parted and let them through as an older man ran up to see what was happening. He stood for a moment and just looked at the Prentices through the small opening in the crowd.

"What happened to them?" he asked pointing.

"Oh, they're just having a bad day," answered Cole in a serious voice, as he turned and headed back to the dance.

When Cole reached the main door, John Prentice and Julie were just coming out. Julie saw Cole and Ballard coming up the stairs in the dim light and said, "We heard there was a fight out here. What happened, did you see it?"

"Up close and personal," Cole replied, holding his handkerchief on his cut. Marlene came up and touched Cole on the arm. "I'm gonna fetch you a towel and ice," she said, and headed into the grange. Cole couldn't help but notice Julie give a quick scowl as she and John continued over to his vehicle.

The fight had lasted less than three minutes, but news traveled through the crowd at a pace that would have made a racehorse jealous. An older man in his sixties came up to Cole, "It's about time someone gave those Prentice boys what they deserve." He nodded his head like he was agreeing with himself. "You watch your back now. They're a mean bunch and they'll be back."

Cole knew he was telling it straight. This was nowhere near over. "Mister, I recognized Lowell Star and the two Prentice brothers, but who was that last fella?" Cole asked.

The old man pushed his hat back a little to reveal a partially bald head. "Well, I'm not plum positive, but I think the guy's last name is Dunn."

"Thanks." Cole felt uncomfortable with his newfound attention. Allen had mentioned finding the plane wreck and graves to a few friends, and now this story was also making the rounds. Cole seemed to have the attention of just about everyone in the grange hall.

Marlene had returned and hung on his arm like she never planned to let go. One of her girlfriends slipped up beside Marlene and whispered in her ear as she giggled. "So Marlene, who's your new boyfriend?"—a comment that embarrassed Marlene and caught Cole totally by surprise, considering he had met the girl a little over an hour ago.

As they stood on the porch, Cole saw Jay and Suzie coming out the grange door and Cole saw the opportunity. "Marlene, I enjoyed the evening, but I need to excuse myself." With that he turned and headed over to Jay and Suzie.

"You're leaving?"

But Cole just kept walking. The fight had taken all the romance out of him, at least for that night.

"I hear you and Ballard wiped out the whole Prentice bunch single handedly," Jay said.

"A few of them, anyway," Cole responded, watching Julie walk away with John Prentice. Several people passed by and congratulated Cole on the fight. He came to the conclusion that he wasn't the only one who didn't like the Prentice bunch.

Sheriff Burris walked over to Cole. "I checked the whole thing out, and it sounds like they started it and you two finished it."

"Last thing I wanted to do tonight was fight, Sheriff, but I had no choice."

"I think everyone has had enough for tonight. We'll talk more when we ride out with Allen and look at that airplane wreck you found. I can't quite figure that one out, but I did seem to remember hearing of a missing plane out of Jackson several years ago. But everyone was looking for it near Dubois, not over here. Anyway, I'll check it out and see you on Tuesday. Keep out of trouble till then, will you?"

Cole saw Ballard over in the corner, showing a small crowd of cowboys how he unleashed hell on those Prentices, and chuckled to himself. The group seemed to be hanging on every word. Cole had never seen this side of Ballard before and was glad to consider him a standup guy and a friend. He hated to interrupt his performance, but Cole was ready to call it a night. His head ached, and he didn't like standing there with a bloody towel plastered to his cheek. "Hey, Ballard, would you mind giving Jay and Suzie a ride home tonight? I'm a little played out."

"Sure, happy to. See you tomorrow." Ballard grinned.

Cole walked up to Marlene. "I really enjoyed meeting you, and I apologize for the fight. It wasn't what I planned, but I need to get going."

Marlene pouted and muttered, "Thanks for nothing." Then she turned and stomped back to her girlfriends. Easy come, easy go, Cole thought to himself, as he got in his truck and started it up. The trip back to the ranch seemed far longer with no one to talk to and the stillness of the Wyoming summer night.

Sunday morning, Cole slept in until seven thirty, awakened by an old rooster that had somehow gotten through the large open window of the bunkhouse and pecked him on the kneecap. Cole sprang out of bed and the bird flew to the floor. Cole cussed and rubbed his knee as he shooed the rooster out the bunkhouse door and dressed for breakfast. He had known for a while what he wanted to do with this day off.

Cole headed over to the Schmitz's around two in the afternoon. The dogs heard his truck coming up the driveway a half mile away and were in full howl as he stopped in front of the small homestead. As he headed up to the front porch, Martha opened the door and greeted him.

"Back already? I think Suzie's in town staying with her folks," she said.

"I didn't come to talk to Suzie; I came to visit with you."

"Honey, I already have a man and anyways, you ain't my type," she laughed. "Come on in and have a seat."

Once inside Cole couldn't wait to hear Martha's story. "Suzie said that as a young lady you worked for Gillis McCabe. That true?"

"Sure did, started work for him in '74 right after the big remodel and worked there for two or three years after he died. Gillis was a nice enough man, but a little on the strange side."

"How so"

"Always working on things behind locked doors, never shared with anyone what he was doing. He was one smart fella, but a person could get old before he would tell you anything. You know, he used to keep rattlesnakes in a big tank in his office? Live rattlesnakes! You never seen such a thing," Martha said. "He got rid of them when he did the big remodel. Boy did that rile everyone up when he did that remodel. For a long while, people here would hardly talk to him."

"Why was that?"

"Work in these parts was hard to come by then, and he hired only men from back East, near fifty in all, I reckon. They came here by wagon, and they worked for more than a year and never were allowed to leave the ranch even once the whole time." Martha took a small sip of her black tea. "No one could figure it out, and when the remodel was done, all those men up and left almost overnight. A few people saw some of men riding out, but they wouldn't talk to no one but each other. Tongues wagged about it for several years around here, and Gillis never did spill the beans on why he done it."

"Did anyone ever figure out what went on?"

"No, not even his family was allowed in the house during the remodel. He rented a house in town. Made them stay there. Said he wanted it to be a surprise. When everyone was allowed back into the house, he had changed nearly half the house and had brought in incredible new stuff from back East, like that fancy staircase. It sure was beautiful, so I guess his wife and son thought it was worth the wait."

"I wonder what the secretiveness was all about," muttered Cole.

"Well, he was a nice enough man, would do a lot to help a neighbor in trouble, but you knew there were things you just didn't ask about."

"What about maps? Did you ever see any maps of the ranch?"

"Only once in a while would you see a map and if you did, he was always holding it. Never saw one just lying on his study desk or anything like that."

Despite Martha's stooped posture and arthritis, her mind remained sharp. "Can I ask a few more questions?" Cole said. "I know that I just dropped in on you, and you weren't expecting to spend your Sunday morning talking to me."

"Sure, fire away."

"When Gillis died, did they find the maps?"

"No, but I don't recall any one looking for maps. They looked everywhere for other stuff, and when they pried open his locked cabinet, the only thing they found was the ranch deed."

"Pried open the cabinet"

"Yep, no one ever found any keys. And that ain't all. They didn't find any of his stocks, money, or nothing. They did find a few important papers, but none of his maps, other important papers, or his safe."

"So he did have a safe they didn't find?!" Cole asked.

"Darn tootin' he did, and a big one at that. Seems no one saw it after the remodel. I don't remember anyone even talking about it until after he died."

"Now that's strange."

Phil walked into the room. "Cole nice to see you again. Are Suzie and Jay here?"

"No," Cole said. "I just came over to visit with your lovely wife." Cole got up and excused himself and thanked Martha for the visit. He had been invited to the McCabes for dinner, and since he still had to go to Meeteetse, he didn't want to be late.

Chapter 9

Hours later on his ride back to the ranch, Cole's mind began to race. Where did the maps, stocks, and money go? Were they in the house, or did he bury them somewhere on the ranch? Why would he hide the family valuables and not tell anyone? McCabe's safe had to have the answers.

He drove up the driveway and pulled in front of the main house, its massive size dwarfing his vehicle. It had taken longer than he had hoped to find the part for his truck he needed and he knew he was slightly late for dinner, but he hoped that they had started without him. He raced up the porch stairs and knocked on the door. Tyler opened the door with a smile and welcomed him. As Cole passed him, thinking he smelled the slightest odor of cigarette smoke. Cole was surprised that Tyler smoked. To his knowledge, no one in the house smoked, aside from the cigars that went with after-dinner brandy out on the porch.

The McCabe family and Allen were well into their meal when Cole sat down. "Sorry I'm late, had a little problem in town" Cole said. Tyler quickly served him the main course of roast beef with hot gravy. Cole dished himself up some mashed potatoes and gravy. "I apologize. I needed to go to town, but I wanted to swing by and talk to Martha Schmitz." He was hungry and glad he hadn't missed dinner.

"So," Wes said, "what did Martha have to say?"

"We talked about her working for Gillis when she was a teenager, and I asked her about seeing any maps when she was here."

"Well did she?" Wes asked.

"Yeah, she said she saw some maps a couple times, at least that is what she remembers, but she has no idea where he kept them."

"You went all the way over there to just ask her about maps on your day off?" Sally asked.

"I think Martha is a fascinating person to talk to. Her description of working here was really interesting, especially when she talked about him building the house and how he handled that."

"What do you mean, Cole?" Sally asked.

"Gillis having the family move to town and hiring only east coast men to work on it in a time when jobs were mighty scarce, that's a little different if you ask me. Do you know why he did that?"

"If we knew why he did that, we would probably know where he hid all the money, stocks, and all the other important papers that haven't been found," Wes answered with a disgusted look on his face. "Hell knows we have torn this place apart looking for them."

"I'd like to talk about this again when we have a chance," Cole suggested.

Wes nodded in agreement.

"So, Cole," Sally said, "tell us about this plane wreck you told Allen about."

"Well, there isn't a lot to tell, really," Cole explained. "It's an old wreck. Been there maybe two or three years I'd guess. There's debris scattered over at least an acre on Decker Mountain. The thing I can't figure out is who buried those people and put in those grave markers. That part is plum strange."

"So, nobody knows who's buried up there, and no one saw the wreck?" Julie asked.

"I sure don't, but Allen talked to the sheriff. Maybe the sheriff knew something," Cole replied, as he looked at Allen.

Allen shook his head. "Sheriff says he doesn't know anything of a wreck or, for that matter, two people missing, but we will know more after we visit the site."

"On a ranch this size, you expect to find an odd thing here or there, but a plane crash, who would have ever guessed?" Sally commented.

Everyone but Julie had questions, and Cole found it challenging to try and sneak a bite in between them. Allen, Wes, Ballard and even Sally McCabe planned to join Sheriff Burris and Cole on their trip back up to the crash site the next day. After numerous questions about the site and how he found the wreck, a new round started on the fight and what happened in Cody. Cole sighed—it was like the interviews he used to have in college for the radio stations after a big game. He answered every question as thoroughly as possible, and then he turned to Wes and asked a few of his own.

"Wes, when visiting with Martha Schmitz, she filled me in on a bit of the family's history, and, well, I was wondering if you would mind if I took a shot at searching for the maps and whatever else I find. It sounds funny, but I'd really enjoy a good challenge."

Wes just laughed. "You know how many people have tried to figure out where he hid those things over the last sixty years? I got to believe that if no one has found anything by now, it just might not exist, but you got me. Yeah, sure, you can look. Help yourself on this one, but do it on your own time."

"Thanks," Cole said. "I appreciate it, but I need some access to the house and a few answers to some questions about Gillis. When you get a chance, can we get together and talk?"

"Okay, but now that everyone is finished with dinner, let's go out on the patio and have a smoke and a brandy. What do you say?"

"Sounds great," Cole said. The men migrated to the patio where Chin had the brandies already poured and the cigar box open. Everyone reached for a cigar except Cole, who settled for just Brandy.

"My granddad, now where would I start?" Wes pondered. "He made his money back East with the help of his dad in the ship business and, for whatever reason, sold out and came to Meeteetse. Probably read books on the Wild West or something, but once he got something under his bonnet, it quickly became an obsession. And sharp? He had a great mind but was a little unusual sometimes. I guess you could call him a genius."

"My father was very intelligent, but Grandpa amazed him with his ability to understand and absorb almost anything he read," Wes continued. "And my father impressed a hell of a lot of people by figuring out a modern power and water system, when a lot of big towns hadn't cracked that nut. Most people would've been pretty proud of their accomplishments, but not my father. He never felt like he lived up to my grandfather's expectations. Grandpa had a number of projects that, for some reason, he didn't share with my dad, which made him feel left out. Grandpa had a strange, reclusive side that no one could quite put their finger on. Sometimes, he would leave the house for days and not tell anyone where he was going. He was his own man and didn't share a lot with anyone, including my dad or his two wives."

"Two wives" a startled Cole responded with surprise!

"Not at the same time," laughed Wes. "His first wife came with him from back East. She was the mother of my father. She died of the fever when Dad was two, and my granddad remarried three years later to a woman from up north of here. She loved Grandpa from everything I heard, but she didn't savor the loneliness of ranch life that much. She spent a lot of her time just like Grandpa, reading all the time."

"After all these years, how do you know what and how much Gillis read?" Cole asked.

"Let me show you something," Wes directed. The group had pretty much finished their cigars, so they headed back into the house, following Wes. He turned and went up the magnificent staircase that flowed up beside the massive fireplace in the middle of the house.

Cole couldn't help but be impressed with the way the architect had brought everything together. "Do you know who the house architect was?" Cole asked.

"My grandfather," Wes answered.

They reached the top of the stairs and took a right into an expansive room that Cole had never seen. The room was lined with bookcases stretching from floor to ceiling. "Some of these are books brought in by other members of the family, but ninety-five percent were brought in by my grandfather."

Cole was amazed at the shear number of books. There were books on about every subject imaginable, all neatly organized into categories. Cole started reading the section names, scanning some of the titles—horse and animal training, poetry, architectural design, and politics. There were hundreds of classics, an unbelievable library for a large city, much less a ranch in the middle of Wyoming. Cole moved to a section entitled Engineering. There were two shelves of books, each approximately four feet long. Some of the books appeared brand new, while others looked almost worn out. Cole reached for one of the older books, *Engineering and Modern Home Design*. Cole thumbed through it and noticed a number of pages that had very light pencil marks underlining certain paragraphs. It looked as if someone had tried to erase the marks.

Cole replaced the book and picked up another title, *Theories of Structural Engineering*. In his quick thumb through, he again noticed certain pages that had pencil marks. Again he replaced the book and looked for another cover that had seen better days. His eyes wandered through the titles until he came to *Thermal Mass and the Design of Fireplaces*. Why would anyone waste their time reading about thermal mass and fireplace design? Gillis must have had trouble sleeping. Wes continued showing the group how organized the library was and how many different categories of books existed. The group rejoined the ladies, and everyone visited and enjoyed the evening, with Cole receiving his share of ribbing on the possibility of finding Gillis McCabe's treasure. Even Cole wasn't totally sure that he was up for the challenge, but he was going to try. Everyone looked forward to Tuesday and the adventure of going up to the plane wreck. Allen and Wes and all the others had their own ideas about who the victims were and what caused the crash. No one had any realistic ideas about who buried the people or built the crosses.

As Cole thanked Sally for the dinner and got ready to leave, Julie approached him. "Cole, are you riding tomorrow?"

"Yes, I am. There's a lot of the ranch I haven't seen yet."

"I'd like to come along, if you don't mind. I need some time in the hills . . ." Julie looked away for a moment. "I have a lot on my mind."

"Sure, I'll be saddling up at six-thirty. If you still want to go, meet me at the barn at six. And I'd be glad to have some company."

The next morning, Cole went into the pasture to get Patch. All Cole had to do was whistle and the mule trotted up to him, and it helped that Cole always had a treat in his pocket. He thought the chances of Julie being up and on time were as good as rubbing two wet sticks together and starting a fire, but he hoped he was wrong. Cole looked at his pocket watch. As he slipped it back into his pants, he looked up at the house, turned and was surprised to see Julie standing behind him where she must have come from inside the barn. "Good morning, Cole. Fine morning for a ride, don't you think?"

"Yes, it is," Cole said. "Hope you packed a big lunch. I don't figure we'll be back until evening."

The drive out to the ridge through the cool morning air was subdued. Julie spent the time looking out the window at the hills.

Cole decided that when Julie was ready to talk, she would, and until then he would respect her silence. The old International did a good job of pulling the homemade horse trailer down the hardpan clay road. Nothing seemed to move as the sun shone on the beautiful valley floor. It was August, and only in the past month had the last stubborn bank of snow left the north slopes of the mountains. When they finally pulled over to unload, Cole said, "It may be none of my business, but if you need to talk, I'm a good listener."

"I'm sorry," Julie said. "Just have a lot on my mind today. I'll try to be better company."

"Well, I don't want to step where I shouldn't . . ."

"To tell you the truth, I really just needed to get out and clear my mind. I feel comfortable with you. You're different than the other men around here."

Cole didn't know quite what to say. "Anything I can do."

Julie saddled Gun Smoke and Cole saddled Patch. Riding Patch hard all summer had added at least a hundred pounds of muscle to the mule's well-built frame and he carried a saddle well. Cole tied on his saddlebags, an ax, and his gun scabbard, then went back to the truck to get his 30.06. The two mounted their rides and trotted to the foothills.

Within ten minutes, they had left the bluish green sagebrush and were entering the scattered timber. A large group of wild turkeys ran in front of them, several launching themselves into nearby trees. The chirping of dozens of birds filled the clean air, and Cole enjoyed watching as the flock disappeared into the timber. Julie stayed silent as the turkeys scattered.

After riding for over an hour, the terrain became rockier and steeper, with the timber becoming larger, but more sparse. Cole had been keeping an eye out for a game trail, preferably one that was well used. He knew that a heavily traveled game trail in this country was the secret to being able to move between the steep rockslides and cliffs. Cole was surprised at just how much use the trail had and wondered why. The trail broke from the forest and turned into a rocky shelf that varied from as wide as twenty feet to as narrow as three, as it made it way up the ridge. As Patch got to the narrowest spot, about three feet wide, the mule stopped and looked over the edge at a hundred-foot drop to the treetops below. Cole spoke to Patch and encouraged him by giving him a little leg pressure with his spurs. After the two had passed the bad spot, Cole turned to Julie and smiled.

"Now, that's what you call a real pants pucker." Julie looked up but didn't say anything. Finally, she smiled, the first time she had done so the whole morning.

The deeply carved trail led back into the thick timber and worked its way up the ridge. The sun hit them in the face again as the trail broke into the open and began working its way through some boulders at the base of a small cliff. Again the trail headed back into the timber and dove into a small meadow filled with tall grass and a loud, flowing creek. Cole's first thought was where does all this water go? It sure as hell wasn't flowing down to the base of the mountain and out into the valley. This was yet another good source of water in August that could possibly be used for the cattle. But it just seemed to disappear somewhere further down the valley. An old cow pie sat on the trail, so Cole knew at least a few cattle had found their way up here from the valley, but very few.

"Let's tie up here for a while and explore this bench," Cole said, as he pulled Patch's reins to a stop.

"Good," Julie said. "You go ahead. I need a few moments to myself." Julie tied her horse among tall grass in the shade of aspen trees. Cole hobbled Patch and then began following the creek down to a point where, like the others, it dove into the ground under a large rockslide. Julie headed up above the meadow to a secluded stretch of ground that was barely visible through the thick aspen. Cole figured at least half the creeks he had found disappeared long before they reached the valley floor. This could only mean that there was one heck of an underground water supply somewhere, and he hoped to find it.

As Cole returned to the meadow, he noticed Julie on the bench above, studying something intently. He quietly walked up an old trail that had been invisible from a distance. At one time, it had been well used, and it still left a depression that meandered through the aspens. When Cole reached Julie, she was looking at an old metal plate and the rusted remains of an ax head that was stuck in the top of a rotten stump. Behind her was a wreck of a cabin, black from age, its roof partially fallen in and a short broken wood door jammed its entrance. On one side a small window had been cut into the logs and it contained the remains of a single pane of glass.

"Look what I found," Julie cried, as she looked up and saw Cole. "It must be one of those old miner's cabins that we've heard about. Dad always said they used to hide out on the ranch, but this is the first one I ever found that looks pretty much undisturbed."

"He must have had a mine around here somewhere. We might be able to find the old trail to it, too. Let's take a look inside."

The inside of the cabin smelled heavily of rat dung and rot. There was only one room, with a table and one chair, as well as a very small rock fireplace, one that would have held only a tiny fire and would have hardly put out any heat. Dusty cobwebs hung from every wall and a few cans, their labels missing, sat on a sturdy shelf. A single bed with cedar posts stood at one end of the room, with the remains of hides stretched over it. On the wall was an extremely faded and yellowed portrait of a young child holding what looked like a ball in a frame made from hand cut birch branches. A rusty shotgun leaned against the corner of the cabin, and beside it sat a large wooden box. Cobwebs and a heavy coating of dust draped most everything not exposed to weather in the room. A small part of the roof had caved in, mainly in the chimney area. But the majority of the cabin was still somewhat protected from the severe effects of the many hard winters it had seen. The picture and the gun, both things of personal value, told Cole that whoever had lived here had certainly intended to return.

By the excited look on Julie's face and her intensity looking through the many items in the cabin, Cole could tell that she enjoyed the find every bit as much as he did. For a moment, whatever was bothering her had vanished, and now her attention was totally focused on the discovery of this old piece of history.

"I'll bet you're right," Cole answered. "This has got to be one of those renegade miners that Gillis used to talk about."

"Great-Grandpa used to tell my dad there were dozens of these guys secretly mining the ranch. I wonder what happened," Julie said.

"I don't know, but it was serious enough that he never made it back. No one would leave his gun and probably the only picture of his son, if there was any chance he wouldn't return," Cole said, not wanting to say what he was really thinking.

From the look of the height of the collapsed door and the opening that now existed, Cole could tell the cabin had lost at least a foot and a half of height from the bottom logs rotting away and the building settling. It had been built to withstand harsh winters, and the joint caulking, for the most part, was still doing its job throughout the structure. If it hadn't been for a number of spruce trees that had died around the cabin, a person could have ridden within yards of it and never suspected its existence.

They spent some time looking at everything from old cookware to several boxes of rusted ammunition tucked under the bed of hides. Several more hides and a number of metal traps hung from the log walls. Cole went over to the large wooden box in the corner and opened it. He found the remains of several unrecognizable leather items, a rusted knife and pistol that were covered in rat dung, and a small empty can of chewing tobacco. Cole took a stick and moved some of the dung to see if anything else was in the box. His stick hit a smaller, slightly rusted metal box that had lodged itself in the corner of the larger box and was not noticeable at first glance. Cole carefully removed the box, aware he was probably going through this man's most precious memories. He thought highly of anyone who was tough enough to live in these hard mountains and try to make his fortune from the land. Cole sat the rusty box on the table and carefully pried it open with his knife. The box was in excellent shape, and neither the rodents nor weather had destroyed its sturdy body. The inside of the box looked almost like new and showed little signs of damage or age.

Cole reached into the box and removed a stack of ten or more yellowed letters, all addressed to Clarence O'Malley or his wife. Most of the letters had been opened and had cancelled stamps. At first glance most appeared to be from his wife.

Cole replaced the letters neatly back into the box and turned to Julie. "Let's read these later. I still have some work I need to get done and some country to see before dark." Cole left the cabin, walked down to Patch, and put the box carefully into his saddlebags.

As he started to untie his mule, Julie walked over. "Before we leave, could we have some lunch?"

"Well sure, I'm sorry. I should have kept better track of the time. I'm used to being by myself most of the time and only stop when I'm really hungry. Usually, it's just long enough to get the mule a drink or grab something out of my saddlebags."

Julie sat in the shade with only her head in the sun, her silken black hair sparkling in its light. She began eating her sandwich without saying a word, staring at the ground. She looked very intense and uncomfortable, like she really wanted to get something off her chest. Suddenly she blurted out, "John Prentice has asked me to marry him."

Cole felt like he had just been kicked in the stomach. He was angry, but he had to remind himself that he had no right to be. Julie sat there for a long time, looking as if she required a response, one that Cole didn't want to give.

"You're really catching me off guard. I don't know quite what to say," Cole said. From the look on Julie face, she didn't care for his answer.

"Did you accept?" Cole asked, feeling a churning in his stomach.

"I told him, 'Yes."

Cole slowly lowered his head and stared at the ground for a moment, speechless. He felt an all-too-familiar sense of loss, a deflating sensation. Something cherished, someone loved, was vanishing from his life. This was all he knew.

Suddenly, the silence between them was broken by the hair-raising sound of howls from a pack of wolves. They were close and moving fast as they came down the hill, obviously in hot pursuit of prey.

"They may be after some of the cattle," Cole said as he jumped toward Patch to get his rifle. From the sound of the chase, if he was lucky, he could intercept them probably a hundred yards above the cabin by the creek. Cole grabbed the rifle, and with the speed of an all-American quarterback, he took off running up the hill. He followed the first part of the old trail up to the cabin and then veered off following a bench slightly above the creek, as he ran through the aspens and ferns toward where he thought they would cross.

Seconds before he saw the prey, he heard it running through the creek, as the wolves closed the distance. By the time he got to the spot where it had crossed, whatever it was had already disappeared down the narrow game trail into some thick evergreens. Puffing from the high altitude and the uphill run, Cole readied himself for a fast shot at the wolves that were quickly approaching. He could almost hear them breathing when he launched himself into the middle of the trail, threw up his gun, and took a shot at the lead wolf. The large gray wolf was pushing one hundred and twenty pounds, and the shock of Cole jumping onto the trail ground him to a stop just long enough for Cole to pull the trigger.

The neck hit was perfectly placed and toppled the large wolf backwards onto the trail. The remaining five wolves, which ran closely behind, turned and tried to make their escape back into the shadows. Cole was able to fire one more shot that missed its true mark but hit a smaller brown wolf in the thigh. Cole knew that he had as good as killed the second wolf because the others would never accept a wounded member back into the pack. The smell of blood and the weakness from the wound would make him a victim of his own kind. Cole lowered the rifle and went to examine the dead wolf. The bullet had caught the bone of the neck, which explained how it had thrown the wolf backwards on impact.

Cole bent down and was looking at the wolf, when he felt Julie's hand on his shoulder. "Are you all right?" she said. "Were they chasing a steer?"

"I don't know, but the muddy side of creek should leave a good track. We should be able to tell if it was a steer or elk," Cole said. The rugged trail the wolves had come down was full of grass and rock and left little sign, so Cole moved down to the edge of the creek. He easily crossed using an aspen that had recently fallen and spanned the roaring creek. From this side of the creek, a solid track in the mud could easily be seen. Cole bent down to examine it more closely, expecting to see a cattle track. Suddenly, he stood up with his an astonished look on his face.

"What's the matter?" Julie asked.

"It's human! These are human footprints."

Chapter 10

Julie quickly climbed over the log to Cole and knelt down in disbelief. It was unmistakably a human footprint. "Who would be up here alone barefoot in this country?" Julie asked, eyes wide in astonishment.

"I don't know. I don't even know where to begin. Alone, being chased by wolves, it doesn't add up." The two of them went back and forth with questions to each other. Who was this person, and how long had he been out there? Cole finally turned to Julie and said, "I think we need to see if we can follow his tracks."

"Will the animals be okay with us leaving? The wolves won't come back, will they?"

"That pack wants nothing more to do with us, at least for a long time, and our stock isn't sour. They'll stand quiet while we are gone." For over an hour, the two tried their best to track whoever had escaped down the ridge. Either by luck or skill, the person left little sign to follow. After an exhausting hour of following small broken branches, bent grass, and partial imprints, the trail was lost for good in a rockslide littered with large boulders that jetted from the mountain's side. Whoever this person was, he was right at home with his environment and was very familiar with the lay of the land. Cole thought to himself that he probably intended to lose the wolves in the rocks, where he would have had at least some advantage.

They quietly backtracked and crossed the creek. Cole took a second to look at the large wolf lying dead in the trail before walking back to the stock. Nothing more was mentioned of Julie's engagement, but it was never far from Cole's mind.

"Cole, where do you think he came from? You don't think he could have been on the plane that you found?"

"I don't know. I don't even know if it is a man or woman, but he certainly didn't come from that plane crash. The largest piece of wreckage on the whole site isn't more than a couple square feet, and nobody could have possibly survived that."

Cole thought for another minute. "Anyway, there were burn marks on the wreckage and some of the surrounding trees. So not only did it crash, but it burned, too. Probably happened in the winter when there was considerable snow on the ground, or it would have caused at least a small fire that someone would have seen." Julie seemed at least a little relieved that some injured victim of a horrible plane wreck was now wandering the wilderness of Wyoming on her family's ranch.

It took about twenty minutes to walk back down the ridge to where the animals waited patiently. Julie's horse grazed on grass at the end of an extended lead rope tied to a tree, while Patch used his hobbles to find the best grass possible within a ten-yard radius of his newfound best friend.

"Should we look for the mine?" Julie asked.

"We can, but we only have another hour, before we need to head back. I don't want to go cross those deadfalls in the dark. I'm not sure what I'm going to tell Allen and your dad about the human track," Cole said.

"Me either. What do you say?" Julie asked.

For the next hour, they searched the ridge and nearby small valley for sign of a mine or trail. The country was beautiful with its thick aspens and juniper ground cover, but there was no sign of any mining operation or, for that matter, even a trail that might lead to one. At the end of an hour, they were both ready to head back to the stock and get going. When Cole and Julie finally reached the animals, both were intently watching something down in the meadow below. Patch's eight inch ears made him look like a hunting dog on point as he watched the young bull moose step into the meadow.

Cole took one last look back toward the location of the cabin. It was very obvious that whoever had chosen this spot didn't want to be found. He had placed the cabin just far enough back into the timber to be completely hidden from the rough trail. Another thing that impressed Cole was that this person had taken logs from another area to build the cabin, as there were no stumps in the area to betray its location. A person could pass by here for years and never think to look for a cabin back in this thick stand of spruce. Cole and Julie tightened their loose cinches, mounted, and began their journey back down the ridge to the truck.

The ride was very quiet, with only a few pleasant comments of little meaning to break the long stretches of silence. Cole was thinking to himself that he had come to this country to lose himself in its vast acreage and, for at least a while, be unknown. Now he had fallen in love with a woman that he had never even had a serious talk with, not to mention the engaged part. He was no longer unknown after the fight he had wanted no part of, finding the airplane wreck, and now finding a barefoot human who was being chased by wolves.

With Patch leading the way, the two gracefully passed the bad spot in the trail, and, within a couple of hours, were back at the truck. They unsaddled, loaded, and were in the truck and on their way in less than ten minutes. When they reached the ranch, they unloaded, rubbed the stock down, and turned them into the pastures.

As she was about to return to the house, Julie turned and smiled at Cole for a second and then said, "I enjoyed our time together. Maybe we can do it again." Then she turned and headed to the house. She walked a few steps, stopped and turned again. "Are you coming to dinner tonight?"

"No, I need some time to myself, but thanks," Cole said.

Julie gave a weak smile and continued walking toward the house. From his saddlebags Cole removed the cabin's old letters and put them under the bed in a small chest he had brought from his parents' house. Then he changed his sweaty shirt and headed over to the mess hall where he joined the other cowboys for dinner. Jay came through the door just as Cole sat down and jokingly laughed, "What an honor to have the two best fighters in Cody in the same room!"

Ballard's head jerked up, he smiled and then chuckled. "I can't say that I didn't enjoy that little discussion we had with those boys." Everyone joined in and laughed at Ballard's comment. During the rest of the meal, everyone relived the fight and asked questions about the plane wreck. Cole was tired of answering, but some of the men had never even seen a plane, much less a wreck. He sure as hell wasn't going to tell anyone what happened today with the wolves and the barefoot person. He was receiving way more attention than he ever wanted and wondered to himself why trouble seemed to shadow him.

After dinner, Cole decided to walk off the big meal he had enjoyed so he started down toward Patch's corral. The mules, for the most part, didn't get ridden much by the cowboys and were used mainly for the packing duties, but Cole believed they made an incredible mountain riding animal as well. A big bay mule had its head over the fence chewing on some long grass. Cole was surprised to see Allen leaning against the fence smoking a cigarette, looking out over the huge valley. "Allen, I didn't know you were a mule lover," Cole said in a disingenuous voice.

"To be honest, I'm not. So what are you doing out here?"

"I just needed air." Cole paused for minute. "Allen, can I ask you something personal?"

"Depends on how personal"

"Well, Julie asked me to go riding with her today and well, she said something that really kind of hit me wrong, I guess."

"Did she tell you she was marrying John Prentice?"

"Yeah" There was a pause, "Yeah she did," Cole said. "What's going on? I didn't even think they were that serious."

Allen struggled with what to say. "Well, it's really none of my business, but if she thinks he's the one, who am I to say anything."

"Do you think she loves him?"

"I don't feel real comfortable with this discussion, but I know you really care for Julie, so I'll level with you. This is the first year the ranch has done well financially for some time, and we can thank you and the end of the drought for some of that. Wes has been borrowing money for nearly eight years from Prentice's bank, and the debt is coming due. To my knowledge, McCabe doesn't have the money to pay all the bills and the notes payable next spring. If he doesn't pay the debt and interest, then Prentice will get the ranch. At least if Julie marries Prentice, the family should be able to keep the ranch, and hopefully the men will keep their jobs."

For the second time that day, Cole felt like he had been kicked in the gut. He had a difficult time gleaning anything good from the conversation. "I appreciate the straight talk, Allen. I'll see you first thing tomorrow for the ride."

"The sheriff was out with Wes today, and he is definitely going with us. See you tomorrow," Allen said, as he turned and headed over to his small cabin behind the largest barn.

It was a dark evening with scattered clouds and sparse moonlight as Cole headed back to the bunkhouse. He sat down on his bed and turned on the single bulb that dangled from the ceiling close to his bunk. He reached down and opened the small chest and retrieved the faded letters from his worn, metal box. He looked at the stack and then read the first letter, not knowing what to expect.

The letter was written by a J.D. Fitterer and started out "Dearest Family" and expressed excitement and optimism about finding a promising site and developing his mine. He talked of buying his tools in Dubois, Wyoming, and how he had built the cabin where no one would ever find it. Cole was able to figure out from some of the letters that apparently some miner had brought a nugget of gold into Meeteetse, gotten into a fight and had died of a gunshot wound before he was able to tell anyone where the mine was. The rest of the letters were more personal and didn't give any real clues to what had happened, just detailed the hardships of being alone up in the mountains.

The last letter was different. From the very start, he could tell the writer was worried. Fitterer talked about how the mine seemed to be promising, but he couldn't shake the feeling that someone was watching him. He was happy that the mine and the cabin were far apart and both well hidden. In the past, it had given him a real sense of security, but now he wasn't quite as sure. The letter spoke of the small amount of gold Fitterer had mined, enough to keep him in food and ammo for the winter. The last letter ended with how much he missed them, and how the diggings were getting better every day. He prayed he'd be home soon.

Early the next morning, Cole packed a lunch for the ride up to the crash site. The sheriff had not arrived, but all three of the McCabes, Allen, Ballard, and Elmer, were catching and saddling their horses and loading them in one of the ranch's two stock trucks. Elmer was in his early thirties and was Cole's idea of a typical German, smart but with a bit of an attitude. He stood only five feet five inches, but worked as hard as any man on the ranch. He was a little overweight, quite the talker and always did well with the ladies, at least the few times Cole had seen him with them. Elmer was a little on the stubborn side and one of the most intelligent cowboys on the ranch, but he shied away from having more leadership, something Cole never understood.

The saddles and blankets were secured to the side racks of the two passenger truck, and a car would carry the extra people. When Sheriff Burris arrived, Cole could see his horse sticking his head out of the sheriff's open horse trailer. Burris stopped just long enough for everyone to load into the vehicles. Wes joined the sheriff in his truck as they led the way up toward Pine Ridge. Cole purposely got in the truck with Allen, and he was sure it was the best choice. There was no way that he wanted to be stuck in the other truck or the sedan for the next hour with everyone drilling him with more questions about the wreck.

Everything went smoothly, but it still took over an hour to drive to the isolated ridge and another thirty minutes for everyone to unload the stock from the trucks and then load the two pack mules. Ballard and Elmer had loaded the extra mules with light loads that included shovels, two axes, canvas sacks, and a pick. If they needed to bring anything down the mountain, then they were ready and would have space.

During the first part of the ride, Cole learned that the McCabes only remembered a couple of times ever seeing a plane flying over the ranch. Elmer had never seen an airplane at all except in pictures. The trip up the mountain was uneventful other than stopping to remove some of the deadfall to make it easier to carry a load back down the mountain, if needed. Patch had been able to just hop over most of the deadfall, but some of the other horses weren't as athletic. With this being a wreck site, Cole was sure there would be many more trips, so the extra work was probably worth the time and effort spent clearing the trail with the crosscut saw and axes. The ride to the site would take about three hours, only because Cole knew the way. The skies were sunny and the views spectacular. It was a perfect day for a ride. Near the top, the wind began to pick up a bit on the hard side, but it was always blowing a little on the hard side. Cole's face had become thick and bronzed due to the constant attacks by the elements of nature, and he looked older and more mature because of it.

Once they reached the crash site, everyone hurriedly tied off and the examination began. The sheriff started the process by walking around the whole site twice, carefully observing everything with a skillful eye. He looked at every piece of the plane's wreckage several times, but time had already eroded much of the evidence that may have been helpful to figuring out what happened. Even to the experienced eye, there were few clues to be found. Finally, Sheriff Burris hollered to Elmer and Ballard to bring a couple of shovels and dig up the smaller grave. Julie walked over. "You're not going to dig them up, are you?"

"Yep, I am. I got to know if there's really bodies buried there," said Burris.

Elmer, Ballard, and Cole quickly removed the rocks and began digging. It wasn't long until they exposed the first bones, mainly shattered and small, leaving little to solving the mystery. They were surprised when they unearthed an intact skull that appeared to belong to a small adult, and the pieces of clothing that were buried with the skull appeared to be that of a woman. Whoever had buried these people had spent considerable time looking for as many pieces of bones as possible, a fairly gruesome task, Cole thought.

The men carefully reburied the bones and restored the dirt and rock to the first grave and then began the careful excavation of the larger grave. The grave contained a larger skeleton that was much more intact, probably a man, but with the exception of a few scraps of clothing, there was nothing that would identify the owner. After another hour, the grave was carefully put back together and the crosses firmly secured back into the ground at the head of the graves.

"That was tough, and we didn't find anything that would identify them," said Sheriff Burris. "All we know is they were probably a man and a woman, not much more," replied Wes.

"I'll start trying to identity these people and the plane as soon as I figure out where to start. I'll probably need to bring in some higher ups later, if that's okay with you, Wes?"

"No problem, I'm sure someone is looking for these people. They're someone's family."

During the trip down the mountain and the ride back to the ranch, Cole enjoyed talking to Allen. They had developed a relationship that was almost brotherly, even though Allen was significantly older. Cole looked at Allen, "You know, Allen, I can't believe how fast time has gone by since I came to the ranch."

Allen just smiled, "Cole, life is just a little bit like toilet paper— the nearer you get to the end, the faster it goes." Both Allen and Cole laughed hard and resumed the small talk.

Once they reached the vehicles, they loaded up and headed back to the ranch. About a mile before they reached the ranch, Cole turned to Allen. "Do you know how much we're talking, money-wise?"

"Are you talking about the bank note?"

"Yes, how much is the note for?" Cole asked.

"I really shouldn't be having this conversation with you. It's the McCabe's business and their business alone," Allen said.

"I know, but I just want to help somehow," Cole said.

"I'm sure you do, but I don't know anyone that has close to three hundred and fifty thousand dollars, and I think that's what they need to square the deal. I'm not sure what they will do. Even if they sell all the stock and everything that ain't nailed down, we still don't have that type of money," Allen said.

"How'd they get so in the hole? Couldn't Wes see this coming?" Cole said.

"I think he might have been okay if the drought hadn't held on so long, but it did. And between you and me, Wes is probably not the best businessman I ever met."

"Nobody is thrilled with what's going on, and I think that John Prentice and the bank are pretty smug with their position. I've known Prentice for years, and, as I told you, I have never really liked the guy. I've never thought of him as a straight shooter." Cole was not surprised with the answer. He felt the same way.

The truck rolled to a stop at the barn's loading dock, a substantially built, three-sided log retaining wall that allowed a truck to gently push up against it without damaging the bumper. Cole helped Elmer and Ballard unload the stock, and then the gear. By the time Cole had finished and come out of the barn, Sheriff Burris was gone and the McCabes were back at the house.

The next three days went by fast and without excitement. Julie had finally told the family about the human footprint, but Wes had decided not to share it with others, and Cole agreed. The chances of finding someone up there who didn't want to be found were practically zero. Cole and Jay had talked the week before about how spooked a couple of the guys were about having to stay at some of the more isolated line shacks. Jay had brought up the subject, because he was being sent to Canvas Creek, one of the most secluded line shacks on the ranch. He was scheduled to be there for two weeks, something that didn't tickle him much. He was to check on the cattle, repair an old log dam, and develop a small spring.

In the past, little energy was given to trying to develop the high mountain pastures and their rotations, but all that type of thinking had changed in the short time since Cole had arrived. Wes and Allen had developed a new energy and had been willing to listen to most of his ideas, and that made Cole's long hours and hard work worthwhile. Cole had shared a lot of this with Jay, and they were quickly becoming very close friends. Even though Jay really didn't want the Canvas Creek duty, he knew this was an area of the ranch that Cole was anxious to see developed.

The past few days, the other hands had enjoyed giving Jay static and joking about his girl and what would happen if he disappeared on the lower forty. It was all in good fun, and Jay knew it. Jay had gear for two pack animals ready, and he planned to head out Monday after spending the weekend visiting with Suzie. He had been told that the line shack needed work, and no one had spent any time there the previous two years, so Jay was not sure what to expect. Allen had talked to him about taking extra tools. There would also be a fair amount of time needed to fix the dam and check out the grass and cattle.

Saturday morning, Cole got up early. He needed some personal items from town and he didn't want to lose the whole day, so he was out of the ranch at the crack of dawn. About two miles from the big house, a large herd of elk ran across the road in front of him, followed by a tremendous bull with seven points to a side. The rack was still partially in velvet, which made the immense horns look even larger. Cole had not thought about fall at all, and the elk brought on many pleasant childhood memories of his father and him hunting as he drove the rest of the way to Meeteetse.

Cole pulled his truck in to the front of the general store and said hello to the old gentleman who had planted himself in the rocking chair by the front door. He still had a good head of gray hair that seemed to blend itself into a long gray beard. He exchanged a few pleasantries and headed inside. A store clerk wearing a white apron, who looked to be in his mid-thirties, looked up, smiled, and wished him a good morning. Cole couldn't find the baking soda, so he walked up to the counter and asked the manager where it was. The store clerk showed him and then eyed him, asking, "You new around here? I haven't seen you before."

"I've been at The Greybull Ranch for nearly six months, but I don't come to town much."

"You ain't that Cole Morgan that found that plane and got into a fight with the Prentice clan, are you?"

Cole began to pull his wallet out and the clerk smiled tightly. "Yeah, that's me."

"Well, your money's no good today," said the clerk. "Never could stand that family. Between you and me, they once jumped a cousin of mine in Cody and beat the guy up pretty bad."

Cole still tried to pay, but the clerk insisted it was on the house. Cole started to walk away, stopped and returned to the counter. "If a person wanted to find out about something that happened around here just after the Civil War, is there anyone he could talk with?"

"There's probably at least three that I can think of that are still around and could tell you a mite, but Floyd, there, could probably tell you as much as most." The clerk pointed to the old man in the rocking chair. Cole thanked him and went out on the boardwalk and greeted the old man again.

"Sir," Cole spoke to the old gentleman. "Would you have a minute for a couple of questions?"

The old man slowly looked up with a little smile on his cracked, gray face, "Son, I have nothing but time."

"The store clerk said that you have lived around these parts all your life. Do you know anything about a Creager family and the possibility of them finding gold?"

"I was a pretty young teenager. I think everyone that lived here during that time and was old enough to understand remembers what happened, at least to some degree. It was the most exciting thing to ever hit these parts," said Floyd.

"Would you mind sharing it with me? I'd sure appreciate it."

"Sure, pull that box over and sit a spell, and I'll try and remember all the details," said Floyd, smiling as if he had a new best friend. "Seems to me it was about eighteen-seventy or thereabouts. The Greybull was a mite smaller then, about half the size it is today. Well, if I remember right, there were these two brothers, Vern and Virgil Creager, and they had a ranch that used to be north of The Greybull, until it got bought and added to The Greybull. Seems to me, I heard Gillis McCabe bought their ranch for just the taxes that were owed after one of them was shot and the other disappeared. Gillis pretty much owned and controlled the access into the area, and no one wanted trouble, so Gillis picked it up cheap like."

The old man paused and spit some chew into the street and then continued. "I guess the part you are really interested in is the gold."

"No, I'm interested in all of it."

"Good," said Floyd. "I like a good tale."

"The way I heard it was Vern and Virgil Creager had started ranching in the valley about ten years or more before Gillis McCabe had come to town.

"There was some bad blood after McCabe settled in. He didn't like the Creagers crossing his ranch with their wagons and cattle, and allowing the cattle to get mixed up, that kind of stuff. Well, everything got a little heated between them, and then about two years before the Creagers were shot, they sold off most of their cattle, and everything seemed to quiet down between the two."

"That's strange. Do you know who shot them?"

"Don't know. Early one morning, Virgil shows up at the Jones's place on the edge of town with a bullet in him. Mrs. Jones, real nice lady, she died a mite back, tried for three days to nurse him back to health, but he had lost too much blood and died right there in their bed. Just before he died, he came around long enough to tell Mrs. Jones about a gold mine he and his brother found and had been working. Says about the time they were taking the gold out of the hills with their mules and loading their wagon, they were bushwhacked at the ranch, and someone stole their gold. Said his brother, Vern, was wounded and got away, but no one ever saw him again. Virgil asked Mrs. Jones to give him his jacket, and he pulled out a large gold nugget, size of the end of your thumb, and gave it to her. He then asked her to get paper and pencil and said he'd give her directions to the mine. Seems he didn't think his brother made it either. Mrs. Jones was so shook up over the whole deal, she didn't take good notes, or at least that's what she said. Creager asked her to share the mine with his family back East. He talked about a bayonet stuck in a large old tree with lots of branches, probably a Limber Pine. He said it pointed to the start of an old trail, but before he got any further, he died. Well, you know how women are." Floyd laughed.

"She told her sister and told her not to say anything. But her sister tells her husband who tells his brother, and, before you know it, everyone in town knows there's this gold mine. The word gets out fairly quick, and a lot of strangers start showing up looking for gold, and most of them trying to find it on McCabe's ranch. Well, Gillis McCabe, he hires some real tough men to help control his property and rumors start to fly."

"What type of rumors?" Cole asked.

"Things like people trying to steal claims on McCabe land and worse, like maybe when Gillis' persuasion didn't work, people would leave their land in pine boxes," Floyd said. "We had a lot of strangers around here, most of them miners trying to hit it rich on and around the ranch and on that government property west of the ranch. For about three years, everything seemed pretty heated up, but no one found the mine or any other gold, for that matter. By the beginning of the fourth year, only the real diehards were still around, and the rest, well, they all seemed to have quietly disappeared. To my knowledge, no one ever did find anything except for maybe the Creagers, and they were dead."

Cole thanked the old man again and went back inside the general store. He reemerged with an ice-cold crème soda and handed it to the man. In the back of his mind, he could only wonder if Gillis McCabe had been as great as everyone had made him out to be.

Chapter 11

It was about noon when Cole returned to the ranch. Most of the way back from town, he had been thinking about where to begin his hunt for the missing maps and other valuables. As he drove up toward the big house, he saw Julie getting into John Prentice's car. He didn't care for Prentice, but he sure liked his car. The Chevrolet created a cloud of dust as it left the yard. Cole headed up to the big house, climbed the wide steps, and rang the doorbell. Tyler invited him in.

"Is Wes around? I'd like to talk to him," Cole said.

Tyler led Cole to a large study, where Wes was working behind a huge oak desk. "Wes, I was serious when I said I wanted to find the stuff your grandfather hid away. I hope you weren't kidding when you said, have at it."

"I wasn't kidding, but I think you're wasting your time. I got to tell you, don't get your hopes up very high. This house has been gone over so many times. Everyone has thought about it and has looked for secret passages, secret rooms, hidden stairways, you name it. Hell, I've spent a fair time looking for it myself. God knows the ranch could use the money, if it exists."

For the next hour, Wes explained some of his theories, places people had looked, and some of his own personal logic and ideas of the situation. "Everyone believed maps and stocks were here, but no one had any idea where. We have literally taken some rooms apart looking for them. When my father added indoor plumbing and electricity, we all thought we'd find something, but we didn't." Cole had always respected Wes, and now he found himself actually enjoying the man. "Cole, I need to leave, but I'll have Tyler show you around and tell him to give you the run of the place while I'm gone."

"Thanks, I appreciate it."

Cole had a game plan, but only time would tell how effective it was. He began by measuring the perimeter of the house and wrote down all dimensions. He had cut a thin board three feet square and attached to it a large piece of paper. He planned to develop an accurate grid map of each of the three main floors. He wanted to save going under the big porch and climbing around in the attic for last, because of the dust and dirt he might track back into the house.

It took him over two hours to develop sixteen cross sections in each direction of the first floor, the number he believed necessary to accurately dissect each floor and not miss anything. This allowed him to address every space down to inches. Cole was looking for a loss in walls of six inches or more. His theory was that this was the size needed to have a hidden panel with enough room to store at least some cash, papers, or stocks. Then, he carefully inspected and measured the height of the high plaster ceiling for any sign of a trap door, but he found none.

It took him another three hours to inspect the second floor with the same diligence that he had done the first. He spent an extra hour on Gillis' study, because he believed that if there were a secret panel, he would find it there. The room itself was grand, hung with several old portraits of the family's grand past and a three-foot wainscoting of finely oiled black walnut rising up from the floor.

Cole moved all the furniture and a small hand-woven rug to one side of the room. He took out a thin, pocketknife and carefully tried to slide the blade between each of the six-inch-wide by two-foot-long, staggered oak floorboards with no luck. The end of each board was securely fastened to the floor by three heavy, counter-sunk, square-headed spikes. Carefully he looked at each board and counted the number of square nail heads per board. Everything was the same, built with craftsmanship and without flaw. Again he had found nothing. He then repeated the exercise on the other side of the room, with the same results. Frustrated, he leaned back against the wall and stared at the ceiling. He knew Gillis McCabe had a reputation as a genius. How would he hide valuables so he could get them quickly without prying eyes? The large deadbolt on the backside of the heavy maple door indicated that, at times, Gillis had secured himself inside for whatever reason. He felt like he was missing something. He needed information on Gillis' mannerisms and how his mind worked.

"Cole, you still here"

Wes's voice shook Cole from quiet thought. "I didn't realize it was so late."

"Did you find anything?"

"Not yet, but I was wondering, did you ever come into this room when you were a boy, before your grandfather died?"

"I may have, but I was too young to remember. Anyway, it's like it was back then."

"How do you know that?"

"Two things: the family wanted to keep it as much as possible the same in remembrance of my grandfather. And because we have several pictures in here with my grandmother, my second one, that show the room as pretty much the same, with that big desk and that couch and chair in the same positions they are now. I remember Dad telling me that Grandpa used to come into this room, lock the door, and spend hours in here, before he did the remodel and built the library. Dad always thought that was real strange. Sometimes he would miss dinner, and Dad said he would get real mad if anyone even knocked on the door."

Cole got to his feet. "Thanks for letting me look, but I'm not done by a long shot. Would it be okay if I looked at the third floor in the morning?"

"That'll be fine, unless you're planning to show up before ten. It takes the missus a little time to eat and get things presentable, if you know what I mean. The master bedroom's on the third floor."

The next morning, Cole headed over to the cookhouse to fix himself breakfast. Sunday everyone had to fend for himself because that was the cook's day off. When he entered, he saw Jay eating a large stack of pancakes with butter and syrup.

"Well, well, good morning. Did you save any of those pancakes for me?" Cole asked.

"Nope, but I did leave you a little batter. Best I could do."

"Are you leaving this morning for Canvas Creek?" Cole asked.

"Yup, unfortunately, it's a long ride. I'll sure miss Suzie for those two weeks, but I couldn't get anyone to trade me."

"Is Elmer driving you to the trailhead?"

"Yeah but it's still a five-hour ride up the mountain to the line shack, and boy is it a lonely place. I did two weeks up there about four years ago when I first started and let's just say it ain't my favorite duty."

"Let me get some pancakes down and I'll help you tie on the packs and load the stock," Cole said.

"Sounds good, Elmer's supposed to meet me at the barn with the truck in a bit," Jay said.

The two finished up breakfast, then walked outside just as Elmer drove up. The three loaded the gear on the truck sides and then the animals. Elmer and Jay both waved as the truck roared to a start, and with a noisy bang and a black cloud of smoke, they took off down the driveway toward the main road.

It was barely nine, and he still had an hour to burn, so Cole decided to spend the next hour down with Patch. He was really getting attached to the mule and thought he'd ask Wes about buying him. Several of the cowhands had their own personal horses and were given free room and board, as they still used a fair amount of the ranch stock for chores.

As Cole reached the corrals, he noticed Julie leaning over the fence petting Gun Smoke. Cole admired her choice of horses, but he had neither expected nor wanted to run into Julie, but when she turned and gave him a warm smile, it did something to his insides.

"Well, good morning, Mr. Morgan. I hear you've been turning the house upside down looking for Great-Grandpa's hidden booty."

"I don't know about that, but I'm trying to do a thorough job."

"Dad was complimenting you again last night at the dinner table. He says you're one smart young man, and if any one can find it, you can."

"I certainly think a lot of him, too," Cole said.

The two talked about horses and riding, but mainly about the human tracks and the plane wreck until it was after ten. Cole excused himself and headed up to the house. Cole was not used to failure, and he was determined to figure this one out.

Tyler greeted him at the door. "Come in, Mr. Morgan," he said without emotion.

"Is everything okay?"

Tyler just looked at him. "It's fine. Are you back to continue your search?"

"Yes," Cole said as Tyler showed him in.

Sally McCabe met him as she came down the wide main stairs by the fireplace. After all the things he had learned about Gillis McCabe, the large painting of him on the fireplace brought new meaning.

"It's all yours, and good luck," Sally said with a strange seriousness.

Whereas Wes had just laughed at his effort, Sally McCabe believed in him and really was taking the whole thing very seriously. Cole took his tools and board and headed to the third floor where he spent another three hours investigating, moving furniture and rugs from one side of the room to the other, while he examined every square inch of floor, walls and ceiling. When he was done, again he had found nothing.

It was almost two when Cole decided to go eat lunch. Allen was just finishing his meal and was sipping on a cup of hot coffee. Cole sat down beside him and with a frustrated voice said, "You know, Allen, I haven't come up with even one clue of what old Gillis did with his booty."

Allen listened for the next ten minutes while Cole explained his thorough search. "I still need to look under the porch, but I really don't believe he'd crawl under there and get filthy every time he needed some of his valuables. I'll check it out, but it doesn't make sense that he'd do that. Besides, when they rebuilt the porch ten years ago, someone would have found something. And that only leaves the attic. I don't think I'm missing anything, at least nothing obvious."

"I know one thing," Allen said. "Gillis McCabe was smart, and there is a reason no one has found his so-called booty, as Julie calls it. He would have tried to hide it different than anyone would suspect. I've thought about this for years, just like everyone else. Gillis would have had to been able to access his money reasonably quick and away from prying eyes. I really believe when it's finally found, it will be right in front of us, and we never seen it." Allen excused himself to go to town while Cole returned to the house.

Again, Cole rang the doorbell, but this time Julie answered, "Back for the booty hunt?"

"Thanks a lot," Cole said with a frown. "I'm just trying to help."

"I didn't mean it that way. It would be the greatest thing if you found it. It would change everything. Anyway, I need to get back and help Mom in the kitchen."

Cole headed to the attic and started measuring. The space was fairly small, at least compared to the rest of the house. On the three wooden walls, he carefully inspected the boards for any movement or sign that they could be removed. Again, he pulled out his small knife and pried on each plank, as he made his way around the room. He then rechecked the wood ceiling and actually pulled several boards loose. With the help of two stacked chairs, he removed the boards and stuck his head in above the attic ceiling. He had bought a new flashlight when he was in town, and now he was glad he did. He shone it into the space, but with the exception of a lot of old torn newspaper insulation, there was nothing.

Cole replaced the old furniture and sat down with his back against the brick chimney wall. He scanned the walls and ceiling looking for anything that he may have overlooked. After more than ten minutes, he got up and looked back at the chimney. The chimney had the brick pattern of the rest of the house, but there was no fireplace on this floor—only the large brick-walled chimney that carried the smoke high above the house's roof.

He began carefully examining every brick, looking for any possible access. He didn't find anything, and the more he thought about it, the more impractical the idea of storing valuable possessions in a hot fireplace became. In frustration, he retrieved his gear and went to the door that led down the stairs to the third floor. As he opened the door, he heard a floorboard squeak on the floor below. Cole headed down the stairs and opened the door, but the hallway was vacant except for the faint odor of tobacco. Had somebody been there? As he slowly closed the door behind him, he realized that of all stairways in this house, only this one had a door at the top landing and another one at the bottom. He wasn't sure if it meant something or not.

Cole went down to the main floor where he ran into Sally carrying a load of laundry. "Did you find anything?" she asked.

"No, but I was wondering if I could look through any old pictures of the house taken around the time of the remodel?"

"Sure, I know just where they are. I'll get them for you right after I get these clothes washed."

"That's great. I still need to go into the crawlspace under the house and look around."

"Be careful under there. We get pesky rattlesnakes once in a while."

"Oh, great," Cole said. "I'll watch out."

Cole walked around to the back of the house and studied the porch. He was glad he had a flashlight. It was a little expensive at a dollar, but when it came to snakes, it was well worth it. He removed the crawlspace door and inched into the four-foot-high, cobweb-filled underworld. He slowly shined his light around the dirt floor, looking for clues. Carefully, he moved each old board, certain he would find a rattlesnake any moment, but there was nothing. After an hour of searching, he was relieved to put the door back on and head over to the bunkhouse for a shower. He was disappointed he had found nothing.

By the time he had showered and changed his clothes, it was time to return to McCabe's house for dinner. Allen and the McCabes had wanted to hear his ideas for Crow Creek, for irrigating the pasture below it. When Cole was at Washington State College, he had taken several courses in irrigation development as part of his range management major. One of the ideas that made a lot of sense to him was an inexpensive irrigation pipe made by hollowing out and connecting large cedar logs and then tightly wrapping them with wire for strength. The theory had been around for a few years, but a new drilling technique had been developed that made it more economical. Cole's idea was to construct a dam high enough up Crow Creek to capture and channel the majority of the water to a level dry pasture half a mile away. Allen and Cole had estimated the cost and believed it would pay for itself in less than three years.

Cole was slightly late again for supper, but everyone politely waited until he was seated. He first explained his plans to pipe water for irrigation and to develop a flooding technique to increase the land's carrying capacity. It took over an hour and a lot of help from Allen to persuade Wes to agree to the idea, for it was still expensive to do. Cole knew that money was tight, but he believed that plans like this would eventually save the ranch. It was certainly a lot cheaper than running metal pipe, and with Wes agreeing to the idea, they now needed to find a large stand of tall straight cedar logs.

When the conversation died down, Sally handed Cole a small package across the table. Cole carefully opened it to reveal a stack of old pictures taken shortly after the remodel, before Gillis' death.

"It's just some old pictures," Sally said to the others. "Cole wanted to see how the rooms of the house looked and were decorated when Gillis was alive. Actually, a lot of them are very good, because he had a professional photographer come in and take them.

"From what I've heard, Grandpa Gillis was so proud of the house, he always wanted some of his friends from back East to come out and visit. According to Wes, no one would visit, because they heard it was so wild out here, Indians and all."

Cole thanked Sally for the pictures and started to get up when Julie walked over. "Would you like to have a cup of coffee on the porch with my folks and me?"

When they walked outside, Wes and Sally were sitting down with their coffee. Wes said, "We're all interested in how hard you're chasing this mystery of Grandpa's treasure. Have you found anything?"

"If you're asking me to point to something in particular, well, no, I haven't. But I haven't lost any of my confidence that I'll find it, if it exists."

"Oh, it exists all right," Wes continued. "I sometimes sound skeptical, but I am one hundred percent sure that does exist, but where, I haven't a clue." Tyler walked out on the porch and refilled empty coffee cups. Wes had already finished his drink, and Tyler leaned over Cole to pour Wes a fresh cup. As he did, Cole recognized the same faint cigarette smell he had noticed in the attic.

"You know, Cole, we've dug around the fountain, torn the wall apart, dismantled furniture, and every time we have an idea, we try and figure out a new hiding place. Ever since I can remember, people have been trying to figure out where he hid the loot," Wes said. "But to tell you the truth, I'm out of ideas. I thought every time we remodeled the house we'd find it, but we never did."

While everyone visited, Cole noticed Tyler quietly stealing around the corner. Cole excused himself and took the photos to the bunkhouse. A nice breeze blew down the valley, and the big weeping willow in the front lawn swayed back and forth in rhythm to unheard music.

Cole lay on his bunk and closed his eyes for a couple of minutes. He then picked up the package of pictures and started going through them. There were pictures taken throughout the house. He decided to start with the study, the most logical hiding place in his opinion. There were four pictures of the study that were in excellent shape, and Cole stared at each one for what seemed like hours. As far as he could remember, everything appeared almost the same as when Gillis had passed away. He decided that if it were fine with the McCabes, the next evening he'd compare each old picture to how the house existed today.

It was a couple of days later when Cole and Wes met and agreed on how to proceed with their new water transfer project. It had been decided that they would start the first stage by clearing the initial path for the pipe, but until Wes knew where the additional funds could be found he would have to wait to complete the entire project.

Cole was up early, ate and was out on Crow Creek an hour before the clearing crew was scheduled to show up. For the second time, he checked the ribbon path of the water pipe down the hill. The day went by fast, and the crew made good time clearing rocks and debris, creating a well-defined route for the wooden pipe. Throughout the day, Cole thought about the layout of Gillis' study, while supervising the construction. His crew did well. A good path had been cleared down the mountain, and soon the men were headed back to the ranch for dinner.

Cole wasted no time getting to the mess hall and was the first one seated for the night's meal. Chin was setting down plates of chicken, corn, and potatoes—one of Cole's favorite meals. As Cole reached to fill his plate with potatoes, the cook gave him a disgusted look. It was no secret that Chin liked everyone starting and, most importantly, finishing at the same time. Cole decided not to take the chance of upsetting the cook, so he backed off and waited a few minutes until the rest of the men showed up after washing off in the bath house. He hurried through his meal, grabbed the pictures of the study and other areas of the house, and hurried up to the front steps of the mansion like a man on a mission. Tyler answered the door and showed him in with another unusually stoic reception.

Cole couldn't figure out the change in Tyler's attitude, but he decided that he wasn't going to let that bother him. "Is anyone in Gillis' study?"

Everyone in the family still referred to it as "Grandpa's study," and no one seemed to be bothered with keeping the name. "No, go right in," Tyler said. Cole had always prided himself on the fact that he noticed his surroundings, and he looked forward to examining and comparing the old pictures with what existed today. Very noticeable were the added electrical fixtures that replaced the candle chandeliers that used to hang from the ceiling. Other than that, at first glance it looked as if Gillis McCabe's study was lost in the past.

The pictures were in excellent condition. After studying them and visually going back and forth from picture to room, it appeared that the only difference was a painting of flowers in a garden had been removed and now a newer family portrait hung in its place. Cole again removed all of the paintings and a black and white photograph of Gillis' parents from the walls and reexamined all of them and where they had hung, but nothing was out of the ordinary. Allen's words about the clues being right in front of him still bothered him, but he was determined to examine everything and miss nothing.

There had to be a clue. The first three of the four pictures taken were definitely meant to show off the different angles of the room, with the furniture, windows, and paintings as the background, and various members of the family in stately poses. The last picture was taken inside the study and showed Gillis standing in the arch of the door, leaning against the doorframe with a long, brown wooden pipe hanging from his mouth. It was obvious to Cole that this was the same door with its inner deadbolt and dark walnut that matched the wainscot interior. Gillis wore a period-style suit, a derby, and tall riding boots trimmed in silver. Cole was looking at the boots, when, all of a sudden, he softly said to himself, "There."

Beside the door was a large, black granite doorstopper shaped like a horse's head with a two-inch brass ring hanging from its mouth. Cole walked to the door and examined the area where the head would have stood. The back of the door had several large dents in the walnut finish that may have been caused by the door being opened too hard and hitting the stopper. There were a number of things that struck Cole as odd about the doorstop. Why was it the only doorstop he had seen in the house? The house was so well built that very few breezes were ever present in the home, so why have a doorstop at all in the room you least wanted people to visit? And why was the doorstopper so large, almost twelve inches high? And where was it now?

Chapter 12

Maybe it was a dead end, but Cole left the room excited and ran into Wes in the foyer. "Just the man I need to see," Cole said. Cole showed the picture of Gillis in the doorway to Wes. "See something in this picture that's no longer there?"

Wes looked a minute. "The old doorstop that Grandpa had made here in town is gone. Boy, I never even knew it was missing until you said something. Is it important?"

"I don't know, but it could be. It's the only thing that seems to be out of place."

"The guy that made it was local and really good at carving horse heads. Shoot, he made horse heads for just about everything," Wes said.

"Do you know where the doorstop is?" Cole asked.

"Wes walked over to a chair and sat down. "Wow, I sure don't. I was just trying to remember the last time I saw it. It must be at least ten years."

"I take it you don't remember giving it away or anything?"

"No, I sure don't, but maybe Sally does. I think she's in the kitchen."

Sally was slicing roast beef when the two men marched in.

"Mrs. McCabe, do you know where the old horse-shaped doorstop is, the black one that used to be in Grandpa's study?"

"What do you want it for?"

"The only thing that I can find different in Gillis' study is the missing doorstop, and I want to follow up every lead I get," Cole said.

"So you think you got a lead because the doorstop is gone?" she asked.

"Well . . . maybe?" Cole said.

"Let me tell you, people were always opening that door too wide and hitting that darn thing, so one day I got so upset, I gave it away," she said.

"Do you remember who you gave it to?" Wes asked.

"I gave it to Martha Schmitz probably ten years ago or more. She really liked it and commented on it most every time she came to visit."

Cole couldn't go over to the Schmitz's until Saturday, which was two days away. Until then, he worked with the men developing the water capture basin near the top of Crow Creek.

On Saturday morning, Cole hurried to the Schmitz house. Like always, the old dog howled to announce Cole's arrival as he drove up the dusty road to the house. By the time he was out of the truck, Martha and Phil stood on the front porch. "Well, good morning, Cole, nice to see you," Phil said.

Greetings were exchanged by all, and Cole headed through the front door into the modest home.

"Would you like a cup of fresh coffee," Martha asked, as Phil put some of Martha's cookies on a plate and offered them to Cole.

"So, what brings you to these parts first thing on a Saturday morning?" Phil asked.

"I came to talk to Martha again," Cole said. "Sally told me she gave you a horse head doorstopper that used to be in Gillis McCabe's study, and well, if I could, I would really like to see it."

Martha Schmitz slowly moved over to her rocking chair and sat down. She took a small sip of tea and smiled at Cole. "So what would you be wanting with that old thing?"

"You probably gathered from my last conversation that I was trying to find where Gillis McCabe hid his valuables. No one can find them, and I'm determined to."

"And what makes you think you can find them, after who knows how many people have tried and failed?" she asked, raising her eyebrows as she took another sip of tea.

"I may not, but it won't be for lack of trying," Cole replied.

"Well, then turn around, because the head you're looking for is sitting on the mantle over the fireplace behind you."

Martha had put a bouquet of wild flowers on each side of the stopper, and its black granite color helped it blend in. Martha slowly got up and walked to the mantle and picked up the heavy granite head. It was all she could do to place it on the table.

"Wait a minute, I'll help you with that," Cole offered.

"No, no, I'm still plenty strong and need to do things myself."

Carefully, she set it down in front of Cole and returned to her chair.

Cole picked up the head, which weighed close to fifteen pounds, and for the next five minutes, he studied every detail. He turned it every which way, checking for anything unusual. The beautiful, sculptured horse's head was a work of art, which softly rested on the table with a thick pad of felt glued to its base. "I guess I drove all this way for nothing."

"Well, you coming and visiting Phil and me isn't exactly nothing" Martha said. "And things aren't always as they seem."

Martha got up and walked to her kitchen cupboard and got a fork. She lifted the fork a foot over the black granite head and dropped it. The fork dropped toward the table but within inches of landing, it turned in mid air and slammed against the horse's head.

"A magnet" Cole shouted with surprise!

"Yup, and a very strong one at that," Martha said.

"Did Sally or any of the McCabes know it was magnetic?" Cole asked.

"I'm sure they must have, but I had it over here for quite a while before I found out," Martha answered. Cole reached over and tried to remove the fork from the granite. The magnet was very strong, and only with a large amount of pressure did the fork come free.

"Can I borrow this for a week or so?" Cole asked. "I think this just might help me."

* * *

When Cole arrived at the ranch, he headed to the barn where he got four feet of rope and a two-inch diameter wooden rod about a foot long. He went back to the truck and retrieved the doorstop, and headed up the stairs to the front door. Cole hit the doorknocker several times and waited.

"Good morning, Mr. Morgan," Julie said, mocking Tyler's formal speech.

Cole was so excited to try his idea, he simply returned the good morning greeting and asked if he could go to the study.

"Hold it right there, Mr. Morgan. Why are you acting strangely? Did you find something?"

"Not yet, but I think I will."

"Really, may I watch?"

"Yes, but you may be disappointed. I just don't know." Cole smiled.

Cole tied one end of the rope to the rod and the other around the black granite horse's neck, leaving two feet of slack between the wood and the head, which allowed him to keep the figurine about an inch above the floor, as he carefully moved about the room. Within several minutes of working the area around the old oak desk, the magnet grabbed at the end of one of floor planks and stuck solid. Cole stopped and just stared for a moment, then jerked straight upwards on the rope.

A two-foot long section of plank smoothly popped out of the floor, revealing a small compartment. Two one inch square magnets embedded in each side the floor board had tightly secured it to equally sized, opposing magnets in the joist. In the center of the board was a strong, three-inch square magnet also embedded in the wooden plank. The fake square nail tops blended perfectly with the rest of the floor. The heavier magnet had allowed Cole to quickly raise the hidden trap door that, by the look of the dust, hadn't been opened for at least sixty years.

Cole was impressed with the craftsmanship and how smoothly the door had popped opened, exposing a small gray metal box approximately twelve inches long and eight inches wide by six inches deep. Julie screamed, "Cole found it! Cole found it!" She rushed over and kneeled down beside Cole for a closer look at the box.

"Well, open it!" she said, as Cole carefully removed it from the sanctuary that had protected it all these years. He stood up and moved over to the desk, where he set the box down.

"Do you want to have your dad and mom in here when we open it?" Cole asked. Grudgingly, Julie sighed. "Yes, they should be here. But don't you dare open it until I'm back!" She went to find her folks, yelling with every step.

It was only a couple of minutes later when all of the McCabes, Chin and Tyler were standing in the study with looks of shock and excitement. Wes beamed at Cole. "You're amazing, son. Please be the one to open it. After all, I don't think we would have ever found it without your help."

The box was of high quality metal and covered by a small amount of dust. Cole took out his red handkerchief and gently wiped the dust away. The latch opened with a slight squeak, but all in all, a smooth motion. Inside the box and on top of its contents sat a small, red velvet cloth.

"Go ahead and take it out," Wes encouraged. Cole opened the cloth and exposed a shiny, silver-plated six-gun revolver with beautiful art work and ivory handle. He carefully picked up the gun and easily spun its cylinder, as he pointed the barrel toward the sky. All chambers were loaded and ready for action.

"Cautious man, wasn't he?" Cole said. Next, he removed a large leather envelope from the box and untied the two leather strips holding it shut. He then turned the envelope over and shook the contents on the table. Cash, lots of it, fluttered down onto the table, while a few bills missed and floated to the floor.

Sally and Julie quickly reached down and grabbed the loose money, while Cole carefully restacked it as if to emphasize its value. Wes quickly counted the bills and finished at $5,100, none of them newer than the day Gillis McCabe had died.

"There isn't near as much money as I thought Grandpa had," Julie said.

"That's because—if I'm right—this is only his petty cash that he kept around to pay day-to-day items. It was easy to get to and was enough to pay for some cattle or payroll or whatever, but it wasn't his main stash. If it was there would be some of the stocks, maps and who knows what else," Cole reasoned.

Wes nodded in agreement. This certainly was part of the lost treasure, but it wasn't what they were really looking for. The money would come in handy, but it was a far sight from the huge sum owed to Prentice's bank. Cole checked the hidden storage area, but there was nothing further to find. Wes put the gun and most of the money back in the envelope and placed it back in the box. Wes shook Cole's hand, complimented him on his find and handing him two old one hundred dollar bills. "I know this isn't enough for what you found, but I need this to help with some of the bills. I really appreciate this and thank you."

Sally gave Cole a short hug as he walked outside. "Thank you, thank you so very much." Tyler followed the two of them out.

"Cole, you're amazing," Julie said, "Who would have ever guessed that you would find any of Grandpa's booty!"

"I do have an idea on where to look for the real booty, as you call it, but it's going to take a little time. If I'm right, it is still out there," Cole said. "He had this in a safe place that he could visit at a moment's notice, yet no one would know where his stash was. No the real valuables are still to be found and I hope to do that."

"I'm going to go talk to Dad, but will you come to dinner tonight, please?" Julie said hopefully.

"How could I say no?"

As Cole left the house, Timmy greeted him. The ten-year-old lived several hundred yards down the road that led to the barns. Timmy's dad Archie, had worked for the ranch for ten years, and like some of the older cowboys were allowed to have their families join them. They lived in one of the nicer houses that Gillis had originally built for guests. Cole rarely saw Timmy because of how early he left for work and how late he got back, but he thought that Archie, as an only parent, had done a good job raising him. Timmy was standing at the bottom of the stairs with a huge smile on his face.

"So what's going on, Timmy" Cole asked.

"I just heard you found the old man McCabe's treasure. That true?"

"I wouldn't exactly call it a treasure, but I did find a little money. How'd you find out already?"

"Chin had me peeling potatoes, and I heard Mr. Tyler and Chin talking. Wow, I gotta tell everyone!" Timmy spun around and headed toward the mess hall.

Great thought Cole to himself, everyone in the county is going to hear about this now. Timmy did tell everyone who would listen the story of how Cole Morgan found the McCabe treasure, and by the time Cole made it back to the bunkhouse, several of the cowboys had emerged with questions and pats on the back.

After twenty minutes of repeatedly explaining the story, Cole cleaned up, excused himself and returned to the big house for dinner. On the walk up, he pulled out his wallet and looked again at the two one hundred dollar bills. Cole had never seen a hundred dollar bill, much less one from the 1870s. The average hand on the ranch made forty dollars a month, but Cole, because of his education, made twice that. Cole hit the doorknocker several times, and, to his surprise, Wes seemed to beat Tyler to open it.

"Come in, come in, I feel like you are more like part of the family every day. Wow, I am just speechless. I never believed anyone would figure out where the money was."

Wes seemed to be more excited than when Cole had first found the metal box. There was more excitement at the dinner table by far than Cole had ever seen before.

"Thank you again, Cole. Julie says you might have an idea where the rest of it is," Wes said.

"I guess I have a few ideas, but nothing concrete yet."

"If Cole found the rest of Grandpa's booty, you think it would be enough to pay off the bank?" Julie asked.

"We owe quite a bit, yet I believe there's a decent chance; but that's not dinner talk," Wes said.

Cole felt better than after a touchdown in college, like he had done something to contribute to this family he had come to genuinely care for.

Part II

The Hunt

Chapter 13

Jay appreciated Elmer Dahm's offer to drive him to the trailhead at Canvas Creek. That would save him over three hours of riding and would allow a decent head start on the trail before noon. Elmer and Jay talked about a number of things, until Old Blue roared to a stop at the widest spot in the road that signaled the start of the trailhead that led to Canvas Creek. Old Blue was a relatively new 1934 Chevrolet two-ton truck that was built to last, and the ride felt like it.

Elmer unbuckled the pack straps and helped Jay lower the mantied canvas packs from the sideboards of the truck. Both Jay and Elmer worked together to unbuckle the large ramp that allowed the animals to descend from the truck bed, then slid it out from under the bed of the truck. The ramp had two-by-fours screwed in laterally every two feet to allow the animals some traction as they walked down to the ground. Jay's stout sorrel gelding, Copper, and his two mules, Limo and Otto, were quickly unloaded. He had chosen to take Limo because he was a ride and pack mule, and that would give him some versatility if something happened to Copper.

It wasn't any time at all until Jay's horse and the mules were saddled and the packs were loaded. Jay thanked Elmer for his help and turned the stout gelding up the trail. In the background, he heard the lonely sound of the truck returning to the ranch. The first part of the trail meandered through thick timber and then up through steep rocks. It didn't take long before Jay came to a medium sized tree that had fallen over the seldom-used trail. The trail had changed its course many times over the years, due to windfalls and mudslides. Normally, a cowhand would just work around the obstruction that was in his path, but here the hillside was too steep.

Jay pulled back the reins and stopped Copper, dropping the reins to the ground. Having a good horse that was trained to ground tie was worth its weight in gold when in a demanding situation like leading a pack train. The sorrel held perfectly still as Jay tied the lead mule to his saddle horn and retrieved his ax from the side opposite his rifle. It took less than twenty minutes and a lot of hard chopping to remove the tree and resume his journey up the ridge. Finally, the string began to line out, and Jay made good time.

He had ridden for a little over an hour and was just above the tree line when he came upon a wide, shallow creek, where the string could get a good drink before heading higher up the narrow valley. Jay gently rode Copper into the creek and almost to the other side before stopping, so all of the animals could drink at the same time. As the three animals drank, Jay noticed tracks in the mud on the far bank. From the look of things, a large grizzly had crossed several days before and its deep tracks were still obvious in the soft, sandy mud. It was not all that unusual to see tracks, or for that matter, to actually see a grizzly, but this was a little different. Jay could clearly see that the paw print was missing a sizable chunk of its front paw, and there appeared to be only three toes remaining. He wondered if the bear had been caught in a trap in the past and had lost part of its foot escaping.

Bears that killed calves on the ranch were often the target of trapping. Jay remembered there had been a cattle-killing grizzly, and the men tried to trap or shoot it for over three years. Somehow, it eluded even the best of them. Several years earlier, he had heard a story of a large grizzly that tore its foot out of a trap, but Jay could only remember bits and pieces of the story. He did remember that they tried to trail the bear for a few days, only to have it vanish in a huge rockslide. There had been no sign of this bear for at least five years now, and the general consensus was it had either been hit by one of the cowboy's long range bullets or had just left the country. The track was clear, but didn't appear fresh and the animals didn't seem to pay much attention, so after a good long drink, the string moved up the mountain again.

For the next hour, the trail snaked through several colorful aspen patches with beautiful fern floors, as it climbed a narrow, thickly timbered ridge. After a full six and a half hour ride, the trail broke over the ridge and into a high mountain meadow that rolled and stretched for half a mile on a gentle grade. In the distance, Jay saw a small herd of cattle grazing peacefully on the opposite hillside. As he rounded the small hill, he came face to face with a large, white-face bull that was lumbering down the trail. The bull looked at the string, bellowed, and then dove to the lower side into a steep draw. The sky was a soft blue with a few faint puffy clouds floating through, and a slight breeze blowing from the west kept most of the bugs at bay.

All in all, it was the perfect day in the saddle. The higher mountains were already snow-capped and gave a solid backdrop to the landscape. Jay could see several bands of pronghorns taking advantage of the lush high mountain grass and the openness that allowed them to see their enemies at great distances.

Around four that afternoon, Jay and the string turned the bend, went over a small bald knob, and saw the valley that was home to the line shack. It was comforting to know he had almost arrived. The shack was simply a rough, small log cabin, built about forty years earlier, with a cedar roof and a small stone chimney. It overlooked a meadow and a sprawling basin. A shallow, fast-moving stream with short continuous drops sent the sound of water throughout the canyon, as it meandered just below the line cabin in some thick aspen. A corral made from old peeled logs blended with the scattered stand of aspen trees sixty yards in front of the cabin, and it would afford the animals enough grass for several weeks.

It felt good to be back, and Jay casually rode up to the front door and tied his stock securely to the slightly sagging hitching rail log that blocked direct access to the front porch. It was obvious that the place hadn't been used steadily for years, and Jay didn't know if anyone had visited in the last three. He carefully unloaded his packs, unsaddled the animals, and stacked the gear under a small cedar shake overhang on the building's downhill side.

Next, he inspected the corral for breaks and spent a little over an hour repairing them with baling wire and spikes. Opening the crude log gate, he led the animals inside, where he untied their lead ropes and turned them loose. Almost immediately, all three were rolling in the thick grass to dry and scratch their wet, itchy backs. Jay hung the lead ropes on what was left of a rotted tree snag and turned back to the cabin.

The cabin door was built of two-inch-thick planks bonded together with numerous cross braces. The door was a bleached gray and held in place by thick, dry pieces of leather attached securely to both the door and its frame. Two thin, rusted pieces of angled metal firmly held a two-inch-thick board across the door. Jay removed the brace, struggled with the door for a minute, then pushed into the cabin. It was just like he remembered.

A single wooden pole-frame bed with pig wire stretched across the opening sat on one side of the room against the wall. To the right was a small blackened metal wood stove with a section of dented stovepipe bending sharply as it rose and turned to meet the stone chimney that allowed the smoke an escape route to the outside. Above the bed was a rolled-up, tattered mattress hanging from a chunk of rope to keep the mice at bay. A few metal spoons, cast iron skillets, and one large, dented, blackened pot hung above a small wooden counter with a forgotten frying pan in the middle. Between the bed and the stove sat a tiny table that appeared to have been made from two old crates, and a solid, lone chair. Everything was in great need of dusting, and cleaning mice droppings would take some time, but Jay knew this was all part of his job over the next two weeks. The dark log cabin had only one small window, but it was large enough to light the room during the day, even with the door closed.

The evening was calm, and the animals had settled in and were quiet as Jay stored his remaining supplies. He opened several metal mouse proof boxes, and removed an old lantern, which he filled with kerosene. He had brought extra fuel, and having light to unpack by and work in the evening would extend his day. It was colder in the cabin than outside in the sun, so he built a fire. This time of year, high country nights often dropped into the lower forties or below. He kept busy dusting and unpacking and setting up the cabin for the next couple of hours. He already missed Suzie.

By eight o'clock he felt pretty organized, so he cooked up some bacon. The smell made him realize just how hungry he was. When Jay was done cleaning after dinner, he pulled out a smoke and took the old wooden chair from beside the table and moved it to the front porch. It was dark so he went inside and hung the lantern by an old wire above the table. The lantern cast its dim glow through the window and out onto the porch, just enough so he could see some of his surroundings. Jay walked out, stretched and sat, leaning backwards on the chair's two hind legs. He enjoyed the quiet night and the bright stars, as a gentle breeze blew from the animals toward the cabin. Some people couldn't handle the isolation of this cabin, but other than being lonesome for Suzie, Jay enjoyed it. They had gotten pretty frisky on that last date in the backseat of his car, so now he wanted and needed more.

His mind wandered to their upcoming spring wedding and how he would see some of his friends that he hadn't seen for some time—but, most of all, he kept going back to being able to make love to his new wife every night. His daydreaming was interrupted by the slight rustle of leaves off in the distance below the cabin.

The sound came from the opposite direction of the stock, which he guessed were silently grazing in the corral. He quietly listened for a few more minutes, when he heard the sound again. He decided to take his 30-30 Winchester rifle and the lantern from the cabin to investigate. Better safe than sorry, he thought, as he started down the line cabin's three steps.

He cautiously walked below the cabin and held the lantern above his head several times to throw light as far as possible. For the next couple of minutes, he stood perfectly still, just barely moving his head and listening, but he heard nothing. Disgusted with the effort, he returned to the cabin and got ready for bed. He had gotten a large pail of water from the creek earlier, and now he poured himself a bowl to bathe from and set it on the stove to heat. A little later, he washed up, and, within minutes of lying down, was sound asleep and snoring loudly.

The next morning, Jay was up early. As he was pulling on his trousers, a small mouse ran across the floor. Jay threw his boot at the rodent, but missed. Breakfast consisted of coffee, a bowl of oatmeal, and a slice of sourdough bread. He finished eating and then went down to the creek, where he filled his pail and canteen. He glanced at the small patch of aspens and ferns, where he thought he had heard something the night before, but he didn't see anything worth examining. He packed a lunch of jerky, bread and some of Suzie's homemade cookies in waxed paper, and stored them in his saddlebags. He put on an extra shirt for the cold morning breeze and headed out to check the stock. All the animals stood by the gate, enjoying the morning sun's warmth. Jay put a lead rope on Copper and led him out of the corral over to the hitching rail, where he saddled up and tied the saddlebags on.

Jay's plan for the day was to survey as much of the country to the west of the cabin as possible and visit the distant spring that he intended to develop for a watering hole. He had also brought ten pounds of salt to lure the cattle to the future watering hole, so he tied the sack to the saddle horn. He would put the salt on an open ridge overlooking the water, and when the cattle came for the salt, they would also find the pool. He started to mount his horse when he remembered his rifle, which he grabbed and loaded into the scabbard.

The ride out was beautiful, and in two hours time, Jay counted over one hundred and fifty head of cattle stretched over the wide horizon. In the past, several lazy cowboys had dropped salt in a meadow only fifty yards from the cabin, creating deep trails in all directions. Jay was a little frustrated with his memory of the area, but finally he found the small, isolated basin that held the year-round spring.

The problem with these high mountain meadows was not the grass but the availability of water in the late summer and early fall. By developing this spring, the hope was to hold the cattle higher longer. Water had to be available to drink within a two- to three-hour walk, or the cattle wouldn't use the area. Jay inspected the gurgling stream and decided the best way to create a long-lasting drinking hole would be to cut some medium-sized spruce trees from a nearby stand and use them as a dam. The mules would make short work of dragging the logs down to the creek, where he would build the dam and then line it with burlap sacks and a thick layer of mud. He mentally inventoried the tools he needed and believed he could complete the whole job in one long day, including travel.

As Jay rode back down the trail, a slight breeze picked up as Jay caught sight of the cabin. Its security felt comforting. The two penned mules began their imitations of mountain canaries to welcome Jay and Copper back. Jay unsaddled Copper and led him toward the corral, but, halfway across the meadow, Copper put the brakes on, refusing to be led any further. Jay calmly stroked the side of his head and talked to him in a soft voice for a full ten minutes, knowing he wasn't going to get an answer. Finally, Jay was able to gently coax Copper back to the corral, but it was obvious that something had crossed the meadow that day, probably a moose, and Copper didn't care for the smell of it one bit. Later, Jay would check for tracks, but right now he was tired and hungry.

Dinner consisted of potatoes, bread and beef jerky, which really hit the spot. Jay made up some sourdough and placed it in a small

Dutch oven to rise. If he got back early enough the next day, he would try to bake some fresh bread. After dinner, Jay checked the stock, and saw they were grazing quietly. He had gotten back a little late, and it was already getting dark, so he began his nightly routine of bringing the chair out on the porch and having his evening smoke. It was amazing to Jay the amount of stuff he could work through his mind, with the total quiet that came with the line shack. He was in his own little world when he suddenly felt an odd sensation, like being watched. He slowly scanned the area around the cabin, but everything seemed normal. The animals didn't seem bothered. Jay laughed aloud for being spooked again and tried to go back to his favorite thing, thinking of Suzie.

There was a slight breeze blowing from the stock toward the cabin that made the porch extremely pleasant, and Jay tried to enjoy it for a few more minutes, when he heard something down by the creek. Again, he grabbed the lantern and his rifle and moved quickly down to the creek for a look. As he stood holding the lantern above his head, another breeze whipped through the trees, and the leaves and ferns danced to its tune. Jay was annoyed with himself for getting spooked over nothing, and he turned back to the cabin.

After a few quiet minutes on the porch, he resumed his letter to Suzie about what he did that day and how much he missed her. He even wrote about looking forward to the wedding and seeing Suzie in her wedding dress, before he became too tired and hit the hay.

The next morning, everything was quiet as Jay headed over to check the horses. Limo was at the gate, so Jay decided that it was a good day to give Copper a break and ride one of the mules. Limo and Otto were easy to catch, and stood there as Jay tied his lead ropes on them. Copper seemed quite happy that he wasn't going two days in a row, and hardly raised his head. Riding one mule and leading the other loaded with supplies and tools, Jay made good time to the spring. Within three hours, he had developed the spring's channel and built a small log catch-basin to pool the flow of water and create a good sturdy place for the cattle to drink. The ride back was quiet and he made good time on one of the more worn cattle trails. That night, Jay baked bread and enjoyed a smoke on the porch—free from the sensation of being watched—and went to bed early.

The following morning, he awoke to a thick fog and the gentle sound of rain on the cabin roof. He started a fire using small branches from a pile on the porch. Jay took his time drinking his hot coffee and eating fresh bread with a little honey. He always carried his rain slicker and chaps, and today they would be needed. The rain turned to a drizzle, but it was wet and cold and the breeze didn't make it any more pleasant. Jay saddled his horse and headed up the valley, where, after an hour, he veered west toward a part of the country he had ridden through only once before. The clouds continued to occasionally blow in, and most of the time Jay could only see a hundred yards. He felt very comfortable with his stocky horse and his own sense of direction and didn't concern himself too much with the fact that he didn't have a plan. Early fall storms didn't last long, and Jay hoped this one passed quickly. He knew he could turn around and ride back to the cabin, and no one would know, but he was being paid to ride and check the cattle, and he was loyal to the brand. For the next two hours, he rode through the drizzle with the clouds rolling in and out, giving him subtle glimpses of the surrounding landscape.

Jay had just worked himself through a mature stand of aspen, when a large puffy cloud blew out and gave him a clear view down into the small valley below. Framed by the charcoal remains of a mature stand of spruce was a very strange rock formation. Jay pulled back on the reins and, with a few slight leg motions, got Copper headed over and down in the direction of the rock outcropping. Over millions of years, the wind had carved an oval hole in the middle of the rock that looked eerily like an eye, and with a little imagination, the rest of the stone looked very much like the face of an old man with a long chin.

At the base of the rock, numerous burnt stumps and logs littered the ground, the result of a lightening strike from the previous year. It was interesting to Jay: without this fire, the chances of seeing the strange rock were probably next to zero. Jay was not a creative man, but even he could clearly see the old man's face in the rock. The outcropping rose from a slightly raised knob and when Jay rode up for a closer look he couldn't help but notice the slight depression in the grass that led straight from the back of the rock towards a steep cliff face several hundred yards away.

He dismounted and led Copper over to the hollow for a closer examination. Jay was certain it was a very old trail that, at one time, had been well traveled—but who built it and where did it go? The more he walked the trail toward the cliff, the more impressed he was with how well hidden and thoughtful was its location. It would be nearly impossible for anyone to see, unless they were almost on top of it. The trail merged with the steep ridge rock face near a large pile of massive boulders and continued along a narrow shelf in the rock cliff. Jay took a minute and looked back. If not for the lighting strike, how would anyone have found this?

Jay realized it was around noontime. He hadn't eaten lunch, and his stomach grumbled. He decided to follow the trail until he found a good spot to tie his horse and eat. There was no sign that any cattle had found the trail, and he saw no tracks, but in his mind he used that excuse to continue. Besides, he always enjoyed exploring, and he was sure this trail went somewhere. In several places the trail had sheer cliffs at its edge that dropped over fifty feet, but the grade of the trail across the hillside was gentle in its slight downward direction.

This trail was a mystery to Jay, and he questioned how well developed it was to have only been a game trail. The other thing that caught his attention was how well hidden the trail was from anyone above or below. If you didn't know it was here, you would never suspect it existed. As Jay rode further, he noticed some places that almost looked like someone had actually used a pick to widen certain spots. After twenty minutes of working along the cliff face, the trail shrank to the point of being so narrow that it wasn't wide enough to even turn a horse around.

Then he saw it! Partially carved into the rock cliff, someone had built a hand-laid stone bridge across an otherwise vertical face. Beneath the bridge was a heavy stand of pine trees that totally eliminated observation from below. The twenty-foot bridge was not wide but well built and had probably taken serious time to construct. Each rock had been carefully placed to develop strength and support, and whoever had built this was a craftsman and planned to get some use out of it. Another riddle, thought Jay. As the stone bridge ended, the cliff faded away and the trail came out into a small opening. The trail appeared to vanish into the thick grass of a small park that was not more than a hundred feet long by fifty feet wide. It had taken far longer to get down the trail than Jay had expected, and he knew if he were to make it out by dark, he would need to eat lunch and head back.

There were several small patches of lush, green grass scattered throughout the ridge, so Jay decided that a small park up the ridge offered the best grass. At the edge of the park stood a giant Limber Pine tree with an unnatural number of thick stubby branches that almost seemed to guard the small mountainous meadow. It looked like the best place to eat and picket his horse. The massive tree was substantially larger than the others in the area, and at least half its thick massive limbs were either dead or dying. Maybe it was because it had fought the harsh Wyoming winters alone for so many winters, or it was just a freak of nature, but the massive tree had twice the branches of its smaller counterparts.

Grabbing his lunch out of his saddlebag, he led Copper up the slope and picketed him on a short rope below the tree. Heading up to a flat rock, he made himself comfortable, and within minutes, the horse and Jay were both busily eating. Jay was almost done when the light drizzle stopped and the sun's rays began to warm his face. Slowly, he leaned back to stretch his back and began gazing up into the massive snag that stood as a lone beacon on the ridge.

At first Jay thought he was seeing things, but stuck into the trunk about twelve feet above the ground was the unmistakable shape of an old bayonet. He took a moment to gain his composure then looked up the ridge. The bayonet seemed to point in the direction of a large rock outcropping further up the slope. Jay had heard the story of Creager's gold many times from Suzie's grandparents and others since moving to the ranch—and the part about the bayonet leading the way—but never in his wildest dreams did he believe that he would find it. He stood up and walked closer to the tree, where he could clearly see that it was a rusty bayonet.

"Oh, my God," Jay said softly. "I found Creager's bayonet."

Quickly, he turned and hurried up the slope in the direction the bayonet pointed, examining everything as he went. Within ten minutes and over a hundred yards, he had found it. Hidden by the branches of an overgrown tree was the beginning of what appeared to be a trail, a very old trail. The deep rut of the trail was clearly visible under the thick growth, and it was obvious to Jay that if he wanted to go very much further, he would need the small hatchet in his saddlebags.

He almost ran down the hill, scaring Copper in the process, to get his hatchet and race back to the hidden trail. It was difficult chopping through the low limbs, and in places it seemed to take forever to make any progress. After less than an hour, a heavy cloud moved back in, and rain began to fall once again. He knew it was time to quit. As he moved back to his horse for his slicker, the sound of thunder could be heard pounding the mountain above him, and Jay knew that no matter how much he wanted to go further, he would need a fresh start in the morning.

The ride back went well in the last of the evening light, as Copper confidently followed the dark path, sniffing the ground frequently. The cold rain was uncomfortable, but Jay only thought of the gold and how his life with Suzie was going to change. He would buy a huge ranch and the newest roadster available, one far nicer than John Prentice's. He spent little time worrying about finding the mine, much less that it existed on someone else's property.

It took four hours before he rounded the bend and rode up to the cabin. Jay quickly unsaddled and turned Copper into the corral. Then he put away his saddle under the lean-to beside the cabin and hurriedly went in and changed out of his wet clothes, built a fire in the stove, and started dinner. He knew that he would easily find the mine the next day, and his excitement was almost unbearable.

After dinner, he washed the dishes and got out the letter he had been writing to Suzie. He needed to share every detail of this day with her. He couldn't wait to hand deliver the letter and see the expression on her face, when she read the part about finding the bayonet and the mine. He folded the letter and put it into a light brown envelope, then put it in his saddlebag to finish the next day after he found the mine and its gold.

A few minutes later, he decided to celebrate and unpack the bottle of whisky he had stashed away for a rainy day and have a drink on the porch. It was still drizzling outside, but he really didn't notice as he sat down and poured himself a drink and began pondering his future. The first one went down quickly, as he made several toasts to himself and his future wife. Jay was pouring a third drink when he heard it again, the sound of something in the leaves below the house.

He went in and returned with his Winchester and the lantern, and headed down below the cabin. After several minutes of searching, he found nothing and headed back to the cabin. He reached down and picked up his bottle, which he decided to finish inside.

He looked over his shoulder and was surprised to see the lantern light reflecting off the eyes of the stock. They must have seen the coyote or whatever it was that seemed to visit most nights. Jay closed the door behind him but, in his drunken state, failed to secure it with the brace. He had turned to set the bottle on the table when the cabin door exploded, tossing Jay against the wall. The last thing he saw was the powerful teeth and claws of a huge boar grizzly tearing him apart. He screamed yet he couldn't feel the pain, but he could hear the sound of bones crunching. Then it was over.

Chapter 14

For two days, Cole had gone to bed to the soft sound of sporadic rainfall on the bunkhouse's tin roof. He loved the soothing sound, and the mellow rhythm seemed to massage his brain into the deepest of sleeps. He awoke to the sound of the bunkhouse door slamming open against the wall, and a bright light snapped him to full attention. Allen Skimming flipped on the lights and turned down his lantern. Water dripped from his raincoat onto the wooden floor. Beside him stood Elmer Dahm, covered in mud, his face dirty, worn and strained. As Cole's eyes adjusted to the light, his mind was frantically trying to figure out what was going on. "Okay, gentlemen, it's time to get up. We need a little help here," barked Allen.

Cole jumped to his feet and dressed on a chunk of old canvas at the base of his bunk. "What's going on?"

Allen took a couple of seconds to answer. "Jay's been gone for two weeks. He was supposed to meet Elmer between noon and two yesterday, but never showed up. Elmer waited until about eight and then searched up the trail a couple of miles to see if he could find Jay. About an hour up the trail, he found Limo, one of the mules Jay had taken, eating in a small meadow beside the trail. He had several cuts on his chest and wouldn't let Elmer near him. I need at least three volunteers to saddle up and ride back up there with Elmer and me." Allen looked around the room.

"I'll go," Cole said.

Allen nodded. "The road will be like grease from this rain. We'll need to take horses, because the vehicles will never make it. Chin's packing supplies and I need some of you men to catch a couple of mules. We don't know what we're going to find."

"What happened to you, Elmer?" Cole asked.

Elmer stood beside Allen with a small cut on his ear and another one over his eye. "When I finally made it back to the trailhead, I jumped in the truck and headed back to the ranch. The road was already greasy and . . . well, I skidded off the road and laid her on her side. I've been walking most of the night," Elmer said with an anguished look.

Ballard, the case hardened veteran, had already started toward Allen, when he asked for volunteers. Everyone volunteered to go, and Cole was impressed with the type of leather this group was made of. Allen quickly picked Ballard, Cole, and Archie to join Elmer and him. The men who weren't chosen hurriedly put their rain gear on to help with the mules, packs, horses, or whatever else they could do.

Everyone worked as a team, with little indication that they had been sound asleep only moments before. It only took thirty minutes, unbelievable time, for the group to saddle and pack everything. A full medical supply pack was put on one of the mules, as well as shovels, extra manties, food, and a small ten by twelve-cabin tent. By the time Allen and his group of five headed down the dark road in a trot toward Canvas Creek, it was a little after four and it had stopped raining.

At five, the sun chased darkness from the eastern sky. Half an hour later, storm clouds blew in, and it began to rain again. It seemed like the cold water fell just hard enough to soak everyone before easing to a drizzle, then quitting. Strong gusts of wind drove ominous thunderheads across the sky. The horses, as well as the mules, had mostly come from quick-paced Tennessee Walker stock. Even in the mud, the small rescue party made good time toward the most rugged part of the mammoth ranch and the Canvas Creek trailhead.

The red clay road was slick as ice, which forced the animals to tread carefully. They veered to the side of the road to get footing on the excess gravel. Several of the previously dry creek beds were beginning to swell from the rain washing down the mountain valleys to the flats. Most of the crossings had small, solid, wooden bridges designed for freak gulley washers. Sheep Creek had no bridge, but its strong gravel bottom usually stayed firm under six to eight inches of water. But now, even from a hundred yards away, the men could see wood debris being tossed about in the foaming brown water. The strong current would be challenging to cross. As they got to the edge of the swollen creek, Allen spurred his large bay gelding into the water.

The rest of the group watched as Allen's horse struggled across the torrent of brown frothing water roaring down the creek, then safely climbing onto the far bank. Cole nudged Patch into the swollen creek, and he handled the challenge like a true veteran. About two thirds of the way across, a small chunk of wood bumped his front leg, then harmlessly flowed away down the creek. Patch stepped up onto the bank and came to a stop beside Allen's horse and next came Ballard on his sorrel. The horse shied at first, but with a little spur from Ballard, he cautiously started across the creek. They were almost in the middle when a large log swirled down the creek and hit his horse in the back leg, knocking its feet out from under him. The force threw Ballard into the water, and he came up splashing wildly, as the water rushed him violently downstream.

In one quick movement, Cole jumped from his mule and grabbed his lariat from the saddle. Dodging brush he ran down the creek to get ahead of the hollering and quickly panicking Ballard. With one well-placed throw, the rope circled Ballard's outstretched hand. Cole tightened his grip and dragged him to the bank, where his horse had regained its footing and stood rider less beside Patch, seemingly no worse for wear. Cole helped Ballard to the shore and sat him on a large, wet log.

"You scared me a mite," Cole said. "I didn't know you couldn't swim."

"Damn log, what are the chances? Must not be my day," Ballard growled as he rubbed the scrabble of beard on his jaws.

Fighting the current, the rest of the crew and the pack mules made their way across the creek. Allen directed them to tie up and build a fire, no easy task with the wet brush and wood. The rain had stopped, but the temperature was probably only in the middle forties. Elmer pulled a small metal flask containing whisky out of his saddlebags, "Take a couple of sips of this, it will warm your inners." He handed it to Ballard. He turned back to his horse and after a moment of searching pulled out another smaller bottle containing black liquid.

Turning, he smiled at Ballard, "This my friend contains some of old Elmer's secret fire starter," he laughed. "To some people, it's just a fine mixture of equal parts used motor oil and gasoline, but its guaranteed instant fire," he hesitated, "comes in mighty handy on rainy nights." Ballard took a large swallow from the flask and set it down beside the small log where he sat.

Everyone helped collect as much dry wood as possible to get a fire started to warm Ballard. After a few minutes the soft sound of crackling old wood began and small flames began to rise above the wood coaxed by Elmer's fire starter. After checking his horse, Allen slowly walked over to Cole and sat down beside him. "Cole, I think Ballard will be fine, but I want you to take Elmer and head up the valley. No telling what happened to Jay, and time ain't our friend in this deal. The rest of us will follow you in an hour or two when Ballard dries out."

Cole and Elmer started down the road, making good time without the pack mules. Within an hour, they came to Elmer's truck lying on its side in the ditch. Normally, Cole would tease Elmer about his driving skills, but today wasn't a normal day, therefore they rode past the wreck without saying a word. Cole thought about Ballard and how close he had come to drowning, and he worried what they would find at the cabin. Cole knew that Jay had been wrangling since he was fifteen, and he wouldn't panic in a bad situation. He hoped he would find Jay in the cabin, sick or with a broken leg, but that didn't explain his scratched up mule running loose on the trail.

Neither Elmer nor Cole talked much as they reached the trailhead and started up. Elmer's tracks from the night before had been washed away, and the trail looked fresh and clean. Even though Elmer was a tough, experienced man, Cole noticed that he was looking a little tired from his ordeal and lack of sleep. Cole knew that Elmer wanted to be there for Jay, and Cole had seen him win the argument with Allen on coming back. Other than Jay, Elmer was one of the few hands who had been to the line shack in the last five years, and knowing the way was important with time not on their side. "How long a ride is it to the cabin?" Cole asked.

"Six to seven hours, if I remember right, depending on how greasy the trail is and how bad blow downs are."

By the time they made the clearing, the wind had blown most everything dry, including the trail, which made easier going. It was close to two when they got within sight of the cabin, and it was clear from the start that something was wrong. The door hung loosely from one hinge, and a dark stain oozed from below the door, across the porch, and down the stairs. As Elmer and Cole got closer, they recognized bloody scuffmarks that disappeared into the grass below the cabin.

There was so much blood that not even the heavy rainstorm had washed it away. As Cole tied Patch to the hitching rail, the mule acted very nervous and danced around. His eyes bulged as he carefully examined every ounce of terrain around them, and his huge ears twitched back and forth, carefully listening for anything out of the usual. Cole pulled out his rifle, as did Elmer, and as they walked to the porch, Cole felt a sick feeling in his stomach. He confirmed that the stain on the porch was definitely blood, grabbed the damaged door and opened it enough for them to get inside.

The inside of the cabin looked like a bomb had detonated. Huge claw marks scored the walls, and there were deep gouges in the cookware and crude furniture. Empty cans, blood and flour covered the floor. The table, chair and bed were in pieces, nothing seemed to have escaped the carnage. Large tears streamed down Elmer's face, and Cole fought back his emotions to keep his guard up. The two took several minutes examining what remained of the line cabin. In a corner lay the torn remains of the bed and some pack gear. Cole moved the bed, half expecting to find part of Jay's body in the corner. But there was nothing more than a shredded blanket, a ripped can of beans, and more blood. He was sure by the claw marks and other signs that he was dealing with a large, powerful bear, probably a grizzly.

Cole and Elmer snuck around the cabin, sure that they would see the rogue bear at any moment. At first, following the blood trail was fairly easy, but the further they went, the less blood they found. "The rain must have washed away the tracks and blood," Elmer said. "Where do you think the body is?"

Cole guessed that Elmer had little experience with grizzlies, even though he had worked on the ranch for at least ten years. "Normally, a grizzly will eat its fill and then drag its prey away somewhere and bury it in a mound of dirt, sticks, and brush," Cole said. He looked back to see Elmer's face go white as he leaned over and threw up. "You better go back to the cabin and wait for me. The next part will probably be worse." An exhausted Elmer shook his head no.

Together they circled the cabin about fifty yards out. Cole wanted to see if they could pick up a trail or other bear signs. They were about three quarters of the way around the clearing, when they spooked a group of magpies by the creek. It was then the men caught the smell of something dead. Cole stepped into an aspen stand and saw the partial remains of a mule. The corpse had a pile of brush and leaves scattered on top of it, and it was lying at the base of a tree. From the sorrel hide, he could tell it was Otto, Jay's other mule.

It appeared that a large part of the body had been eaten, but, for some reason, the neck and head were still intact. Otto had been a tremendous mule: smart, strong and a better companion than most people Cole knew. Now this beautiful, old, sorrel mule lay dead and partially eaten by a killer bear. Cole was cautious not to let the gruesome site take his full attention, because he knew the bear might still be close. Next, they moved in front of the cabin and noticed the far end of the corral had collapsed. "Looks to me like Jay's horse, Copper, may have gotten away," Cole said to Elmer.

They completed their first circle, then began a wider search a hundred yards farther out from the cabin. They had almost finished the second loop, when Cole noticed scuff marks in a gravelly section of ground. There wasn't any proof, but Cole's gut feeling was this path was where the bear had taken Jay's body. If he were right, the bear had killed Jay first and then went after the livestock.

Cole stopped and looked around, focusing on a large boulder that stood six foot high with a flat spot on top. "Elmer, you stand over there on top of that rock, and if you see anything move, holler," Cole said.

Elmer nodded and climbed up on the six-foot-high boulder that had a commanding view of the area around the back of the cabin. Cole waited until he was in position to cover him, plus Cole didn't want Elmer to see what he believed would happen next.

Carefully, Cole picked his way down into the thick aspens that were mixed with a spattering of young spruce trees from five to eight feet tall. Slowly, he opened the bolt of his rifle and again checked to make sure there was a bullet in the chamber, then replaced his thumb on the safety and his finger on the trigger. His old 30.06 was a good rifle and boosted his confidence as he crept through the trees. The dense foliage by the creek made the area darker than Cole would have preferred. He moved with great care and alertness, and soon sweat beaded on his forehead, as he stalked deeper into the thick aspens. It was Cole's sense of smell that led him to the decaying body of Jay Taylor, buried in a mound of mud, leaves, and sticks.

At first glance, the only thing Cole could make out for sure was a hand connected to a small section of arm covered with a bloody shirt. A boot laying several yards from the mound looked as though someone had neatly removed it and set it there to dry. Cole slowly looked around. The pungent odor of the bear hung in the air. Cole knew it was bear scat deposited around the mound. Several times, he walked slowly around the pile, suspiciously looking at anything that could possibly hide a bear. After three minutes that seemed like forever, Cole started back to the cabin to find Elmer. He took one step and kicked something with his foot—Jay's rodeo buckle.

Jay had proudly told him the story of his uncle earning the buckle for staying eight seconds on a bull named Blue Nose at the Cody rodeo. Cole picked up the buckle and noticed a large imprint in a soft soil several feet away. Despite the rain, Cole could clearly make out a deformed bear paw. He looked at it for several minutes, burning its shape into his mind forever, and as he placed the buckle in his pocket, he vowed to himself that he would hunt down and kill this monster. Over the years, Cole had enjoyed seeing bear, but this one was a brutal killer, and he knew it would kill again.

Cole cautiously continued back up the trail, where he met Elmer climbing down from the rock. "I found Jay. The bear—"

"Where, where's his body? I need to see him."

"You can see him later. For now, let's go back to the cabin and get you some rest."

Elmer paused for a second and then nodded his head in agreement. He looked terrible: tired, sick, and so emotionally drawn that he could hardly talk. It had been a mistake to let him come, no matter how bad he wanted to be there for Jay. Jay had been one of Elmer's closest friends, and Elmer was just barely keeping it together.

"He's been dead for at least a week," Cole said. "There wasn't anything we could have done for him. We'll deal with this after the rest of the guys get here. In the meantime, why don't you sit down while I grab the axe and some rope and go fix the corral. We'll be staying for the night."

It didn't take Cole long to find some new logs and repair the corral. Then he unloaded the saddles off the two horses and released them into the corral. The horses acted nervous at first, but soon had their heads down and were eating.

Cole walked back to the cabin and leaned his rifle against the hitching rail. Walking up the stairs felt eerie as he continued through the doorway into the blood stained cabin. Carefully, he began removing items that were destroyed beyond repair. He next built a small fire thirty feet in front of the hitching rail and burned everything from the blood soaked mattress to the many food cans that the bear had ripped apart. Cole knew the metal wouldn't burn, but he wanted all the food scent to disappear. Then they would sort through the fire and bury the cans deep and away from the cabin.

Inside the cabin, he righted the stove and reconnected the dented stovepipe. He couldn't find a pot that didn't have a tooth or a claw hole in it, but he did find a metal pail on the porch, and with that he went down to the creek with his rifle to fetch a bucket of water.

After he had boiled the water, he began to clean up the cabin floors and walls. Elmer seemed slightly better when he came back over after checking the stock, but he was still visibly shaken and in no shape to go looking for the bear. Cole knew the bloodstained cabin was too much for Elmer, so he had him gather some more wood for the night. Cole planned to burn the campfire all night in case the bear decided to come back.

It was four hours later when the rest of the crew rode into camp. Ballard looked like a boxer, with a large purple bruise over his left eye, probably from hitting a rock in the stream. The three riders pulled up their horses to the hitching rail in front of the line cabin and quietly surveyed the torn door and burn pile twenty yards away. When they saw the bloodstains on the front porch, the men's faces turned ashen.

Allen climbed off his horse. "Archie, unsaddle the animals and get them in the corral." Allen took a long look at Elmer and then at Cole. "Can you help me get Ballard down and up on the porch?" With great care, they lowered the huge man from his horse, and then, with one man on each side, walked him up the stairs onto the porch. "Plant yourself here until I tell you different," Allen ordered.

"What the hell happened here?" he asked.

"A grizzly bear," Cole replied. "It must have hunted and killed Jay in the cabin and then dragged him away. I found his body about a hundred and fifty yards down by the creek and it ain't pretty."

"Hell of a guy," Allen muttered in a soft voice. "Nobody should die like that. I don't look forward to telling Suzie."

"I'm glad you're here," Cole said.

Allen looked at him for a moment. "That's not our only problem." He pointed at Ballard. "He didn't tell anyone he felt like his chest was going to explode, until he fainted and fell out of the saddle about a mile back. I think he's got some broken ribs. We had a hell of a time getting him here. We tied his chest up with canvas strips from a manty, but he's still in a lot of pain. That water tossed him around like a rag doll and who knows how many rocks he hit."

"Is he going to be all right?" Cole asked.

"Hell, I'm no doctor, but he's one tough son of a bitch. With some rest, I think he'll be fine." Cole followed Allen into the cabin. "My God," Allen said softly. "I've never seen anything like this." Cole could see Allen's eyes well up as he bent down and picked up a piece of what once was part of Jay's shirt. "Hell of a waste of a good man. Hell of a waste."

As Elmer comforted Ballard, the rest of the group continued to clean up and prepare for what could be a very difficult night ahead. It took well over an hour to finish cleaning the place enough that they could rebuild the bed for Ballard for the night.

After they were done, Cole walked over to Allen. "It's too late now to get Jay's body. We'll get it done first thing in the morning and wrap it in canvas for the trip out. Besides, it probably isn't the smartest thing to have something bloody that close to the cabin if the bear's still around."

"I understand," Allen said. "We aren't in any hurry. I'm not leaving here until Ballard feels like he can ride without it killing him. What I'll probably do is send Elmer and Archie back in the morning to get a few more men, and then we'll start hunting that bear. In all the years on this ranch, I can't remember anything like this. We've lost a few men in horse accidents and the like, but nothing like this. Jay Taylor was a good man and a good cowboy and will be missed by a great number of people, especially Suzie."

Cole nodded in agreement and turned toward the cabin.

It took Cole and the other cowboys several more hours to finish rebuilding and organizing the cabin. Allen had brought plenty of medical supplies for Jay, and now he found himself using them to tightly bandage Ballard's chest. It wasn't pretty, but the cabin should work for the night to keep Ballard warm and, hopefully, as comfortable as possible.

After a light dinner of jerky, coffee and bread, Cole, Allen and Archie moved closer to the fire. As night set in, they took turns stoking the fire and patrolling the grounds with their rifles. Elmer kept Ballard company in the cabin, until he fell asleep on the floor from total exhaustion. Cole had rebuilt the bed and made Ballard a makeshift mattress out of the horse and mule blankets. The starry night stirred with a slight breeze, and the only sounds were the men's snoring in the cabin and a distant coyote. The other three men sat quietly together on a large log a few feet from the flames.

Allen broke the silence. "Cole, in all that's happened today, I forgot to tell you Sheriff Burris stopped by with a message. He and a government agent returned to the plane wreck to look for clues. They found several burned gauges, a piece of landing gear, you know, odds and ends and the like. That Federal guy took the tail section to somewhere in Missouri to try and determine the owner."

"I hope they figure it out. I can't understand why things happen like they do. It makes no sense," Cole said softly. "You know, Jay was one of the finest guys I ever knew. He had a great outlook on life, a wonderful girl—why him?"

"If I had a good answer, I'd tell you, but I don't. No one ever said life would be fair," Allen said.

"You can say that again," Cole muttered, his voice filled with frustration. Very little else was said that night, because the impact of Jay's death had a sobering effect on everyone.

The next morning everyone was up early, and Ballard appeared to be feeling a little better, but far from riding condition. Allen handed him his rifle and ordered everyone to help him to the porch bench. "Now, you sit here and watch the stock while we go down and get the body, OK?"

Ballard hesitated, and then nodded his head in agreement. The four men silently walked down to the creek carrying shovels, a canvas, rope, and their rifles. When they reached the grizzly's burial mound, Cole examined the immediate area but found no new tracks. Putting their handkerchiefs over their faces, the men began digging the decaying body out of the mound. It was a gruesome job, and the smell and flies were overwhelming. It took over thirty minutes to carefully remove the body and secure it in the heavy canvas.

"I guess that's it," Allen said. "Let's get back to the cabin and see how Ballard's doing."

Nobody spoke a word until they got back to camp. Once there, Allen said, "Elmer, you and Archie saddle up the horses, and Cole, you and I will lead the mule down to Jay's body." Cole put the packsaddle on the small bay mule named Rosie and led her over to the cabin and tied her to the hitching post. Elmer and Archie filled their canteens and made sandwiches for the long ride back to the ranch, as the four men led the mule to the body. The mule didn't like the smell of the blood or the bear, but it was well trained and stood fairly still while Allen tied several diamond hitches over the manty to keep Jay's body secure.

"May he rest in peace," Cole softly whispered.

The group walked back to the cabin, where Elmer and Archie mounted their horses. "I'll see you in three or four days," Allen said. "Tell Wes I need at least five men with supplies for a week. And new supplies for the cabin, a new mattress for Ballard . . . and get some real good bear dogs if you can. See if you can hire that government trapper guy, I think his name is Herman. Rich Herman, if I remember right."

"Will do, boss," said Elmer, as he turned and nudged his horse lightly with his spurs. There was a strange, lonely feeling seeing them leave, and Cole shrugged it off to the ever present threat of the bear.

Cole thought of Jay and poor Suzie, and a familiar gnawing emptiness knotted his gut. "I'll get some wood for tonight," he said. "I want to have plenty for the stove and the campfire. Who knows what that bear is up to."

"Good idea," Allen stated as he turned and went back into the cabin to make a hot lunch for the three of them. Allen repaired the cupboards, and while cleaning the debris he found Jay's saddlebags under some stove wood in the corner. He added them to Jay's belongings that he intended to give to Suzie.

"That smells good, boss. Never known you could cook," Ballard said.

"Well, you better enjoy it, because it will probably be the last trip I cook for you. Start mending those sorry bones of yours, so we can go home where there's real cooks." The three ate beans, bread and a little cooked beef for lunch. Allen placed hot coffee and a plate on the small stand beside the bed and helped Ballard sit up. He was real sore and hadn't slept well. "Maybe this will put some color back into that pale face of yours," Allen quipped with a smile.

"Thanks, guys, I really appreciate the meal. Sorry I haven't been more help," Ballard moaned. "Hell, I haven't been any help to tell the truth."

"Hell, if nothing else, we needed you to sit on the porch and scare that bear," Allen said. Ballard moved slightly to get up, and the pain doubled him over. Allen and Cole helped him back to the sitting position on the rebuilt bed, and Ballard ate a little before he lay down and snored softly on the mattress made of horse blankets. For the rest of the afternoon, with rifles close by, they chopped wood for the cabin and the fire out front. They didn't know if this would stop the grizzly from coming back into the small camp or not, but it made them feel a bit more comfortable having a well lit camp and a fire to warm the man on guard.

"We need to try and get some sleep," Allen said. "Hell, we sure haven't got much the last few nights, and we got a hard hunt ahead of us. I think that monster is one smart bear. This ain't going to be easy."

"I agree. I've looked around a little, and I found bear scat in a number of places several hundred yards from the cabin. I think the bear was waiting for just the right time to kill his prey," Cole said. "I think we'll have our hands full just finding him, much less killing him."

Allen looked down at his coffee cup.

Cole paused. "But we will, I guarantee it."

"You go in with Ballard and get a little rest. I'll come in about four hours from now, and you can relieve me," Allen stated. Cole headed in the cabin and quietly closed the door. He made himself as comfortable as possible, leaning up against the wall in the only open space in the cramped cabin. There was no real comfort to the hard pine floor, but he had grabbed his saddle for a hard pillow. His mind wanted to remember Jay, but his exhausted body won out, and soon he was asleep.

Cole felt Allen's gentle hand on his shoulder. "Time for your shift, I gave you a couple of extra hours. I think you needed it. But I'm starting to fall asleep myself, and I could sure use a little shut-eye."

Cole stood and got his bearings. He didn't remember sleeping that hard for a long time. "Sorry, I guess I was more tired than I knew," Cole said, as he headed toward the fire. He found the dry spot on the log that Allen had been using and sat down. Even though the others slept only thirty yards away in the cabin, Cole lost himself in the stars, thinking of his childhood and running around his folk's old cabin with his dog. Since their funeral, he had not allowed himself to visit those memories for the wounds they opened. He loved both of his parents very much, and being an only child made them even closer. He remembered the Christmas when his new dog tore up his dad's present and was caught red-handed. And how his dad chased the dog around the Christmas tree and knocked it over. He had heard, but never understood until recently, that the mother was the main person in a boy's life as a child, and the dad was the special person in a man's life. He had fished and hunted with his dad as a boy, but he didn't find that special bond with him until his late teens. Their memories, the memories of his dog, and now the memories of Jay all brought him both joy and pain. Jay had been one of the first people to extend himself as a friend when Cole had first come to the ranch. He hadn't realized how much that friendship had meant to him, and now it was gone like so many of the other special people in his life.

The embers barely glowed, so Cole grabbed a big handful of branches and tossed them on the fire without really thinking, his mind in the past. The flames licked the branches with new energy, and they got Cole's immediate attention. Suddenly, he realized what he had done. A larger fire constricted his pupils, hurting his ability to see into the darkness. Now, the brightness of the fire filled the meadow, and Cole could no longer see further than the perimeter that the light cast. He turned his back to the fire. It would take a while for his eyes to adjust to the darkness, and he hoped he hadn't made a mistake that would cost him dearly.

He sat on the ground with his rifle in his lap. How stupid can I get, he thought? Several minutes went by, with only the crackling of the fire breaking the night's silence; his eyes slowly began to readjust to the darkness. Another few minutes and I should be fine, he thought, and then he heard it: the snap of a branch several hundred yards into the woods.

Chapter 15

Cole heard nothing for several minutes. He thought it had been the wind, until he heard another sound, this time softer and closer, then another branch crackled nearby. Cole thought about hollering for Allen, but his instincts told him to be quiet. He might never get a better chance to kill this monster. He began to breathe heavily as every muscle tightened, and he made sure his rifle's safety was off. Cole stared into the woods for a bear shape, but with all his efforts, he couldn't see any movement. Time seemed to stop as the intermittent sounds came closer. Sweat beaded on his forehead and his finger tightened on the trigger. Every time he heard a new sound, he adjusted his position and readied himself for an attack. The subtle movement of leaves and the occasional snap of a branch told him the grizzly was close, real close.

Cole followed the sounds for over ten minutes, when suddenly the rustling shifted to his left and toward the stock. He jumped to his feet and lit the lantern. It seemed to take forever for the little flame to start to glow. Carefully, he crept along an interception course. It was awkward to carry the rifle with one arm and hold the lantern in the other. Part of him wanted badly to shout to Allen, but he was afraid a startled bear might charge. A sleepy Allen would end up in the middle. No, he decided, he must do this now, by himself, and make the best of it. He had great faith in his gun and its knock down ability, and he would stay with his plan.

Sneaking forward with all his stealth, he suddenly stopped and laughed. Here he was with a lantern sneaking through the trees, worrying about the bear hearing him, when he knew it sure as hell could see the light from the lantern.

The realization helped him regain his composure, and he lowered his tired rifle arm. He had not heard any new sounds for several minutes, and now he wasn't sure where his enemy lay in the vast darkness. One thing he was sure of, this killer wasn't going to get another one of the animals, especially Patch. It surprised him, the emotional bond that he had for this young mule. It equaled a close relationship with a dog or another human. Cole was quietly moving toward the rough corral when it happened, a branch snapped not fifteen feet to his right. Cole whirled to meet the charge, but there was only silence. He froze with his rifle up and slowly raised the lantern to extend the light further into the woods. The creature hunkered at the edge of the lantern's light beside a mature aspen. Cole raised his rifle in one swift movement, but something was wrong. The dark shape didn't move, and it didn't look like the round body of a bear. Cole took two cautious steps closer, so the light would illuminate the area better. The strange shape took one step forward and then several more toward the corral.

Suddenly, he recognized the shape. It was Copper, Jay's horse! Cole's whole body relaxed, and, for the second time in minutes, he laughed at the situation. Cole took several minutes to regain his composure, then in a quiet voice began talking to Copper and moving toward him. The horse was spooked, but seemed ready to join the other animals. Cole led the horse, who still had his halter on, over to the gate and the waiting mules and horses. Turning, he headed back to the fire and sat down, leaning the rifle against the log beside him. Cole took a deep breath. He felt drained. He reached for his canteen and took a long sip, then closed his eyes for a minute to regroup.

A camp robber landed on his hat, and Cole jumped to life as the bird flew away. He had fallen asleep, and it was sunrise. Cole was extremely angry that he had fallen asleep. It was his job to protect the camp. What would have happened if the bear had come back? Cole stood up and noticed the fire had gone out, and he was surprised the cold hadn't awakened him. He must have been totally exhausted.

Allen opened the cabin door as Cole relit the fire. "Good morning. How did it go last night?"

"I kind of screwed up and fell asleep. Sorry, it won't happen again," Cole said. Then Cole explained what had happened the night before. Allen listened intently and then began to laugh.

"So old Copper probably put a lump in your shorts, did he?"

Cole nodded his head. "How's Ballard?"

Ballard showed up at the door, smiling. "So, you got the shit scared out of you, did you? To tell you the truth, I think I would have, too." Though Ballard winced when he laughed, he moved better, and he seemed in less pain. Allen and Cole fixed breakfast, and Cole took a hot cup of coffee over to Ballard, now planted in the chair on the porch. Cole set his coffee down on the porch and leaned his rifle against the cabin, then headed back over to the corral to take a better look at Copper in the light. He grazed amongst the horses and looked up when he heard Cole coming. Copper only glanced up long enough to convince himself that everything was fine, before lowering his head and continuing to graze. The beautiful horse had a few scratches on his flank and shoulder but looked healthy otherwise.

Allen brought out some jerky and bread to go with the coffee and tossed some sticks on the fire. The floor of the cabin had not been easy on Allen, and he looked a little rough. Even though his hair had just a touch of gray in it, his thick, three-day beard was as almost a shiny silver color. Cole had taken a seat beside Allen on the porch, so they could talk to Ballard without hollering.

"I don't think Elmer and the crew will be back until tomorrow afternoon at the earliest. With your permission, I'd like to go out and see if I could pick up the bear's trail before we get some weather and lose it. I won't take any chances, but I think if I don't try, we might lose our only chance of finding him."

"Are you sure you don't want to wait until we get some of the boys here? That bear's a killer, and I think he stalked poor Jay for a while," Allen quietly said.

Cole shook his head. "No, I'll be careful. I really need to do this. I can't see myself just sitting around another couple of days and waiting for reinforcements. I'll take Patch. That mule is great at spotting—better than any guard dog I've had—and I really feel comfortable with him."

"Don't take any unwarranted chances. I think you know what I mean."

"I do. And thanks—I really need to do this," Cole replied.

They all ate a hot breakfast, then sat around and talked about what had happened as they sipped on their coffee. Ballard was starting to move better, but he was still in bad shape. After breakfast, Cole went to the corral and whistled to Patch, who was eating grass in the thick area of the aspens. When he heard the whistle, his head jerked up and he came trotting over to Cole. Cole talked to him in soothing tones as he put his halter on, attached the lead rope, and led him through the gate to the cabin where the saddles were stacked.

He then remembered they had taken the blanket into the cabin, so after retrieving it, he saddled up, packed some jerky and bread in his saddlebags, and slid his rifle into the scabbard.

He stepped into the stirrup, which creaked as the cold leather of the saddle stretched, and turned to Allen and Ballard, who were taking their time nursing their coffee. "I'll see you sometime late afternoon or tonight. It will depend on how fast I can pick up the trail," Cole said. He turned his mule and headed down the path to where they had found Jay's body.

Cole carefully watched the mule's reactions. Patch's long ears were quick to detect even the slightest sound, and his great vision did the same for movement. Away from the safety of the herd, the mule had to rely solely on himself and his rider. As they rode down the trail, Patch's ears constantly moved from side to side, scanning for any abnormal or threatening sounds.

When they got to the spot where they had found Jay's body, Cole gently pulled back on the reins and dismounted. There were still spots of dried blood, and Patch nervously twitched his ears. The ground was torn up, with the tracks of the men, bear and the mule muddied together.

Cole tied Patch to an aspen about fifteen yards from where the body had lain and began to carefully study the ground. Old bear tracks were everywhere. Obviously, the grizzly had been using this area for a while. There were so many tracks, it was impossible to determine which route the bear had most recently taken. After thinking about it for several minutes, Cole decided to lead Patch and circle the area several hundred yards further out to see if he could cut fresh sign. Cole led Patch toward a larger meadow also surrounded by aspen and pine. The grass in the meadow was tall, but not high enough to hide a large bear, something that Cole sought comfort in. He mounted his mule, pulled his rifle from his scabbard, and laid it on his lap as he rode. He knew any minute he might meet up with the bear, so he readied himself.

Riding through the meadow, he weaved among sparse aspens and hit a game trail that headed west across the valley to an open hillside. He had only ridden for five minutes or so, when he noticed the tracks. They were at least several days old, but they were definitely bear. For the next sixty yards, the bear tracks paralleled the trail, then crossed and headed up the steep hillside to Cole's left. A very clear track lay in the mud of the trail—a deformed bear paw.

Both fear and excitement filled Cole's body. He could quit and head back knowing the location of a fresh track, or he could follow the track as long as possible hoping to catch a glimpse of the bear. He sat in the saddle for a moment and thought. By the stride of the track, the bear was moving fast, and the chance of overtaking him in a good spot was slim. Cole decided to do neither. He would mark the trail by tying his handkerchief on a small evergreen tree, then head up above the trail onto a high ridge. Hopefully, by gaining some elevation, he could spot the bear from a vista, and chances were, from a distance, he probably wouldn't spook him. For over an hour, Cole rode Patch up the ridge, meandering back and forth to keep the mule as fresh as possible on the steep climb. The hill was mostly void of trees and became even steeper and rockier the closer he climbed toward the top. Cole decided to tie Patch to a small tree and climb the rest of the way on foot. He swung his gun over his shoulder and started working his way up through the rocks. It didn't take long before he found a sheep trail that appeared to angle its way toward the top of the ridge, and he found it easier going than hiking straight up. The path was rocky and steep, but it wound its way through the many slides that seemed to block access the closer he got to the jagged rock crest. He felt damp sweat on his body and wished he were in better shape, and he tried to ignore the dull ache in his bad knee.

As he reached the ridge crest, he slowly poked his head above the rock just high enough as only his eyes could be seen by anyone or anything on the other side. He carefully scanned the huge valley below and the many smaller branching ridges that were contained within it. Five hundred yards across the valley, a herd of mule deer grazed on an open hillside. If the big grizzly were anywhere near them, Cole knew they would be at full alert, but for now, the warm morning sun and the thick grass seemed to be the only thing that mattered. He had a great vantage point and decided to wait for awhile. A gentle breeze was blowing up the valley into Cole's face, so he wasn't worried about the bear catching his scent from below.

He was nearly nine thousand feet high in altitude watching and puffy white clouds floated in and out of the little mountain ridges and valleys. As one of the clouds blew off a small ridge about seven hundred yards away, he noticed a large mule deer buck bedded on a rock shelf. The deer had blended perfectly with the terrain, and if it hadn't been for the cloud and the way it accented the point, he would have never noticed him. Even at this distance, Cole could make out the buck's heavy rack, and he wished he were on a hunting trip. He was admiring the large buck, when he noticed movement below it, the undeniable shape of a large grizzly moving across the hillside over a thousand yards away. At that distance, he could barely make out the shape, but he knew in his heart he was looking at Jay's killer. The bear ambled below a large rock outcropping in the general direction of the bedded mule buck, which had not yet sensed the grizzly.

Over the course of ten minutes, the bear had moved within a hundred and fifty yards of the buck, when a large, puffy cloud blew in and blocked Cole's view. The lingering cloud took almost five minutes to finally float away, and when it did, the giant buck lay dead at the feet of the grizzly. Cole was shocked at what just happened. Somehow, the huge bear had crept up a steep, rocky ledge without making a sound, traveled over a hundred and fifty yards in less than five minutes, and still was able to kill the buck in his bed. His ability to silently sneak up and kill an animal known for its keen sense of smell and awareness was impressive. The hair on the back of Cole's neck stood up, as the bear tore apart its prey.

Cole turned and slowly slid down the hill, so the bear couldn't pick up any movement. He sat for a couple of minutes, thinking about this animal he so desperately wanted to kill. The bear could see, hear and move better than he could, and this one was smart. If Cole quietly made his way down the ridge, he might be able to get within four hundred yards of the bear without being detected, but a shot at that range with open sights was anything but a sure thing. Left alone, the bear would take a few hours to eat and perhaps hang around for a day or two. Cole's desire to kill the creature overrode his common sense to wait for the other men's help.

For several hours, Cole glanced over the rock every fifteen minutes to aim his rifle at the bear, but the dot on his sight completely covered the beast. During the time spent sitting out of sight, Cole found his mind wandering strangely to Julie, and he realized how much he cared for her. He wished he had met her under different circumstances. He found a comfortable clump of grass at the base of a flat rock and rested. He very much wanted to go down the ridge to get as close as possible for a one-shot kill. He knew his chances were slim at this distance with the wind and drop of the bullet, and he wasn't exactly sure how far away the bear was. Dealing with a wounded, smart bear didn't excite him, and the thought of putting other cowboys in more danger bothered him even more. Again, he decided that the best thing he could do was stay with his plan and wait until he had backup. Cole decided to take one last look at the bear before dropping down to his mule and heading back to camp.

Carefully, he climbed to his vantage spot and slowly peered over the rock to where the bear had been all afternoon. The bear was gone, and so was the deer carcass. Cole spent the next fifteen minutes scanning the site, but there was nothing, so Cole carefully picked his way back down the hill to where he had tied Patch to a small tree. After thirty minutes of hiking, he reached a spot where he could look down and see the tree in the small meadow, but Patch was nowhere in sight.

A sense of dread overwhelmed Cole. What if he had been watching the wrong bear? What if there were two of them? Could the grizzly have circled around him? Cole covered a lot of ground quicker than was safe. He was anything but quiet, as he raced the last fifty yards down the hill toward the meadow. Just before he got to the meadow, he slowed to a stop and jacked a bullet into the chamber, then carried it in a ready position. The majority of Patch's lead rope still hung from the tree, missing only a small piece that connected it to the halter. On closer examination, Cole could tell that it had been chewed off. Suddenly, a twig snapped behind him. Cole swung his rifle around with almost unbelievable speed to see Patch walking out of a small clump of the evergreen trees that had concealed him. The sorrel mule had a large wad of grass in his mouth, and the other end of the lead rope hung from his halter.

Cole felt himself go limp with relief that he had not lost another thing dear to him. "You mangy, long eared mule, what in the hell do you think you're doing chewing your lead rope in two? I thought I trained you better than that!"

He wanted to convey his anger, but he was so happy to see him that he had to turn and smile to himself before he returned to scolding the mule. Patch stood there intently listening as if he were taking the whole thing in, then he took his snout and gently pushed up against Cole's chest. Cole could no longer keep up the act. He gave the mule a little hug around the neck, tightened the cinch, and then started getting organized by putting his gun in the scabbard and the remains from the lead rope in his saddlebag.

Both Cole and Patch knew the way back, and they went cross-country, choosing not to follow the longer, meandering trail. Cole was pleased that he had found the bear's trail. Hopefully, the men and the hounds would get there sometime tomorrow. If luck were with them, the bear would stick around that area for a while. Suddenly, a couple deer jumped up in front of them, startling Cole. Patch took control and needed very little guidance, as he carefully picked the fastest and best way back to camp and the other stock.

It was several hours past sunset when Cole rode into camp. Allen and Ballard were sitting around the fire talking and smoking hand-rolled cigarettes. They were relieved to see him. Cole dismounted and stretched his back. He leaned his gun against the porch, then led Patch to the side of the cabin. He brushed the mule down, led him over to the gate of the corral, and turned him loose with the rest of the herd. When he turned around, Allen was standing there with a plate of beans and bread and a cup of coffee. Cole sat down, and Allen joined him with another plate of steaming beans. They were hot and good, but Cole had already eaten the same dinner for the last four days, and the beans were starting to get to his system. While he ate, Cole told the other two what he had seen that day, and they agreed he had done the right thing by waiting.

When Cole was done eating, Ballard reached over, grabbed his plate, and said, "I can't seem to do much, but I sure as hell can do the dishes."

"Thanks," responded Cole. "I appreciate it." Allen just smiled, nodded, and lit another cigarette.

"Allen, you remember telling me about that ranger that went missing ten, fifteen, years ago?" Cole asked.

"Sure do, that was the talk around campfires for several years after it happened," responded Allen.

"Do you think there is any chance that may have been a bear—this bear?" Cole asked.

"I don't rightly know, real hard to say, but I guess it could be. Must have been at least fifteen miles from here by how the crow flies and a lot further by horse," Allen said. "I can't rightly recall the missing ranger's name, but I do remember meeting him years ago. Nice guy, short, with the brightest red hair you ever saw." Allen moved to pour himself another cup of "mud," a term he used to describe Ballard's strong coffee.

"It sure does seem strange that we'd have two deaths up here exactly alike and it's not be the same culprit," Cole said. "Real strange to me and wasn't that ranger killed in a cabin just like Jay?"

"I can't rightly say, because they never found that poor bastard's body or what was left of it, but from what I remember, the cabin had some blood in it, just like this one," replied Allen.

Chapter 16

With the help of his stick, Ballard carefully walked out of the cabin, down the two porch steps, and sat by the crackling fire tended by Cole. He was through washing dishes and enjoyed the company around the campfire. From his movements, Cole could tell that Ballard was beginning to recover.

A cold wind whipped from the south down through camp, and Cole thought how lonely this country could be. The three moved out to the log by the fire, and the rest of the evening was filled with many conversations, all of which included bears. No one finished a story without being interrupted by the loud sound of someone's fart, as the beans worked their magic.

That night, Ballard shared in the guard duty, but he stayed on the porch except to occasionally stoke the fire. Cole slept well and was awake at the first crack of daylight, feeling more rested than in the last three days combined. He made a fire in the stove and then put on the coffee pot. After checking the stock, he grabbed his gun and the bucket, then headed down to the stream to get some fresh water. The forest was alive with the sound of birds and other creatures, and though Cole was careful, he really didn't believe any threat was nearby. Allen and Cole cut more firewood and then took turns shaving and taking a bucket bath, as they were as ripe as an overused outhouse. Cole, Ballard, and Allen sat on the log talking about how well Patch had done for a young mule, until Cole changed the subject.

"Allen, I know the rest of the crew won't be here until tomorrow, even if we're lucky. I'm going to go nuts just sitting here waiting, and I don't think that bear is going to be coming back this way, at least for some time. Would you mind if I saddle up and just go the opposite direction, check for cows and get a handle on what's going on?"

"Hell, no, I think that would be a great idea. Who knows what else has happened up here. We sure have a little time to find out," Allen said.

With that, Cole saddled Patch. After packing a lunch in his saddlebags, he slid his gun into its scabbard and stepped into the saddle. For several hours, he followed an old trail that meandered up the ridge above the cabin. The day was sunny with just a slight of breeze, and the views were spectacular looking down over the huge valleys. Cole hoped that Jay enjoyed at least one of these beautiful sunny days before he died.

He crossed a small creek, where Patch paused to drink, and Cole scanned for sign. The trail ended as suddenly as it had started in a large meadow on a ridge top overlooking low, grassy, wind-swept hills. The trail must have been created by cattle over the last sixty years and vanished into the grass as the cattle had fanned out to graze. With no path to guide him, Cole studied the mountaintops for bearings and took off cross-country to the southeast. From the cabin, Cole had seen a few distant cattle grazing on some of the ridges and a herd of over a hundred at the head of a deep, rocky basin across the valley, but here he hadn't seen any new sign for over two hours.

As he crested another small ridge, he jumped a herd of five elk. The bull looked like he was just going into the rut, with strips of velvet still hanging from his horns, and upon seeing Cole, he let out a high-pitched bugle that echoed throughout the basin. The big bull stared for a moment at Cole and then herded his cows down the mountain and around a smaller knob below them. Cole gently nudged Patch, and they slowly made their way down the small ridge to watch the majestic herd as long as possible before they disappeared. As the last cow elk leaped over a rise, Cole noticed a very interesting rock outcropping framed by the charcoal remains of a recent fire. The angular rock looked like a strangely shaped face staring up toward the sky. Cole slowly rode down the hill and entered the burnt patch of spruce to get a better look at the unusual rock. The old spruce stand appeared to be the victim of a lighting strike in the last couple of years. Had the trees survived, they would have hidden the rock formation entirely.

Cole smiled at how much this rock looked like a person and especially where the wind had created a hole that looked very much like an eye. On the fringe, there were a few unburned spruce and a small mix of aspens surrounded by lush grass. About twenty yards past the strange rock, Cole picketed Patch to one of the aspens to feed while he ate his lunch. Cole sat on a boulder between the burnt stand of spruce and the rock and examined it while he ate his jerky and bread, washed down with water from his canteen. After lunch, he untied Patch and mounted, wondering how many cowboys had been on this very ridge and missed the rock completely.

The ride back was scenic and slow by design, for there was no direct route, and Cole arrived back in camp just as the sun was setting on the small valley.

"Look what the cat drug in," laughed Ballard, as Cole rode over to the campfire where he sat with Allen. Cole was getting to like and understand Ballard.

"Hungry?" Allen asked.

"You bet. What are we having?" Cole asked, as if he didn't know.

"Well, sir, we are having the finest beans known in these here parts, because I cooked them myself," grinned Allen.

"Great, I can hardly wait," Cole replied. "I always like different foods."

Dinner tasted good, even though it was the same thing he had the night before and night before that, prompting Cole to hope the others carried a variety of grub with them.

That night around the campfire, Cole told the others about seeing the cattle, elk, and the strange rock shape that reminded him of an old man. Ballard and Allen enjoyed poking fun at Cole about the rock and suggested next time he find one pointing to where the bear had gone. "I'd sure like that!" Ballard laughed. He always laughed harder at his own jokes than he ever did at anyone else's.

It had been dark for about an hour and a half when Cole heard a hound's bay echo up the valley. Allen turned and looked at Cole, "boy am I glad to hear that sound."

The train of five men, including Archie, Dodge, and Nick, three pack mules, and five dogs entered the cabin area, exchanging restrained greetings. All but the trapper and his brother had spent serious time with Jay. He had been well-liked and they were angered by his death.

Archie led the group to the front of the cabin and climbed down from the lead horse. "Sorry it took me so long," he said to Cole and

Allen. "This is Rich Herman, and this is his brother, Buck, and their dogs."

Rich was a large, bearded man in his fifties, known for his trapping, tracking, and hounds. The group unloaded and unsaddled their stock, then began setting up a large fourteen by sixteen canvas tent with a stove, bed rolls and eight cots, putting even the largest hunting camp Cole had ever seen to shame. After the tent was set up, Rich Herman walked over and sat down beside Cole. "So, you're Cole Morgan. It's nice to meet you. I'm sorry about Jay. I didn't know him well, but I knew him. He was a good man."

"I appreciate you and your brother helping find this bear," Cole said.

"Not a problem. I've heard a few things about you in town." Then he laughed. "All good" Cole just smiled. It seems everyone had met Rich before except Cole, but he seemed to be a pleasant man.

Not only was Rich tall with broad shoulders and a thick chest, he moved with surprising agility. He was dressed in an old cowboy hat that had seen way too much rain, sweat, and waterproofing oil. He had tied his five dogs up to different trees around the campfire, and they slept quietly. His outgoing personality was something that Cole had not expected. A large bobcat pelt was sewn over the shoulders of his heavy oilskin coat and there was enough hide left over to tie around his neck if the weather got rough. His light, blondish red hair tumbled over his shoulders, but the color suited his wind-leathered, freckled face.

"You guys sure must walk on the right side of the street for catching me. I was driving in to Meeteetse with my dogs to meet up with my brother there. Buck and I were going to chase this old black bear that had been killing chickens over at the old Stevens place on Rock Creek. Turned out that it not only killed his chickens but also killed his dog, and then it came up on the porch of the cabin. The rancher, he shot it dead after I had already taken off for town. So, I arrived to meet up with my brother, and he tells me that a man was killed by a grizzly on The Greybull Ranch, and they were trying to find me. And to make a long story short, here we are, Buck and me."

Ballard walked over, leaning on a stick. "Nice seeing you again, Rich. How have you been?"

"A mite better than you," Rich chuckled, "heard you had a hell of a run in with a raging creek."

"You might say that." Ballard rubbed his chest. "Nice looking dogs, what's their names"

"Well, that one there is Bishop. That one is Brandy, and that's Bruiser, Pepper and my main dog, Boozer," Rich said, as he pointed to the dog sleeping closest to the group. "They're all first class bear dogs, some of the best in these parts. At least the older ones are."

"Why'd you name that one Boozer?" Cole asked.

"Well it's a bit of a story, but the short version is I bought him as a puppy and I was sitting at home cleaning my gun and drinking a beer out of a large mug. I needed to use the outhouse and when I got back, that darn little pup had drunk that mug clean dry and could hardly stand up. Actually, it was kind of funny watching him stumble around and run into things. After that, my wife Abby and I took to calling him Boozer. He's turned into the best darn bear dog in this part of the country. He's twelve now, and he's a lot smarter than he used to be. Been sewed up so many times, I'd swear he could do it himself! Yeah, old Boozer is lucky to be alive. He sure is one cold nosed son of a bitch."

"What do you mean, cold nosed? What does that have to do with anything?" Dodge asked.

"The colder the nose, the better they can pick up a scent. Old Boozer isn't the fastest or strongest, but he is the best I got at picking up an old trail," replied Rich, as he stretched his back on the old log by rocking back and forth.

The rest of the evening was spent listening to Rich telling about some of his bear chases. "Most black bears will tree with a pack of dogs on them, but those old grizzlies will often stop and fight and that ain't ever good for the dogs. I've lost more than one dog to bears that way. That's why I like to send Boozer after them first, to tell me what's going on, and then I send the rest of the pack. Boozer's smart, real smart. He's been on over three hundred bear hunts, and he knows what he's doing. He lets the younger, more aggressive dogs get hurt, and he just sits back and howls, great dog. Not sure what I'd do without him." Rich rearranged his position on the log. "Surely don't know."

Everyone enjoyed having the cots to sleep on. The new, fresher guys from the ranch drew guard duty, and Cole didn't take long falling asleep. When he awoke in the night to relieve himself, the amount of snoring reminded him of the bunkhouse.

Waking early the next morning, Cole found Rich and Buck feeding the dogs. The hounds seemed well mannered and responded to every command. There was a fresh cold in the air, and the sun's rays were several hours away. The air was crisp, and the starry night foretold a clear day. The dogs wolfed down their food like they were sure the dog next to them would get theirs if they didn't.

"Let's get this show on the road," Rich said to Allen, as he came out of the tent. Buck had already begun saddling their horses, while Rich finished taking care of their dogs. It had been decided that Archie would stay with Ballard, and he'd fix breakfast and lunch while everyone else got ready. It wasn't long before everyone was having breakfast and talking about the hunt, and—thank God—the meal contained no beans. The horses and Cole's mule looked ready, and the dogs were yapping and wagging their tails. All of them seemed excited for the day's challenge. Rich smiled as he worked with his dogs, each one responding to the sound of his voice.

The troop left camp with Cole leading the way to where he had seen the bear two days earlier. Next followed Rich, riding a horse and carrying a long leather leash connected to Boozer. His brother, Buck, followed, with the rest of the dogs walking single file, held together by leashes. Nick led Buck's horse, and then came Allen and Dodge. As they reached the point marked by Cole's handkerchief, Rich signaled for everyone to stop. There was almost no talking, and everything was in whispers or sign language.

Rich stepped down from his horse and examined the spot. The old track was still clearly visible in the dried mud, and he took his time analyzing it and then turned and walked back to Allen. "That's one big bear, probably in the eight hundred pound range, looks to me like he tangled with a bear trap and lost part of his foot. He'll be smart and wary toward anything human." Rich spit a dollar-sized wad of tobacco juice onto the ground. "This trail is at least four days old, but Cole said saw him in another canyon. I think we should head over there and see if we can find fresher sign. My Boozer is good, but there ain't much here to work with." Rich petted his dog's head.

All the dogs had a piece of short leather tied around their snouts to keep them from howling before Rich was ready. Surprise was important in not letting the bear know he was being tracked too early. For an hour, the group followed the trail, choosing not to go cross-country until they were closer to the site where Cole had seen the bear. Finally, Cole signaled to Rich that they needed to climb, and everyone began zigzagging back and forth up the hill to the site of the deer kill. With Patch leading the way, the group crested the small ridge to within twenty yards of the last place Cole had seen the bear. Cole looked at Boozer and saw his hackles rise. The dog's whole body language had changed, and Rich watched his every move. Cole dismounted and walked around the rock to take a look. The mule deer's carcass was partially eaten and buried beneath grass and dirt.

"I think it's time," Rich said, as he released the leather tie and the buckle that was on the dog's collar. "Get 'em, Boozer!"

The dog took off with a short "Boooo," tail wagging and nose to the ground. Rich turned to the group and said, "Now, if any of you get a chance to shoot, you better shoot, it maybe your only chance. This is a big, smart, bear, and it ain't going to be easy. We'll wait until Boozer really gets a solid trail, and then I'll let the other dogs loose. These younger dogs are more aggressive, but a lot less experienced, and I want Boozer to have a solid head start."

About ten minutes later, the sound of a distant *"Booooooo"* could be heard, and Cole noticed how the other dogs' tails began wagging faster. Rich and his brother turned the rest of the dogs loose, and within minutes, all of them were out of sight around the ridge. The sound of all these dogs bawling was surprisingly exciting to Cole. He felt the adrenaline surge, and he caught himself nudging Patch to keep pace with the fast-moving dogs. After another twenty-five minutes, the group came to a spot where the bear had obviously spent some time.

One of the dogs, Bishop, had chosen to stay and smell the strong, musky odor of the bear a little longer than the rest, but as the riders got within a hundred yards, he let out a deep bawl and chased after the rest of the dogs. A large pile of bear dung lay beside the flattened grass, where the bear had spent the night. How much of a head start the bear had wasn't exactly known, but it wasn't more than half a day at best. The group headed up a small ridge that would give them a vantage point over the next valley. It was too steep and rocky at the top for the horses and mule, so they were ground tied, while the men hiked to the top for a better view. Allen brought out his spotting scope and scanned the large valley ahead of him. All of a sudden, the bawl of one of the hounds rang out across the valley.

"Boozer is close, real close. That's his bawl when he's caught up to a bear!" Rich yelled. "Hopefully, the others won't be far behind. We need to move now and hurry! We don't want those hounds hurt if that bear decides to fight."

"Look!" Cole cried. "Over there, it's a couple of the dogs, and they're headed down the ridge toward that timber."

The dogs weren't much more than specks, but their location helped the men home in on the bear's location. Quickly, everyone mounted and walked the horses down through the rocks as fast as possible in the direction of the dogs. It took almost twenty minutes to cross the small valley, and they made good time following a well-worn game trail. As they crested the last ridge, they heard the hounds bawling in the timber below. The country was now extremely rocky, with timber growing between the boulders and deadfalls littering the hillsides. The hounds must have caught up to the bear, because they weren't moving. Cole led the way, because Patch was better than the horses at maneuvering over the rough country.

The hounds were less than two hundred yards away. Cole jumped down, tied Patch to a tree, and grabbed his rifle from his scabbard. Rich rode up beside him and hollered, "Put as much lead in him as you can. Don't assume he's dead. It might be your last assumption!"

Cole heard the dogs and bear fighting, and he knew he needed to get there fast. He ran as fast as he could, hopping logs and dodging trees. Then, he heard the screaming cry of one of the hounds, the roar of the bear, then a hound's death bawl. The last fifty yards took him several minutes, and then he was there. He could hear the other men breaking branches and hollering as they drew closer.

Cole stopped and climbed up on a large stump for a better view. In front of him, in the bottom of a small basin, lay the bodies of two dead dogs. One of the dogs was almost torn in two, and the other one's head was covered in blood. Cole swung his gun around, but the bear was nowhere in sight. The spot was the perfect ambush site. The dogs, in their haste, would have had to jump down into the small opening that was probably twelve by twenty with steep sides. Cole scanned the timber for a moment, hoping to get a glimpse and possible shot at the bear, but the grizzly was gone.

Cole met Rich as he came around a small spruce tree. "Rich, I'm sorry. I was too late. They were dead when I got here." Cole knew these dogs were a huge a part of Rich's life, and he could see small tears welling up in the hard man's eyes. Rich climbed down into the small, banked enclosure and slowly picked up Brandy, one of the hounds. The limp body of the dog draped over Rich's arm, as he lifted her up and gently hugged her.

"My poor Brandy and Bruiser, what have I gotten you into? I'm so sorry, I'm so sorry." It was then that Rich's brother, Buck, showed up with the other men. Buck had two of Rich's younger dogs, Bishop and Pepper, on their leashes. They had retreated to the security of the men when the fight broke out.

"Rich, I got Bishop and Pep—"

Buck's sentence died on his lips when he saw Rich kneeling beside the two dead dogs. Cole felt like he had been kicked in the stomach again, a pain he had felt far too often.

"Where's Boozer, where's Boozer?" Rich screamed at no one in particular.

Boozer was nowhere in sight, so Cole wondered if the bear had carried him off. Cole slid down into the sunken basin created by the rocks and deadfall and put his hand on Rich's shoulder. "I'm so sorry. I know how you cared for your dogs."

Cole reached down to pick up Bruiser's body, when he heard the quietest of whines coming from the basin's corner behind some limbs and a small pine tree. He looked closer and could see a small patch of sandy brown hair behind a chunk of log about the size of a dog. Rich was still talking to Brandy when Cole walked over to the log and saw Boozer lying in some spruce needles, bleeding in several places. It was clear by the size of the puncture marks, that the dog had been bitten and then thrown to the side against a rock and under the tree. The other two dogs must have come to his rescue and paid for it. Boozer's cuts weren't terrible, but they would need stitching, and he would live to fight another day. As soon as Rich saw Boozer, his whole expression changed as he gently laid Brandy down and went and hugged Boozer for several minutes. Then, in almost a whisper, he started scolding him to be more careful. Cole climbed out of the pit with Bruiser and carefully laid the carcass on the ground by the log before he went back for Brandy.

"What now?" Cole asked Allen.

"I'm not sure. I'll ask Rich in a few minutes."

Cole could tell that this whole thing was really wearing on Allen, and he hoped it would be over soon. Buck went down to his brother and helped carry Boozer up and out of the pit.

"Sorry Allen, but I'm done. I need to get Boozer to the vet, and these two young dogs don't have what it takes to go after that bear. In all the years I've hunted, I've never seen a bear set a trap like that. He's a killer, and he's smarter than my dogs," said Rich, wiping his nose with the sleeve of his jacket. "I'd appreciate it if you and your men would help find some rocks that I can pile on the bodies of my dogs. I don't want anything eating them, and I want to head back to town as soon as I can with Boozer. Sorry we didn't finish the job. I didn't know Jay well, but at one time I was a good friend of Suzie's mother, and that kid deserved better in this world."

For the next hour, Cole and the men dug graves and covered them with rocks, while Rich and Buck made two crosses out of spruce branches. Cole had been attached to his dog, but he was really touched by the love these two men had for their animals. After the dogs' graves were completed, Rich and Buck spent a little silent time over them and then turned.

"Allen, Buck and I are heading back to the cabin now. I sure am sorry we weren't better help."

"I understand, and I really appreciate you trying. I'm real sorry about your dogs," Allen said and then turned to Cole. "I think we should probably head back, too. I really don't think we can catch that bear without dogs."

Cole paused for a second, "Allen, I'd like to at least follow his tracks for a while longer and make sure he's not doubling back." Cole spoke firmly. "I owe Jay at least that."

"I don't think it's a good idea, but I understand. Take at least one man with you and be back tonight, so we can figure out what we're doing tomorrow," Allen said.

"Will do," Cole said. He turned and hollered over to Dodge, "Are you up for trailing this bear for awhile?"

Dodge, who was sitting on a large rock, stood up. "You bet I'm ready. Let me tie my horse beside your mule, and I'll be ready."

Dodge was a little older than the other cowboys and sported a scraggly brown beard spotted with gray. His wiry frame was deceivingly strong, and Cole had been amazed at some of his arm wrestling victories against much bigger cowhands.

The two took off and began trailing the bear across the timbered hillside. The going was slow because of all the rock, deadfall, and steep slopes. The big bear was easy to track, with its huge claws tearing up both ground and logs as it ran. Cole and Dodge noticed that it wasn't unusual for the bear to cover twelve to fifteen feet with each hurried stride, even in this tough terrain. A half mile later, the bear had slowed to a walk but still was covering a lot of ground. Their pace was brisk, and soon they broke out of the timber onto an open, south-facing hillside, mainly grass and rock, where one could see a fair distance. The steep hillsides were tough for walking, and Cole wished he weren't wearing his cowboy boots. It took them almost forty-five minutes to make it half way up the steepest part of the open ridge. Cole had no idea how far they were behind the bear, or how they could possibly catch up to him.

With sweat running down their faces they stopped and sat down on a flat rock for a break. Cole rested his 30.06 rifle between his legs and took a drink from his canteen, as the sweat rolled down off his forehead. They talked for a few minutes about how much further they could go and still be back at the cabin before dark. Cole slowly scanned the hill up to the top of the ridge. He couldn't believe his eyes; there stood the grizzly at three hundred yards. He just seemed to appear from behind a tree and was now staring back at them. The bear was huge, his thick hair several shades of brown accented by the sun's rays, as it stood on a light colored rock that jutted out from the ridge crest.

"There he is!" Cole hollered as he jumped to his feet and raised his rifle ready for a shot. The bear, which had been watching them, saw the movement and turned into the shadows. Cole only had seconds to aim, judge the distance, and squeeze off a shot.

The rifle shot echoed into the valley. "I think you missed," Dodge said in a low voice. "I think I saw a chunk of bark come off that tree just above him."

Dodge and Cole hurried, slipping on the steep slope, as they scrambled up the last part of the open ridge to the boulder that only a moment before acted as a perch for the killer bear. As they worked themselves across the slope, a game trail suddenly appeared that took them nearly to where the bear had stood. The torn ground around the rock showed that he had been there watching for a while, something that made them both a little nervous.

The tree the bear had been standing under, had a fresh chunk of bark missing five feet above the ground. Both Cole and Dodge stood and took a second to look at the bullet's damage and then checked their guns again to make sure they were loaded. The trail and the tracks continued over a small ridge and then headed uphill for about fifty yards, before going onto a trail and into the thick north-facing timber.

"I want you to watch our backs as we go down there, and I'll lead. If you see the slightest movement or something that doesn't look right, holler at me loud," Cole whispered to Dodge. The two slowly began down the game trail and entered the thick timber. The shadows and deadfalls that littered the ground made the going very treacherous, and the two men carefully examined their surroundings as they made their way deeper into the timber. The bear tracks were clearly visible and easy to follow. Sweat ran down Cole's face. Suddenly, Cole stopped and motioned for Dodge to be quiet. A clicking sound could be heard somewhere in the distance. It went on for twenty seconds, then it was quiet for close to a minute before the clicking sound resumed. They listened for several minutes before Dodge whispered, "What the hell is that?"

"The bear," Cole whispered. "He's mashing his teeth. It's his way of showing that he's angry. I've seen black bears do it."

Dodge just looked at him and shook his head.

Cole whispered again, "What caliber is your gun?"

"A 30-30" responded Dodge.

"Pretty damn light for grizzly bears."

"Well, this is one hell of a time to point that out," Dodge replied louder than he should have. Down the trail a twig snapped, and conversation ceased.

Chapter 17

The woods were getting darker, and the shadows made it harder to detect anything, as they ventured further into the timbered hillside. The trail was well worn from game in the area, and, with the exception of a number of deadfalls, a person could have actually led his horse down it. The two crept seventy yards further on a trail carpeted with old pine needles and dead branches. The silence was suddenly shattered by the snapping of branches on the hillside below. It brought both of them to full alert. Dodge cautiously scanned every dark shadow in the general area of the sound, as he slowly turned to Cole.

"Pard, I think we need to get some daylight between us and that bear. The way I see it, he has the odds big time in his favor. That bear could just quietly wait for us, just like them dogs, and we wouldn't have a chance."

Cole returned the look and said, "I hate to say it, but I have been thinking the same thing. But boy, do I hate not going after this devil. It's obvious that he's been hunted before, and he knows what's up. Let's slowly back our way out of here and see if we can get a few men tomorrow and make these odds just a bit better."

The men turned, and with as much stealth as possible, made their way back up the trail toward the ridge's rim. At the first deadfall, they stopped and scanned the site for several careful seconds. They knew this would be their most vulnerable time, while maneuvering over the log. It was almost like they felt the bear's eyes on them as they carefully moved through the shadows projected by the tree canopy.

Then they heard it, the crack of another branch not fifty yards below them, followed by a low growl echoing through the woods. The hair stood up on the back of Cole's neck and a drip of sweat ran down his forehead into his eye. Dodge and Cole saw the light from where the trail entered the woods. It was probably twenty yards to the opening and then another fifty yards to the ridge crest.

"That bear is tracking us," Dodge said.

"I know. I think he is trying to circle us before we can make it into the open," Cole replied.

"I vote we make a dash for the open before the bear gets between us and the ridge!"

"Ready?"

"Hell, yes!" Dodge snorted. They sprinted up the trail toward the crest of the open, rocky ridge. They had almost reached the top of the ridge when Cole stopped and swung his rifle around ready to pull the trigger if necessary. But there was nothing behind them.

"Hey Dodge, hold up, I think the bear gave up!" Cole hollered.

At that moment, Cole realized he was wrong as a shadowy figure moved between two large trees. The grizzly positioned itself further down the ridge, closer to where the forest met the grassy hillside. Then they heard it again, the teeth mashing and low growl that surged adrenalin through Cole. Both men raised their rifles, hoping for a shot that wasn't there. They saw nothing, but heard claws raking and bark savagely being torn from trees.

"Back your way into those rocks at the crest," Cole said, pointing at a rock outcropping that provided a good view of the country below. Dodge turned and slipped several times as he moved up the hill toward the rocks. "Cover me!" Cole turned and with several graceful moves made it up beside Dodge. "Now at least we have a fighting chance."

"That reminds me," Dodge said, as he pulled a large wad of chew out of a small can in his shirt and put it in his mouth. "If'n I'm going to die here, then at least I'm going to have one last chew. God knows I deserve it."

Cole smiled. Dodge's comment helped him regain composure, so now he scanned the timber through the sights of his rifle. For the next twenty minutes they carefully watched the timber for any sign of movement. The rock ledge they had chosen allowed them an excellent view up and down the ridge for at least a couple hundred yards in each direction, but that didn't stop Cole from asking Dodge to move a few feet and check the back side of the ridge. After several minutes, Dodge came back and sat down next to where Cole was standing. Cole rested his gun on a large rock and kept it pointed toward the timber. "Cole, since we can see at least a hundred yards and there ain't nothing moving, why don't we make a break for it?"

Just then, another loud growl came from the woods, and Cole saw the shape of the large bear moving further down the tree line. Cole carefully drew a bead on the shadowy figure and touched off a shot. A loud growl and the smashing of branches echoed up the ridge. Then everything was quiet. "I think you hit him!" said Dodge. "If you didn't kill him, he's going to be really pissed."

"I took a quick shot, and to tell you the truth, I don't know. He was in the shadows and I shot where I thought his heart was, but, well . . . I just don't know." The two waited a couple more minutes, but traveling back to the horses in the dark was not a good idea. "Let's start across the hillside and see what happens," Cole said.

Dodge nodded his head in agreement. They slowly slid off the rock and followed a game trail that would be faster than picking their own path. Every couple of minutes, the two stopped and checked behind them as well as the timber they were headed towards. They moved well and covered the same ground in about half the time it had taken them to get up to the ridge. When they were only twenty-five yards from the timber, they heard it again, the distant growl of the grizzly. Cole and Dodge looked back to see the large grizzly close to the rock outcropping they had just vacated. The mammoth beast was swaying sideways back and forth, chomping its teeth. The clicking sound reverberated across the open hillside and both Dodge and Cole felt their stomachs tighten up.

"So, what do we do now?" Dodge asked, as the two of them just stared at the bear.

"He's sure as hell out of range, and I don't plan to go back up there, so let's slowly and quietly melt back into the trees and see if we can't make the last half a mile or so to the horses before that bear can circle us," answered Cole.

"I've done one hell of a lot of hunting in my life, but this is the first time that I ever felt like the hunted," said Dodge as he turned and headed for the nearby timber.

"Let's move and see if we can get to open ground before that bear catches up," Cole said, as he turned and hurried into the woods behind Dodge. They began a quick jog, hurdling logs and rocks as they moved through the trees, closing the gap between them and the horses.

"I got to stop," Dodge moaned breathlessly. "I need a second to catch my breath."

Cole nodded his head in agreement, for he was exhausted, too. Then they heard it, an animal in the bushes about twenty yards ahead of them on the game trail. Both men raised their rifles and thumbed off their safety catches. Several seconds passed, and then a large blue grouse came strutting out into the trail, saw them, and flew off. Both men breathed deeply, as they once again began to jog toward their animals.

Finally, they found the small clearing where they had tied their stock and were glad to see the horse and Patch quietly standing by the trees. It only took seconds to retighten their cinches, untie their mounts and hop on. Dodge and Cole made good time going back to camp, because the horse and mule were more than ready to go. It was hard keeping the animals out of a fast trot, as they made their way up to the trail that led toward the camp. An hour and a half later, just as night fell, the two rode in to camp. Rich, tending his dogs, was the first to see them and gave a shout to the rest of the men.

"How did you do? You look kind of wore out if'n you ask me," Archie said, as he grabbed the lead rope on Dodge's horse as Dodge got down.

"Boy, do we have one hell of a story to tell!" Dodge dismounted his horse and led it over to the saddle pile.

"What happened?" Ballard asked with a new spark in his eyes.

"Yeah, what happened?" Allen asked anxiously. Nick, who had made dinner, brought over hot plates of food after Cole and Dodge had unsaddled and put their animals in the corral.

"Well, we had a little go around with the bear," Cole said.

"You caught up with him?" Allen asked.

"I'm not sure so much that we caught up with him, or he didn't set another trap for us."

"Yeah, if it wasn't a trap, it sure felt like one. Cole got a shot off and may have hit him, but we're not sure," chimed in Dodge. For the next hour Dodge and Cole shared their day, with Dodge doing most of the talking. After they were done, everyone but Rich had questions.

Finally Rich, who had been strangely quiet, said, "He's a killer and not afraid of men. My guess would be that he's killed at least a few people, maybe more. We had a killer one time down near Jackson. It killed a rancher, his family, and even his dog. But we got lucky on that one, caught him swimming a small pond, and six of us got on him at the same time. Killed him dead, but when we cleaned him, we found human remains in his stomach and at least twelve old wounds in his hide. One tough, mean, son of a bitch that bear was, and nowhere near as big as this one."

Cole had done little of the talking, and it had taken him far longer than the others to eat his plate of beans, beef, and bread. Dodge had already left for the tent, and everyone was calling it a night when Cole got up and walked over to Allen. "I need to talk. Can we go over by the corral?"

"Yeah, sure," Allen said as he looked into Cole's pale face.

The two walked quietly over to the corral. Cole leaned on one of the cross poles and stared into the pen of grazing mules and horses. "Allen, I turned and ran today. I mean I completely lost it and panicked. I thought that bear was going to kill me and I ran like a scared rabbit." Allen moved closer to Cole and leaned on the same log. "How can anyone depend on me if I can't be trusted not to run? I don't know what happened up there."

Allen stood there and listened, not wanting to say anything until he was sure Cole was finished. "Cole, there isn't a man alive that hasn't turned away from danger at one time in his life. We're human, and we make human mistakes."

"But I ran like a scared kid," Cole said in a shaky voice as he dropped his head and stared at the ground.

"You just lost one of your closest friends to that bear, and you've sure seen a lot of death in your life. You were probably on overload. Hell, Cole, I don't think there's anyone in that situation that wouldn't have run. You're no coward, and you need to quit beating yourself up over this. We've all had our nerves stretched with this killing, and every one of us is fighting to keep our emotions in check. You're a young man and you're tackling some mighty tough hills, but you're doing fine. What happened out there today wasn't being a coward. It was having the kind of sense that you need to fight another day. I like you, Cole, and I like the make of your leather. There's no one I would rather stand with against that bear. I want you to forget this, now let's get some sleep. We're moving out early tomorrow."

With that, the two of them turned and headed back toward the fire. As they walked, Allen put his hand on Cole's shoulder and said,

"It'll be fine," then turned and headed past the fire up and into the cabin.

It took them the rest of the evening to devise their plan. They decided that Rich would take Boozer back to town to get him stitched up. Buck and Ballard would stand guard at the line cabin with the remaining two dogs. Allen, Nick, Archie, Dodge and Cole would head out again first thing in the morning after the bear. Two guards, each with a dog, took turns patrolling the camp, and even though all was quiet, no one slept well.

At daybreak, everyone was up, anxious and grouchy. Buck and Ballard made breakfast. The rich aroma of stout black coffee seemed to soothe their spirits as everyone else saddled the horses. The day was sunny with a slight breeze—good weather for tracking a bear.

"If my dogs were a little older and had a bit more experience, I'd have Buck take Boozer back and go with you. But I think they'd cause more trouble than they would help, 'cause they really don't know what they're doing, yet," said Rich, as he watched the activity. You could tell he felt bad and a little guilty that he wasn't going, after all that had happened. After breakfast, everyone mounted up with their rifles fully loaded in their scabbards and enough supplies for several days. Rich half-heartedly waved goodbye, as he headed down the trail to Canvas Creek with Boozer up in his saddle. The rest of the group returned to where Cole and Dodge had last seen the bear. Ballard sat on the porch, contemplating the smoke he was rolling, and Buck held Pepper, as the group disappeared across the meadow.

After a couple hours, the riders entered the small meadow where Dodge and Cole had tied their animals the previous day. Everyone brought their mount to an abrupt halt and focused on the large pine tree in the middle of the meadow. It had been torn to pieces overnight. "Wow," Allen said. "I've never seen anything like this. He's sure as hell telling us what he thinks of us."

Cole and Dodge got down, removed their guns from their scabbards, and began examining the area. Cole found no blood. It looked like the bear had spent a fair amount of time there, and then his tracks retreated to the cover of the woods. A large pile of bear dung sat in the middle of the meadow, and the smell was making all the animals nervous and hard to control. "Cole, can you tell what he's doing?" Allen asked. "I don't think he's close, do you?"

"No, I don't. There's a set of tracks heading slightly up the hill and they look like the freshest," he replied. "But, boy is he pissed, never seen the like."

Dodge mounted his horse and Cole led Patch for a while, following the trail up into sparse timber and then onto an open ridge. The marks left by the bear's huge claws tore up the grassy hillside as he traveled and made tracking fairly easy. Cole remounted, and for the next couple of miles everyone rode in silence as they scanned every hillside and valley for movement. Normally, a wild animal's trail meanders as it travels, but it was obvious the bear was headed straight for something, but what, no one knew. At a small mountain creek, the group filled their canteens and let their animals drink. The bear's tracks angled up the hill toward an alpine pass above them. "Think that bear's headed for the pass?" Dodge asked.

"Sure as hell seems like it," Cole responded. The terrain had gotten steeper as the group worked its way along the many game trails, edging their way closer to the pass. The route had a number of ancient deadfalls, rockslides, and impassable terrain. Cole found that Patch had an almost uncanny ability to find the best possible route through the jagged terrain, and he made the journey easier for everyone. If there was a game trail, he found it.

Finally, they entered the head of a steep, rocky valley covered with several inches of snow. Sometimes the bear stayed on a game trail and sometimes he traveled cross country, so the tracking took longer than expected. As the trail rose up the mountain, Cole noticed a clear pond nestled into a small basin below them. Stomachs were rumbling and legs needed stretching. This would be a great place with both water and grass for the group to stop for some lunch. Allen signaled the group to drop into the basin.

Cole pulled a roast beef sandwich out of his saddlebag and sat down on a dry, granite boulder. As he peeled back the wax paper, the aroma made his mouth water. He hadn't realized just how hungry he was. While the others had rested at the last stop, Cole had scouted the bear's path and made sure that he wasn't doubling back. He had packed several homemade cookies, dried apple slices, a small slab of cheese, and a chocolate bar, a real treat that he didn't often get. The men talked while they ate, and it didn't seem to bother anyone that they launched food onto their beards or bellies as they spoke.

Everyone chatted about what the bear might do and how they should proceed, but they all knew that only Allen called the final shots.

"Pack it up," Allen said. "We'll lead the stock from here."

The bear's trail remained strong and easy to follow. In places he had crossed several small patches of snow, and the prints from his huge tracks reminded everyone of the seriousness of their task. For the last mile or so, the bear had lengthened its stride, moving quickly toward the pass. None of the cowboys knew the bear's final destination, but the group was close enough at times they could smell the pungent odor left by the bear's passing. A fairly well-defined game trail nearby meandered up through the rocks and disappeared around a large rock outcropping several hundred yards up the trail.

Allen said, "Cole, you take Patch and lead, and be sure to have your gun ready when we go around that big rock up there. I sure as hell don't think that bear is done with us yet." The group fell into an orderly line, cautiously leading their stock single file up the steep, rocky trail. Cole could tell by Allen's pace that he was getting winded, so he began taking more short breaks to give everyone a breather. The pass was over ten thousand feet, and some of the men weren't in any better shape than Allen. Unlike most of the others, the high mountain air seemed to inspire Cole. As the group started around a large rock that hid the next section of trail, Patch stopped and his big ears twitched to full alert, like a well-trained bird dog. Then he took several steps back until Cole yanked on the reins.

"What's going on?" Dodge asked quietly, while moving up beside him.

"I don't really know, but Patch is telling me that he heard something behind that rock." Cole pulled his rifle from his scabbard. "Wait here and hold Patch while I check it out." Cole handed the lead rope to Dodge, then turned and began walking up the trail.

He was just rounding the rock when he heard the crash of stones. With the quickness of a superb athlete, Cole chambered a shell as he raised his rifle, clicked the safety off, and took aim, all in one quick motion. He found himself staring into the eyes of a very old, startled, gray-faced Rocky Mountain Bighorn Sheep with a wad of grass tucked in its mouth. Cole's movement had caught his eye, and he was now standing looking directly at Cole, with his body on total alert. Cole slipped the safety back on and slowly lowered his rifle. The fact that the sheep had been relaxed disturbed him. This sheep had literally been standing on the grizzly's trail. Cole knew the group was at least a half day behind the bear, farther than what he had originally thought. Cole turned to Dodge, who had followed Cole up the trail. He waited for Dodge to move up beside him. At that point, the ram decided there was way too much activity up there for him and ran up the trail and out of sight over some rocks.

Dodge laughed. "Only one of those damn sheep, huh?"

Cole looked at him with a sigh of relief and said, "Yeah, one of those damn sheep." They remounted and rode on.

At the crest of the ridge, the ground opened up to reveal a small, sheltered basin on top, with a shallow pond created by melting snow. The pond was about a half an acre in size and had a patch of green grass surrounding it. The meadow was large enough that the whole group and the pack mules would be able to stop and graze for the night. Cole walked up to Allen and in a quiet voice said, "That bear is at least three hours ahead of us, maybe more. I saw a couple of drops of blood on the rocks coming up here. I must have hit him when I shot at him yesterday, but I don't think he's hit bad. I'm not sure what he's doing now, but if I was to guess, I'd say he's trying to put some distance between us."

Allen looked at him for a couple of seconds and then slightly kicked the ground.

"I would say you hit him all right. I bet he's really smarting from the wound, and my guess is all he wants to do now is get away. There's no way we'll catch him before nightfall."

Cole nodded. "But I do think we need to try, Allen. I'll go and see where his trail goes, so we are ready when everyone catches his breath." He knew the only one still breathing heavily was Allen.

There were three game trails meandering into the meadow besides the one the group had followed. One trail led up and one down the ridge, but it appeared the bear had taken a rocky trail that fell off into a granite basin below them. The torn earth at the beginning of the trail was easy to follow, but the sharp, jagged rock would make it impossible for the horses to continue without putting them at risk of injury or even death.

Cole explained the situation and then suggested that three men follow the trail until dark, while the other two stay with the stock in case the bear doubled back.

"Why don't you and Dodge go and take Nick. He has a .44 magnum and I think you need the firepower, just in case. I'd love to go, but to tell you the truth, I'm tired and I wouldn't want my being out of shape to put you three in any kind of jeopardy."

Cole led the way, with Dodge and Nick following closely behind. With its large boulders and cliffs, the trail was probably used by little more than mountain goats and sheep. After an hour of walking down into the valley, the trail entered the timber. The trees had grown slowly, and most were deformed from the pounding wind and heavy snows that made survival in these mountains difficult at best. It seemed amazing to Cole that even in the harshest environments, the trees and grasses could still find a way to eke out some sort of an existence. Cole raised his hand for the group to stop. He bent down and checked for sign, but there wasn't any. For the next twenty minutes they backtracked, looking for the slightest sign that the bear had been through the rock-filled path, but there was none. Cole tried circling the site for a while, but still he found nothing. Somehow the bear had totally lost them, and for now, had won.

"We need to head back to camp before it gets dark," Cole said to Dodge and Nick. "This bear knows he's being trailed, and like a smart elk or deer, probably walked along the rocky trail to some point, where he jumped to one side or the other and vanished."

"I'll bet you're right," said Dodge. "I'll feel better when we're back at camp. The thought of wandering in the dark with that bear doesn't excite me." Both Dodge and Nick were breathing hard from the climb back up the mountain, but they were still willing to go if needed. After an hour of hard walking, the small group finally came to the top of the ridge and the camp where Allen was cooking dinner.

"Didn't see him, huh?" Allen said with regret in his voice.

"At the bottom of the hill we got into some pretty big rockslides and his trail disappeared. That bear must have decided that trails weren't for him and changed direction. Anyway, we didn't find him, and we lost the track," Cole said, as Dodge and Nick nodded in agreement.

Allen sat on a large boulder with a nice flat spot. "Unfortunately, I think we're wasting our time if we think we are going to catch up with that bear. Who knows when he's going to quit running, and I don't think we can follow him through this terrain. We camp here tonight, so let's set guards. We pack up and leave for the cabin at first light."

The wind was cold, but the group settled into a little sheltered opening in the rocks just big enough for them and a small campfire. Buck had volunteered to get wood with the mule down the ridge at an old lighting strike. He ended up coming back to camp a little after dark with a load. But, even with the fire, it was cold and no one slept more than to nod off periodically.

At first light the horses and mules were either hobbled or picketed out to graze, while the group ate a little breakfast before the long ride back to the cabin. Dodge cradled a hot cup of coffee in his hands and enjoyed the heat it generated. "I never would have believed that bear would get away when I volunteered for this here job. I was just sure we'd kill him, that bastard. Jay was one hell of a guy and that bear needed killing for what it done." Dodge sat, looking at no one in particular.

"We'll find him. When we do, he won't be so lucky," Cole snarled.

The ride back to the cabin took almost the whole day, and the group arrived an hour before sunset. Buck and Ballard walked out to greet them, but they could read the look on the men's faces and didn't ask them how it had gone. That night over a campfire, Allen told Buck and Ballard what had happened.

The next morning was brisk and clear, and everyone was up early, cleaning the cabin and loading the mules. Ballard was moving better and even helped hold a mule while it was loaded. It took a couple of hours to break camp, but soon the group started down the trail that led to Canvas Creek. Because they had either used or left a large part of the supplies, a couple of mules rode empty as the string made its way down the mountain. In the quiet of the solemn ride, Cole wondered what each man was thinking. If they were like him, they were thinking about going to the funeral and what they were going to say to people who asked about the bear. There were no good answers, and Cole felt defeated—a feeling he didn't much care for.

The group rode into the ranch in a light drizzle several hours after dark. After unloading their gear and putting away the stock, most of the men headed for the showers and quickly to bed. It had been a rough trip. Allen went up to the big house and disappeared inside.

Chapter 18

The next morning, Cole awoke to find Smokie, the ranch cat, curled up on the blanket above his ankles. Why it had chosen his bunk over all the others was a bit of a mystery, and its movements had awakened him. He reached down and petted the old cat. After dressing he headed for the barn to check on Patch and the other animals that had been on the trip. He scratched Patch's ears for a while, then gave them all some oats before releasing them into the big pasture. The mule had lost a little weight on the trip, but nothing like the horses. His ability to eat everything from weeds to leaves allowed him to get something in his stomach along the trail. As he walked into the barn, he met Julie coming out.

"Cole!" She hugged him and then looked in his eyes. Quietly, she said, "I can't tell you how sorry I am. Everyone else is, too. Jay was loved by a lot of people. I listened while Allen told Dad the whole story. I know you didn't find the bear, but you men did your best. I'm so sorry. I wish there were more I could do for Suzie. She's been a mess since this whole thing happened. She's staying at her grandmother's house, and she asked to see you when you got back. The funeral's tomorrow."

"I'll do that, thanks. I appreciate you telling me. I'll take off right after breakfast."

"Would you mind if I went with you? Maybe I can help with something."

"I'd appreciate some company. Can you be ready in thirty minutes?"

She nodded and returned to the barn to feed her horse. Afterwards, she turned it out into the pasture, and headed back to the house to get ready.

Cole pulled his truck in front of the McCabe house, and as soon as he stopped, Julie was out the door and down the steps. Cole thought to himself how beautiful she looked with her flowing brown hair blowing in the wind. She got into the truck and slammed the door. "Sorry I didn't mean to do that."

"It's okay. I don't think any of us are thinking real clear right now." The ride over to the Schmitz ranch took about thirty minutes unless the weather was bad, but this day the sun shone brightly as the little truck purred along the road leaving the ranch. Cole was thinking about what to say when they arrived as he turned to Julie. "Have you spent much time with Suzie? How's she doing?"

"She's a wreck. I try to comfort her but what do you say? There isn't anything fair about this whole thing. She really loved Jay."

Cole nodded his head in agreement. "I understand."

With the exception of a couple of jackrabbits running across the road ahead of them, the trip was uneventful. Cole found it comforting to talk with Julie, and he wished the two of them were driving somewhere else under different circumstances.

They pulled into the Schmitz ranch, and Phil got up from the porch swing, waved, and walked out to greet them. "Thanks for coming." He looked tired but sincerely happy to see them as he showed them through the front door. Cole and Julie entered the main room, followed by Phil, and saw Suzie sitting on an old couch in the corner, looking at pictures. Her eyes were red and swollen. Several seconds passed before Suzie realized they were even there. Finally, she turned her head and made eye contact, which seemed to snap her out of her daze.

She jumped up and hugged Cole and then Julie, and tears began to stream from her face. They sat around and talked for over an hour about what happened and how sorry they were. Martha entered the room and gave both Julie and Cole a hug and motioned for them to have a seat. "Suzie, Phil and I want you, Cole, to be one of the casket bearers at the funeral tomorrow."

Cole paused for a second, and then said, "It would be an honor." He felt uncomfortable with the conversation, and it brought back bad memories. Down deep, he wished he had something magical to say that would make all her pain go away.

Julie and Suzie had wandered into the kitchen when Martha Schmitz in her old slow way came up beside him and said quietly, "May I see you in my room for a minute? I need to show you something."

Cole was hesitant, but he felt she must have some reason for being secretive. Cole followed Martha into her bedroom, which was furnished with a beautiful, old, heavy maple bed and two small but comfortable chairs. "Please sit, I have something important to show you." Cole took a seat as Martha slowly walked over to a small dresser and opened the drawer. Inside the drawer was a set of well-worn saddlebags, which she took out and passed to Cole. Then she sat down beside him. She looked him in the eyes and said, "You know these were Jay's saddlebags, don't you?"

"No, I didn't," Cole replied.

"Well, some of your boys brought these when they delivered the rest of Jay's belongings a couple days ago. Jay didn't have anyone but Suzie. You remember one of our talks about four months ago and me telling you about some of the old stories about the ranch? Well, one of those stories we didn't talk about happened in the seventies when some ranchers were bushwhacked after they came down from their mine and were loading a wagon with gold. Apparently they didn't think anyone knew about their mine, but they must have been wrong. One of the miners, Virgil Creager, was found just outside of town bleeding badly from gunshot wounds, and the lady that found him tried to nurse him back to health. Well, he was shot way too bad and he knew he was going to die, so before he did, he gave this lady a gold nugget from his jacket, telling her a story of a mine and an old bayonet that was stuck in a tree that showed the way to the mine. Even though lots of people looked, no one ever found that mine, the bayonet, or the gold or Creager's partner and brother, Vern," explained Martha.

"I have heard parts of the story before, but why are you telling me this now?" Cole asked. Martha reached over, put the saddlebags in her lap, and undid the buckle on the right one to pull out a crinkled brown envelope, which she handed to Cole.

"You need to read this. It's a letter from Jay to Suzie that he wrote in the cabin. I don't know exactly when, but just read it."

Cole slowly opened the unsealed letter and began to read:

Dearest Suzie,

Today will change the rest of our lives. I've decided to write everything down so I can share every moment of this special day with you. This morning I went out riding to check for cattle and I ended up riding a lot further than I intended. I guess I was daydreaming about you. Well, I was riding this ridge and I saw this rock that looked like an old man's face, it was really something.

I went down to take a closer look in a stand of mountain spruce that had burned up in a lighting strike and exposed the rock and if those trees had been growing and healthy I would have never seen it. I got off my horse and decided to walk over and get a better look. The rock was amazing but then I noticed what looked like an old trail on the other side of it that seemed to dead end into a cliff about a hundred yards away. The trail kind of meandered into the ridge and through the rocks and into the trees. Well, I had time and I was curious so I decided to follow it.

Once I got into the trees the hillside got real steep, but the trail was good and ran with a consistent grade before it broke out on the other side. I was surprised at what a good trail it was, not your ordinary game trail or anything. It came to a place where it was sheer cliff but the strangest thing— someone had built a small stone bridge wide enough that I could ride my horse across. There were trees growing up beside the trail that made it almost invisible to the valley below. I thought to myself that whoever built this here trail didn't want it found.

Well, I followed it until Copper and I came to a rocky ridge with a small meadow where I thought I would have lunch. I picketed Copper out and sat down to enjoy my lunch when I happened to gaze up into this great big old pine snag. Probably fifteen feet up was something sticking out of the snag that just didn't look right and there it was. At first I couldn't tell what it was except it wasn't part of the tree and then I knew it was that dang old bayonet that everyone had heard about for so many years. I had almost forgotten the story and when I remembered it, well I about came out of my skin. There it was, that bayonet!

Well it was getting late but I still went up the hill and after a while I found the old trail that I think goes to the mine. The trail is too heavily over grown for me to clear it with just my hatchet, so tomorrow I plan to go back with an ax and clear the trail good enough that I can find it later.

"That's the end," Martha said. "I don't think he finished it. At least, that is all that was in the saddlebag."

"Wow," Cole said in a quiet voice. "What am I supposed to say to that?"

"Probably nothing right now, but I needed to tell someone, and I trust you, and Jay trusted you. Maybe that mine really exists and maybe it don't. But maybe Suzie might get a small share and get a chance to go to college and get out of here. I don't know, but I needed to tell someone, and right or wrong, I believe it needed to be you."

Cole sat back and looked ahead. He was thinking that he might know that rock, if it were the same one he had found. "I'll think about it and get back to you after the funeral. But for now, everyone has plenty on the table, so let's keep this under our hats."

On the ride back to the ranch, Julie and Cole were silent as they struggled to come to terms with death. It was after dark when Cole's International pickup drove up in front of the McCabe house. Julie got out, thanked Cole, and headed into the house. Cole parked the truck and had started for the bunkhouse door when he heard Patch do his mountain canary imitation. Even though there were probably twenty-five mules on the ranch, Cole knew the sound of Patch's bray.

He turned and walked the hundred yards by moonlight to where Patch stood with his head leaning over the fence. Quietly, Cole stroked his head and talked to Patch about the day, about Jay, and how Suzie was doing. It surprised him the amount of relief that flowed out and it didn't make him feel stupid, sharing his emotions with a mule. Patch was a good listener and never seemed to interrupt. Cole thought of the many conversations he had with Jay, and even though he hadn't ever shared anything really deep, he felt like they had bonded. He missed him badly, and he needed someone to talk to, someone to share with. A single tear rolled down his cheek, the first one since his folks had passed away.

The next day, Cole got up and helped with a few chores around the barn and talked to Timmy, who had met him at the barn door. "Well, how's that rabbit doing? Been a while since I seen him, or for that matter you," Cole said.

"Well, sir, it's not a him. It had babies a couple of weeks ago, and she is doing fine," replied Timmy. Cole and Timmy talked for a while longer, and then Cole excused himself. Later that afternoon, Dodge, Elmer, and Cole got dressed for the funeral and took off early in their suits for the church in Meeteetse. Cole's suit looked good on him, but Dodge's sleeves were half an inch too short, and the stitching on Elmer's jacket shoulders needed repair. Allen had told them the other pallbearer was a man out of Casper named Matt Jones, but Cole had never met him. He had been a close friend of

Jay's, before he had left Casper to go to work on another ranch closer to his folks.

The three entered the church to see the pastor setting up the candles on a shelf above the piano. "Pastor, sir, we're here for Jay Taylor's funeral. What would you like us to do?" Cole asked. Cole hadn't spent much time in a church for years and hadn't met the pastor before.

"Just a second, my son," the pastor turned, smiled, shook each man's hand, then explained the whole service. Jay's friend, Matt Jones, joined them as they took a seat in the front pew. The service was painfully long, the church was packed, and it hurt hearing about Jay's dreams and goals and how he would be missed by all. Cole closed his eyes as the pastor spoke of riding for the brand and The Greybull Ranch. He remembered Jay's joking smile and how fun he was to work with, and how he was the first man in the bunkhouse to offer his hand. Cole was jolted back to the moment by an elbow from Dodge.

"It's time," he whispered. The four men got up, took their positions around the casket, and in unison picked it up and walked slowly down the aisle. Cole kept his head and eyes straight ahead and tried to look as formal as possible. He really didn't want to have eye contact with anyone, but he couldn't help a quick glance at Suzie, who was boldly staring ahead with large tears rolling down her face. Further down the aisle, he saw Julie, who was standing beside John Prentice. Even in black, she looked beautiful, but her eyes were swollen.

The burial in the cemetery behind the church was over quickly, and soon the group moved to the park to celebrate Jay's life. Suzie and Jay had once talked about what they wanted when they died, and Jay had said he wanted a picnic after the church service where everyone smiled and remembered him. A little stand had been erected for anyone who wanted to talk about Jay and his memories. There were a number of people who came forward and talked about how he touched their lives, but Cole wasn't a public man and chose not to speak.

Cole, Dodge, and Elmer went over to where Allen and the McCabes had set up a table and began talking with the family. Sally had made a huge lunch with plenty of extra food and drink for all. Cole took some chicken, headed over to a large weeping willow tree by the river and sat down to eat. Elmer followed him, but Dodge was in a deep conversation with Sheriff Burris and a man Cole had never seen before.

A voice startled Cole. "Well, Cole, I hear you were sent running by the bear that killed Jay. I thought you had a little more leather in you than that. I guess everyone thought too highly of you," scoffed John Prentice, who had walked up from Cole's blindside. John looked smug and in control as he stared down at Cole.

Cole continued to eat his chicken and then slowly looked up and back at him and said, "Well, Mr. Prentice, I am surprised to see you here. From everything I've heard, no one would have wanted you at their funeral, but I must have been wrong, too."

"You son of a bitch, you're damn lucky we're at a funeral, or I'd kick your sorry ass," Prentice sneered.

"I agree that one of us is lucky, but I don't think it's me. I guess one of these days we'll find out. And for your information, that bear and I aren't done."

"You know, Cole, when I marry Julie and take over the ranch, the first person I'm going to fire is you—"

Prentice was interrupted by Julie's voice.

"What's going on here? I can't believe you two are trying to start a fight at a funeral. I think you both badly need to grow up!" Julie, face flushed and fists clenched, stormed away. For the first time, Cole was glad she was riding with Prentice back to the ranch.

Cole headed back to McCabe's table, and Sally asked, "What was that all about?"

"Sorry ma'am, he's just like a burr under my saddle. I need to let it go."

"What did he say?"

"It doesn't matter. This is Jay's day, and it needs to stay that way." Cole turned and walked toward the church, where Allen was talking to Wes.

Ballard witnessed the exchange between Cole and Prentice, smiled and said, "That's going to be one hell of a fight. Sure hope I get to see it."

About halfway over to Allen, Cole heard Sheriff Burris call his name. "Cole, do you have a minute? I'd like to introduce you to someone. This is Will Connor. He's a deputy over in Cody, and he's been helping in the investigation of that plane crash. They figured out what kind of plane it was."

"I'm impressed. There wasn't much more than some burned out metal and some scrap left. How in the hell did you do that?" Cole asked. Deputy Conner took a step closer and shook Cole's hand.

"Glad to meet you. Sheriff Burris has told me a lot about you and finding the wreck. We dug around and were able to find a couple of gauges, including the altimeter. Our contact in Missouri was able to identify them as gauges from a nineteen twenty-nine Curtis Robin, a pretty expensive plane. Whoever crashed it had money. But the strange thing is that we can't find any reports of a missing plane, much less the people. Normally, a person with that type of plane is important and has money, and people would notice if they were missing. If we had all the information off that tail section you found, we could probably identify the owners, but, as of right now, we don't have a lot of answers."

"I appreciate you keeping me informed. When they said some strange things happen on this ranch, I guess they weren't kidding," Cole said.

Sheriff Burris smiled, while Deputy Connor had a bit of a blank look.

"Nice meeting you, and if I can be of any help, just holler," Cole said as he went to talk to Allen. Allen and Wes were finishing with their conversation when Cole walked up and everyone greeted each other.

"Is there anything that you'd like me to do before I head back to the ranch?" Cole asked.

"Not really," Allen replied.

As Cole turned toward his truck to leave, out of the corner of his eye, he noticed Tyler walking toward some other vehicles parked beneath one of the large, spreading willow trees. At first, he didn't think anything of it, but he stopped and watched as he disappeared behind a small delivery truck that blocked him from view. Tyler had taken a second to look over his shoulder, like he were checking to see if anyone was watching him.

Cole slowly changed direction, and when he came even with the end of one of the many small buildings, he ducked behind it and used it to get close to where Tyler had disappeared. It took several minutes to figure out where he had gone without giving away his own location, but when he finally got close enough, he could hear two men arguing. One of them was Tyler, but he couldn't quite make out the voice of the other man, and from where he was, he couldn't see them without being seen himself. Cole couldn't make out much of the conversation, but he recognized the word "promise." The voices, though quiet, were tense and sounded angry. Soon Tyler walked to his car, got in, and slammed the door. The other man seemed to have disappeared. Cole leaned against the building and wondered what just happened.

Cole's ride back to the ranch was consumed with thoughts of the bear, Jay's funeral, and the look on Suzie's face. He also wondered whether he should take more time off and search for the mine that Martha believed existed.

* * *

The rest of the week was made up of long and hard days, but they went fast, as Cole attacked the many tasks he had neglected while trying to help Jay. At the end of the week, Cole saw Allen walking across the barn yard and approached him.

"Allen, I need some time off. I know I missed a lot of work because of that appendicitis and the bear, but I need to take some time and go back up there."

"By yourself, you want to go after that bear by yourself? Are you really that crazy? We just buried one of your best friends. Do you want to be next?"

"No, I'm not crazy. It's something I need to do, and I can't talk about it," Cole said.

"Won't you at least take Dodge or Elmer with you?" Allen asked.

"No, I need to do this myself, and I need to borrow two mules and some supplies." For the next five minutes, Allen tried his hardest to talk Cole out of going, but in the end Allen acquiesced. Cole planned to leave in the next three days, but only after he paid one more visit to Martha Schmitz.

It was late afternoon two days later when Cole returned to the Schmitz Ranch with a lot of questions for Martha. Cole pulled up in the front of the porch, and he got out just as Suzie opened the door. She looked much better than the last time he had seen her. Her hair was tied with a bow, she had a nice dress on, and she was smiling.

"Cole," Suzie said, as she gave him a hug. "After what Grandma told me, I thought you might show up here this week. I don't want you to go up there."

Cole looked at her then said, "Is your grandma in?"

Suzie opened the door and they both entered the house. Martha Schmitz was knitting something that Cole thought was a hat.

"Martha, I have a number of questions before I head back up there looking for the mine. I need you to fill in as many gaps as possible."

"Well, Cole it's nice seeing you again, but unfortunately, I don't know that I have any really good answers to give you. I'll try. But I have changed my mind after talking to Suzie. We don't want you going back up there. We've grown attached to you, and who knows where that damn bear is?" Martha replied.

"If it's the place I am thinking of, it's probably ten miles at least from where we lost his trail, and I wouldn't go by myself if I thought there was too much danger," Cole said. He knew he could run into the bear, but didn't think it likely. One way or another, he knew he would someday even the score.

"You know where Jay was talking about?" blurted out Suzie.

"Yes, I think I do, but I never saw a trail behind the rock. To tell the truth, I wasn't looking. And being that far away from the last place we saw that bear tells me the chances of me running into him again are slim to none. If that mine exists, I'd like to find it for a number of reasons. One is to help you, Suzie, but the other is to help the McCabes. They've been like a family to me. If something doesn't change, they're going to lose the ranch," Cole slowly said.

"That explains a lot," Martha replied as she quietly listened.

"What do you mean, Grandma?" asked Suzie.

"I think it explains why a beautiful, smart girl like Julie would agree to marry some SOB like John Prentice. Yeah, sure, he's got money and prestige, but he's no good and never was, even if it's none of my business to say so," Martha replied.

"Then you see why I want to go so bad. I have to, for not only Suzie's sake, but I have to do it for the McCabe family." Cole took a breath and then began again, "If I do this and anyone finds out, then I may have a big problem. Prentice is already counting his cows, if you know what I mean."

"Yeah, both Suzie and I have had many talks on just that subject. We think Prentice is dangerous, and the McCabes would be in a bad way after John and Julie were married. I can see we won't be talking you out of this, so how can I help?" Martha asked.

For the next twenty minutes, Cole asked a number of questions about the original Creager story, but he got no good answers. Finally, he said, "Is there any more to the story than you have told me? I mean *anything*?" Cole asked.

"Well, there's one thing I remember from when I was a kid. There was some kind of hidden cabin in the canyon where the mine was. I heard that a couple times when I was a kid, but that part seems to have dropped plum out of the story when I hear others tell it. That's the only thing I can remember that's different. Hope it helps."

"At this point, anything helps. Thanks. I need to be getting back. I've got to pack tonight, and I plan to leave early in the morning."

* * *

At The Greybull Ranch bunkhouse, Cole quietly put some gear together and then went by the kitchen to get some supplies from Chin. Cole knocked on the back door and Tyler answered.

"Hi, Tyler, is Chin in?"

"Yes, just a minute and I'll get him. Is there anything I can do?"

"No, Chin has some supplies for me. I need to be gone for a couple of days on business," Cole replied. Chin appeared, walking down the hallway toward him, and for some reason Cole was relieved not to have to explain any more to Tyler.

"Well have a good trip," Tyler said, as he turned and headed back toward the kitchen. Chin handed him a bag full of enough food and supplies to last four days and Cole thanked him. He had started to turn away when he stopped and turned back toward Chin.

"You watch over everyone while I'm gone, okay?" Cole said.

Chin smiled and said, "Yes, boss."

Chapter 19

It was an hour before sunrise when Cole mounted Patch and began leading his small pack train of three mules down the road toward Canvas Creek. Cole wanted to get away from the ranch before he drew any unwanted attention and had to answer questions about what he was doing or where he was going. The train shook their heads and put up a small fuss as they crossed in front of the courtyard to the house. After the first thirty minutes, the mules settled down as they normally did, and they began clicking off the miles. Cole thought to himself that there was nothing more beautiful than a good string of mules working together.

It took nearly four hours to reach the trailhead, where they turned up and started the long, gradual ascent to the line cabin. Cole was not excited about staying there by himself, but if the bear came back, the cabin offered the best protection. He was determined to remain focused at all times and not let his guard down even for a second.

Cole stopped at the first creek they came to and examined the mud. With the exception of a few deer and coyote tracks, nothing had crossed. The further up the hill he went, the more the wind blew, and it grew colder. Cole worried he might not be able to find the trail to Old Man Rock, as he called it. At every open section of mud on the way up, Cole checked for tracks, but saw nothing. After over ten hours of hard riding, Cole rode into the small meadow that surrounded the cabin. Nothing seemed to have changed since he left. He carefully unloaded and brushed the mules by the porch, with his rifle no more than ten feet away at any time. Then he led them to the corral, opened the gate, and corralled them for the night. Cole watched the mules roll and then settle down and begin grazing, before he returned to the cabin. He thought to himself how great a watchdog a mule was, with its incredible eyesight and those long ears for hearing. He felt safe, knowing their only concern was how good the grass was.

At the porch, Cole carried the rest of his supplies into the line shack. He hadn't been sure how much evidence of Jay's death would remain inside, so he was pleased to smell the clean air that a slightly open window had left, but there were still numerous claw marks on the wall to remind him of the power of the vicious attack. Cole reached down and picked up his rifle and a bucket, so he could get some water for the cabin and stepped out on the porch. In the quiet between gusts of wind, he heard the howl of a distant wolf. Dusk was thirty minutes away as Cole headed down to the creek.

Once there, he stopped and looked around for several minutes, examining the brush and the creek bank for fresh sign. After he determined it was safe, he sat the bucket under an old wooden down spout that someone had made by hollowing out an old cedar log. It hadn't been used for years and was clogged with green moss, but enough water streamed through it to allow a person to fill his bucket without dunking it in the shallow creek. It took almost three minutes for the bucket to fill, and all the time Cole cautiously examined his surroundings. Maybe it hadn't been the best idea to come up here alone but if people learned they may have found the mine, there's no telling who would be up here and what they would do to get the gold. After all, the original miners thought they were alone, too.

Cole slept peacefully, and the next morning he walked out on the porch into fog so thick he had a hard time seeing the corral. He heard the mules breaking branches to get some of the last good grass that was left between fallen aspen trees from an earlier windstorm. Cole didn't like not being able so see more than thirty feet. If the bear were nearby, he could stalk Cole from any direction.

After several minutes of standing out in front of the porch, Cole decided to cautiously walk over to the mules and get Patch. He knew he would feel better with his smart mule beside him. Cole brushed Patch's thick coat, which was becoming heavier due to the cold, autumn nights. The saddling went well, and Cole tied on his saddlebags and his rifle, then mounted. On the ride out, Patch's ears swiveled back and forth, searching the area for unusual sounds. It took a little searching but finally he found the trail leading up to Old Man Rock. The fog bothered Cole, but after fifteen minutes of riding, they broke out of the low hanging clouds, revealing a beautiful blue sky with a bright warm sun. Cole relaxed as he scanned the jagged ridges in front of him. The clouds looked like a dirty cotton ball floor that stretched as far as the eye could see.

For several hours Cole followed the trail, trying to remember the path to Old Man Rock. As the trail veered slightly uphill, Cole noticed a small, odd shaped rock at a turn in the trail, and he recalled that this was the place he had changed direction and meandered down the ridge. He had learned young from his dad to always try to visually remember the small things as he traveled in the woods, because sometimes, like when fog settles in, even the smallest detail could save your life. It began to look familiar as he rode further down the ridge and on to a faint trail that worked its way through the rocks and grass.

The clouds were now beginning to break, and Cole could see ridges exposing themselves further down into the valley that only moments before were hidden. He thought about how much time he had spent on a horse and how Patch was measuring up in his ability to find an old trail, one that he may not have ridden for months and then only once. Cole was able to ride right to the burned patch of spruce and then around it to Old Man Rock. He wasted very little time looking at the rock then tied off Patch to a small aspen tree. He immediately dismounted and climbed the rock, and it didn't take long for him to see what Jay had seen earlier: an old, but very well-defined indentation that seemed to wind across the mountainside toward the steep timbered ridge to the east.

From the ground the trail was hidden by tall grass and rocks. A man would have a hard time seeing it from horseback or just standing on the site, but the elevated view from the rock allowed Cole to make out the faint track. Whoever had built this trail had entered from many directions, an old prospector's trick. The terrain in front of him was wide open and didn't look like an entrance to anything, much less a trail. The closer he walked towards where he thought the trail began, the more the terrain in front of him looked rocky and impassable. Then suddenly the deeply carved imprint of a trail seemed to appear just over a small rise. Whoever had placed this trail had done a great job of hiding it.

Cole slowly began down the path, which seemed to get slightly better the further he went. Patch seemed comfortable with the straight, gentle trail and started making good time. Once in a while, there was an old snag, or a rock had rolled out onto the trail, but in most cases he could see where Jay had led his horse around it. Cole was impressed that, in bad spots, Patch would slow and carefully take the best route around the obstacle without any instruction. It was eerie thinking about Jay and this being one of the last places he had ridden, but Cole remained focused. A man alone on a steep mountain trail is in enough danger without daydreaming.

The trail slowly narrowed and worked its way through the rocky terrain, with a variety of large boulders lining both sides. Being on the northern face, this part of the trail spent most of the day in shade, and the wet, mossy stones made for difficult footing. Finally, he broke out of the rocks and was greeted by an overgrown patch of grass that was more in the sun but fairly well treed, with steep banks on both sides. The ponderosa pine trees were old and large and totally blocked Cole's view of the valley below. A couple of times, he came to a place where Jay had used his hatchet to clear a deadfall. Small chips of wood littered the trail in spots and somehow made Cole feel he was, in some strange way, sharing this adventure with Jay.

As he rounded the corner, an old, narrow, rock bridge suddenly appeared in the trail. Whoever had built this had intended it to last. It was wide enough to ride a horse across and was built up against the steepest part of the ridge face. The builder had been a craftsman and had spent precious time tightly fitting each stone. The trail had to lead to a mine or something of great importance, for someone to have spent so much time constructing the bridge in the middle of nowhere. With the exception of a few areas where rolling rocks from above had damaged it, the bridge was in incredibly good shape.

Twenty minutes after crossing the bridge, Cole emerged into a small, sunny meadow on the ridge with a picket stake up to his right. The fresh, splintered wood on the stake showed someone had hammered it into the ground recently. That, as well as several piles of horse manure, told Cole that this was where Jay had tied his horse. Cole removed Patch's bridle and hung it from a snag's dead limb in clear sight, where he could easily find it in the dark, and picketed Patch in the same spot Jay had used. Somewhere nearby was where Jay had to have found the bayonet, Cole thought, as he slowly scanned the terrain.

He pulled his rifle from its scabbard and grabbed his canteen. One large snag that stood alone above the meadow caught his attention, and he climbed up the hill about twenty feet to where it stood. The giant Limber Pine was old and thick with hundreds of dead branches, but only a few with needles, and it looked like it had seen better days. The small, torn patches of old bark and the lack of new growth showed the great tree had served its time with honor against the wear and tear of the high mountain winds and snows. Cole walked up on the ridge and looked back at the huge monarch. It took only minutes to notice the bayonet about fifteen feet above the ground, just as Jay had said. It protruded about ten inches away from the bark and was very rusty, but you could definitely tell what it was. I found it, Cole thought. Now I need to find the trail.

He began hiking up the ridge, distracted by a camp robber bird that kept flying ahead of him and scolding him on his journey. Finally, it flew to a big branch on a Limber Pine tree and stopped. Cole had paused to look at the bird, when he saw it—a small red handkerchief partially hidden on a low branch, the beginning of a trail, an old trail.

Once Cole got under the tree, he could clearly see where Jay had worked branches back into the entrance to disguise it. The trail had not been used for years, and the number of cut branches showed that it had taken some time to clear the initial debris for the first hundred yards, and then the clearing stopped. From that point on, the trail was heavily overgrown, and Cole could see how hard the task of clearing had been. It would be impossible to get a horse or even a mule up to it without a significant amount of additional work. Now the going would be harder, and several times he thought of going back and getting the short axe that he had packed, but his desire and curiosity to find where the trail led were far more powerful.

After an hour of fighting his way up the hill, the trail broke out into lightly timbered hillside, and Cole took a minute to enjoy the newfound elbow room. The path was cut into a steep hillside and again showed the craftsmanship of its builder. The farther he went, the steeper the slope, until it entered a small canyon with vertical rock walls. At this point, the trail was cut into solid rock in some places and then worked its way through massive rock outcroppings. Cole thought that a person would need a hot air balloon or to be half mountain goat to find this place.

On the downhill side of the trail was a cliff and the sound of waterfalls echoed up from the canyon belly. Cole looked over the side—it had to be at least a hundred feet to the bottom. This would be a great trail to avoid at night, even with a lantern. The flat part of the trail was three to four feet wide and, with the exception of a little debris that had collected over time, was clear and passable.

For the next twenty minutes he walked carefully up the path, creeping around the blind corners that continually presented themselves on the winding trail. Several times he checked for tracks in the soft gravel of the trail, but he found only the sign of deer and small animals. It appeared that no human had been in this canyon for a long time, and Cole was convinced that Jay had not traveled this far. Farther up the trail, he came to a large boulder that forced the path to detour, and at this point it narrowed to three feet for over thirty yards.

At the end of the straight stretch, the trail widened again and appeared to end. Two rotting timbers stood on either side of a four-foot wide entrance ahead of him, flanked by crumbling, waist-high, hand stacked rock wall. The wall had lost a few rocks, but Cole was impressed with the placement. Both posts, probably twelve inches by twelve inches square and over six feet tall when they'd been installed, had rotted, until one was only a little over two feet high and the other four feet above the walls. At one time, Cole surmised from the rusted metal hinge hanging from the taller of the two old posts, this had probably been a gate.

He reached the wall, stopped and tried to figure out exactly what he was looking at. The area behind the wall was spacious compared to the trail, and it appeared to have been built for protection or to keep livestock in or out, but these were only guesses. After several minutes, he continued cautiously up the narrow canyon, and soon the trail widened again—but this time into a thick, lush meadow at least sixty yards wide with numerous ancient, large, rotting stumps. Cole scanned the terrain in front of him and then looked up but all he could see were the steep faces of the ridges that hid this valley from the rest of the world.

He slowly entered the grassy meadow as ground squirrels scurried for safety. Several of them stood on one of the many old stumps that littered the valley, and they allowed Cole to get close before letting out a high-pitched peep and running back down into their holes. He had just passed one of the old stumps when one of the ground squirrels chirped right beside his foot, and Cole jumped and looked around. It was then he saw it, a small log cabin neatly tucked under a large rock overhang. The cabin was difficult to see because of the number of small trees that had grown up around it, almost totally camouflaging the structure. The remains of a large spruce tree lay bound over one side of the cabin, caught on part of the huge rock shelf that covered over half of the building. It did a good job of further camouflaging the cabin's outline. The wood on the cabin was black from age, and it appeared to have a small window on at least one side. The front had a sturdy, plank door with two rusted bars that held it together, secured by heavy bolts. The roof was made out of heavy cedar shakes, almost completely intact. Cole didn't want to put caution aside, so he slowly turned and continued up the valley a bit to make sure that he was still alone. Then he backtracked to the cabin.

The plank door was built to last. It opened inward, as with most cabins, and Cole could see through a crack part of the heavy hinges that still supported it. Cole tried to shove the door open with his shoulder, but it wouldn't budge. Then he hit it with his foot, with the same result. There was no keyhole or lock on the door, so either the building had settled on the frame, or the door was jammed or bolted shut from the inside.

Going around to the window on the side of the cabin, he found his view blocked again by wooden planks that had been added to the inside window frame, much like an outdoor shutter. Cole made his way around to the back of the cabin, but there were no windows or door—the cabin was built right up against the steep, stone face of the canyon wall. He turned around and went back to the front door and reexamined it. A stone fireplace of angular granite stood beside the door, and the chimney extended four feet above the roof of the cabin. Finally, Cole walked around to the last side of the cabin.

This side was difficult to see at first, because of the dead tree that straddled the roof and the dead branches that hung down to the ground.

He found another window about the same size on the other side, hidden by branches. Carefully, he broke off a large branch to allow himself to climb closer and look into the window. It was shuttered from the inside like the other window. Cole walked to the front and looked for something to use as a battering ram and found a log that he felt would do the trick. After several failed attempts, he said out loud, "Damn, that's not going to work." Next, he took his ram to the first window and broke several of the old panes of glass. He tried again, bashing the window boards, but with no more success than he had on the door. Cole was about to give up when he decided to try the final window. After several attempts, he decided the builder was equally gifted in construction on all three openings. He sat down, and looked at the last window and thought, who was this guy, and how did he get out of the cabin?

With several branches of the large snag touching the roof, Cole decided to climb up to see if he could get a better vantage point. He moved his rifle closer to the snag, leaning it against the cabin. He found the snag easy to climb, and within seconds he was above the roof looking down. The damaged roof had an opening the size of a man's waist from where a tree branch had pierced the shakes. The tree must have twisted when it fell, making the hole slightly back and protected under the rock overhang. Cole broke off another chunk of the snag and tried to widen the hole, so he could either look into it or lower himself down into the room.

After three branches and numerous attempts, he was impressed with how strong the roof was, far stronger than the aged branches he had tried bashing against it. Its solid strength made him feel comfortable in his next venture of sliding across the roof, while spreading his weight over an area equal to his body. Cautiously, he inched over to the hole and looked in.

It was almost pitch black in the room, and Cole couldn't see much more than outlines of furniture and the old fireplace. He inched nearer the hole and had stuck his head a little deeper to get a better look, when he heard the creak of lumber. With a crash, Cole found himself lying in a pile of shakes and dusty broken boards on the floor of the cabin. "That hurt," he said softly. "I guess that wasn't one of my better ideas."

Cole used his cowboy hat to slap the dust off, and with the exception of a skinned knee and a little lost pride, he was fine. He continued to dust himself off as he walked to the door. The light from the new opening filled the inside of the cabin to the level of a bright, full moon. Cole saw that several large timbers had been lodged in the jamb to secure the door from the inside. That's strange, he thought, as his eyes adjusted to the low light. He removed the plank and, with great effort, opened the door wide enough that he could exit.

Now that he knew that he could get out, he turned and started examining the room, as his eyes adjusted more to the darkness. A small, single bed lay in the darkest corner, and Cole went over and looked as closely as possible to try and figure out what was stacked there. At the head of the bed he touched a round object that was smooth on top. Why didn't I bring a lantern or flashlight, he muttered to himself? At first, he just touched the round object on the bed with one finger, and then he reached down and let his hand wander around it. Suddenly he jerked back. He had just realized his finger was in the eyehole of a skull.

"Okay, that's enough of that." Cole walked to the door and squeezed out into the full light. It took him a minute to catch his breath, and then he grabbed the log he had used for a battering ram, wedged it into the doorway and pried the door totally open. "That's better."

The room was twice as bright as before, even with the shadows. Cole reached down, picked up the skull off the floor, and replaced it in its original position on the bed. The room smelled musty, with mouse droppings on the bed and the floor. He moved slightly and felt his boot brush something on the floor. He looked down and saw a pistol sticking out from under the bed. He carefully picked it up and stepped back into better light. It was a single shot, pre-Civil-War-era gun, rusted but intact. It appeared to be loaded.

Fluffy chunks of mattress created by rodent activity lay on the bed around what looked to be a full, human rib cage. Cole decided on his next trip he would give this man a decent burial, for he knew if the tables were turned, he would have wanted the same. He thought how odd this situation was; finding the remains of a body this long after the person had died. He walked back outside, sat down on a rock, and looked at the cabin. For the first time, he realized it was lunchtime and that he was hungry. Cole took a drink from his canteen and then pulled a sandwich wrapped in wax paper from inside his shirt. The sandwich was thoroughly smashed from the roof cave in, but it tasted fine. As he sat there eating, he looked at the valley and wondered if this could be the skeleton of Vern Creager, Virgil's brother, or someone else. Whoever it was, his loved ones never knew what happened to him, and that was just plain wrong.

Cole ate and scanned the valley for any movement, but there was none. Finally, he got up, grabbed his gun, and proceeded up the beautiful little valley. About twenty yards past the cabin, a small waterfall spouted out of the cliff's solid rock. Where it landed, it had created a pond with a narrow creek that ran down through one side of the valley. It was small but would have provided plenty of water for a couple of people and their livestock.

It was obvious they had built the cabin with trees from the meadow, but they had also created pasture, which would have allowed them to feed livestock and remain unseen. Cole was totally fascinated at how much planning and work had gone into this project. The valley soon narrowed where a lot of the original timber still stood. The trees were so thick that the valley floor was devoid of plant life, and an old trail meandered under the branches. Cole continued on and noticed another building tucked beside the canyon wall in a small opening.

Little remained of the old building. Many of its boards had rotted away, and the roof was decayed and mostly gone. The door lay on the ground a few feet from the building. It had been well built of planks, but now it was rotted and sat broken in three pieces. Cole stepped around it and peered inside to see that the room had shelves and several long, narrow tables. Cole had seen ore separating tables before and believed this was what he was looking at. Several rusted lanterns hung from log beams on the one wall that was still intact. The other wall leaned badly and had a number of chunks of rotted leather attached to it, but Cole had no idea what they were for. He could easily see most everything inside the building, so he decided not to enter—it wouldn't be the first time an old miner booby trapped his mine shed. He walked to the back to see if he had missed anything, and with the exception of a large pile of old tailings he found nothing.

Suddenly, he felt something looking at him, and it made the hair stand up on the back of his neck. In one quick motion, he swung around with his rifle, but nothing moved, and the only sound was distant birds chirping. He thought the old skeleton must have spooked him, and he needed to regain his composure.

He returned to the trail, which grew more difficult due to the abundance of overgrown branches which he broke, pushed aside or crawled under. After another five minutes, the trail finally emerged into the open, and Cole found himself on a narrow path similar to the one coming into the valley. In open country he felt much more relaxed as he walked and only periodically turned and looked at his back trail. Everything appeared normal and, at least for the time being, he could see well. The trail was in excellent shape, and he made good time following it up the canyon. The track led closer to the cliff edge, where the creek below roared from its many small waterfalls.

The rock hillside to Cole's right rose straight up over a hundred feet, and as he looked over the rim to the creek below, he saw it was about the same distance straight down to a bottom of huge boulders, dead trees and whitewater. What an amazing trail, Cole thought to himself, as he continued his journey up the valley. He was careful to keep his gun ready as he went around each rock that could hide anything, but every time he examined the ground for tracks, the largest he saw were from a Rocky Mountain Bighorn Sheep. After seeing the new tracks, he figured there was probably another way out of the valley, even though it may be extremely difficult. He was excited and his imagination wandered. He knew that it was just a matter of time now, before he found the mine and could help pay off the ranch and—

A rock the size of a football landed five feet behind him. Cole jerked to the side and immediately looked up, just in time to see a small man disappear out of sight. Then he saw the beast behind him, the huge grizzly charging only ten yards away. How had he gotten so close without Cole hearing him? Cole leveled his rifle for a shot but was too late—the bear crashed into him. Cole felt the blow, and the bear's horrid breath hit his face as it roared. The last thing Cole saw was blue sky and the bear's open jaws as he fell over the steep cliff. Then it was dark.

Part III

Creager's Gold

Chapter 20

Cole slowly opened his left eye to a dark sky and a cold night. Dried blood glued his swollen right eye shut. He tried to use his fingers to open the eye, but when he did, sharp pains shot down the length of his arm. The cold had already begun to seep through his jacket. His head felt like it had been pounded into the dirt. He was confused and didn't know where he was, but he heard falling water below him. He carefully moved his toes and then all the fingers on both hands, wincing at each movement from the effort. At least everything moved. From what he could tell, he was about fifteen feet below the canyon rim on a narrow rock shelf that jetted out from the cliff wall. His body was caught between the cliff and enough of an angular shaped rock in the ledge that his body hadn't rolled off. Through his daze, he looked to each side and carefully tried not to fall the remaining eighty feet or so to the rocks and creek below. With every bit of strength he had, he tried to sit up, but his body wouldn't budge. Nausea forced him to lie back against the cold rock.

Events slowly came back—he remembered hiking up the valley and someone throwing the rock that warned him to turn around, just as the bear charged. He remembered the horrible smell of the bear's breath, and seeing blue sky and the bear's open mouth as he fell backward, but nothing more. He gently felt his swollen lip with his tongue. It hurt and he tasted dried blood. From what he could see in the twilight, there was blood on his clothing, and the way he felt told him he had at least one broken bone in his arm. There was no way he could climb the steep cliff back up to the trail, Hell, he couldn't even sit up it hurt so bad. Isolation and helplessness flooded over him, and he decided to at least yell for help, even though he knew no one could hear.

"Help!" The pitiful squawk that came out of Cole's mouth didn't sound like it had come from the powerful man who had set several football records in college. The cry sounded more like a person about to die. The pain from yelling pierced his body, and he passed out again.

When Cole awoke for the second time, he found himself not on the ledge, as he had remembered, but in a small hollowed out spot in a rock cliff. A small fire crackled in front of him and he felt the heat radiating off the rocks behind him. Someone had placed a ratty blanket over him, something for which he was grateful. He reached up with his good arm and felt a bandage on his head that covered the cut, though it continued to pound unmercifully. Again he tried to sit up, and again he became dizzy and nauseous. His left arm had been splinted with two sticks bound together with leather strips. The cuts, bruises, and broken bones were easier to stand than the over whelming nausea. He tried one more time to sit up, but only made it a few inches before he collapsed and fell back to the ground and back into the darkness.

Cole's next realization was light and warmth. He opened his eyes and saw the sun in the middle of the sky. The fire crackled with life and a small pile of branches lay close by. In addition to the blanket, someone had added an old, heavy coat, and Cole really appreciated the additional warmth. He lay awake for another twenty minutes before he fell back into another deep sleep.

He opened his eyes to darkness. A small tin can, the size normally used for beans, sat full of water in front of him, as well as small chunks of meat on a small piece of deer hide. Cole had no idea how long he had slept, but the woodpile beside him had increased since he was previously awake. His head still hurt but didn't pound uncontrollably like before. It seemed to Cole that someone had cleaned the blood from his swollen eye, and he didn't feel as dirty. Cole started to remember more of what had happened, but the pain in his body made it hard to focus. He remembered the bear, the sky, and the ledge but couldn't figure out how he got there or who was helping him. He drank a small amount of water and ate a little meat, then he lowered his head back down and was out once again.

The sound of birds chirping stirred Cole awake. The fire barely smoked, so with great difficulty, Cole added a few branches from the large pile beside him. For the first time, he noticed his bed, which was made from an animal hide laid over branches and leaves. The way it was placed in a small depression in the rock allowed the heat of the fire to radiate off the rock wall back onto his bed. It comforted

Cole that more food and water had been set out. At least he knew that someone cared if he lived or died. Whoever his savior was, he was very experienced at living in the wilderness.

It was the first time that Cole had stayed awake for more than a few minutes and the first time he felt he was going to survive. For the next hour, he lay still and looked at the small camp. The bed of leaves smelled like an animal's bed. The small fire had rocks stacked around it, and judging by the amount of charcoal that stained them, the camp had been used for quite a while.

He slept, awoke, ate and drank and then fell asleep again. The pattern continued, with Cole adding wood to the fire every time he woke up. How long he had been here, he had no idea. The woodpile was nearly gone, as were the food and water. Whoever had been his savior seemed to have abandoned him.

The sun's warm rays woke him and he was thankful for the heat. The fire had died out, but the blanket and old coat were warm enough that he had slept through the night. Cole's mind was starting to clear, and he noticed the little opening in which he laid contained several wooden boxes—where they had come from, he couldn't guess. There was a small pile of wood about fifteen feet away beside the cliff. Cole wondered if there were enough coals to start another fire. He sat up too fast and was dizzy. He tried to stand using his good arm, then awoke minutes later, still lying on his bed of leaves. He quickly realized that if his savior didn't come back soon, his chances of surviving were slim to none. He drank what remained of his water, ate the remaining chunks of meat, and lay down.

He opened his eyes to a crackling fire with the stars just visible beyond it. Across the fire sat a small man with long, matted bright red hair and a beard of the same color. He was eating something, probably a piece of meat, Cole thought. The red-bearded stranger wore an assortment of clothing from hides to a brightly colored, button-down shirt and modified jacket. He wore no hat, and his jacket had deer hide covering the shoulders. His pants also appeared to be made of hides, and he was barefoot. His face and body were dirty, and even at a distance, Cole could smell him. It didn't appear that he had seen Cole crack open his one good eye.

Cole watched him eat and then said, "Good morning." The red-headed man jumped back and looked at Cole for a moment, moving his head slightly to one side, and then smiled with a mouth half-full of yellow teeth. His head showed an old injury: at least three inches of the skull was sunk and scarred, and only scar tissue remained where the normal curve of the skull should have been. The man soon returned to the fire, squatted, and continued to eat.

"Thank you," Cole said quietly. "You saved my life." The skinny stranger didn't acknowledge Cole, but he didn't seem uncomfortable with his presence either. He walked over and picked up the bean can, then disappeared from sight, returning moments later with a can full of water, which he placed in front of Cole and then moved away. This time he brought what appeared to be dried fish. Cole chewed a piece and was surprised to taste salt. Where had he gotten salt? Who is this guy?

"What's your name?" Cole asked. The small, red-headed man just continued to eat as if he hadn't heard anything. Cole tried a little louder, "What is your name?" But there was still no response. "Well, if you're not going to answer me, then I'm going to have to call you something. How about Red? I hope that's all right with you."

Again, the stranger continued eating and didn't respond.

"We're getting nowhere fast," Cole muttered. Even though he had been awake for less than thirty minutes, the warmth from the fire and his full belly made his eyes droop. He laid his head back onto the bed and soon he was asleep.

Later, he awoke to the fire crackling back to life, as Red stoked it. It was late afternoon and Cole figured he had been gone from the ranch for at least four days. What had happened to the mules back in the corral? What had happened to Patch when he ran out of grass in the small meadow where he was picketed? It really tore Cole up that he had no answers and couldn't do anything about it. He tried standing with the help of a thick branch. It was a struggle, but for the first time he stood and was able to control his dizziness. He walked a short distance from his bed and looked out over the valley. He remembered the first time he had awoken in the leaf bed and how bad it smelled. He must be getting used to it because it no longer took his breath away.

The next day, Cole felt stronger with less chest pain. With the exception of his arm, which was a ripe yellowish purple, he felt better. Cole knew the arm needed to be set by a doctor, but he also knew he was lucky to be alive. That night, as Red squatted across the fire from him, Cole took a drink, pointed to the can and said,

"Water." There was no response. Then he did the same thing and with food, but again Red only showed his gap-toothed smile.

Several days later, when Cole was able to move around better, he decided to explore his little camp. Red had left as he normally did midmorning, so Cole grabbed his walking stick and climbed to his feet. They seemed to be on some type of rock shelf that jetted out from the cliff wall, for he could tell they were at least twenty feet above the valley floor. He worked his way over to some small trees that hid his view of the valley and could see the end of the rock shelf and the cliff that dropped off to the forest floor below. Red had picked a very good campsite. No wolf or bear could possibly climb the steep wall to the ledge. Cole had noticed that when Red went for food or water, he disappeared behind a large rock that divided the ledge. It took some careful walking, but he finally reached the large rock that separated the camp. The rock jutted out onto the ledge and reduced the width to only four feet. At that spot, Cole had an unobstructed view of the long, narrow valley below.

On the other side of the rock was another ledge approximately twenty feet wide by forty feet long, with a tiny creek that sprung from the rocks. To his left was a hut made from logs, boards and hides, with a small door and a rusted stovepipe jetting above the roof. Cole walked over to a rivulet of water that fell from a crack in the rock, forming a small pool at its base. A soft mud bank surrounded the pond, before it turned into a stream that cascaded over the ledge. Cole looked down at the water and saw a footprint in the soft mud. It looked to be the same size as the track left by whoever was being chased by wolves, when Cole was with Julie several months earlier. It had to have been Red.

Cole noticed a pile of hides to one side of the door and a pile of bones on the other. Apparently, Red skinned a lot of his kills here. Cole hobbled carefully up to the door. It opened more easily than he had expected and was well fitted to the opening. Inside was an old mattress on a wooden frame that allowed Red to sleep off the cold ground. There were pots and pans, but little silverware. The cups were old cans like the one Cole had used for drinking. He figured Red must be one tough son of a bitch if he lived up here throughout the year. Numerous strings of dried meat hung from logs that spanned the ceiling. The back of the room appeared to be the remnants of an old mine or cave. Immediately, Cole's mind raced—

he had found the Creagers' gold mine! But after ten minutes of closer examination, he determined that there had been little to no mining, and there wasn't any gold. Finally, he sat down. All the movement had exhausted him, and his body hurt all over.

He realized just how foul Red smelled as he scanned the room. The guy obviously never took a bath. A lantern hung from the ceiling, but it was covered in cobwebs. Cole thought to himself that if he had matches, he could still try to light it, but he didn't. He was continuing to examine the tiny cave, when he noticed what looked like a very old painting of a bear on the wall—by the hump on its back, a grizzly. An Indian petroglyph, he thought. The cave had probably been used for hundreds of years.

Cole looked at the mural for several seconds, and mumbled to himself, "Looks like they had trouble with those damn bears even way back then." A pile of old clothes lay in one corner and Cole picked up a bright blue shirt with flowery yellow highlights on the shoulder. It looked a lot like one of those wild shirts that Ballard wore. Then he put it back in the pile with the other clothing. He tried to pick up the pile to look under it, but it was way too painful. In his effort, he saw a lone shirt with a nametag sewed on it. It was olive colored, badly worn, and showing dark red stains that could have been blood. The name had faded over the pocket, but he could still read, "Wilson." He spent about ten minutes in the little shelter, before he decided he needed a breath of fresh air and went back out into the sunshine. As he left, he carefully closed the door of the small shelter, and that's when he noticed an old monarch of a spruce leaning out over the cliff to the valley below. Time had not been kind to the giant, but it still had a lot of green branches. Something in the tree caught his eye, but Cole wasn't sure what it was. He walked under the tree and looked up.

A light blond, wooden oval hung next to a rope, which was tied to a stout limb. He finally realized that he was looking at a wooden block and tackle set. One of the ropes from the pulley hung down within Cole's reach, and he pulled on it to see if he could get the rest to drop. With one weak tug, the lower part of the block and tackle fell from the tree and landed on the ground in front of Cole. Cole picked up the pulley block and saw the faint letters "USFS" burnt into the block. So, he borrowed it from the Forest Service, did he?

Cole thought. This must be how he got me off the ledge and how he got me up here.

"Whew! What a smart little guy," Cole whispered under his breath.

From Cole's vantage point, standing and holding a crutch, he noticed handholds someone had cut in the cliff. Red must have been using them to access the valley. When he had anything larger than he could carry on his back, he would use the block and tackle to bring it up or down. Red was intelligent and a craftsman. How had he gotten out here and why had he lived this life of solitude? Was it the injury? He could only guess at the answer, but for now, whatever the reason, Cole felt happy Red was here.

He painfully headed back to his bed and slept the remainder of the day. That night he was awakened by the sound of Red using the block and tackle to lift something up the cliff. He patiently waited, and soon Red hiked around the corner with the hindquarter of a mountain sheep. He set it by the fire, added a few larger branches to the coals and then began cutting strips of meat off the sheep, hanging them on a wire above the fire. Red continued for over an hour without looking in Cole's direction. Finally, he stood up, cut several pieces of cooked meat, and handed them to Cole. Red stared at him for a couple of seconds, smiled, went back and sat down. Cole was humbled and thankful for everything and in a quiet voice said, "Thank you. Thank you, Red."

Red did not acknowledge him.

That night, the throbbing pain in Cole's arm kept him awake. He also seemed to be running a low fever. At one point, he unbuttoned his coat and opened his shirt to look at his chest. The effort was painful. There was a single, bloody claw mark. Thankfully only one had made it through his jacket and into his flesh. It was a shallow cut, but it looked red and angry, and Cole was sure it was infected.

A thick blanket of fog had begun to creep up the small canyon valley below, visually devouring the moonlit landscape in its path. Cole slowly opened his one good eye as the fog rolled over the ledge and slowly encompassed his small fire and leaf filled bed. Red was nowhere to be seen, and Cole wondered what had awakened him. Then he heard a strange sound. Something was out in the fog and seemed to be coming from beyond the reaches of the steep ledge that protected him from the valley below.

* * *

A faint voice came through the billowing clouds and Cole tried but couldn't pinpoint its source. It was almost like the voice floated in space, and as he listened, the voice drew closer. He couldn't tell if his eyes were playing tricks on him, but the rough shape of a man seemed to suddenly appear. He seemed to drift silently in the fog toward him. Suddenly, Cole heard it again, his name being called very softly as the form seemed to materialize. For some reason, Cole felt no fear or panic, as the voice sounded familiar and comforting, but how could it possibly be? The figure walked to the edge of the fire and momentarily stared at him with heavy, loving eyes.

"Dad, dad, is that you?"

The strong figure answered, "Yes, Son, I'm here." There was a pause. "I've always been here with you."

"How could you be here, Dad?" Cole asked.

The figure was twisted and sad and stared at Cole for a moment before saying, "I'm here because you need me, Son. You're in danger and must leave this place tomorrow or you may never leave."

"But Dad, how. . ." The apparition across the fire seemed to just fade into thin air as Cole spoke, leaving only the silence of the night behind.

* * *

The next morning, Cole woke up to snowflakes drifting into his face. With a shock, he realized it was morning, and an inch of fresh snow covered the ground. Suddenly, he remembered his father's visit from the night before, and he knew he had to leave immediately. Red sat in his usual place across the fire, stoking it with more wood. Cole didn't know quite what to do, so he spoke to Red in a louder voice that he hoped would get his full attention.

"Red," Cole said, "I need to leave." As he talked, he pointed at himself and then pointed down the valley. "Do you understand?"

Red looked at him and then turned his head slightly out of level, like he did so many times before. "Is it all right if I take some of this meat for my trip back?" Cole asked, as he pointed to the meat. This time Red smiled, and for the first time, Cole believed he understood. The snowflakes tapered off and then stopped, but the message was clear. He rolled strips of meat in a piece of shirt that was lying by the bed and then placed it inside the old coat Red had used to blanket him.

He then drank all the water in his can and wished he had a canteen or another way to carry water, for the fever was making him thirsty. Getting up, he reached for his walking stick to steady himself and then headed for where the block and tackle hung from the tree. Even the smallest movement hurt, but Cole knew he had to get out before snow blocked the trails. He was stiff and sore, but he was not going to give up without a fight. His arm was totally useless, and he knew that getting off the cliff would be difficult at best. He hobbled his way around the rock, over to the small shelter, reached down and picked up a piece of hide that was about a foot square, and headed for the giant Limber Pine. Red followed Cole, not saying anything, but following his activities with interest.

"I'm leaving now, but thank you, thank you for saving my life. Is there anything I can get you?" Cole said, as he made eye contact with Red.

For the first time, Red, with great difficulty, said something. "Yellie."

Cole had no idea what that meant, but he nodded his head and turned to face the cliff. Cole grabbed a three-foot-long chunk of thick rope that, by the looks of the fresh blood, had recently been tied to the mountain sheep. He had to assume the rope was securely tied above in the tree, as there would be no way that he would ever be able to climb up and check. He tied the rope around his body, and when the rope went over the bear's claw mark, Cole moaned with pain. Then, he connected the bottom part of the block and tackle to the rope. He threw his walking stick down over the cliff close to where he hoped to land.

Using the hide to help slide the rope through his one good hand, he watched as the pulley slowly lowered him down off the ledge. The pulleys squealed as the block and tackle began gently lowering him to the ground. Cole was worried about how weak he had become from his ordeal, and he could barely hold the rope as it slid through his leather wrapped hand. It was only a twelve foot drop, but it seemed like forever before Cole felt his feet touch the solid ground. He was concerned that the sound from the pulley would alert the bear of his departure. Once down, he took several deep breaths, then grabbed his walking stick using his good hand and his teeth to place the deer hide over the end of the stick, and tied it with a thin piece of leather he had gotten from his pocket.

Cole looked up and saw Red standing above him looking down expressionless. Cole waved, then turned and took several steps and stopped. He looked back at Red and said, "Yellie?"

Red smiled and replied, "Yellie."

Cole left and began hobbling through the trees on a faint path that he hoped would lead him to the main trail down the valley. After what seemed like hours, the secondary track merged with the main trail, and Cole heard stream water dropping over the cliff. It reminded him of his thirst. The main trail was fairly clear of obstructions, and Cole made good time for another twenty minutes until he came to a small creek where he took his time drinking, washing his face, and resting. He had not seen Red since he started down the trail and assumed that he had not followed him, something that he had hoped would happen.

A crow cawed and Cole jumped as the low-flying bird screamed above him on its way down the valley. He gathered himself up and continued down the trail, somewhat refreshed from the ice-cold water and the break. Soon he rounded a corner and saw his rifle lying in the moist dirt in the middle of the path. Cole wanted to take the rifle, the rifle his father had given him, but he knew he didn't have the energy to pack it back, so he stepped over it and continued down the trail. To the right were three, twelve-foot tall, four-inch poles tied together with thick leather. Now, he knew how Red had gotten him off the cliff shelf—he had used the block and tackle and a tripod, no small feat for a person only two-thirds Cole's size.

For several hours, Cole carefully worked his way down the trail through dense timber and open meadows, stopping only when he felt he couldn't take another step. He used the branch as a crutch, and that helped until his armpit became so sore that he couldn't stand it any longer. It bothered him that he had chosen to leave the rifle, but now he had to concentrate on surviving. If he met the bear again now, the rifle wouldn't help him. Sweat beaded his forehead from the worsening fever, and Cole felt chilled. Somehow, he kept going, past the old cabin, through the meadow, and down the hill. Cole didn't even take a moment to look over at the shack, because he knew he had to stay totally focused. He didn't know if he could make it to the small meadow where he had left Patch, but he needed to free him so he wouldn't starve. Hell, he had no idea how long he had been up here. He knew it had been more than five days, but it could have been longer.

Cole watched for fresh bear tracks, but he wasn't sure what he would do if he saw any. The dry rocky trail now turned into the thick trees, and Cole knew he was near the meadow where he had picketed Patch. He was exhausted, but reaching the timber had given him new energy. Slowly and carefully he made his way around and over the deadfalls that blocked his way. He couldn't remember a time in his life that he had felt so completely tired. Maybe it would be good to have the bear find him and end this misery.

Suddenly, he saw the opening of the small meadow. He stumbled forward hoping to see Patch, but he was nowhere in sight. Cole walked painfully over to his picket rope and picked it up. The rope was chewed through, and Patch was gone. Cole was exhausted, dizzy, and he felt like throwing up. He slumped to the grass and immediately passed out.

Chapter 21

When Cole awoke he was shivering badly, and large snowflakes had begun to accumulate up on his clothing. He didn't remember ever feeling so cold, and he knew it was the fever. He was stiff and sore, and as much as he wanted to get up and head toward the cabin, he knew there wasn't enough energy in him for the journey. He stared out over the snowy landscape and thought, if I have to die this is a beautiful spot to do it. He thought about his folks and how he missed talking to them, especially his dad, and it would be good seeing them again in Heaven. He thought about Jay and his warm smile and personality. The last five months had gone so fast and yet he had come to feel he belonged on this ranch—it was home. He had needed that feeling, and now he was going to die in these empty mountains. He thought about the old mansion and Julie, when a large branch cracked behind him. Cole decided he wasn't going to fight. He hoped the bear killed him quickly. The sound of the bear became louder, as Cole heard gravel crunch under its large paws.

That doesn't sound like the quiet movement of a bear, he thought. Hooves! Cole twisted around and saw Patch lowering his head down to be petted. The saddle had slipped to one side but remained on his back. With all his energy, he stood up and gave his mule a huge hug. "Patch, thank you, Patch, I missed you too, boy."

Cole could not believe his luck. He tried to fight back the emotion, but the dam broke and tears rolled down his face in abundance. He stood there for several minutes just hugging Patch, then, with his one good hand, he straightened the saddle and tightened the loose cinch. The bridle hung from the snag where he left it, but Cole wasn't sure that he could put it on one-handed—so, with great difficulty, he mounted Patch without it. Using only his leg pressure, he pointed Patch toward the old trail and gave him a little kick of encouragement. The landscape around them faded under a blanket of snow, as the sturdy mule walked quickly through the timber up the trail and toward the rock fields.

For the next hour, Cole tried to hang on as Patch walked back to the line cabin. He could no longer ride upright, but leaned forward against Patch's neck. It was like the mule sensed that something was seriously wrong and was careful with each step. Suddenly, dizziness overwhelmed him. Patch was walking by Old Man Rock, when Cole slid to the ground unconscious. The snowflakes landed on Cole' still body, his mule beside him as if he were on guard duty, protecting his rider, his friend. The thick-falling snow had begun to cover Cole's body when Patch raised his head and let out a loud bray, and then another, and then another.

* * *

Cole remained unconscious as the small group of riders led by Rich Herman rode down to Old Man Rock and saw the silhouette of Patch standing guard over a lump in the fresh snow. Rich, Allen and Dodge jumped off in unison and rushed to Cole's side.

"Is he still alive?" Dodge asked. Allen put his arm around Cole's back, tilted his body to a sitting position, and then began brushing the snow off Cole's stone white face. Allen put his finger on Cole's neck, searching for a pulse.

It took several minutes for Allen to find a pulse before he turned to the others and spoke. "He's alive, but barely. Help me load him on my horse and then throw a blanket over both of us. We need to make it back to the cabin fast, if we're to have any chance . . . any chance at all." The group worked like a well-trained unit and had Cole on Allen's horse and heading up the ridge in less than a minute. The snow fell harder, and it looked as if the heavy storm would continue.

* * *

A day and a half later, Cole finally opened both eyes. The swelling in his right eye had gone down enough that he could see with both. The room was warm and he could hear the wood crackling in the stove. Daylight shone through the cabin's only window, and from his bed he could see it was lightly snowing. Cole closed his eyes and thought, I made it, I really made it. Allen was sitting in the chair next to him, and when Cole shifted his arm he jumped up and faced Cole.

"Well, partner, I was wondering if we lost you," Allen said. "You gave us a hell of a scare, worst I've had for a while. Hell, I think I kinda got a little used to having you around." He took a rag and wiped Cole's forehead before he started talking again. "Why in the hell did you go after that bear again? You've got yourself about three quarters dead, and if it hadn't been for that mountain canary of yours braying his head off, we never would have found you."

"Patch braying?" Cole said.

"Yeah, the mule of yours must have heard us at least five hundred yards away and started braying. With all the wind and snow, we barely heard him. And when we got there, you would have thought he was on sentry duty, the way he guarded you. Strange…real strange," Allen said. "I do have to give some of the credit to old Rich Herman, hell of a tracker. He was able to follow your seven-day old tracks all the way up that hill, but you must have turned off somewhere, and with that snow, well, we lost your tracks. Hell, you could hardly see anything up there, much less a trail that old."

"Seven days?" Cole asked.

"That's right, seven days; you were supposed to been back a couple of days ago," Allen said, as he took out a washcloth and dipped it in a bowl of hot water that was sitting on the stove. He was carefully wiping Cole's face when they heard a knock at the door.

"Mind if I come in? I heard some talking in here and figured Cole must have woke up" said Dodge, as he closed the door behind him and began dusting the snow from his shoulders and hat. He smiled and said, "What in the hell were you doing all by yourself up here, partner?"

Cole was in no mood to discuss it, so he just replied in a hoarse, soft voice, "I needed some quiet time." The answer caught Dodge by surprise, and then he smiled and laughed and replied "Hell of a quiet time, if you ask me."

"We need you to eat a little soup before you go back to sleep," Allen said. "It'll make you feel better." Cole tried, but he could only eat half a cup before his eyes drooped, and within seconds he was back asleep.

Allen walked out on the porch where Rich was finishing a hand rolled cigarette. "By the look of his clothes, the boy's been through a lot," commented Rich.

"Yeah…yeah, he has," replied Allen. "His body is at least fifty percent black and blue, and he has some wounds the doc should look at. I haven't asked him how he put a splint on his own arm, but he sure did a hell of a good job of it. Otherwise, I think he could have lost that arm. It looks like a clean break, though it looks old, like he did it at the start of the trip. There's one cut across his chest that could be a claw mark, but I haven't asked about it. To tell you the truth, he hasn't really said much."

Rich just lowered his head as if looking at the ground and took a puff on his cigarette. "What'll we do if it keeps snowing?"

"I don't know. He ain't in any shape to ride and probably won't be for another couple of days."

"The snow's eight inches deep, and it don't look like it's going to slow down for a while," Rich said between puffs.

"Yeah, it doesn't look good. The three of us will decide what to do tomorrow morning, but for now, we just got to ride it out. Keep knocking the snow off the tent so you two have a place to sleep tonight. I'm staying inside with Cole." Allen smiled the tent was a ten by twelve cabin style with four foot sides. Dodge had set up the stove and a couple of cots with bedrolls, and a large pile of wood for the night. The fire kept the inside of the tent reasonably warm, but a person had to get up every so often and knock off the snow, and feed the fire or the tent would collapse.

Allen made dinner and Dodge woke Cole to get him to eat more soup. Everyone went to bed early, for they knew it might be tough going the next day. Several times in the night, Allen was awakened by Cole's nightmares. He screamed loud enough one time that Rich and Dodge came running into the cabin to see what was wrong. Each times, Allen was able to get Cole to drink some water and eat a little mix of beans and ham. It was a long night.

The sun rose to a beautiful, snow covered camp. The storm had blown over in the early morning, and everything sparkled from the deep snow and bright sunlight. Part of the tent had collapsed in the early morning hours, but not enough to wake the men. Allen put some water on the stove, and then stoked the fire in it. He opened the door to see Rich and Dodge knocking the snow off the tent and yelled, "Why don't you two get your sorry butts in here. I'll have coffee going in just a minute or so." With a clear sky, the atmosphere in the camp improved. It would be extremely difficult to ride down the slick, steep trail, but at least for the moment they knew what they were dealing with.

Eighteen inches of fresh powder lay on the ground and covered the previous night's tracks. Allen handed everyone a cup of hot coffee and then began, "I don't know if he's strong enough to ride all the way down to the trailhead, but if we get another snow tonight like we had last night I don't know if any of us are going to get out of here. That trail down the mountain is way too narrow for us to rig up some kind of a sled. If we're to get him out of here, we're going to have to ride him out."

Cole's fever had broken overnight, and he awoke to damp clothes but no shivers. Allen, Dodge and Rich stood over his bed drinking coffee. "Well, good morning, Sunshine," Rich said to Cole as he opened his eyes. Cole looked beat up, with several cuts and bruises to his face and a hollowness in his normally strong features.

"Good morning to you," Cole murmured. "Can I get you boys anything?" Everyone laughed at Cole's sense of humor. With Cole awake, the group started discussing the trip back when Cole interrupted and said, "Well, let's saddle up and get back to the ranch. I could use a nap."

Allen smiled and looked at Dodge and Rich. "I guess he said it. Let's pack up."

"But how are we going to get him down?" Dodge asked.

"We can ride double on my horse," Allen said. "He's big and strong, and I think he can carry us both, at least most of the way. I'll put him in front of me and hold him in the saddle. If he passes out, I can keep him from falling. I'll need a couple of saddle blankets to sit on the back of the saddle and a blanket to wrap around Cole and me to keep him warm, but I think it'll work."

Several hours later all the stock was saddled, and the tent and the rest of the gear was packed and loaded on the mules. It was hard working in the deep snow, but everyone was experienced and the task went well. The warm sun almost made it seem hot as the men worked to close up the cabin and prepare for the ride down. They decided that Dodge would lead with the mules and stop halfway at Decker Flat and make a fire, so when Allen and Cole rode in, they could get some hot soup down Cole. Rich would ride in front of Allen to help break the trail better and would be close by in case Allen needed any help with Cole.

Decker Flats had long been used for a midway camp between the valley and the high mountain pastures, and for years it was a main stop on the trail. But since the cabin had been built forty years before, the campsite had seen almost no use. It was out of the wind, and had numerous dry snags for firewood, and would be a great place to rest Cole.

Rich and Dodge dressed Cole in their extra set of long johns and other clothing, in case they ended up being out a lot longer than anyone planned—experience taught them that things seldom went as planned. Then they loaded Cole into Allen's saddle and neatly placed two blankets behind Allen's saddle to get the height of both riders about even. It was a lot of weight for the big horse, but there was really little choice. Cole couldn't ride by himself, and they needed to get out before the next storm hit. Allen's sorrel gelding was built stout with thick bones and weighed roughly twelve hundred pounds, a decent size horse in anyone's book. The stock swayed and pawed at the snow, anxious to get on the trail.

Dodge allowed the mules to set a fast pace as they left the cabin, with Patch in the rear. They weren't shod, and the lack of slick metal on their feet made their footing much better than that of the horses. Allen wished he had brought a shoeing tool to remove the horse's shoes, but in their haste, no one had thought of it. They would need to be careful and do the best they could on the slick, narrow trail. The plan was to give Dodge a little room with the mule string and then carefully follow their worn trail. Rich helped put the blanket around Allen and Cole and then mounted up himself.

The first hour of the ride went as planned, but Allen could tell that Cole was having a hard time staying awake. His head soon drooped uncontrollably to one side, which forced Allen to balance both of them as they rode down the hill. By the time they reached Decker Flats, Allen was exhausted, and his arms were numb from being in one position too long. Dodge had made it to the small campsite twenty minutes earlier, and he had a nice warm fire going in the clearing as Allen, Cole, and Rich rode in. "Help me with Cole," Allen shouted to Dodge. "I can barely feel my arm."

Rich tied off quickly and helped slide Cole out of the saddle. Dodge had a blanket on the ground for Cole and some soup and coffee warming by the fire. Cole looked pale, and the sight of his unconscious form worried Allen.

"Cole…Cole…wake up," Allen said, as he gently slapped him in the face. The first couple of slaps did nothing. "Cole, you got to wake up!" Allen slapped him again. "I'm not letting you die on my watch!"

Slowly, Cole's eyes opened, and for a couple of seconds Allen could tell he didn't know where he was. "Its okay, Cole, you're fine. We're getting you down the mountain to a real bed." Rich and Allen tried to get Cole to drink some hot soup, but were only somewhat successful. After an hour the group reloaded and decided that Cole would ride with Rich. Allen was thankful for the break. As much as he wanted to help Cole, his body just didn't have the strength. Rich was bigger than Allen and just as strong, and he rode a stocky sure-footed Morgan. Allen looked at his lathered up gelding and knew he had made a good decision.

Five hours later, Dodge emerged from the trailhead to see Elmer sleeping in one of the ranch's two-ton flatbeds. As Dodge got closer, Elmer awoke to the sound of stock and piled out of the truck to help him with the mules. "Man, am I glad to see you. I've been waiting here for the last two days. Did you find Cole?"

"Yeah, but he's in bad shape, really bad shape. Let's tie up the mules and the horse over in those trees," Dodge said. "And take one of those hay bales from up top and spread it around in the back corner of the truck for a bed for Cole. The others should be here in another twenty minutes or so."

Time seemed to stand still, but finally, over a small ridge emerged the horses with Rich holding Cole with Allen following a few yards behind. "Quick, get Cole in the back of the truck on that hay, and let's get back to the ranch house," said Dodge, as he helped Elmer and Allen unload Cole from Rich's horse.

"Dodge, can you and Rich get the stock back to the ranch" Allen asked, "I know it's another three hours, but I don't think we have much choice."

"Don't worry none about us. You save that boy." Rich answered and Dodge nodded in agreement.

On the ride back, Elmer did his best to miss as many holes in the road as possible, but some were unavoidable. Elmer hit a large bump, and jolted Cole awake. "Where are we?" he asked.

"On the road back to the ranch, we'll be home soon. Just keep quiet and rest. You'll be asleep in a warm bed soon," Allen answered.

"Hell, it seems to me like about all I have done lately is sleep," Cole said in a groggy voice. "How did you know I was in trouble? How did you find me so quick?"

"You sure you want to talk right now?" Allen asked.

"Yeah, I need to know."

"Well, it was kind of creepy. Five days after you left, Slim had to drive up to the old ghost town to check on a bull that has pink eye, and on his way back that afternoon, he found a . . . message of sorts in the middle of the road. There was this three foot wide by two foot tall stack of rocks with a large branch poking out the top."

"But what made you think I was in trouble?" Cole asked. "Well, on top of the stick was your hat and it had blood on it." Cole just closed his eyes and quietly said to himself, "Red."

Chapter 22

Cole floated between deep sleep and foggy dream while he lay bandaged on the bed. His mind wandered between dark memories while cold sweat dampened his forehead and body. In one dream, Cole found himself sitting on a vast ridge, looking out over an immense valley below. A wisp of fog blew up the ridge and turned into the face and then the body of Julie. She was smiling as she bent down and softly took his hand in hers and at that moment he felt warm and protected. Her lips didn't move but he could hear her voice saying, "You'll be fine. I won't let anything happen to you." She gently kissed his cheek and vanished into the fog.

As Cole opened his eyes for the first time, he heard voices coming from another room. He recognized Julie's, and he thought the other might be Wes McCabe's. He listened for a moment longer and heard Allen telling Julie that the doctor was just driving in. Cole felt different bandages from his head to his thigh, and he felt soggy in his sheets. He switched position, and the pain from the slight motion made him moan. He had never felt so miserable in his whole life. Seconds later he could hear someone coming.

"I thought I heard something," Julie said as she entered the room. She wore a soft white dress with a yellow flowered belt that accented her shapely body. Cole thought to himself how beautiful she was and wished he had found the mine for her sake. "You're finally back with us. You had me worried. Everyone worried. The doctor's here to check your progress," Julie straightened Cole's bed a little. "You okay?"

"Thanks. I'm all right. Progress," Cole said with effort.

"Yes, progress. He worked on you for over two hours the day before yesterday. This is the first time you've been awake since the men brought you here. Doc Knight said to let you sleep, as that was the way your body was dealing with all your injuries. That bear must have really beaten you up," Julie said.

"How did he know it was a bear?" Cole asked.

"For one thing, you had a huge cut across your chest that looked like it was from a bear claw. Besides, everyone knows you went back after that bear. I got to tell you Cole, that was the stupidest . . . " Julie was interrupted as the doctor entered the room.

"Thanks for rescuing me, Doc. I sure do appreciate it," Cole said.

"What does he mean rescue" the doctor asked Julie with a puzzled look on his face.

"He's just giving me a hard time, because I was discussing the intelligence level of a man who would single handedly go hunting a killer bear, that's all," replied Julie, and she took a step back to give the doctor room to examine Cole. The doctor pulled back the covers to Cole's thighs, exposing his chest, stomach, and the pair of underwear he was wearing.

Cole looked at Julie and said, "Can't a man have a little privacy around here?" "Privacy, who do you think has been giving you your bath for the last two days? I'll tell you who, my mom and I. And we've taken turns sitting by your bed since you got here!" Julie stormed from the room.

"She's right, you know," said the doctor. "You were in nasty shape when you got here—dried blood, dirt, infected cuts, broken bones, black and blue areas. Should I go on?"

"No, I get the point. I guess I owe her and her mom a load of thanks," Cole said.

"Well, to tell you the truth, you owe a lot of people from the way I hear it, but especially Julie and Allen." Doc sat on Cole's bed and began checking his bandages.

"Allen is alright?" Cole asked.

"Yeah, more or less, but his arm is giving him a lot of trouble. Seems that while riding you out, you passed out, and he had to hold you in the saddle for close to three hours. You probably passed out from that infection in your leg. And he lost some of the feeling in his arm," replied Doc.

"Will he get it back?" Cole asked with concern in his voice.

"I think so. Can't be positive, but I think it's just a pinched nerve, least ways it's acting like one. But now I want to get back to you. You have torn a lot of ligaments in your chest and back, your head has a severe cut that required seventeen stitches, your arm is broke—but amazingly you set it yourself—and your leg is infected. You have at least ten areas that I stitched up. And your thigh, not to mention your whole body, is badly bruised. You need to seriously rest for a couple of two weeks, probably more."

The doctor finished changing Cole's bandages. "You amaze me, son. When they brought you in here two days ago, I would have bet you wouldn't have made it, but sure as shucks you did. You got one tough body," the doctor said, as he put away the remaining bandages and his scissors in his bag and closed it.

"Thanks, Doc, I appreciate everything. I'll try harder to stay out of trouble."

"I'm getting a little too old for all this excitement. That's twice in the last six months that you have almost died on me," Doc Knight said, as he turned and started walking toward the door. He stopped short of the door, turned back to Cole, and said, "You know, son, the third time's a charm. You better think about that before you do anything else as stupid as what you just did." Cole just listened. There was no way to tell the doctor the truth about his mission.

Cole's entire body ached, but that didn't bother him nearly as much as the thought of him hurting Allen, and the worst of it was that he hadn't accomplished a thing. Cole let his head melt into the pillow and stared at the nightstand picture of Gillis McCabe and his wife on vacation. They were posed with Mrs. McCabe sitting on what looked to be a park bench and Gillis standing proudly beside her in his high boots and derby hat. He held a light brown cane with what looked like a bronze hog's head on the handle. The picture was old and a little faded, but the frame was beautiful and looked to be hand carved.

"Mind if I come in?" Julie asked. She set a tray with soup and a glass of milk down on the nightstand. "The doctor says you might live. And if you do, it'll be because of the wonderful work Mom and I did." She looked at him with an exaggerated smile as she tilted her head unnaturally to one side to show Cole her unhappiness with his earlier comment. Cole knew better than to say anything. "Now you need to get some food in you." Julie dipped the spoon in the soup and began feeding Cole.

I guess this isn't all bad, he thought to himself. At least she has to spend time with me. Julie kept scolding Cole about his intelligence until he changed the subject. "So, Julie, is that a picture of your grandfather or great grandfather?"

Julie paused for a moment, knowing so well what Cole was doing, but she decided he had been chastised enough. "That's my great grandparents on vacation in Chicago. I think the second year after they moved out here. She was Great Grandfather's first wife— the one we're descended from. They made a cute pair, didn't they?"

Cole nodded. They were a cute couple, but they could have been dog ugly and Cole would have still nodded, for he was too beat down for any kind of an argument and was just glad that she backed off scolding him. He knew he should keep the conversation moving away from him, so he asked in a very soft, quiet voice, one that he knew she would feel sorry for, "Had your great grandfather built the original house by then?"

"Why, yes. It wasn't totally complete then, though. I think I told you Great Grandfather totally remodeled it about a year after he had married his second wife."

The conversation continued another couple of minutes before Sally McCabe walked into the room. "Why Cole, it's nice to see you awake. You sure had a lot of people concerned. How are you feeling?"

"Like I've been at the rodeo for a week straight, and the bull died on top of me."

"Well, it's good to see you awake, and I hope you're feeling better anyways," said Sally.

"Thanks for the help. I really appreciate everyone's efforts."

Sally turned to Julie, "We need to get going if we're going to make it to Cody by noon and find the material for your wedding dress. After all, it's Friday and we have that appointment."

Julie looked at Cole and responded, "Mom, I want to put the trip off for a little while until Cole feels better. This whole thing has taken a lot out of me, and I'm tired. Would you mind if we did it next week?"

Sally shook her head. "Well, no, but I would have thought you'd be more excited for your big day."

"I am excited, but staying up with Cole all night just wore me out, and I would just like to have everything perfect for this day and not be tired," responded Julie.

"That's fine, dear, we'll go next week." Sally spun around and left the room.

Julie walked back over to Cole's bed and sat down beside him. She put her hand on his head. "You're not telling me everything are you, Cole? I hope someday you will." With that she got up and left the room.

For the next couple of days, different visitors made their way in to see Cole with a variety of questions. Cole wanted so badly to tell someone that he didn't go after the bear, that he was looking for the mine, and was real close to finding it when that stupid bear came hunting him. But he couldn't risk the rumor of gold getting out.

On the third day, Allen came to see him, looking good with the exception of his arm, which dangled unnaturally at his side. He had not gotten its use back, and his face showed that it bothered him. He walked over to the bed with Julie behind him and said, "Well, partner, that was a close one, a real close one. Hell, you just about killed both of us. I knew I shouldn't have let you go. That was a fool thing for me to do." Allen looked down at Cole, and Cole noticed the dark circles under the older man's eyes. The trip had clearly worn him out.

"You had no choice," Cole said. "I would have gone no matter what, because it was something I had to do." Cole wanted to tell Allen so badly, but he knew he couldn't. News like that would blow the lid off the ranch if it got out, and Cole was in no condition to stop it. "Thank you for helping me. You guys saved my life." There was a pause and then Cole asked, "How's your arm?"

"Oh, I think it'll be fine in awhile. I guess I overdid it. Tell me something, Cole, who's Red?"

"That's a long story. I'm not rightly sure, but I'll tell you about Red as long as both of you swear to me that, for now, you will keep it a secret— I'll tell you both why as soon as I can."

Allen and Julie nodded in agreement.

"He's a guy who lives up there off the land. He looks and acts about ninety percent wild." Cole went on to tell Allen and Julie the majority of the story, conveniently leaving out the cabins and the old mine.

Cole turned his head toward Julie and asked, "Remember that day we went riding and found that cabin and heard wolves? Well, Red, as I call him, is a perfect match for the footprint we found in the mud. Red helped me a lot. If it wasn't for him, I wouldn't have made it. The guy's head looks like it's been damaged in an accident or something, but he's got to still be really smart, or he couldn't have rigged up that block and tackle set and pulled me off that rock shelf or up to his camp. Smell, my God does he smell. But the funny thing about that was, by the time I left, I was almost getting used to it. He didn't help me get down from his camp, but he sure didn't do anything to stop me either. As I was leaving, he said the first word I had heard him say the whole time. I had turned and asked him if he needed anything, and he said 'Yellie.' I have no idea what that means, so I smiled and left. Whatever yellie is, he sure wanted it."

Julie began to laugh. "What's so funny?" Cole asked, while Allen looked on with a puzzled face.

"Do you remember as a small child eating peanut butter and yellie sandwiches? Well, I bet he does," replied Julie, "He wants jelly!"

The three of them laughed even though it hurt Cole's chest terribly.

"Were you able to figure out who he is?" Allen asked.

Cole looked at Allen, "Well, I'm not sure, but didn't you tell me something about a Forest Service guy who disappeared?"

"Yeah, it was around fifteen years ago when a guy named Wilson, a wilderness ranger, disappeared. All they found was some blood in the cabin, no body. I'll bet that bear had something to do with this injury, now that I think about it."

"Well, in his belongings I found what looked like an old uniform shirt, all stained, and there was a name tag over the pocket. It was Wilson," Cole said.

"Sounds like Red might be Wilson," Julie said.

"I don't know, but there sure seemed to be a lot of Forest Service tools around Red's camp. But there was a lot of other stuff that could have come from anywhere," responded Cole.

"His size, build, and color of his hair sure match Wilson's, but from what I heard, he was a real sharp thinker, nothing like what you're describing, but possibly the injury changed him," responded Allen. The group talked about Red for a few more minutes, but couldn't come up with proof one way or the other. Cole tried his best to remember and tell the rest of the story, but some parts were blurrier than others, and some parts had to remain secret for now. All the activity exhausted him, and he talked himself to sleep. Four hours later, Cole awoke to see Ballard asleep in the big, comfortable armchair across the room.

"Wake up, you freeloader, this is my room," Cole hollered as loud as he could and paid for it with a sharp pain to his chest. The sound that came out was a far cry from a shout, but the strength in his chest was returning, and it was enough to wake Bob.

Ballard checked his watch. "Sorry, Cole, I've been waiting for a little over two hours, and I must have fallen asleep."

Cole could see by the white band at his neckline that Bob was still wrapped in bandages from busting his ribs on the first go around after the bear. "Well, are you feeling better?"

Ballard laughed. "That's great, just plum great. You're almost dead and asking me how I feel. Cole, what did your mother make you out of, pig iron?"

Cole smiled, then they both chuckled, Ballard reached down and grabbed Cole's hand that stuck out from under the sheet.

"You know, when you first came in, I thought you were going to be some kind of a spoiled brat college kid, but I was wrong, dead wrong. I just want you to know that you can ride with me anytime, and I'm glad you made it, even though what you did was one of the dumbest things I can think of. You going after that bear by yourself," said Ballard. "Hell, I would have gone with you, ribs or no ribs."

The two talked quietly about what happened for a while, and then Cole asked Ballard, "Have you ever owned a bright blue shirt with flowers on the shoulders?" Ballard stared at him for a moment before asking, "Do you know the son of a bitch who stole it?"

"What do you mean, 'stole'?" Cole said.

"Well, I went to the dance in Meeteetse a couple of years back, and I got some blood and beer on it, so when I got home I scrubbed it good and then hung it on a rope up behind the barn so it could dry out. When I came back, it was gone. Some son of a gun stole it, right here on the ranch."

"Well, I think I know who took it," Cole said.

For the next hour Cole retold his story to Ballard, who listened intently. When he was done, Ballard just looked at him for a moment and said, "The hell you say." Then he paused again for almost a minute before continuing, "So you say this feller really stunk? Probably my shirt ain't worth getting back, but boy that was my favorite." Cole smiled and Ballard laughed as Julie interrupted them when she walked into the room with a tray holding a glass of milk and a small sandwich.

Tyler Raines stuck his head through the doorway behind her and said, "Nice to have you back, Cole. Hope you're feeling better." Then he disappeared down the hall.

Over the next week, Cole slept most of the time, while Julie and Sally did most of the work tending to him. He was getting better, but the torn ligaments in his chest were slow to heal. One time, while talking with Wes McCabe, he sneezed, and the pain made tears come to his eyes. Cole had asked Julie to bring some of the books from the library to let him read, specifically ones on engineering and architecture that were no newer than eighteen seventy-five, the date the remodel was done.

Most days, Cole woke up and ate and then would spend several hours reviewing books. During the week, he read the majority of the McCabe's library on both architecture and engineering. He found some books with passages underlined in pencil and then erased. He paid special attention to these and he examined the formerly highlighted areas closely. Allen had once told him that he thought whoever found Gillis McCabe's secret would find the clues right under their nose, and Cole believed with a little work, Allen would be right. Cole read and studied for a few hours after dinner and then fell into a deep sleep.

It was the middle of the night when Julie heard Cole scream. Her room was the closest to his, so she jumped from her bed and headed to him. She turned on the light. Cole lay on the pillow breathing hard, sweat all over his face. As she entered the room, Cole moaned, "No . . . no."

Julie quickly grabbed Cole in her arms and held him, saying, "It's all right, it's all right, I'm here." All of a sudden, Cole opened his eyes. His face was against Julie's chest and he could hear her breathing.

"You're having a nightmare, Cole. Are you all right?" Julie asked gently. For a second, Cole could feel her breast against his cheek, before he pulled back and took a second to clear his head.

"Sorry, I was having another bad dream. That bear was so close I could smell his foul breath. Thanks for getting up. I'm sorry I woke you," Cole said.

"Oh, Cole, you've been through so much. It's no wonder you're having nightmares. I think anyone would." He appreciated her soothing voice and her soft warm body holding him, even if for only a few seconds. He wondered if he would ever get a chance to tell her the truth.

The next day, the warm rays of the sun came through the window, as Julie brought a tray of food and a book. Julie helped Cole eat, even though in the last couple of days his strength had come back enough that he probably could have done it himself. They visited all the way through breakfast, and Julie told him that this was the last book in the engineering section of the library. When Cole was done, Julie said her goodbyes and took the tray back to the kitchen.

Cole lay back on his pillow and opened today's book, *Specialty Locks and Their History*. Cole slowly scanned the pages until he got to Chapter Fourteen, Secret Locks. The title had a penciled star beside it, and a quick scan of the chapter showed where numerous pencil marks had been erased, scuffing the page. The chapter explained dropping ball valves and how to hide a lock. It detailed the value of different key lengths and how long keys effectively prevented unwanted parties from having access to the actual lock. There was a special paragraph about the difficulty of hiding long keys. Cole read the chapter twice and then set the book down beside his bed to reread the next day. He was about to take a nap, when there was a knock on the open door. It was Sheriff Burris.

"Cole, nice to see you're alive and kicking. From what I've heard, that bear came within a hair of killing you, son."

Cole was happy to see Sheriff Burris. His well-trimmed beard and gentle manner hid the high energy that the sheriff threw into everything he did. "Well, Sheriff, it's nice to see you, too," Cole quietly laughed. "Have you found the identity of the pilots yet?"

"To tell you the truth, while you were hunting bears, I went down to Nebraska and hunted pilots—so, yes, I have. But I'm not sure I've really solved anything. It appears the pilots of our plane were named Dunn— Leroy and Thelma Dunn. They owned a large ranch in northwest Nebraska in isolated farm country. We, well at least the guys that were working on it in Missouri, identified all the numbers on the tail section, and with the other clues, they traced the plane from the manufacturer to the Dunns. We went to the nearest town, which was thirty miles away, and the storekeeper remembered them. He said they quit coming in the store nearly four years ago, and he hadn't seen either of them since. When we drove into their ranch, we found it was large but had seen better days. The foreman came out, and we introduced ourselves and started asking questions.

"It appears that the Dunns left the ranch in their plane and never returned. The foreman didn't know where they were headed, but he did tell us that he was told to not talk about their trip to anyone, and he hadn't until then. According to him, they had done very well on their ranch and had bought the plane just before the stock market crashed. Apparently, they lost almost everything. The foreman didn't seem to know anything else. But the Dunns had a contact wherever they were headed. The fact that we found their bodies seemed to change everything for the guy. He volunteered that they had a twenty-year-old son, who had left about a year before they did and only wrote once in a while to organize things. The son's letters came from Cody."

"Cody, really"

Sheriff Burris nodded. "We talked about the plane and what they thought was going on with the son's letters. Later, we talked with the local sheriff about what we found, and he said he would look into everything he could. According to him, the Dunn family pretty much kept to themselves most of the time. They had a huge ranch and a big house, and from what I could find out, their family showed up in those parts some time after the Civil War.

"But unlike most post-war people, they had more money than they knew what to do with. Sheriff Davis said he knew a couple of old timers that might be able to tell him more, and if he found out anything else, he would write."

"Thanks, Sheriff," Cole said, as Burris finished and left the room.

Chapter 23

Cole had been in bed for eight days and was beginning to reap the benefits of the great care he was receiving. His body was healing, and though he had numerous extremely painful spots, it was tolerable for the most part. Cole found himself changing positions more often. His chest didn't hurt nearly as much with just normal breathing. How he had made it down the mountain to the meadow where he had tied Patch was simply a miracle. At the time he had had no idea how badly he was hurt, which was probably a good thing.

Julie walked into the room and greeted him. "How's my cowboy today?"

Cole had enjoyed being with her. Everyday they would spend at least a couple hours talking, and Cole was beginning to feel a bond. He wondered if she were feeling it too. It was late afternoon on what Julie told him was a Saturday. She said she needed to go get ready for something, so he asked, "What?" Cole found that even when he closed his eyes he saw Julie, and the thought of her with John Prentice was more painful than living with the pain of the accident. He tried not to think about it.

Julie said goodbye and planted a soft kiss on Cole's cheek. It was the first time she had shown any physical affection toward him, but Cole didn't know what it meant.

Some time after she left him, there was a knock on the front door and Cole heard Tyler say, "Good evening, Mr. Prentice. I assume you're here for Miss Julie?"

Cole heard the door close and some muffled conversation, but nothing he could understand. He heard Wes greet John and something about a loan, but they seemed to be walking away from Cole's room, and he couldn't make out anything more. When they returned, Wes said he would go and see if Julie was ready. A few minutes later Cole heard Julie greet Prentice with, "What did you say to my father?" Then they walked out of range. Shortly afterwards he heard the door close and there was silence in the house.

Cole turned his head. Images of Julie in Prentice's arms danced in his mind until he fell asleep. Several hours later he was awakened by Julie yelling, "Who do you think you are, telling me what to do? Get out!" The main door slammed, followed by the sound of footsteps climbing the stairs toward Julie's room, where another door slammed.

A bird chirping on a limb outside his window awakened Cole. For the first time in a while he had slept through the night, though it bothered him that something had gone on with Julie. Tyler brought him breakfast that morning: bacon, eggs, toast, jelly, and a glass of milk. "Good morning, Cole. I hope you slept well last night."

"Yes, I did. I'm starting to feel a lot better, probably due to the great care I've been receiving. By the way, where's Julie? She normally brings me breakfast."

"There's been a slight problem, so I will be helping you for awhile until you get better. Mr. McCabe believes it would be more appropriate for you to be moved back to the bunkhouse tomorrow," Tyler said.

Cole didn't know what to think. He had almost felt like one of the family, and now, just barely able to stand, he was being put in the isolation of the bunkhouse. What happened? It was a long morning without Julie's visit, and the whole house felt different. That afternoon, Cole heard the doorknocker and Tyler opening the door. He heard soft voices at first indistinct and later he heard Julie's voice. She was greeting someone cheerfully and they went into another room and closed the door. An hour later Tyler walked into Cole's room and said, "Mrs. Schmitz and her granddaughter are here and would like to see you, if you are feeling well enough for visitors."

"Sure, bring them in. I'd love to see them."

Seconds later Martha walked through the door followed by Suzie, who hurried around her grandmother to the other side of the bed and gave Cole a hug. Martha sat down on the near side of the bed, holding a cane in one hand.

"Cole, we're so happy you're all right. If we would have ever thought that bear was gonna—" a clunking noise from outside of the room interrupted Suzie.

Cole pointed at the hallway. "Why don't you close the door, Suzie? I need to talk to you and your grandmother." Suzie got up and peered into the empty hallway, shut the door, and returned to her chair.

"Sure sounded like someone was out there, but I didn't see anyone," she said as she sat down. Cole told them the whole story, including the cabins and Red, leaving nothing out. The two women were amazed and terrified at the way the bear had stalked both Cole and Jay like prey.

"It feels so good to finally share the whole story with someone. Everyone thinks I was a fool who went hunting that bear by myself. I wouldn't mind hunting that bear, but not alone," Cole said.

"We know you didn't do it for yourself and I know if everyone knew the true story, they'd think different of you. We wanted to give you some time before we came to visit. We heard you were really in bad shape, that you almost died," Martha said.

"Well, I didn't. But I hope I never go through something like that again. I think I found the mine, or at least I'm very close. It's no wonder no one has found that canyon. It's completely hidden by steep cliffs, and the trail is almost impossible to find unless you know exactly where it is. Even then, it's darn hard to follow at first. I'm amazed that Jay ever stumbled upon it. You could have ridden by that spot a hundred times and never suspected there was a trail there, especially before the lightning took out that clump of spruce."

Martha held Cole's hand. "Suzie and I have talked, and we don't want you going back up there. It's too dangerous."

"I won't be going for awhile. It's going to be at least a month until I can get around, and by then the trail will be snowed shut, if it hasn't already been by now."

"We don't want anything to happen to you," Martha said, and Suzie nodded. They talked for a few more minutes about Cole's ordeal, then Martha handed him the cane she was carrying. "By the way, Julie wanted you to borrow this until they can get into town and get you a new one," said Martha.

Cole studied the old cane and it looked familiar. It was polished a rich dark brown with a metal cougar's head on the top. "Isn't this Julie's great grandfather's cane?"

"Yes, it is, and she wants you to use it. It's very special to her," Martha replied.

"Well, why didn't she bring it down herself and give it to me?" Cole asked.

Suzie answered. "There's a problem with John Prentice. He doesn't like you at all. He told Wes McCabe to move you to the bunkhouse with all the other hired men, and he doesn't want Julie seeing you."

"When did he start calling the shots for the ranch?" Cole asked.

"He and Julie are getting married in four months, and he's taking over the day-to-day operations."

"Wait a minute, why?"

"Because the McCabes owe the bank a whole lot of money with interest and Wes doesn't have it. So Prentice is taking over now as opposed to later. It's got everyone upset."

"When's the note due?" Cole asked.

"I'm not sure, but I heard it's within a couple of months of the wedding, or at least sometime around then."

"So Prentice is really putting the pressure on, is he?"

"Yes, unfortunately you're right. I don't know what anyone can do about it either," Martha muttered.

They talked for a while longer, catching Cole up on other news from town. Martha said they needed to be heading back before dark, got up from her chair, and started walking with Suzie toward the closed door. Before she reached the door, though, Martha stopped and faced Cole. "You once asked me if I remember Gillis McCabe ever doing anything strange while I worked for him. Well, I did remember something. It may be nothing at all, but I thought you might be interested. It was the first week on the job and I wanted to make a good impression, so I thought I would go up on the third floor and clean the floors without being told. Well, I started to work and noticed what appeared to be a stain behind the door at the far end of the hallway, so I decided to start there. I opened the door and knelt down on the floor with the door partially open, and I started scrubbing. Then I heard footsteps and peeked around the door to see who it was, and it was. Gillis McCabe opening the door that led to the attic. He looked my direction, but I must have been in the shadows, for he didn't see me. For about ten minutes I waited for him to come down, but he didn't. I decided to ask him if he wanted anything else cleaned up there. Gillis had blown out the candles, so I relit them and took one up the stairs to the top door. I opened it and it was dark, so I called to Mr. McCabe, but he didn't answer.

"I walked in and looked around the room. There was only one window, but it was bolted shut. Mr. McCabe wasn't there, he had just disappeared. So I took the candle and walked back down the stairs, closed the door behind me, and went to the bottom landing, blew out the candles and went back to my cleaning. I was beginning to think I was seeing things when about twenty minutes later I hear another noise, and I peered around the door again. I saw Mr. McCabe holding a candle and shutting the door to the attic steps. Then he went back downstairs. I never asked anyone about the attic, nor did I ever go up there again until several years after Gillis McCabe died in that robbery over in Powell."

"Wow, that's quite a story," Cole said. "Thanks."

"I had to dig deep to remember it, but somehow it just popped back in my mind the other day, and I thought you needed to know. Maybe it'll help." Martha smiled and left with Suzie.

About five o'clock, Tyler hurriedly brought Cole a dinner tray with mashed potatoes and butter and ham cut in small pieces. It smelled good and tasted better. Cole talked to Tyler for a while after dinner when he wasn't so busy with the family. The meal made Cole feel full and tired, he drifted off to sleep early in the evening. Cole slept well for most of the night, but then the giant bear visited him again with its horrid breath and roar. Cole was running, running, running, and then he was awake.

"It's all right, it's all right, Cole, I'm here." It was Julie, and she was holding him in her arms. Cole felt the sweat on his face, and he was panting from the terror. The embarrassment he felt at Julie rescuing him from a nightmare was soon forgotten, as he enjoyed feeling of her arms around him. There was no more special woman in the world, and he enjoyed every moment of her touch. "Are you okay, Cole?" she asked in a soft, soothing voice.

Cole looked up without speaking, and then he kissed her lips. At first she stiffened a little, but then she held him tighter and kissed him back tenderly. Never had Cole experienced such a kiss, and it made him feel like he was on top of the world.

Then Julie pulled back and smiled. "I shouldn't have let you do that. I'm engaged."

"I know, but I'm not sorry. I wanted to do that from the first time I met you," confessed Cole.

"I have to go. Dad says I'm not to spend time with you, and he'd be furious if he found me here. I'll try and come see you in the bunkhouse." She got up to leave, then turned back around and planted a gentle kiss on Cole's cheek before she slipped out the door.

It took Cole several hours to fall back to sleep, and when he did, his dreams were full of Julie, with John Prentice laughing and laughing at him. Morning seemed to take forever to come. "Good morning, Cole. Did you sleep well?" asked Tyler as he entered the room with a breakfast tray.

Cole only smiled and nodded.

"After breakfast we are moving you back to the bunkhouse. It's wonderful you've recovered enough. We're all happy you're feeling better."

"Yeah, that's fine," answered Cole.

Tyler nodded and left the room, leaving Cole alone with his thoughts. At least he would be around the men again, and it was time for him to start pushing himself.

About an hour after breakfast, Elmer and Dodge showed up at the door to move Cole, and with one on each arm they carefully moved him back to the bunkhouse. Cole had recovered some of his strength, and his wounds were slowly healing. The two brought Cole to his bunk with a newly built table beside it for him to keep his things within easy reach. The men carefully helped Cole, but he was getting better and was able to swing his leg and use his good arm to help with the process of getting into bed. Elmer walked in behind them with about eight books.

"What's all them for?" Dodge asked.

"Julie says he likes 'em," responded Elmer. "She wanted me to bring them over with this cane, so I did." They talked for a while and then said they needed to get back to work, but Chin would be over with lunch.

After all the activity and chatter, it was stone cold quiet, and Cole felt alone and abandoned. He decided he couldn't afford to feel sorry for himself, though, because there was too much to do. He grabbed a book on fireplaces and thermal mass, and with the aid of old Gillis' cane, struggled to the chair beside his bed and began reading by the light coming from the window above the chair. For the next three days, he read from the books and studied their contents. He was fascinated by a book on passages and hidden locks, with its descriptions of hidden rooms and their designers. Several days later, one passage in particular caught his attention. It said unusual keys required unusual, but accessible hiding places.

One thing that had surprised Cole about Gillis' hidden booty, as Julie called it, was that no one had ever found a key. Now Cole wondered if Gillis had hidden the key the same way he hid the opener to the compartment in his study in plain sight. After hearing Martha's story about seeing Gillis going into the attic, he just knew there must be a doorway to a secret treasure room in there somewhere. Maybe, just maybe, it opened like the study, with a magnet. The original black horse magnet was still in the McCabe's hallway, and it would be easy to test his theory if he used someone capable of lifting the head and have them run it all over the room. He might be wrong, but he had to give it a try.

The next morning he asked Elmer and Dodge if they could help him for an hour, and they had agreed, though they didn't yet know what they were in for.

"What are we doing?" Elmer asked as the two of them helped Cole to the front door.

"You'll find out," Cole said, as he hit the doorknocker on the McCabe's front door. This time Wes answered.

"Cole, good morning, what can I do for you?"

"Well…" Cole paused for a couple of seconds. "I have another theory on your grandfather's secret room, and I was wondering if I could come in."

There was a slight hesitation, then Wes stepped aside and with his arm motioned them in. "What's your idea?" he asked, as Julie and her mother came around the corner.

"What's going on" Sally asked.

"Cole thinks he knows where grandfather hid his treasure." Wes had more than a little skepticism in his voice.

"Dad, he found Great Grandfather's cash box in his study. You should at least hear what he has to say," Julie said.

"I'm sorry, you're right. It's just that people have been looking for that room for the last sixty years, and no one has found a clue. I don't know why Cole thinks he can find it after being here for seven months."

"Can we at least see if I'm right?"

"Well all right" muttered Wes after a slight pause.

"Elmer, would you grab that black horse head door stopper and take it up to the attic?" Cole asked. Dodge helped him move to the staircase, while Elmer nodded and started up the main stairs.

"I have to apologize, but I'm going to need some help making it to the attic. My leg is still bothering me and sometimes it goes out on me," Cole said.

"Sure, Cole, I'll be glad to," responded Wes, as he put Cole's arm over his shoulder and helped Dodge get him up the stairs, step by step. Once the group reached the attic, Cole asked Elmer to take the head, with the help of the rope Cole brought, and to move it systematically across the floor. After thirty minutes the large magnet had found nothing, and Cole had Elmer go carefully over the fireplace, which reacted to nothing except for the metal bands that were used to structurally hold the chimney intact.

"I'm sorry, Wes. I was darn sure I'd find it," Cole said.

"I think we're all disappointed," Wes said. "A lot of people have thought they knew where it was, and everyone has failed. Let me help you back down the stairs, and then I have some important things I need to do," Wes said. His emphasis on "important things" was not lost on Cole or Julie. She lowered her head, obviously bothered by her father's lack of faith in Cole.

Elmer and Ballard helped Cole back down the stairs and over to the bunkhouse, where he sat on the porch bench. Elmer went in and brought out Cole's cane, gave it to him, and said, "Sorry, Cole. I wish you had found it for everyone's sake. But here's your cane, in case you get tired and need to get back to your bunk. I need to get back to work now, sorry."

Cole ignored him, taking the cane and staring straight ahead. He had been sure he would find the door.

He sat there with both hands on the cane and stared into the courtyard, trying to figure out what he had missed. When Allen had said the solution would probably be right in front of everyone, he was right. That horse head doorstopper had been in front of everyone for over fifty-five years, and not one person had thought it was the key to finding the secret stash in the study. Gillis McCabe was able, in a matter of seconds, to lock the door, move the horse head, open the trap door, and get his cash box. Now he was sure the key wasn't a magnet, but what was it?

Cole fiddled with the cane in his hands as he blankly stared toward the house, then something snapped and he thought he had broken it. In his frustration, he had squeezed the cane, and something had come loose. The wooden shaft that connected the bronze cougar head had separated slightly. The head appeared to be connected to the shaft by a small leather strip decorated with small brass tacks. Cole looked down and felt terrible for breaking Julie's great grandfather's antique cane.

His first thought was maybe he could repair it, so he carefully examined the damage. One brass tack wasn't a tack at all, but some sort of ball bearing that, when pushed down, released the shaft of the cane from the head. Cole slowly and carefully separated the brass head from the wooden shaft and found a narrow metal rod connected to the cougar head that extended nearly a foot into the shaft. Cole laid the wooden shaft at his feet and looked at the cougar head and rod. Looking at it on end, the metal rod was shaped like a star and kept the head from rotating on top of the wooden shaft. Cole thought for awhile, trying to find what was tickling his memory. Then he remembered, when he was in bed looking at the picture of Gillis in Chicago, he had had a very different cane—one with a shaft of what looked like bird's eye maple and it had a hog's head for decoration.

Cole needed to talk with Martha Schmitz immediately. He hobbled into the mess house and took a seat by Ballard, who already had half his meal eaten. "Ballard, I need a favor. I know tomorrow is Saturday and you're probably busy, but I was wondering if we could take my truck and drive me over to Martha Schmitz's ranch. I desperately need to talk to her."

Ballard looked up from his plate and smiled. "You bet, I'm always ready to help, for a small fee." They both laughed.

"Your ribs must finally be feeling better," Cole said.

Ballard responded with a chuckle. "It only hurts when I laugh." They both laughed even harder.

Early the next morning, Cole hobbled to his truck, which Ballard had parked at the front of the bunkhouse. They talked about the bear, Red and what changes would occur when Prentice took over the ranch. Everyone knew about the note, and it was no secret that Prentice would likely be taking control of The Greybull soon. Soon they were in front of the Schmitz ranch and headed toward the porch. Phil Schmitz was sitting on the porch as usual and greeted the two by name. At almost ninety, he got around well and was still plenty sharp to talk to. After the proper greetings, they entered and found Martha starting a pot of coffee, something Cole needed since the two had missed breakfast.

Cole and Ballard walked over to the table and took a seat.

"So what brings you over here first thing in the morning?" Martha asked. The last time they had talked at The Greybull, Cole hadn't noticed how slow her movements had become. But her mental wit was as sharp as the day she and Phil had tied the knot.

"Martha, I really need to know something. When you worked for Gillis McCabe, did he always carry a cane? And did he have that cane when you saw him go into the attic?"

Martha adjusted her hair. "Wow, that's going back a ways. Let me think." Several minutes went by, and then she looked at Cole and said, "Gillis always had a limp. I think he hurt his leg in a riding accident about three years before I got there. And as I remember, I never saw him without that cane."

"One last question before we have to leave. When you were little, did you ever hear of the Dunn family?" Cole asked.

"Dunns? Yes, there was a Dunn family that lived up the valley. I never met 'em, but they owned ground at the far end of the valley. Gillis must have bought their ranch, because it's now part of The Greybull. They sold out when I was young, and the only reason I remember them is my dad used to tell me if I walked around the back of the horses and spooked him I could get kicked and killed like the Dunn boy. I don't know if that's the same family, but they're the only Dunns I know that lived in these parts." Martha finished and refilled the men's coffee cups.

The four visited for another ten minutes, and then Cole and Ballard headed back to the ranch. Cole spent most of the drive silently mulling things over, but finally Ballard interrupted him and asked, "I don't mean to crowd you, but what are you thinking?"

Cole smiled. "I know where and how to find Gillis McCabe's secret treasure room, and this time I'm sure."

Chapter 24

On the drive into Meeteetse, Ballard continued to quiz Cole for more information about the secret room, but all Cole would say is, "When it's time." They arrived at the Red Rooster twenty minutes later and ordered breakfast. Ballard gave up on finding out anything more until Cole was good and ready, and he took his frustrations out on two large plates of eggs, toast, and bacon. When their plates were clean, Cole picked up the hefty bill with the same hand that held his cane, hobbled to the cash register, and paid the older waitress who had served them. With one hand holding a cane and the other arm broken and in a sling, Cole didn't look like much of a cowboy as he hobbled toward the truck.

On the way back to the ranch, the conversation returned to Prentice's takeover and what life would be like under his watch. Greybull Ranch had been a lot of men's livelihood, men who dedicated their lives to working for the brand, something Bob was sure Prentice knew nothing about. Bob shared that the men had been talking about something going on at the ranch for the last week. Prentice had shown up twice and both times walked with Wes around the grounds in intense discussion. "Rumors are flying high, and I sure wish I knew more. I'm pretty sure a number of men won't be working for Prentice, either by his choice or theirs," Bob said, as they turned the corner at the fork in the road that led to the ranch.

"Yeah, I know," Cole hesitated for a moment. "If you don't mind, just let me off in front of the bunkhouse, park my truck out back, and leave the keys in her." Cole paused for a second. "And thanks for helping me this morning. I know I've been more than a little trouble for some."

Ballard smiled.

Cole climbed out of the truck, and with the help of the cane, made his way back to the bench on the porch of the bunkhouse. His leg felt stronger, but the combination of the deep bruise and the cut had caused him some real pain. It hadn't seemed to heal nearly as fast as some of his other wounds. It had been almost three weeks since the men had packed him down from the mountain, and he was sure by now that all the high trails were snowed shut and would be until late spring. Even if he were healthy, he still couldn't make it to the mine—even if he could find it. Not to mention he didn't know if the gold existed or not, because he hadn't seen one ounce of gold from this mine. He had only heard stories, but so far, what he had found matched Martha's memories.

Cole wearily sat down on the weathered bench on the porch of the bunkhouse, tired but full of thought. He knew Wes was no longer going to jump for joy if he asked for one more try. Life on The Greybull was changing fast, and Cole was frustrated and angry that he couldn't figure out what to do. Julie's wedding to Prentice was scheduled for early spring, at least a month before he would be able to get back up the mountain and into the secret canyon. If he did find a gold mine by then it would be on Greybull property, and Prentice would own the ranch.

Cole scratched his broken arm inside the sling. The bright purple had started to fade and Cole felt much better than the first time he awoke back at the ranch. The doctor had taken off the splint and put on a cast, and that had helped tremendously. The morning of extended activity had worn him out, and he was tired of fighting an uphill battle to save the ranch. Maybe it would be best if he left. But if he didn't try, then Julie would suffer the most. Did she love Prentice, or was she just trying to be the perfect daughter and save the ranch through marrying him? Had the early morning kiss really meant something, or was it just a fleeting romantic moment? He didn't know, but he did know he loved her. After another thirty minutes, he convinced himself that he had to try one more time.

At that moment, John Prentice drove into the driveway and parked his Master Deluxe touring car. Cole had to admit the vehicle was beautiful and impressive, far better than anything he could ever buy. Prentice got out and cut a fine figure in a fitted blue suit. Cole could see why some women might love the guy, while here he sat, barely able to walk, with a broken arm and bandages on his head, and bruises on most of his body. The doctor had told him that he could probably take the bandages off his head in another couple of days, but he would like to check the progress first and make sure it had healed well enough to be exposed. Cole had never felt so down and frustrated, yet he knew he had to continue. He had never quit in his life and he'd be damned if he would now.

* * *

Julie was making the bed in her folks' room on the south side of the house. The room was warm because of the bright sunshine coming through the window. Normally, the large willow that stood in the side yard would have shaded the house, but in winter the tree no longer had leaves and provided little cover. Julie moved to the window, opened it a couple of inches, and thought to herself that she needed to remember to close it when she was finished, or it would be really cold in there that evening when her folks went to bed. The soft, cool breeze felt good as it worked its way into the room as Julie worked.

In the distance, she could hear Timmy's dog barking and wondered who was coming. She changed rooms and looked out the window to see the unmistakable car of John Prentice coming up the driveway. She wondered why it didn't excite her; after all, he was her fiancé and a great catch. She returned to her parents' room and continued making the bed. As she fluffed the pillow, she was distracted by the sound of voices below the window.

Normally, the fairly airtight building didn't allow conversations to drift into the house, but the crisp fall air and open window allowed the sound below to travel easily into the room. Julie slowly and carefully pulled back the curtain and peeked out. Tyler was talking to John Prentice. She pulled back. That's odd, she thought, why would Tyler be talking with John? Her curiosity was too much, and she found herself against the side of the window listening. The voices were surprisingly easy to hear, even though it was obvious that the two men were whispering. "I need to know," said Prentice. "You have to keep me better informed until I take possession."

"I'm trying," responded a frustrated Tyler. "Sometimes it's awkward for me to just barge into a room during a conversation, but I will try and do better."

"Just remember, your daughter's ranch note is still behind, and I've been very lenient with you and your family," barked Prentice.

Then the two moved toward the front door. Moments later, she heard it open, and shortly afterwards she heard her father talking to

John. Was Tyler really spying on the family? Tyler had worked for the ranch almost as long as she had been alive. He couldn't possibly do anything that would hurt her family.

Julie quietly moved out into the hall to the edge of the steps, where she watched her dad and John Prentice walk into the study and close the door. She crept stealthily down the stairs to the study and put her ear to the door.

"Wes, I understand you went to Cody a couple days ago and tried to refinance the ranch with a couple of my competitors. I'd have thought you'd know better by now. We don't stab each other in the back. The banks have good relationships with each other. Everyone knows you can't afford to pay back the money. Hell, this ranch hasn't made a dime since before the drought. No one but me is going to help you. Besides, you're still going to be able to live on the ranch with Julie and me."

Behind Julie, Tyler said, "Miss McCabe, is there anything I can do for you?"

She jumped. "Oh, no I just wanted to know who was here, and I had a question for Dad." She paused. "It can wait." She spun and went back upstairs. At the top landing, she stopped and looked back. Tyler was still standing there with an inquisitive look.

About twenty minutes later, Julie had a knock on her door. "Julie, its John, can you come down and go for a ride? It's a beautiful day." Julie opened the door and did her best to hide her earlier emotions with smiles and charm. The two talked about nothing in particular for a few minutes, put on their coats, then got into the car and took off toward town.

Cole could see John Prentice holding the door open for Julie as she quickly slipped into his car. Staring bleakly forward without a target he thought, what was I thinking? Obviously the two of them were in love and happy, the best thing he could do for everyone was to back away quietly and let whatever will be happen. He felt he was on the verge of making so many things happen. He had fallen in love with not only Julie, but the ranch and the people that made the Greybull what it was. He had needed that connection, but all of a sudden everything had fallen apart. He would try one more time to ask Wes if he could look again.

Cole was about to hobble over to the house, when the door opened and Wes came out, putting on his coat. He stopped for a minute, making eye contact with Cole, then started walking straight toward him, scowling the whole time. He hesitated, and then said brusquely, "Cole, I have some bad news for you. I'm going to have to let you go. I liked you from the moment you came on the ranch when Allen introduced you, but things have changed around here, and I can't do a thing about it. I'll give you a week's extra pay, I'll have one of the men to drive you into town this afternoon and help you get settled in the hotel. I'll pay for your first week's rent, until you feel well enough to travel back to Montana."

"Hold on for a second—you mean I'm fired?"

"Yes, that's one way of putting it. Damn, I hate this whole thing, but they're the cards I've been dealt. I wish things were different, but they're not." Wes extended his hand. Cole looked in his eyes as they shook hands, and he could see the hurt. Then Wes turned and headed toward the barn.

A short time later, Dodge and Elmer walked over to where Cole sat. They stood a moment in front of the porch before Elmer said, "Sorry, Cole, we didn't see this coming. Wes told us to take you into town, and he meant right now. We'll help you pack your things and load them." Cole could tell his good friends were hurt and confused, but the shock of the whole thing hadn't hit him yet, and he was dazed but polite as they loaded his gear. For over seven months he had lived, worked and shared time with these men, and with the drop of a hat, everything was over. His dad had always told him life wasn't fair . . . and he had been right.

Elmer drove Cole into town and talked about quitting and moving on, and he wondered what Dodge thought as he followed them in a ranch truck behind Cole's rig. Once in town, Elmer and Dodge helped Cole up the stairs of the hotel and into his room, then they retrieved his gear. Wes had not asked for the cane back, but Cole planned to return it when he could. Cole sat down on the bed and stared at the ceiling. Probably the thing that bothered him the most was that he didn't even get to say goodbye to anyone, especially Julie and Allen. How could everything have gotten out of whack so quickly? Would his life be nothing but bad from now on?

The room was chilly, and the only window faced the north side alley, which kept it in shadows. The furniture was old and worn, with cigarette marks from past tenants and a large brown stain on the rug. There were two yellowed light fixtures hanging from the ceiling, and with both of them on, the room was still dimly lit. At best, the room was a little dark, at worst, depressing.

Cole spent the next two hours thinking on the bed. He had never felt so depressed, angry, and forgotten as he had being escorted from the ranch like some kind of crook. This had Prentice written all over it. Cole wanted to physically tear him apart, piece-by-piece, until there was nothing more than a pile of bones and blood. Never in his life had he felt so much anger, yet there was little he could do with a bad leg and broken arm, not to mention a beat up body. Finally, he concluded that sitting in the room wasn't going to accomplish anything, so he decided to eat supper at the Red Rooster and think about his future—and maybe think up a plan.

The walk over to the restaurant took awhile and it tired him, but Cole felt better than the week before. He ordered a chicken breast with potatoes smothered in gravy. Even though he didn't feel good emotionally or physically, his body still demanded food. The waitress asked if he needed anything else, but Cole smiled and shook his head no, not really wanting to talk to anyone. His thoughts turned to Julie, Allen and the whole McCabe family and how he had enjoyed his time with them. Even after all that had happened, he still liked Wes and knew this wasn't his doing. Wes simply wasn't a strong man and definitely not a born leader like his grandfather. Finally, Cole made his decision. In a few days, he would pack up and head back to the Bitterroot Valley. He was ready for a fresh start and to hell with this place.

Cole finally finished with dinner and began his tiring journey back across the street to the hotel. The cane helped him balance, and he appreciated having it, even though he hoped he would only need it for another couple of weeks. He wasn't a drinking man, but the saloon was beside the hotel and a whisky sounded good. He hobbled into the bar which was mostly empty because of the early hour. He carefully worked his way over to the large, dark walnut bar and ordered a whisky straight up, planning on one drink and then rest. Cole was admiring the large variety of liquor that the bar stocked, when he heard a familiar voice.

"Well, look who's here boys our good friend, Cole Morgan."

It was John Prentice, Lowell Starr, Jake Prentice and Jake's younger brother. Cole knew things were about to get ugly. He had laid his cane on the counter and picked up the whisky in his free hand, while his other arm hung in the sling. Right then and there Cole decided that no matter the odds, he wasn't going down without a fight. John Prentice walked up within a few feet of Cole and then motioned to his party to clear the room of its few patrons, as if he had done it before. As people hurriedly left the saloon, the bartender reached below the bar.

"I wouldn't do that if I was you," said Prentice. "I'd advise you not to take sides, friend. It could get real bad for your health." Prentice smiled and looked the man straight in the eyes and in a commanding voice said, "Move away from the bar now!"

The bartender backed off.

"Well, Cole, this ain't your day is it?" Prentice stood just out of arm's reach, while the other men had moved to within ten feet of Cole.

"I've been telling the boys how much I'm going to enjoy being a husband to Julie and running the ranch. They sure are excited about their new positions at The Greybull. You know, Jake here is going to be the new ranch manager taking over Allen Skimming's job. Should be a good position for him, don't you think, Cole?" Prentice smiled.

Cole ignored him and sipped his whisky.

"You know, Cole, you look in real poor shape. I think all of us would enjoy this a lot more if you were healthy and could at least throw a punch, but what the hell. There's a rumor out there that you think you can still find Gillis McCabe's secret treasure room. I doubt you could, but if you did somehow it would screw up my plans, and you know I wouldn't appreciate that. My family has been planning for a long time to get that ranch back, and since I told Wes we were pulling the note early, he has to march to a different tune, if you know what I mean."

Behind the Prentice boys, Cole noticed the saloon door quietly open and Allen, Dodge, Ballard, and Elmer slipping into the back of the room. Cole threw back his whisky and said loudly, "Bartender, I think I'll have another. I'm not sure this is going to be a fair fight, John," Cole said as he raised his shot glass and took a small sip of whisky.

"No, but I'm okay with it," Prentice sneered as he turned and looked back at his group of men for their approval. For the first time, he noticed Allen and his group. Prentice hesitated for a moment and then turned to face Cole again. As he turned back, Cole threw his whisky in Prentice's eyes and then, with unbelievable quickness, grabbed the cane's shaft with his good hand. With strength born from pure anger, Cole buried the cane's brass cougar head deep into Prentice's cheek. The sound of breaking bones cracked across the room, as Prentice's eyes rolled back and he collapsed onto the plank floor with a crash. For a second, everyone looked on in astonishment as the right side of Prentice's face was misshapen and squirted blood. Then all hell broke out.

Chapter 25

Prentice's entire gang lay bleeding and unconscious on the floor. Allen had made short work of the largest one, and Dodge and Elmer had finished off the other two.

"Damn it!" said Ballard. "I hate fights this short. I wanted more action."

Cole smiled, limped over to the bartender and offered to pay for the two broken chairs and the large table that lay shattered on the floor. The bartender only smiled and went to the unconscious Prentice, reached into his suit pocket, removed his wallet and took out a hundred dollars. "This'll cover it," he said, as he headed back to the bar. "Now, I think you guys need to get out of here before I call the doctor. I'll tell the sheriff it was self-defense. I never liked these guys, anyway."

Cole thanked him, turned, and headed outside to join the rest of the group. "Thanks, guys. I thought I was dancing solo tonight."

"Hell, we wouldn't let you leave The Greybull Ranch without throwing you a good going away party," laughed Ballard, as he gently slapped Cole on the back.

"So you guys knew Prentice was going to fire me?" Cole asked.

"Hell, yes, we did," answered Allen. "Now let's hurry and get back to the ranch and find that secret room."

Cole was stunned by what had just happened. "What about the McCabes?"

"That's no problem. Wes and Sally are at Martha's visiting Phil. They think he's real sick," answered Allen.

"How bad is he?" Cole asked in a concerned tone.

"Not bad, not bad at all. In fact, he's not sick. We set them up and then came looking for you," replied Allen.

Allen got behind the wheel of Cole's truck, and the rest got in Elmer's old sedan and drove to the ranch. "I need to know a few things," Cole said. "How did you know I was in the bar and needed help?"

"We didn't," Allen said. "We needed to find you fast and everyone but Julie decided to come looking for you. We saw the Prentice group heading into the bar and Elmer said maybe there was a chance you were in there and could use some help. So we sneaked a peek and there you were, in need of a little assistance."

"Julie, you said?"

"Yes sir, this whole thing was her idea. Chin heard one of the boys say that you knew where the secret room was and told Julie. Then Julie found me and told me her plan to get her parents out of the house and you back here. Her parents have been lifelong friends of the Schmitz family, and she knew they would go and help if they were asked. Time is not on our side, and we needed to find you fast and get you back."

"How did Julie find out I thought I knew where the room was?" Cole asked.

"You told Ballard that you were sure you knew, and he told Elmer and Elmer told Dodge and, well somehow it got to Chin, and he told Julie."

"Prentice also said he heard that I knew where the room was. How did he learn that?" Cole asked.

"For that, you can credit Tyler. He's been keeping Prentice informed of everything he hears at the ranch," replied Allen.

"But he's been with the family since Julie was a baby."

"That's true. But Julie heard Tyler telling Prentice about the ranch."

Cole shook his head. "Wow, this is a lot to take in. Is Tyler still at the house?"

"Yes, but Julie and Chin said they would take care of everything and not to worry."

"Okay. We need to get up in the attic and find the secret room as fast as we can. If we can do that, and if there's really money and stocks in there, then it's all good."

Allen smiled, "Pretty much."

For the rest of the ride, Cole sat quietly in the passenger seat, rubbing the cane with his good hand and wondering if his mouth had gotten not only himself, but half the ranch in more trouble than anyone could imagine. Timmy's dog barked as the truck pulled up to the house, and Julie ran out on the porch. As soon as she saw Cole, she raced down the steps and helped him out of the truck, then hugged him so hard he lost his balance and fell against the truck.

"How dare you leave without saying anything to me! I've a good notion to—"

"We don't have time for that," Allen interrupted. "Time's short and you can yell at him later." The crew went through the front door and found Tyler sitting in the middle of the room, tied and gagged in a chair. Behind him sat Chin, arms folded, holding a twelve-inch cast iron frying pan. Chin smiled and waved as the group hurried past him and up the stairs.

Julie helped Cole with the stairs on one side, with Dodge on the other. As they climbed up three flights, Julie asked excitedly, "Do you really know where the room is or are you guessing again?"

Cole looked at her as he worked his way higher, "Hell yes I know, just get me up there." He only wished he were as confident as he sounded.

"I'll carry the cane," said Elmer, observing that it was obviously not helping the two assisting Cole.

"Okay, but keep it close," Cole replied. We'll need it in a minute."

After much effort, sweat and help, Cole breathlessly entered the attic. Dodge, who was helping to pull Cole up, turned on the lights. Cole had not planned on how dimly lit the room would be at night, and he hoped it wouldn't be a problem. "Can one of you go down and get a flashlight?" Cole asked.

"I know where they are. I'll get them," responded Julie, and she hurried back down the stairs.

Allen turned to Ballard and said, "Go with her just in case."

"In case of what"

"I don't know, just in case."

Ballard shrugged and followed her down the stairs.

Cole stared at the fireplace and then turned to the group and pointed to the wide metal strip that banded the huge hearth and chimney. "See the six inch metal band? If I'm correct, one of those rivet tops is fake. What I want you to do is try to move each one. One of them should pop out." The group quickly got to work, aided in the dim light by the three flashlights that Julie and Ballard brought up.

"I think I got something!" Elmer shouted, and everyone rushed to see.

A rivet head was shaded from the light. Cole limped over and said, "Let me take a look." The large brick fireplace, like everything else Gillis McCabe had built, was ornate, with recessed panels of brick every four feet to give the wall more visual impact. The loose rivet was directly over one of those slightly recessed panels. Cole felt the rivet. It seemed to be attached at the top but with a little pressure swung to one side exposing a round, dark hole.

"Let's see your flashlight," Cole said to Ballard.

With it Cole peered into the hole but couldn't see anything. "Hand me the cane!" Cole shouted, and Elmer hurriedly gave it to him. Cole pushed on the one ball bearing that released the cane's head and separated it from the shaft.

Julie exclaimed, "The cane! The cane is Great Grandfather's key, isn't it?"

Cole smiled and inserted the metal shaft into the hole and worked it for a few seconds. Finally, it seemed to pop in another inch or so with a click. Then he tried to turn the brass cougar head, but it wouldn't budge.

"What the heck's going on?" Ballard asked.

"I don't know," responded Cole. "Maybe I—" His sentence was interrupted by the sound of a car's tires driving over gravel and a screech as it stopped the front of the house. Julie raced down the stairs, looked out the window and returned while everyone remained still.

"It's my parents, they're back."

For a minute there was only silence in the room while everyone tried to figure out what to do, but it was Ballard who stepped forward. "I haven't come this far to stop now." With that, he grabbed the brass cane head with both hands and turned. In the silent room, the sound of the click was like a gunshot. Everyone waited with anticipation, but the click didn't cause anything to open. Suddenly, Wes McCabe's voice could be heard in the great foyer, upset and yelling at Chin.

In panic, Julie looked at Cole. "Just get the damn thing open! I'll delay Dad for as long as I can." She left and took off downstairs.

Cole turned to Allen and blankly said, "I'm not sure what to do now." He looked pale and exhausted, and Allen knew he needed to step in, and step in fast.

"Back away," Allen shouted, as he took his boot and kicked with all his weight into the hollow area created by the recessed brick.

"What's going on up here?" shouted Wes McCabe, as he stormed into the room, Sally on his heels. Everyone looked at Wes and then back to where Allen had just kicked. A panel of brick four feet by four feet had pivoted eighteen inches into the fireplace, exposing a small brick-lined passage. Wes burst through the group, freezing when he saw the open brick door and the passageway. He looked at Cole. "What's this?"

"Cole found the secret room," Julie explained. "Sorry we tricked you. It's my fault, but I knew Cole would find it."

Wes stared at the floor as he listened. Finally he raised his head and looked at Julie, then Cole. "I'm the one that needs to apologize. But why do you have Chin guarding Tyler downstairs?"

"Dad, Tyler's been spying for John."

"Yeah, we didn't want any snakes spoiling the evening, so to speak," said Ballard.

"Wow," Wes said. "I wouldn't believe this if I wasn't seeing it with my own eyes." He turned to Cole. "Lead on."

Cole had dreamed of this moment so many times since he had come to the ranch, and now after finding the hidden passage, he wasn't sure he was strong enough to continue. Ballard could tell Cole was fading and stepped forward, looked at Cole, and said, "This is your ride, and I aim to take you on it even if I have to carry you on my back."

"You just may," Cole said with a tortured smile. With all his heart and energy, Cole wanted to go, but he wasn't sure he could make it. "Help me. I need to do this."

"Don't worry, you'll be fine," said Ballard, as he pushed the heavy door open wider. The passage was made entirely of brick, the ceiling arched and full of dusty cobwebs that hung to the floor. Allen led with a flashlight and began knocking the cobwebs down with Cole's cane as he entered the walkway. Elmer entered next with one hand on Cole's arm and the other one free to balance and carry the flashlight. Ballard followed, supporting Cole's other arm. A deep layer of dust and grit lay undisturbed on the floor. The hallway ended after ten feet at the edge of a rusty set of circular stairs. The air smelled stale and everything was dusty, but it wasn't cold.

The metal stairs were sturdily built, and Allen thought there was no risk to descend them one person at a time. The old stairway creaked and moaned from lack of use as Allen slowly walked down the first three steps. He stopped and shook the railing, but again everything seemed solid and secure, and Dodge agreed that time hadn't damaged its integrity. For eight continuous circles, the stairway spiraled down the tight, cobweb filled space, falling three floors and then more to well below the house's foundation.

Allen reached the bottom as Julie, Wes and Dodge started down. The landing was wide, and an old, rusted lantern hung on the brick wall to one side. Directly across was the beginning of another passage, with a large chunk of granite sitting in the center of a roughly built brick arch. Allen took a few steps inside to make room for the people coming down the stairs. It took some effort, but finally Elmer and Ballard were able to help Cole reach the bottom.

"This is quite the journey," said Dodge from the stairway above, and everyone laughed, breaking the tension. Dust from the stairs drifted down on the ones already at the landing, causing them to cough and sputter. Allen decided to continue down the stone passage instead of waiting for the others. The hallway went straight for about fifty feet and then took a lazy right hand turn and ended at a large wooden door with heavy metal braces across the top and bottom.

Allen tried the door and was surprised that it opened with little effort. Inside he found a large room, twenty feet by twenty feet with a ten-foot ceiling. There were dozens of boxes and a pile of neatly stacked papers in one corner. Everywhere he looked there was something of interest. One wall looked like a pegboard with holes every eight inches from floor to the ceiling, each containing a bottle. A number of large candles adorned the walls, and Allen took out a match and lit several that brightened the room almost immediately.

Finally, everyone had entered the room and was looking at all the unique items. Julie moved to one side of the room and raised her voice, "Cole, Dad, look—an old filing cabinet."

Wes deliberately brushed the dust off the file case door, uncovering a yellowed tab labeled "Stocks." He opened the drawer with a squeak. "Wow, look at all the certificates. There must be over a hundred in this drawer alone." They were yellowed with age, but in prime condition.

Elmer's attention was drawn to bottles in the peg wall. After removing several and dusting them off with his shirt, he said, "I don't know much about wine, but this Scotch is premium and it's got to be at least sixty years old."

Dodge walked into the room and bumped into an old rifle leaning against the wine case, but he caught it before it fell. He cocked it open and noticed it was loaded.

Wes turned to Allen. "I need everything that looks like a stock or a bond to be boxed up to take to the stock broker in Cody tomorrow. Prentice told me yesterday that he was calling my note next week, but nothing was in writing. I don't want Prentice to know about us finding the room until after we have the stock broker value this."

Cole, who was sitting on a dusty bench looking pale, perked up and said, "Wes, I'm pretty sure you don't need to worry about Prentice for a least the next couple of days. He and I came to an arrangement."

Wes turned to Allen and said, "Now, what does he mean by that?"

"Cole whacked him pretty good in the chin" said Allen and then he went on to explain the bar fight.

"Is John dead?" Julie asked.

"No, but I'd guess he might want to be for a couple of weeks. I'm pretty sure Cole broke half the bones in his face. I don't imagine he'll bother anyone for quite awhile," grinned Dodge.

Elmer went upstairs to get boxes, while the others kept searching through the dusty room.

"Wow, look at this," Dodge said as he took a small metal box from an open safe and raised it up to waist level. "This room is so hidden; Gillis didn't even lock his safe." Dodge laughed as he carefully opened the box to expose a pile of old twenty, fifty and hundred dollar bills. Julie screamed with delight as he emptied the bills onto the desk. When they counted it, they found fifteen thousand dollars in all. Cole noticed some maps that lay above a cabinet beside the desk, but didn't have the energy to examine them yet.

Ballard clapped Cole on his good shoulder and said, "I thought I'd seen everything, but I never imagined a room like this!"

"I had given up ever finding my family's money," Wes said, "I don't know how to thank you." Cole only smiled as the group continued to comb through the room's treasure for several hours before calling it a night.

"I don't think this old room will give up all its secrets tonight," Wes said, "but Allen and I need to be out of here and headed to Cody with all the stocks by four o'clock tomorrow morning. Julie, will you and Dodge help Cole up to bed in the guest room? It's the best I can do for the man who may have saved the ranch."

Julie and Dodge helped an exhausted Cole back up the long staircase to the attic and then back down to the first floor. All Cole remembered was putting his head on the pillow, and then the room was full of sunshine; a lone sparrow chirped in a bush outside his window in the mid morning sun.

* * *

Hours earlier, Wes and Allen had left for Cody.

"You sure have a lot of stocks," commented Allen, as he drove toward Cody. "I would have thought you'd be more excited than you are, considering what happened."

"I'm a little worried," replied Wes.

"What about?"

"Well, those stocks are mighty old, and a lot of companies have gone down since 1929. I don't have any idea whether we have anything of value here. I didn't recognize many company names when I scanned the first bunch."

* * *

Back at The Greybull, Ballard waited until noon to open the door and finally let a tired and angry Tyler out of the barn stall. Ballard looked at him and said, "Why'd you do it, Tyler? The McCabes trusted you. You were a member of their family."

"I had to. Prentice threatened to take my daughter and her family's ranch if I didn't keep him informed. He was blackmailing us, and now I've lost everything."

With that, Ballard drove Tyler to Meeteetse with a single suitcase and left him standing in the snow staring at the departing pickup with The Greybull's lazy G logo.

Chapter 26

On the way to Cody, Wes and Allen talked about their years together and what had happened to them and the ranch. "You know, Cole has been one of the best things that ever happened to this ranch. He has new ideas and ain't afraid to try them," Allen said.

"I'm ashamed to say, I was going to let her marry that bastard, just so we could stay on the ranch. You know, I seriously doubt that would have worked. Julie told me she really didn't love him, and I told her it was normal to have doubts about marriage. I feel like a first class jerk, putting the ranch ahead of her happiness. How could I have done that?"

The firm Stamper, Stamper, and Stamper didn't open for another ten minutes, so Allen and Wes waited in the car. Wes knew Harold Stamper through a mutual acquaintance, and even though he hadn't talked to him for over two years, he considered him a friend.

"Do you think we've got anything really valuable in there?" Allen asked, hoping to hear at least something a little more positive.

"I didn't recognize any names, but I only went through the first box," replied Wes.

He was looking at one of the stocks, when Allen noticed a lady flipping the sign in the door from CLOSED to OPEN.

"It's show time," Allen said. He got out of the car and opened the back door to unload the boxes.

"We should know pretty quickly if we have anything," Wes said, as he opened the other rear door, then started up the sidewalk with his box toward Stamper's. A cold, late October breeze hit them as they neared the stenciled door.

The tall woman who had changed the sign greeted them and showed them into a well-furnished office. "It'll be just a minute. I'll see if Mr. Stamper is ready for you."

"That'd be great," replied Wes. Several minutes passed, and a heavyset gentleman of Wes's age entered the room.

"Wes, nice to see you again, it's been too long. Come in, come in." He motioned them toward a large room with a big oak table surrounded by tall worn leather chairs.

"Yes, it has, Hal, too long," Wes said.

"Mind if we set these here on the table?" Allen asked.

"Not at all, so what's going on with all this?" Harold asked as he motioned them to sit down and took a seat.

"It'll take a few minutes to get you up to speed," replied Wes.

"Go ahead. I don't have another appointment for two hours." Wes tried to tell the abbreviated form of the whole story, including his grandfather's additions to the house and the circumstances of his death, finding the treasure room, and the part John Prentice played in all this.

"I need you to know that Prentice wants my ranch as much as any man has wanted anything before," Wes said, as Allen nodded in agreement.

"Well, John has made a lot of friends in Cody, but between me and you, I'm not one of them. I always thought the guy was way too full of himself, and I didn't care for the way he treated some of his business partners either. Seems to enjoy seeing people go bankrupt just so he can swoop in and get a great deal," replied Harold. "Well, let's get started and take a tally of what we got."

Harold pulled the first certificate and shook his head. "This was really a good stock, but the company failed during the Depression. If you could have sold it twenty years ago, you would have made some real money. You do know that I can't be exact with the value. It'll depend on the day to day price in the market, but I can get close." Harold called for a couple of assistants to come in and got them to work immediately making a list of the stock and its value. Wes and Allen stood and watched as the three men began developing the inventory. "There we go," cried Harold. "Now we're talking—Con Edison."

"Con Edison stock" Allen asked.

"Yes, Con Edison is a good stock—not great, but really good. Your grandfather had quite a few shares, too," replied Harold. "I'm not going to be able to get through all of these by the time I have to leave for my next appointment, but it will only last about an hour, and then I will be back to help. In the meantime, my assistants will keep going, and I will have another one of my staff check what their value was as of yesterday." With that, Harold disappeared down the hall. Except for a couple of bathroom breaks, the two assistants worked through the papers, looking up only to send a finished pile to another room for processing. It was after 11:00 when they finished going through all the papers, and Harold had yet to return. Then, Allen and Wes heard the back door open and heavy footsteps in the hall before Harold reentered the room.

"Sorry it took me so long. I decided to stop and talk to a friend of mine who works in a bank that does a lot of business with Prentice. It appears that they know all about your ranch and what Prentice is doing. Apparently, Prentice had a chat with the president and got him to agree not to loan you or your ranch any money if you came in, and his bank isn't the only one. This jerk is one tough person to deal with, real shady."

"Dirty and devious," Wes said. "I didn't know this kind of stuff happens."

Harold shrugged. "Unfortunately, it happens more than you'd think. I think you guys need a good lawyer. My friend knew all about your foreclosure note. He said it was mailed last week, and even if you didn't get it, I think Prentice will say you did receive it and try to foreclose anyway. I asked him for the exact amount you owe, and I couldn't believe it when I heard it was over three hundred forty thousand dollars. That's a lot of money. How did he get in to you so much?"

Wes looked down for a moment and then raised his head and said, "Well, I borrowed quite a bit for some ranch improvements, and then when the drought hit, I borrowed more. I made a few bad business decisions and, with the interest piling up, it all kind of snowballed. I probably deserve to lose it."

"That's ridiculous," said Harold. "Before you give up hope, let's see what we got in all those stocks."

"Albert, do you have the totals yet?" asked Harold.

"We're just about done. Give me another two minutes and I'll have it," the clerk replied. Wes and Allen moved their chairs up to the table in anticipation of the final numbers. Harold took the sheets that Albert had given him and studied them for what seemed like hours. Harold crunched the numbers. Finally, he looked up at Wes and Allen and said, "Most of these companies went bankrupt or close to worthless because of the Depression. At one time your grandfather had a lot of great stocks, and if you could have cashed them in before the Depression, I don't think you would have ever had to worry about anything. As close as I can tell, two thirds of the companies are gone or close to it, but some, like Con Edison, have really bounced back." He paused and checked his notebook. "Your total is two hundred and ten thousand, as close as I can tell, minus your transaction costs.

"That's a lot of money," Allen said.

"But not enough to pay the note off in full, especially if Prentice has it rigged so I can't borrow from any of the other banks," replied Wes.

"Well, we have another fifteen grand in cash from the box from the secret room, another five from the study and a few thousand of operations money. But we still have a long haul to get to three hundred and forty thousand," Allen said.

"Yeah, I know," agreed Wes.

Wes and Allen went over the figures with Harold and at the end asked him to liquidate everything he could as soon as possible. Finally, Wes said, "Harold, do you have any recommendations on a good, honest attorney?"

"I don't usually use "honest" and "attorney" in the same sentence, but there are a few. Why don't you try one named King? His office is a block south of here. From what I've experienced, he's good and he's also honest. I'll start liquidating your stock tomorrow."

"Well, we'll be in touch. We sure appreciate the help," Wes said, while Allen nodded in agreement.

"Oh, I almost forgot something. I need to run out to the car and get it. I'll be right back." Wes headed out the door and moments later reappeared with a bag in his hands and handed it to Harold.

"What's this?" asked Harold.

"It's a present. I remembered how much you liked Scotch, so I brought you a bottle."

Harold thanked him and sat the sack on the table without inspecting it. "I'll try this tonight after dinner," he said, as he smiled graciously and thanked them.

The two then walked the few blocks to the attorney's office. Within minutes, they were in front of a black door that read King and Sons, Attorneys at Law. Allen opened the door, and a soft bell rang inside the spartanly furnished room. Immediately, a slender middle-aged lady in a dark gray suit walked out from a small side door. Wes and Allen couldn't help but notice the sound created by a long metal brace that supported her left leg and extended beneath her skirt. "Good morning, can I help you?" she asked.

"Yes, we're looking for Mr. King," responded Wes.

"One moment please, I will tell him you are here."

A heavy set, elderly gentleman in a light checked suit entered the room and greeted them with a wide smile and asked softly, "Good morning and how may I help you today?"

"Mr. King, Harold Stamper recommended you to us. Would you have some time that we could visit?" Wes asked.

"Sure, come in. I'm open this morning, so let's visit." The three entered a small conference room complete with five wooden chairs and a table in dire need of refinishing.

Wes cleared his throat. "We need some legal help." He took the next half hour explaining their predicament.

"Do you have the money to pay the note?" was Mr. King's first question.

"Not yet, but we have a good start."

"That's good. But this is not like horseshoes—close doesn't count, and please call me George."

"Will you be able to raise the money? And when exactly is the note due?" George asked, and, without giving them time to answer, continued. "I need you to fill out a power of attorney letter for me, so I can confirm everything at the bank and examine the note. Prentice is a powerful person and someone most people like to steer clear of. I had a client a few years ago. Somehow, Prentice got his ranch and then sold it six months later for double what the debt was." George pinched his chin. "Between you and me, Prentice is worth less than a mangy coyote."

For the next hour, the three talked, and in the end, George said, "From what it sounds, I doubt you'll get the money from any of the bankers here for two reasons. One is Prentice and his connections and the other is the fact that all your collateral is tied up in the note. You don't seem to have anything of real value that isn't pledged. On that deal I told you about earlier, my clients were supposed to close their loan on a Monday and then pay the bank off on a Wednesday. When he showed up to the closing, the bank said there was a problem and couldn't fund the loan, and he didn't have time to find another lender or couldn't, so he lost the ranch. When a bank calls in a note, basically you've got ninety days to come up with the money, or it goes to auction under a foreclosure judgment."

"With no banks willing to help, that might be a steep mountain to climb," Wes said.

"I'll need two hundred dollars for my retainer fee. Is that a problem?"

Wes shook his head and pulled out his wallet. "I was expecting to have to pay today."

After the attorney wrote down all the important facts, he turned to Wes and said, "Go back to the ranch. I'll get in touch with you in the next day or so as to what I found out. I don't want to discourage you guys, but you're probably wasting your time with any banks here. I agree with Harold, Prentice probably has already greased the skids with all of them. Your biggest problem will be finding that money in the next three months or so. I wouldn't be very surprised if they call your note here pretty soon, with what you have told me."

Allen and Wes agreed, thanked the attorney, and headed back to the car. "Let's check one of these banks for shits and giggles," Allen said, as Wes started the car. "It can't hurt." The two drove over to a smaller bank on the far side of town headed toward Powell.

"At least this bank seems to be a little further from those others," Wes said. "If anybody hasn't heard about this deal by now, it would probably be them." The two walked into the bank and the teller greeted them with a friendly smile. "What can I do for you?"

"I would like to see someone about getting a loan for approximately one hundred and forty thousand dollars," replied Wes. "We've got a large ranch to put up as collateral."

"For that much, I need to get the manager. I'll just be a moment," responded the teller. Shortly after that, a skinny bald man in his forties with a small moustache joined them and extended his hand. Wes told the manager about the note and the ranch equity and that he needed the money to pay it off.

"Would you mind giving me a few minutes, so I can call the bank with the note and verify the numbers? I'll just be a second." The manager rose from his chair and started to the door.

"You think he's being square with us?" Allen said to Wes.

Wes shrugged his shoulders and rubbed his temples.

When the manager returned, Allen and Wes both noticed that his demeanor had changed, and he seemed uncomfortable with them. He sat down with his eyes on the papers on his desk and said, "There seems to be a problem with your note. Some of the things you said don't seem to match your bank's records. I would suggest for this sum of money you talk to one of the larger banks. I'm sure they'd be happy to work with you. For now, we're sorry to say we aren't in a position to assist you."

Wes rose from his chair and tried to look into the manager's eyes, but he didn't seem interested in making eye contact.

"No problem, sir, we'll show ourselves out," Wes said.

"Yeah, thanks a lot," Allen said, as he noisily slid back his chair and followed Wes out. Both men were quiet as they got into the car and headed back to Meeteetse as a few snowflakes fell from the sky. "Well, what do you think?"

Wes shook his head. "I'm not sure. The only liquid asset we could sell that fast and anywhere close to that type of money would be the cattle, but it's the middle of winter. If we try and sell now, we'll get pennies on the dollar compared to what they would be worth in the spring. Everyone's got his hay for the year, and nobody is going to buy unless we guarantee we'll feed them for the winter or something like that," Wes said. "We don't have any good choices. If we sell the number of cattle needed to pay the rest of the debt, how do we start up again in the spring? It'll take our whole herd if we'll be lucky enough to get forty-five dollars a head."

"Maybe if we pay off the note, we can borrow the money for new calves in the spring," Allen said.

"I wouldn't want to hang my hat on what the bank will do."

Chapter 27

There was little conversation on their long ride from Cody back to the ranch over the snowy, windswept road. Both sat staring out the windshield in deep thought, trying to figure out the best course of action, only occasionally asking each other a question or making a small comment.

The sight of Sheriff Burris's truck sitting in front of the house caught them off guard. The Sheriff, Cole, and Sally stood on the porch talking, and by the looks of things it wasn't a pleasant conversation.

Wes quickly stopped the car behind the sheriff's, slammed on the emergency brake and shot from the car. "What's going on?" Allen opened the other door and followed him to the porch.

Sheriff Burris faced them and handed Wes an envelope. "It's from Hamilton and Clothier, attorneys out of Cody. I have to serve these papers. It's the law, but I'm not happy about it. You're good folks, and this kind of thing isn't supposed to happen to good people."

Wes opened the envelope. "What is it? Is it the note being called?"

"Yeah, it is, at leastwise that's what the agent from Cody who gave it to me said." Burris shuffled his feet. "Those attorneys work for the bank Prentice owns, and unfortunately, this isn't the first time I've seen one of these."

Wes read the letter. "What does it say, Wes?" Sally asked anxiously.

"The sheriff's right. It's a letter from the attorneys saying the bank is foreclosing on our note. We have to pay up in the next ninety days, or the ranch goes to public auction on the courthouse steps in Cody. It'll be sold to the highest bidder to service the debt on April 15th, 1938."

Everyone was quiet for a few seconds before Sheriff Burris broke the silence. "Sorry, Wes and Sally. I hate like hell delivering this. If there's anything that I can do, I will." With that he went back to his truck and proceeded down the road.

"Damn it," Wes spit out. "I always thought I'd work this out. I never thought this could happen." He lowered his head.

"I know that attorney," Allen said. "Don Hamilton, a real low life. Talk about an arrogant jerk, he takes the cake."

"Let's talk inside. We don't need to air our laundry out here," Wes said, leading Sally to the front door. He held the doorknob, turned and said to Cole, "Come in. You always seem to come up with good ideas. Anyway, I consider you and Allen family. Let's go to the study and figure this thing out."

Wes led the group into the study, and everyone took a seat except Wes. Wes cleared his throat for a moment, then looking at Sally, he spoke, "I haven't been the leader my grandfather was, but that's going to change here and now. I had a long time to think about this whole thing while Allen and I were coming back from Cody. I'll be damned if I am going to let Prentice and his bunch of coyotes steal this ranch. The first thing I need to happen is for no one to panic— we still got a lot of options out there, and we just need to find which ones work. I want everyone to handle this calmly, and don't let your emotions spill over so all the help sees it. We need to act normal. We'll get through this."

"Allen, tomorrow I need you to go over to the Schmidt's ranch and ask if we can phone our attorney in Cody. Tell them we will be glad to cover all the charges. Also, find out if they will take messages for us when we get calls. I know they will, but I feel better asking. Then I need Dodge to head over there every day and check for messages. That'll be a lot shorter than driving to town. Dodge is loyal to the brand and he's not a talker. I'm good with him. We got ninety days, but ninety days is going to go fast, and we got one hell of a lot of hurdles to climb. Allen, I want you and me to make a list of all the ranches within fifty miles of here. Contact Sheriff Burris and find out if he has any suggestions. Tomorrow I plan to head to Thermopolis and check with the banks there. The bottom line is I need everyone to do his part and act normal. I don't want any bank we are talking with to think we're running scared." Everyone seemed reassured with the way Wes took control.

The next morning, Cole woke up sore and could barely get out of bed. He felt the painfully slow recovery. The good news was that most of the deep purple bruises on his arm had turned yellow, and some had nearly faded away.

"Good morning, Sunshine," Julie said when she brought him a cup of coffee. "Mom and Chin fixed a great breakfast of bacon and eggs, and we were hoping you were awake enough to enjoy them."

Cole stared at Julie for a second, enjoying her beautiful smile.

"Once we finish, I want to go back to the treasure room and check out those maps and see what else is down there."

"Okay," Cole said. "But do you think it's just a little strange that your great grandfather built an almost solid brick room underground like that? No wonder no one could find it. Who would have ever thought to look ten feet underground?"

"You did," Julie responded with a smile.

"Well, no, I didn't, at least not on purpose. I thought the chamber would be in the chimney, and I thought it would be a whole lot smaller. I had no idea that there would be a whole stairway leading to a huge room below ground. There had to be some good reason that he spent that type of money and time to build it that way."

"Maybe, but I'm just happy we found it. Now get out of bed, and let's get some breakfast." Julie shut the door to give Cole a little privacy to dress. Cole wondered if Wes and Sally had told Julie about the letter of foreclosure yet, but it wasn't his place to ask, at least not yet.

After breakfast, and with Elmer's help, they returned to the attic. Julie had told Elmer that she was worried about Cole going up and down the stairs, but he seemed to manage better than the night before. Cole undid the cane and unlocked the secret brick door in the chimney, and Elmer pushed it open. Now that everyone knew the way, it didn't take long for the crew to make its way down to the small basement landing. They brought extra candles to replace the old ones but found most were still in good shape. Elmer helped Cole into the old chair in front of the large wooden desk against the wall. For being underground, the landing and large chamber were comfortably warm. Cole suspected this was due to heat from the chimney and some type of heat transfer system.

Julie began opening boxes they hadn't gotten to, while Elmer examined the old bottles in the liquor wall. Cole noticed the air in the chamber was far fresher than the passageway, but he didn't know why. Dodge and Ballard had asked to come down and help, but Julie felt that three people in the room made it way too cramped to lay things out and examine them. Besides, someone needed to keep a watch for Prentice until the sheriff sorted out everything.

There were a number of letters and papers in neat piles on the desk and above the cabinet. Cole began opening them one at a time, reviewing their contents. Some were letters to Gillis McCabe about his attempts to enlarge the ranch, and the negative responses he received. Reading them was like going back in time, and Cole began to enjoy the experience. He took several maps down from the cabinet and thoroughly examined them. They were part of an 1868 survey and were surprisingly detailed. After he put them down, Cole went to the last drawer. It opened as easily, as if it had been used every day for the last sixty years. There were a variety of items inside, but an old, worn envelope in the back caught his attention. Cole checked the date on the postmark: it read 1877. He opened the letter, taking care not to rip the fragile paper on which it was written. The letter was from George Lawrence, Attorney at Law, in Cody.

Cole's absorption in the letter got Julie's attention. "What is it Cole? Is it important?"

"It's a warning from an attorney, a Mr. Lawrence, saying that he had a visit from someone who overheard three men talking in a bar about planning to kill some rich fellow in Meeteetse. The man said he didn't recognize the other two guys, but the one doing all the talking was Vick Dunn. He said he had heard nothing but bad about Dunn, and was afraid for himself and his family. If Dunn ever learned he had overheard the conversation, the man felt he would be next. But he couldn't stand by and not tell anyone, so he told the attorney. He told Lawrence, on the condition that his name was not revealed. There isn't much more," Cole said, as he looked at Julie. "Apparently, Gillis had some enemies, maybe some he didn't even know about."

"And maybe some friends," Julie responded.

"You know, this might explain why your great grandfather built this room underground." Julie just nodded her head in agreement.

"On another subject, there are over six hundred bottles in this wall," Elmer said. "Apparently this guy liked his liquor."

"I'm sure he just had it for guests," Julie responded innocently and Cole and Elmer laughed under their breath.

The threesome worked through lunch, cleaning and inspecting the items in the room. They found several handguns, a gold watch, several boxes of old deeds, a brass telescope, numerous books on boat construction, and a large hollow brass lion that stood almost eighteen inches tall. It was almost five when Sally checked on them again, saying they needed to quit for dinner, now that Wes was home. The three of them made their way up to the attic door, and then Elmer helped Cole down the three flights of stairs.

The front door opened, and Wes and Allen walked in. "Long day," Wes said.

"Well, what did you find out?" Sally asked.

"For one, John Prentice is even more connected than I thought. Somehow he seems to have all the bankers buffaloed. I think what he's doing is giving out false information on the status of the ranch and our financial history to everyone that requests it. Right now, I don't see any bank coming to our rescue," Wes said.

Chin passed through the hall with a large tray of food and set it down at the table. As he started back down the hallway, a knock came from the door. Chin opened it with a greeting. It was Dodge, Ballard, and Elmer, who had been invited over to hear what was happening.

Cole listened intently throughout dinner as Wes and Allen told about their day. Then he told everyone about the letter he had found. He asked if it might be the same Dunn family that Martha Schmitz said used to live up the valley, and sold their property to Gillis McCabe in the early seventies. Could they possibly be related to the people who died in the plane crash? There were a lot of ideas and questions discussed at dinner, and Wes felt a little reassured that he at least had a plan.

That night, Cole's nightmares returned. His mind replayed the bear attack, the savage paw hitting his shoulder, and his bloody body being flung over the cliff like a rag doll. He felt the air rushing past his face as he fell and fell and fell until . . .

"Wake up, Cole, wake up! You're having a nightmare again," Julie said. She sat on the bed and held Cole. Shaking and wet from sweat, he slowly opened his eyes and looked at Julie—the dream had seemed so real. She wore a heavy yellow robe with a narrow white sash that she hadn't bothered to tie in her rush to help Cole. He looked at the silky white nightgown she wore beneath it. She bent down enough that the swell of her breast touched Cole's chest as she softly kissed him on the cheek. Julie put her hand on his head and gently stroked his hair. Cole thought that even in the middle of the night, she was an incredibly beautiful woman.

Cole put his hand on Julie's small waist and gently pulled her to him. He kissed her, and warmth spread throughout his body. She arched into him, and he caressed her back. Her lips were soft and moist, and her touch made his heart pump extra blood to every part of his body. Just touching her made him feel like a man, and he wanted time to stand still so he could enjoy this moment forever. Julie didn't speak, but he knew she felt the same way. Cole slowly pulled her silky robe off her firm, large breasts, exposing her body. Julie shook out her hair, closed her eyes and tilted her head back as Cole ran his hands over her body. There was no doubt that Julie wanted him as much as he wanted her.

* * *

The next morning brought two inches of fresh snow and a light wind. Allen and Wes got up early and continued developing their lists of potential cattle buyers. Allen's list represented most of the larger ranches south of Meeteetse, and Wes's list was mainly ranchers between Meeteetse and Cody. They had talked until late the night before and both came to the conclusion that, in the short run, selling the cattle was the only way to quickly raise the money needed to pay the debt. They would have to figure out later how to buy some cattle back and get the ranch on its feet. The plan was simple, sell enough cattle to raise the needed money in the next three months. Then, with the help of their attorney in Cody and the money from the stocks, they would go into Prentice's bank and pay off the note. They agreed that it was unlikely the bank would try to pull some last minute antic with the attorney present.

It was hard, humbling work to find buyers who had cash available this time of year, and it was becoming obvious each day that it would be an uphill battle.

* * *

The following morning, Cole moved back to the bunkhouse, because he had begun walking without a cane. The cane was now carefully hidden in Wes's closet behind some of his suits. The hidden chamber had been cleaned, and most of the documents and maps had been removed and studied. Cole had hoped they would find more information on the early Dunn family, but he was disappointed. His arm was feeling stronger every day, and the doctor believed it would be totally back to normal in another three months, which would put him back to work in the middle of April. Everyone on the ranch seemed to know that somehow there had to be a rabbit pulled out of someone's hat, to raise that much cash. There were a few interested buyers who would have purchased different sections of ground for good money, but they weren't interested unless they got a clean title, something Prentice wasn't going to allow.

It was the end of January when Cole heard a truck come up the driveway. At first, he thought it might be the doctor checking in, but he was surprised to see Sheriff Burris getting out of his pickup. "Cole, just the man I came to see. How are you feeling?"

"Great, I'm feeling better every day, and in another couple of months or so I think this arm will be good as new. What's up?"

"I had to come out this way anyway, so I thought I'd come by and share some new information. The sheriff down in Nebraska wrote me last week and had a little more history on the Dunns. Most of it was of no value, but a couple of things were awful interesting."

Cole perked up, and the sheriff knew he had his full attention.

"Around twenty-five years ago, one of the Dunn boys loaned his best friend a gold nugget, and his friend started showing a few people. Pretty soon the whole town was talking about it. I guess the nugget was worth almost a hundred dollars. The boy's dad made him return it. But everyone knew about it, and the Dunns wouldn't answer any questions on its origins.

"The sheriff said it wasn't all that long after that, a couple of lowlife thugs tried to rob the ranch. The robbery was a mess, and the two robbers where killed in the attempt. What was really interesting was that the owner's wife was killed, the mother of the kid who gave away the nugget. She was a Dunn, but she had married, and now her last name was Prentice, Mary Prentice. And that's not all. She was the older sister of Leroy Dunn; one of the people we believe was in that plane you found in the mountains. Pretty interesting, isn't it?"

"Yeah" Cole paused. "Yeah, it is."

"One more thing, after the lady's funeral the son who was about nine was sent away and no one knew where for sure. But you might be interested in his name." The sheriff took a breath. "It was John Prentice."

Chapter 28

Every day, Cole's arm felt stronger, and his leg was as good as ever with the exception of his old college injury. He knew he had lived through something a lot of men wouldn't have. He felt blessed and thankful, and looked at life differently. Every day, he gave Patch a little oats and a lot of petting. If it hadn't been for Patch sticking around, Cole wouldn't have survived. The mule had a thick winter coat and always seemed to be comfortable, even in the harsh Wyoming winter. Cole knew that a mule's hide thickened in the winter for warmth and thinned in the spring, allowing the hide to breathe easier and keep the animal cool. Cole wondered if his body did the same thing. He knew that to some he appeared a little weird, talking to a mule like it was a person, but truthfully Cole didn't care.

As he walked back to the bunkhouse, he saw both Allen and Wes come out of the house and leave in separate vehicles. Since the middle of January, with the exception of Sundays, they left every day at the same time, trying to sell cattle or get a loan. As winter wore on, Wes had given up on the banks and was now trying to find private lenders.

Cole had picked a windless, warm winter day to drive into Cody, thus avoiding snowdrifts that sometimes shut down the road. He enjoyed the drive, and stopped at the beautiful stone county courthouse which stood above Cody's other buildings. After negotiating with a clerk at the *Cody Sentinel*, he got an old file for the time period of Gillis McCabe's death. It took another hour to finally find the faded yellow news clipping of the robbery and murder. The article talked about the isolated little grocery store just outside the town of Powell.

It was the scene of two horrible murders—that of a well-liked store owner, Christopher Nielsen, and the wealthy Meeteetse businessman, Gillis McCabe. Most of the information in the article he had already learned from Wes or Martha and Phil Schmitz, but another interesting thing caught his attention. The article said that the sheriff was surprised the robbers hadn't taken the wallet from Gillis, who was shot when he accidentally interrupted the robbery. The sheriff credited his untimely presence as the reason the robbers lost their nerve and fled.

After Cole finished at the courthouse, he drove down the street and entered Smith's Gunsmith Shop. The building had originally been a home but had been remodeled into a business with bars on the windows and reinforced doors.

"Are you Leroy Soelberg?" Cole asked the middle-aged bald man working on a gunstock.

The man stopped and looked Cole over, then said, "Yes, I am. Can I help you?"

"I'm Cole Morgan. I sent you a letter about a month ago asking you to build me a gun. Is it done?"

"You're the one that wanted that modified bear gun right, finished it two days ago. Let me grab it." The gunsmith went to the back room and returned with a sawed-off, twelve-gauge pump model.

"I modified it to hold six shells in the magazine and one in the chamber, and redid the sights to meet your requirements—one drop of shiny polished brass on the front sight. I also got four boxes of shells, two buckshot and two slugs. Mighty mean medicine, if you ask me."

"That's good," Cole said, "Because I plan to kill a mighty mean bear." Cole paid the man the rest of the money he owed and returned to his truck.

On the way home, Cole tried to put together the details of the article and robbery. Why had Gillis McCabe been so far from home, and "just happened" to stumble into the middle of a robbery? Then, the robbers not taking any of the money didn't make sense, no sense at all, unless it was a set up. There was no way to prove it, but Cole was sure Gillis had been murdered.

Cole spent most days working to get the ranch ready for spring. Wes and Allen hadn't shared much lately on how they were doing raising the money, and no one had purposely asked the question. He remembered their last Sunday dinner conversation, when he had brought up the idea of buying some additional piping to develop a spring.

"Wes, what would you think about developing that spring in the bottom of Pine Ridge? It would cost..."

"No. No more little projects. We don't have the money, Cole." Wes took off his napkin and left the table, Sally following him out of the room. Julie took Cole's hand and said, "Don't worry about Dad. He's having a hard time with this."

That night Cole lay staring at the ceiling trying to figure things out. He knew that both Julie and Sally were very upset over the whole thing, but nobody seemed to have a good handle on where Wes was.

* * *

It was late March when Cole came out of the barn and noticed a blue sedan coming up the driveway, at least half a mile away. It seemed to be having difficulty with the rutted road, the vehicle getting tossed from one side to the other. During spring breakup, the road was difficult at best and sometimes impossible to travel. The driver seemed determined to make it, and finally he pulled into the drive and parked in front of the house. An older man in a well-tailored suit got out and headed to the front door. Wes answered the door and showed the gentleman in. Cole decided to see what was going on. Inside the house, Wes was greeting the man and introduced him to Cole.

"Harold, this is Cole Morgan. He's the one who found Grandpa's secret room. This is Harold Stamper."

"Nice to meet you, sir," Cole said as he shook the man's hand.

"I'd really like to thank you again, Harold, for all your help."

"No need to thank me, Wes, it's my job. In all honesty, I should be thanking you, and that's part of why I'm here."

"Why's that?" Wes asked as Sally and Julie entered the room. Wes introduced Sally and Julie and then turned back to Stamper. "So, why should you be thanking us?" Wes asked again.

"Well, the Scotch you gave me, that's why," he responded. "You must have known it was seventy-year-old Glengyle Scotch, some of the best in the world, and that old, it's unheard of. When I read the label, I decided not to open it for at least a month; I thought it would make a marvelous gift for my brother in Chicago. He runs a large company, and we always enjoy a glass of Scotch together after dinner. The first night, I pulled out your bottle and poured each of us a glass. He took a sip then went on and on about how impressed he was with the taste and smoothness of this Scotch. When I showed him the bottle, he practically went nuts. He couldn't believe I had such an old bottle of Glengyle. To say the least, he loved it so much that I told him about your grandfather's secret chamber. He told me it was extremely unusual to find an old cellar like this. The last time something like this happened, it was in France about twenty years ago. Some farmer found a cavern where some monks had hidden their cognac. Well, the demand for two-hundred-year-old cognac was unbelievable, made the farmer a rich man, and that's why I'm here." Stamper finished looking pleased with himself.

"You mean to tell me that the bottles are really valuable?" Wes stammered.

"Yes, my brother said that if you allowed him to sell them for you, your cut would be at least thirty dollars a bottle. Are you interested?" Stamper asked.

"Hell, yes. I'm not sure how many bottles we have, but there are around six hundred. Probably half is wine that's got to be the same age or older," Wes responded.

"Really" Stamper said.

"Yes, we haven't really paid much attention to the wine yet, but I was planning to break open a bottle after Sunday dinner. I may have to rethink that!"

"Wait until Cole finds out about this," Julie said, as she opened the front door and headed to the barn. Julie ran to where Cole was repairing a tire for one of the ranch trucks. "Cole, Cole, guess what! The Scotch we found in Great Grandpa's chamber—it's worth a fortune!" she said as she hugged him. The hug quickly turned into a full-blown kiss that Cole thoroughly enjoyed.

That night Cole, Ballard, Allen, Dodge and Elmer joined the family in celebrating the newly found source of money. Wes cracked opened one of the few bottles of Scotch he decided not to sell, and everyone enjoyed the amazing flavor and smoothness it had to offer. In the morning, they counted the remaining bottles: three hundred and six bottles of Scotch and two hundred and sixteen bottles of wine. All in all, according to Harold's calculations, the Scotch would bring about nine thousand dollars and the wine would bring another three, and that was with them keeping five bottles of Scotch and the same of wine to enjoy for special times. Several days later, a custom padded transfer truck and Harold Stamper's sedan showed up at the front door. After careful packing, the liquor was on its way to Cody, and then to Chicago.

* * *

Two weeks later, Julie walked over to the bunkhouse and asked Cole, Dodge, Elmer, and Ballard to come to the house for a special dinner.

An hour later when they arrived, Wes, Julie, Sally and Allen greeted everyone at the door and showed them in.

"Have a seat men. I have something special to tell you." Wes motioned to the chairs. "As you all know, Allen and I have been working very hard since the middle of January to raise the money to pay off the bank. We sold most of the cattle, some at a fair price and some well below market. But with the money we got from the stock certificates Cole found, the money from the study, the cattle, some operations money and now the Scotch and wine, we are within eleven thousand of raising the money.

"Last week, I talked to an old friend of mine that I have known for years, Wilson Stulc. He owns a number of small ranches, most of them around Lewistown, Montana, but one of them is up north of Powell, and I happened to catch him there. Though he isn't a rich man, but he has agreed to lend me the remaining money, but there's a catch. He doesn't have that type of money just lying around, and he probably won't have the cash until late Tuesday evening, the day before the auction. That's the fourteenth and only five days away. We have to have the money to the bank and the loan paid by eleven the next day, the fifteenth of April, or the property will go to auction. It's Friday evening, and that only gives us five days to make this happen.

"I want everyone to go about your usual tasks until Monday morning, and then I'm sending Allen and Dodge to stay with Wilson and make sure nothing unexpected happens. He'll put you up for a couple of nights, and then you three will drive in early Wednesday morning and meet me, Cole, and our attorney, George King, at the bank at ten when they open. I'm working closely with King, and I have been driving over to the Schmidt's at least once every other day to call him and discuss what we are doing and how to do it. Elmer and Ballard, I want you to stay here at the house and make sure nothing happens while we are gone. I have no idea if Prentice has been monitoring our progress.

"But now I want to celebrate and propose a toast to the ranch and all the friends of The Greybull," Wes said. The rest of the evening was enjoyable, and everyone seemed relaxed and excited, knowing they had a fighting chance.

Several hours later, everyone called it a night and Cole headed for the bunkhouse. The nightmares were slowly fading, and many nights he slept all the way through without waking, something the other men in the bunkhouse greatly appreciated. On Saturday morning, Cole woke early and lay in bed for a few minutes. He had dreamed about finding something in the old desk. He couldn't remember what, how or why, but he remembered finding something. Maybe he had spent too much time reading old documents, or maybe his dreams were now trying to remind him of something he had forgotten. He wasn't sure, but he decided to at least check out the old desk one more time.

There were still a number of unanswered questions from the past that Cole wanted to clear up, and he hoped the room might give him some clues. Was it the Dunns who jumped the Creagers? If they did, that would explain the nugget John Prentice gave away in Nebraska when he was a kid. Were they looking for old cabins using the plane? Not a bad idea, Cole thought to himself, not bad at all. Cole had never ridden in an airplane before, but he had stood on many high peaks, and the usefulness of views from the high elevations was not lost on him. Being Saturday, about half of the ranch hands had headed to town, while Cole lay sorting his thoughts on his bunk. Twenty minutes later, he rose to his feet and headed over to the big house. He wanted to see if Julie would explore the chamber with him again and look at the desk one more time.

He knocked on the door.

Chin answered.

"Is Julie in?"

"Yes, yes, come in," Chin said. When Cole had first met Chin, he hadn't thought the man had much backbone, but now he knew the strength of fire in the little man, and he respected him greatly.

Julie, who must have heard the door, came down the stairs and greeted Cole. Chin quickly excused himself back to the kitchen.

Cole told Julie about the dream, knowing that he wanted to be alone with her every bit as much as he wanted to look at the desk. Julie excused herself and was back shortly with Gillis' cane. "I know where Dad hides it," she said, smiling at Cole.

The lock and the brick door opened easily, due to the hinges being oiled and the fact they were being used on a regular basis. The pair quickly descended the circular staircase to the small room at the entrance of the passage and then entered the main chamber. Inside, they lit a number of candles and an oil lamp, and for the first time Cole noticed how romantic it was being alone with Julie with the candles gently flickering. He examined the desk for any kind of hidden drawer, but after twenty minutes he gave up and sat down on the desk facing Julie.

"Did you find anything, Cole?" Julie asked.

"Yes, I did."

"What?"

"I found one beautiful lady in a candle-filled room, who really needs a kiss from one lucky cowboy." Cole pulled Julie close and kissed her with tremendous passion. They hadn't been at it for more than a couple of seconds, when they heard footsteps coming down the stairs. It was Chin.

"Mrs. McCabe is looking for you," Chin told Julie. He stared into the room that had remained a mystery for so long. Julie smiled at Cole, and the three headed up the stairs.

Cole turned to Chin and said, "Chin, your timing's terrible, but thanks. I'd much rather have you disturb us than Sally McCabe." He followed Chin back up the stairs.

After lunch, Cole and Julie went for a long walk. "Dad's nervous, but he thinks he has a pretty good plan. He's at the Schmidts' right now talking to the attorney. I'll be glad when this whole thing is finally over, and we can go back to the way it was," Julie said.

Cole nodded in agreement.

"You know, Cole, in a way I really miss Tyler. He helped raise me. Why do you think he did it? You know, sell us out and all?"

"Money does strange things to people, and I think there was a price to his loyalty. I don't believe in the beginning that he intended to sell you out. We best be getting back—I promised Allen I'd help him with some things." They walked back to the porch, and he kissed Julie on the cheek. "See you at dinner, gorgeous."

That night at dinner no one talked about the bank or the auction, and no one was very talkative. After an hour, Cole thanked Sally for dinner and excused himself. Wes pulled back his chair and followed Cole to the foyer. "Cole, can we talk for a minute in the study?"

"Sure." Cole followed Wes into the beautiful room trimmed with oak and bright wall coverings.

"Can I pour you another drink?" Wes asked.

"No, I'm fine."

Wes turned his back to Cole for a moment and stared out the large window into the darkness. "I don't know why, but I got a bad feeling about this. It bothers me that no one has seen or heard from Prentice since the fight. To tell you the truth, that's not what I want to talk to you about. I've seen the look on both you and my daughter's face when you two are together, and I want you to know that Sally and I already think of you as a son. You have been special since the first day you set foot on this place, and well, we just want you to know we're happy for the both of you and you have our blessings."

Chapter 29

The next day at noon, Wes and Allen invited Cole, Dodge, Ballard and Elmer over to the house for a meeting. They had lunch and then met in the study and closed the door. Three times they went over the plan from start to finish. Everyone understood it the first time, and Wes felt comfortable that they all knew their parts.

Before daybreak the next morning, Allen and Dodge drove out of the ranch courtyard and down the road toward Powell. It was their plan to be through Cody at first light and to Wilson Stulc's ranch by half past seven that morning, stay there until the money arrived, then accompany it back to Cody. It was Monday, and the rest of the ranch hands wouldn't be up for another hour and a half, so only Wes and Cole noticed their departure.

Throughout the morning, Cole maintained his normal routine. After lunch, he was walking back to the bunkhouse, when Julie came up and gave him a hug. "Dad wants to see you. He sure seems nervous. I hope everything is all right."

Cole grinned. "I'm sure all's just fine."

Julie reached down and took his hand and the two walked toward the house. They entered the house, and Cole headed for the study.

Wes was sitting behind his desk doing paperwork. "Cole, come in and close the door. I've changed my plans. There's way too much at risk to overlook anything. Tyler's spying really bothers me, and even though I know everyone here's loyal to the ranch, I have to be more careful than ever. Instead of leaving early Wednesday morning, we're going to take the money and leave Tuesday right after dark. Sheriff Burris is going to follow us to a place that only I know. Take your new bear gun and feel free to use it if the need arises. I feel very comfortable with Sheriff Burris, I've known him for twenty years or more and the man is straight. We can trust him. He volunteered to help guard the money until this whole thing is over."

"I have just the gun, and you know, Wes, that I'll do whatever it takes to help you and the ranch." They talked a little longer, then Cole walked back to the bunkhouse.

That evening, Cole joined Wes, Sally, and Julie for a quiet dinner, during which no one discussed what would take place in the next couple of days. Cole excused himself early and turned in. The next day was Tuesday, and it would be a long one, so he needed to be at his best. He still tired a little easier than he would have liked, but he was now at least eighty percent of what he had been before his run-in with the bear.

* * *

It was eight o'clock in Cody, and the wind-whipped street was dark and empty. A black sedan pulled up to the edge of the street and parked with the motor running. Twenty yards away, a much older car parked, and a woman got out. She walked to the sedan, where a window had been partially rolled down, and a dark, gloved hand reached out and placed a brown envelope in the woman's outstretched hand. As she returned to her car, the clanking of a metal brace was all but lost in the wind's howl.

* * *

Cole had hoped to sleep well that night, but didn't. The next morning he got up, went to his pickup truck, and removed his modified shotgun from its blanketed protection. He inserted six shells, keeping the chamber open, then put another six shells in the jacket he intended to wear that evening when they left. He fueled up his truck at the ranch's tank, before parking it in its original spot behind the barn.

He ate a quiet lunch with the other men, then headed up to the house to see Wes. When he knocked on the door, Julie answered with a hug. "Dad had just asked me to go find you. I guess great minds think alike. I need to pack you guys some sandwiches and stuff," she said, as they went to the study. At the door, Julie paused for a second and looked at Cole, then turned and hurried in the direction of the kitchen.

"Come in, Cole, and shut the door," Wes said. "Are you ready for tonight? I want to leave about eight-thirty."

"That works fine. I've got my gun in the truck and we are all gassed up and ready to go."

"Good. We'll leave tonight as planned. I drove over to the Schmidt Ranch and called Wilson Stulc. Allen and Dodge made it fine, and everyone is on hold until the money gets there from Montana."

It was dark when Wes met Cole at the vehicles. "You ready?" Wes asked.

"Couldn't be more ready," Cole replied. They got into their vehicles and headed out the gravel road toward Meeteetse.

At the edge of town, Sheriff Burris was parked on the side of the road, waiting with his engine off. Wes pulled up beside him and rolled down his window. "Everything's a go," Wes said.

"I'm ready," Burris replied.

The sheriff fell in line behind Wes and Cole, and they headed south away from Cody. After an hour of driving, they came to an old road in the middle of nowhere and turned into an abandoned barnyard. Everyone shut off their motors and got out.

"Pretty isolated spot you found here," Cole said.

"Yeah, an old friend of mine that died ten years back used to farm this place. But since he passed away, they don't seem to do anything with it any more. It's the perfect place. You can see headlights for miles and hardly anyone comes this way. We'll take turns standing guard, and at first light we'll take the back way into Cody."

It was just sunrise when Wes woke everyone up from a restless sleep. They ate breakfast and made coffee over an open fire, and by eight they were headed to Cody. An hour later, the caravan of vehicles reached the office of attorney George King. Cole and Burris stayed with the money as Wes went to the front door. When Wes opened the door, George was standing by his secretary's desk. "Everything okay here?" Wes asked.

"It's been real quiet. I see you brought the sheriff."

"You never can have too much help at a time like this."

"You ready to head down to the bank?" George asked.

"Yeah, I brought one of my men, Cole Morgan, in addition to the sheriff. I'd rather be overly safe than sorry on a deal like this."

The trip down to bank took a little less than ten minutes, and because the bank wouldn't open for another forty minutes, they parked right in front of the First Bank of Cody, the note holder. The bank was a two-story brick building painted white with a large awning over the front. It needed another paint job, as missing paint exposed a rich, red brick color beneath it. The date of its construction was clearly visible above the door- 1889.

* * *

At the Stulc Ranch north of Powell, nobody heard the friendly ranch dog's sad yelp as it died quickly from several knife wounds. An hour later, when three men left the house with a sack of money, Wilson Stulc stopped and looked around. "That's strange, I wonder where Blue is. Ain't like him to not greet me in the morning." That was the last thing he ever said, as a hail of bullets cut the three men down. Within seconds, a man sprinted in and grabbed the open bag of money before too many bills blew away in the stiff wind.

* * *

Wes sat in his sedan with the attorney, George King, while the sheriff joined Cole and the money in Cole's truck. "Allen, Dodge and Wilson should be here any minute," Wes said. "They're supposed to meet us right at ten when the bank opens."

"I know, Wes," George said. "Relax, everything is fine."

Wes checked his watch again, as someone in the bank flipped the CLOSED sign to OPEN. "Where are they? It's ten. What could have happened?"

"Nothing happened," George said. "They're probably running late for some reason. They'll be here."

It was ten thirty when Wes jumped from the car and looked down both streets in search of Allen's vehicle. "Where in the hell could they be?"

"Maybe they had car problems."

"No. The plan was to take two vehicles in case one broke down."

Cole and Sheriff Burris got out of the truck and joined Wes and George. "What are you thinking?" Cole asked.

"Cole, go to Wilson's place and see what's going on. Here's a map to his ranch." Wes opened his vest and pulled out a small piece of white paper. "George, how long will it take us to get to the courthouse?"

"Six to ten minutes, not long. Want me to go now?"

"Not yet. Cole, you take off for the ranch. Sheriff Burris, George and I'll take the money into the bank. That way when they arrive everything will go smoothly."

When they got to the bank, George asked for the manager. Soon a thin, older gentleman showed them to a small room with a large table and several chairs. George took the lead and explained in no uncertain terms what he expected to happen in the next twenty-five minutes when the money arrived from the Stulc Ranch and how he needed a receipt for the money they were about to deposit. It took the next ten minutes to carefully count out three hundred and thirty thousand dollars but when he was through, everyone agreed with the count, and a signed receipt was handed to Wes. Now, all they could do was wait.

Wes stood up again and walked through the front door out onto the sidewalk. He looked both ways and swore under his breath. When he turned, Sheriff Burris was standing in front of him. "Anything I can do?"

"What time do you have?" Wes asked.

"Same as your watch one minute to eleven."

George King walked to Wes and put his hand on Wes's shoulder. "I'm sorry, Wes, I'm sure the auction has started."

* * *

On the thirty-five minute drive to Wilson Stulc's ranch, Cole thought about Wes McCabe. He had been to an auction like this before, and there were usually several pieces of land being auctioned at the same event. He wondered where The Greybull stood on their docket.

As he drove into the yard, he noticed some men and a woman bent over several bodies on the ground. Cole slammed on the brakes and jumped out. In front of him lay Wilson Stulc, his shirt stained a crimson red with his leg bent unnaturally beneath him. The second lifeless body he saw was Dodge, slumped against a bullet-riddled car fender. Cole pushed back the people and dropped to his knees and looked at Dodge. His white face showed surprise, and by the look of his wounds, he had died quickly. Cole jumped up and grabbed one of the men by both arms, "Where's Allen?" he screamed. "Where's the other man who was here?"

The cowboy pointed toward the house.

Cole ran for the ranch door, and for a moment searched the house, until he saw Allen lying on the living room couch. A blood-stained bandage was wrapped around his head, and several more bandages covered his chest. Cole raced over to the pale man and grabbed his hand. "Allen, can you hear me? Can you hear me?" Cole squeezed his hand while he talked and finally Allen cracked open one eye.

"Cole, I let them down. Never saw them skunks until it was too late. Tell Wes and Sally I'm sorry." Allen's eyes slowly closed.

Cole felt his neck for a pulse—it was weak but still there. As he asked the woman for a wet rag to wipe his head, several men in white uniforms and red crosses on their hats entered the room with a stretcher.

* * *

The previous two properties had sold for prices well below market value, and now the piece everyone had been talking about would be going up for bid. The court representative read The Greybull's legal description, then the auctioneer began his chant. "Let's start the bidding at two hundred thousand. This is one of the prettiest ranches in all Wyoming. Do I hear two hundred thousand?"

An older man in the middle of the crowd raised his hand and then someone toward the front said two hundred and ten thousand. The bidding had slowly worked its way up to two hundred and ninety thousand, when a gentleman in a three-piece suit raised his hand and said, "The First Bank of Cody bids three hundred and twenty thousand."

The auctioneer made eye contact with the bidder and said, "We have a three hundred and twenty thousand bid by Mr. Don Hamilton, representing the First Bank of Cody. Do I hear three hundred and thirty thousand? We have three hundred and twenty thousand do I hear three hundred and thirty? Going once at three hundred and twenty thousand, going twice at three hundred and twenty thousand . . . "

"Three hundred and twenty nine thousand!" shouted a winded Wes McCabe.

There was a momentary pause and then the auctioneer hollered, "We have a bid for three hundred and twenty nine thousand, do I hear three hundred and thirty-five thousand?" The auctioneer repeated himself. "I have a bid of three hundred and twenty-nine thousand, do I hear three hundred and thirty-five?

"Three hundred and forty-one thousand," said a smug Don Hamilton as he scanned the crowd to see their reaction.

"I have three hundred and forty-one thousand do I hear three hundred and forty-five thousand? The bid is at three hundred and forty-one thousand, do I hear three hundred and forty-five thousand? Three hundred and forty-one thousand going once, three hundred and forty-one thousand going twice, sold to Mr. Don Hamilton representing the First Bank of Cody."

Wes looked sick, George grabbed one arm and Sheriff Burris grabbed the other as Wes vomited all over the sidewalk. They helped him to the passenger's side of George King's car. "I'm sorry, Wes. I wish I could help in some way, but everything was legal. There's nothing more I can do for you. I'm truly sorry. Please come back to my office until you recover. I'll drive if you'd follow me, sheriff."

The two cars slowly drove to George King's office. The men helped Wes up the walkway and into the front door. George swung open the door with one hand and started in, while the secretary jumped from her desk. "Oh my, what's happened?"

"It's all right Miss Bright. Mr. McCabe fainted at the auction. They lost their family ranch. He needs some rest, would you mind calling the doctor just in case."

"I'm so sorry. I'm so sorry," Miss Bright said.

"We're all sorry, Miss Bright. Please collect yourself and get some cold water for everyone. Everything will be all right." Miss Bright turned and headed into George's office to call the doctor.

"He's so pale, I hope he isn't having a heart attack or something," Burris said. "After Miss Bright is through calling the doctor, I'll call the Schmidts and tell them what happened. Sally and Julie should be here." The two phone calls were made, and when the phone was put down, it rang again and the sheriff answered. After a brief conversation, he hung up and in a soft voice said, "It was Cole. Wilson Stulc, Dodge, and Allen were gunned down and the money stolen. Allen is holding on by a thread, and they have him in the hospital in Cody. Cole is at the hospital, and he's going to stay by Allen's side for now."

It had been almost two hours and the doctor was just finishing looking at Wes, when Sally and Julie entered the law office followed by Ballard and Elmer. "Is he okay?" shouted Sally as she hugged Wes.

"He's doing as well as we could hope, knowing what happened," the doctor said and handed Sally a bottle of pills. "Give two of these to him later if he becomes too stressed. I'm sorry about what happened. I wish there was more I could do. I gave him some sedatives earlier and they knocked him out. He'll be okay." With that, the doctor said goodbye and left.

Ballard drove Wes and Sally back to the ranch, and Elmer left for the hospital with Sheriff Burris. Once there, Elmer scanned the patient list for Allen's room, and they found Cole sitting beside Allen's bed. "How's he doing?" Elmer said.

Cole straightened up in his chair and stared at them for a moment. "They shot him three times, and he's still alive. He's tougher than a tick, and the doctor says if he makes it through the night, then he might survive. It's touch and go until then. He's in surgery right now, been there for the last hour."

"I'd like to catch the bastards that did this," said Sheriff Burris.

"We all would," Cole replied.

Two hours later, they wheeled Allen back into the room, still unconscious. After a couple of hours, Sheriff Burris patted a tired Cole on the shoulder. "I've got to head back to Meeteetse. I still have a job to do. Wish I could stay longer and keep you company."

In a tired, slow voice, Cole thanked the sheriff and then turned to Elmer. "I think you should go back to the ranch. There are some hard decisions that you could probably help with. I'll be fine without you and I will call the Schmidts if anything happens."

That night, Cole listened to Allen's labored breathing, and he leaned over him and said, "If it's the last thing I do, I'll get even with Prentice for this. I know if you were awake that you'd call me the dangest fool you ever met. But I'm going back up there to where Red lives and see if I can find that gold mine. I can't tell anyone for several reasons. Hell, one is the McCabes don't even own the property any more, and second, if anyone thinks there's a mine, there won't be any stopping people trying to find it. You know, Red saved my life, just like you and the boys did, and I'll never forget that. If people start looking for gold all over those hills, Red will probably be the first one shot. I got to do this alone and without anyone knowing, except for Julie."

Allen never moved. He just lay peacefully on the bed.

The next evening at six, a light tap on Allen's door woke Cole. He hadn't fallen asleep until around three that afternoon, and he could just barely open his eyes. It was Julie and Sally with a small pot of soup for Allen and Cole.

"Cole, how's Allen?" Julie asked.

"He made it through the night. Hopefully, the worst is behind him."

Julie looked at Cole and started to cry. "The sheriff came by this morning and served mom with a letter from the bank. We have two weeks to have everything cleared out. He felt terrible about doing it, and there were tears in his eyes."

Sally and Julie's visit lasted over an hour. Allen never awoke during their stay.

"Julie, can I talk to you in the hall for a minute before you leave?" Cole asked. "I've got something important to tell you." In the hallway, he said, "I need you to stay with Allen. He has to have a face he recognizes when he wakes up. I've got to find that mine for everyone's sake—there's nothing else left to do."

"Cole, you're not healed all the way. You can't go." Tears ran down Julie's face. "The last time you went up there it almost killed you, and I couldn't live if I lost you, too."

"I'll be fine, don't worry. I feel great and won't be gone long, but I have to leave now and head up there tomorrow."

The drive back seemed to go in slow motion, as Cole fought to stay awake. He kept thinking what he could have done differently, but how would anyone fore seen this? Dodge was one of his best friends, and to lose him after Jay and now possibly Allen, he didn't know how he would keep it together if Allen died. He stopped at Meeteetse for supplies and arrived at the ranch just after dark. There were several trucks partially filled with ranch gear and furniture. Cole opened the door of the bunkhouse and saw Ballard. "Cole, are you okay?" he asked. "You look like hell. You really need some sleep. How's Allen?"

"He's fighting the battle but time will tell if he makes it or not. Those bastards shot him three times in the ambush. Allen's made of pretty thick leather. I can't believe they killed Dodge and Mr. Stulc. That guy only tried to help a friend—they didn't deserve this."

"Nobody deserves this," Ballard said while he walked with Cole over to his bed. "You need to sleep. We could use your help moving. A bunch of the neighbors have been here the last couple of days, and Wes is doing okay. He found a place to rent and a place to put the cattle and their belongings until they find a new home."

"Ballard, I need you to tell Wes that I'll be gone for a few days. I have something I have to do. I'm leaving before first light. I don't want you telling anyone, you got me, promise?"

Ballard nodded his head. "I promise Cole."

Chapter 30

It was still dark on a Saturday morning when Cole loaded his pack mule, Pumpkin, and mounted Patch.

"Pumpkin and Patch," he said aloud. His pack contained three jars of strawberry jelly—tightly packed in socks and then rolled together in a spare shirt—as well as the gear needed for the trip. The road was dry, and Cole made good time in the dark. At sunrise he hit Canvas Creek and headed up the trail.

Cole spotted two sets of recent horse tracks. Apparently, some of the ranch hands had already been at the trailhead rounding up stock. The ride up the hill went smoothly, and Pumpkin lined out well behind Patch as they meandered up the mountain. Cole felt safe with his new twelve-gauge shotgun in the scabbard, loaded with six shells and an extra one in the magazine, alternating between buckshot and slug.

Cole reached the line cabin before noon. He chose to spend the night in its modest protection and catch up on sleep. He unloaded the mules and put them in the old corral, where lush new spring grass covered the ground. For the most part, the snow had melted except in areas with high drifts, which would melt in a couple of weeks of sunshine.

Cole lit a fire in the stove, and reheated some stew that he had packed in a mason jar. The hot stew hit the spot, and before dark, Cole circled the cabin looking for bear sign but found none. Then he walked down to the creek with his gun in one hand and the bucket in the other. The mud around the stream showed a lot of deer sign, but no bear. That night, the grizzly dreams recurred, and Cole awoke in the middle of the night drenched in sweat. The dream was so real and his mind so preoccupied that Cole spent the next two hours staring at the ceiling before he fell back to sleep.

An hour before daylight, Cole relit the stove. After several cups of strong black coffee and the rest of the stew, Cole went to the corral where the mules grazed peacefully under a large aspen. He had left their halters on so he could quickly catch them, and in a couple of minutes Patch and Pumpkin were hitched to the rail. Soon he was packed and headed up the mountain. The trail was slick in some spots but had held up well over the winter.

At the top of the ridge, Cole pulled back on Patch's reins and studied the trail behind him. Everything was quiet, as it should be, so he nudged Patch forward with his knee, and they headed cross-country to where the stone face appeared on the burned hillside.

Cole carefully watched for both bear and horse tracks but there weren't any, and soon he reached the strange Old Man Rock that hid the trailhead entrance. Patch swung onto the trail with Pumpkin close behind. Cole couldn't remember falling off the mule or the crew finding him, but from what Allen had told him, he had been found beyond Old Man Rock, therefore, no one should know the trail location. The ground was soft, and it bothered Cole that he left more tracks than he would have liked. Hopefully, he'd find what he was looking for and be back to the ranch before anybody noticed. He tried to have the animals walk on the rock or taller grass, but Cole knew a really good tracker would easily follow their sign.

About an hour and a half later, Cole arrived at the ridge where the huge Limber Pine with the bayonet had stood. The winter had been long and harsh, and like a giant lifeless porcupine with thick wooden quills, the great tree now lay rotting on the ground. It took a few minutes, but finally Cole found the rusty bayonet lying in a large patch of tall grass. He appreciated the fact that if it had been a year later and without a landmark, the trail's entrance would have been lost for eternity.

He tied up the mules, unloaded Pumpkin's packs and unsaddled both of them. He hobbled Pumpkin and released her, then tethered Patch on a long, soft rope in a large area of bunchgrass. He loosened the rope on the firmly tied pack box and removed a pack board and a soft pack, two heavy bags, rope, flashlight with one set of spare batteries, three mason jars of jelly, an axe, and many numerous smaller items including food for three days. Cole kept one eye on the mules for any sign of alarm. If the bear or anyone else were around, they would sense it first.

He then hid the saddles and blankets, the pack bags and the rest of the gear behind a low-hanging pine tree, out of sight at the edge of the meadow. He covered the gear with a heavy canvas manty and stacked freshly cut branches over the whole thing. Then he threw the pack board and loaded pack on and began hiking up the hill to the second trail. He had only gone a couple of steps when he realized he had left the bayonet on the trail. Not wanting to lose it, he stuck it in the ground beside the fallen pine giant, where he'd remember it upon his return.

The pack weighed close to thirty pounds, not counting the axe and shotgun, but he felt strong enough to carry the load. Cole slung the shotgun over one shoulder and carried the axe in one hand, while keeping the other one free. It had been too long since Cole breathed the mountain air, and he inhaled deeply as he walked across the grassy bench to the trail's entrance under the tree.

Cole made good time up the trail, always keeping an eye out for bear signs or people. He hoped to see Red again. He owed the little redheaded guy his life. Finally after an hour or so, he broke from the thick timber onto the more visible, narrow rock trail that wound its way up from the bottom of the steep canyon. Cole stopped several times and listened, looked for sign, and watched the movement of the birds—everything seemed as it should. An hour later, he walked through the old rock entrance that had at one time been a gate, and proceeded into the small meadow where the old mining cabin was located. He carefully walked around the small valley, giving it a closer examination than he had on his first visit, but found nothing. Then he went back to the cabin and opened the old wood door, which creaked with an eerie screech. If it hadn't been such a beautiful sunny day, the sound would have gotten under his skin. Even so, his last visit to the valley weighed heavily on his mind. Cole took the flashlight from the backpack, then grabbed his shotgun and entered the cabin.

The cabin smelled, not of decay but more like the old dusty smell of an unused attic. Cole slowly shined the light around, but the sunshine coming through the window made it almost unnecessary. Picking up the pistol he had examined earlier, he took a long second look before placing it on the floor in its original position. The room was in good order. Cole was impressed that the Creagers had packed panes of glass all the way into the mountains to make cabin windows. Obviously, they intended to use the place for a long time, or they wouldn't have made such an effort. But what was most amazing was that the glass, with the exception of the one pane he had broken, remained intact after all these years.

Cole moved to the bed and examined the skeleton. The mattress, unlike most of the room, had a slightly pungent odor. With the flashlight in hand, Cole carefully picked up the skull and looked at it. It appeared to be unmarked, but when he laid it down, he noticed something lodged into one of the vertebrae.

After examining it, Cole was sure that he was looking at a bullet, probably the one that killed the man who had spent his last night on this rough old bed. He carefully and respectfully placed the bones back on the bed and then examined a dusty wooden box in the corner. The label on the box had long since disappeared, but it opened easily. The inside was empty, with the exception of one envelope stuck against the frame. Cole lifted out the letter and brought it into the sunlight. It was yellow and had a faded postmark from an unreadable town in Iowa. It had already been opened, and Cole removed the letter.

The correspondence confirmed it was the Creagers' cabin. It was to Vern Creager from his wife. She wrote about the neighbors losing their house to the bank, how much she and their daughter missed him and how great it would be to have him home. She told him to be careful, to keep up his guard, and that she was glad they were almost done and coming home, for she needed him. The rest was about how lonely she was and how she appreciated how lonely he must be, working while Vern watched the ranch. Unfortunately, the personal details didn't give Cole any new clues as to location of the mine. He took the flashlight and looked around one more time, but the cabin was small, and he felt like he had found everything of importance.

He took the letter out into the sunshine and laid his shotgun and flashlight against the pack. On a flat rock he sat and read the note one more time. It never mentioned gold or a mine, but Cole was sure that was what Vern's wife was referring to. He suspected they had had some type of code. The letter answered another question—if there were two of them working on the mine, then why only one bed? Of course, they worked in shifts on the ranch and at the mine, which allowed for fresh supplies to be delivered and each one of the Creagers to make appearances, so no one got suspicious.

The more he thought about the Creagers, the more impressed he was with the two brothers. They were craftsmen and smart. They built a trail that they probably used at least once a month, and no one saw them for several years—or did they? Cole sat there thinking that would explain the heavy wagon with the fake bottom at the Creager's ranch. They were going to use that to take the gold to where they weren't known. Cashing in a large amount of gold would draw too much attention, and they had thought that through thoroughly.

These were two smart men, but like most plans, theirs had a flaw, a deadly one. Someone had discovered their secret, and they paid for it with their lives. Vern died here, and Virgil passed away in Meeteetse, both killed by the same thieves—the Dunn family, their neighbors to the north.

Cole was about to stand up when he heard a twig snap. In an instant, he rolled for his shotgun that lay only yards away. Time passed in slow motion as he dived forward, already planning his next move as he flew toward the gun. With one motion, he grabbed the twelve-gauge and pointed it in the direction of the sound. There, with a frightened look on his dirty face, Red stood looking at Cole. Cole lowered his shotgun and felt his whole body relax.

Almost a minute went by before Red moved, and then he spoke in a soft voice. "Yellie?"

Cole laughed and pulled one of the well-wrapped mason jars of strawberry jelly from his pack and handed it to the now smiling Red.

"You really got me going," Cole said to Red. "Next time can you at least give me a little warning you're here?"

Red immediately sat down and unscrewed the jar, then stuck his hand in and shoved a large lump of jelly into his mouth. Within minutes, Red had smeared jelly all over his face in an attempt to wolf down the whole jar.

"Slow down, these are yours, and no one's going to take them from you," Cole softly said. "Relax and enjoy yourself."

Red looked at him for a moment and then picked up the two remaining jars.

"Yes, those are yours," Cole said, nodding.

With that, Red turned and disappeared back into the woods without a word. His exit was so quiet and so quick that even Cole was impressed with his skills.

It was after lunchtime, so Cole decided to have some jerky and dried apple slices before he continued up the trail. The sun felt good and warm, a stark contrast to the day he had been hurt and cold as he tried to make it back to the mules. However, his mind filled with the thought of Allen lying in the hospital bed and Julie's family losing their ranch. After a few minutes, he repacked his gear and began walking to the head of Creager's meadow. He stopped for a moment at the small creek that flowed through and took a long drink, always keeping one eye out for trouble. He continued past the remains of the collapsed sorting shed, not needing to stop and inspect it.

The trail again broke from the forest, and the sound of water crashing over boulders from the spring thaw was almost deafening. After another ten minutes, he reached the spot of the bear attack where Cole's rusted rifle lay embedded in the moist soil of the trail. He gently nudged the gun with his boot, then picked it up and leaned it against a boulder on the side of the trail. The trail widened here, and a few small Limber Pine trees grew in the sparse soil.

Cole followed the path for another thirty minutes as it became rockier and less vegetated. He decided to leave his axe behind, now that he was out of the heavy timber, and he placed it against the side of a big rock in plain sight beside the trail. It was someplace he could easily find later, even in the dark; and by doing so, he could carry his shotgun in both hands. The trail branched, with one route following the raging creek and the other going up a much smaller, secondary canyon. Cole thought he recognized the trail going up the smaller canyon as the route he had taken from Red's camp. At the time, he was hurt, cold, and feverish, but he had taken enough time on his journey to check his back trail. He didn't believe that was the route to the mine, so he decided to stay beside the creek.

The trail remained free of debris, with only a few large rocks on it, the product of years of freeze and thaw cycles. Once in a while, a damp spot in the trail presented itself and Cole always took his time to examine them for any tracks. So far, only birds, small mammals and occasional bighorn mountain sheep had left their marks. Cole rounded a bend in the trail and found a large fallen snag blocking the path. He wished he had his axe. It would be difficult, but after breaking a few limbs, he thought he could crawl under the log. It took some doing, but finally he continued on the trail that was now quickly becoming more dirt than rock. Cole stopped and looked to his left. On the far side of the creek was a small draw where another creek entered the canyon and what appeared to be a faint trail following the creek.

Cole took a moment to ponder the situation. The main trail continued, and for all intents and purposes, looked pretty much the same as the trail that he had used to arrive at this point. The only thing that had probably traveled this trail in the last sixty years were deer, sheep or Red, but none of them would have left much evidence. Cole stared across the canyon again. It was a little over twenty feet wide, and he thought he saw the remains of a heavy wooden beam sticking out of the opposite canyon wall. The rest of the bridge must have been lost years ago to spring runoffs.

Cole wasn't the least bit sure, but he had a hunch that this trail would take him to the mine. Now all he had to do was figure out how to get across the steep canyon filled with roaring whitewater. A number of logs were caught in varying positions in the creek, and after awhile Cole decided that, with a little luck, he could make it. The first thing he did was to pull out his rope. After six tries, he lassoed a boulder on the far side of the canyon. With great effort and caution, he worked his way down and onto a slick log that allowed him to cross to the other side.

The mist rising from the churning water left Cole wet and clammy by the time he was across. He was glad he had lassoed the boulder, because the canyon wall was slick and hard to climb without the rope. Once he reached the top, Cole shook the water out of his jacket and then headed up the narrow footpath, leaving the rope for his return. In places, the trail narrowed to less than a foot wide and he could see where someone in the past had done some maintenance by using carefully placed large rocks to shore up the damage. This gave him hope that his journey was worth the time and effort.

The path was narrow, but the majority of it allowed for safe travel as Cole cautiously made his way up the canyon. The fact that pieces of the trail had tumbled into the creek fifty feet below was not lost on him, and he knew that if he slipped, the chances of surviving were almost zero. How in the hell did anyone ever find this place, much less dig a mine up here? His softly spoken words were lost in the rush of the water below as Cole rounded a small bend, and there it was- the mine.

Chapter 31

The mine entrance was on the opposite side of the canyon, but over the years a bridge of large rubble had accumulated in the canyon between the trail and the mine. A layer of wood debris covered the rubble, which enabled Cole to carefully walk to the other side. The water found a channel through the deep pile of debris and emerged in a large pool, where it joined the raging creek twenty feet below. As Cole got closer, he could see where the mine entrance had been enlarged from a small cave opening. Cole entered the mine, and immediately saw faded Indian petroglyphs decorating the cave's ceiling. Small weathered rock, dirt, mouse droppings and silt created a reasonably flat floor that led to a small room just inside the entrance. Cole could see where fires had burnt in the past, and he wondered how long since the cave had been used, and by whom. He didn't know if it was the Creager's mine or someone else's, or even a mine at all.

Cole stripped off his pack and retrieved his flashlight, then continued into the cave with the light in one hand and his shotgun in the other. Holes for torches had been bored into the walls and by the amount of carbon that remained on the walls and ceiling, the cave had seen a lot of use. Occasionally, portions of the old torches still stood in their holders, wrapped in dusty cobwebs.

Cole followed the tunnel another twenty feet until it split into separate passageways. He randomly chose left and followed the shaft upward as it narrowed to less than four feet. After another thirty yards, the passage ended in a large cavern over forty yards wide. Cole walked to the edge and peered into the sea of darkness below his feet.

If he hadn't been paying attention, he could have easily fallen. Cole could see level ground on the other side and thought maybe the passage continued, but if it did, it would be almost impossible to know for sure. He couldn't see any signs that anyone had tried to span the chasm, so he made his way back to where the main tunnel had split. He followed the other passage until it narrowed slightly and then gently turned left, but there was plenty of headroom to walk comfortably.

He had gone only about fifty feet when the passage veered back to the right, and Cole noticed something against the wall. He walked closer and found a rusty pick and old shovel amongst piles of rubble and chunks of rotten wooden shoring. He picked up the shovel and looked at it for a moment, trying to see a brand or date, but there was nothing. The passage meandered deeper into the mine, but Cole's attention had been caught by an old ladder that appeared to be going up and through the mine's eight-foot ceiling. Slowly, he followed the light of his flashlight into the dark, small opening in the ceiling. As much as he wanted to climb the ladder, he decided to check out the shaft first.

He would feel more secure if he knew what was down that way before climbing into the dark hole and possibly trapping himself. The small, three-foot hole didn't look the least bit inviting, nor did the heavy old ladder that creaked when he tested the first rung. The farther he walked down the passage, the wider it became until it spanned twenty feet. Suddenly, it broke into three tunnels. Cole examined the walls and floor but couldn't see any signs of excavation, footprints or torches, so he turned around and headed back to the ladder. Wherever the other passages led, it wasn't worth the risk for Cole to explore them by himself. All the caverns looked similar, and Cole could see how someone could easily get turned around and lost. If he had brought more flashlights and batteries, he may have looked at things differently. After all he had been through he had to be running low on luck.

Cole walked back to the ladder, then out to the mine entrance and began gathering firewood. It would start getting dark in another couple of hours, and in the steep canyon, probably sooner than that. There was plenty of wood debris on the rock bridge, and most of it around the edges was reasonably dry. Cole gathered three times the wood he thought he would need, something his father had always stressed when camping in strange country. The fire should keep him warm and protected, as long as he didn't fall asleep for too long and let it go out. In a short time, the small fire crackled to life, and the slight breeze from deep in the cave acted as a natural chimney that sucked the smoke out and up the canyon.

Once the fire was going strong, Cole took his shotgun and flashlight back to the ladder. It was old, but stronger than he had first thought, with three-inch poles cut into rungs and hammered in with spikes. The support legs were built from two sturdy, six-inch diameter logs and disappeared into the silt-covered floor. Cole wasn't sure the old wood of the ladder would hold him, so he climbed up one rung and jumped in place. The ladder creaked loudly but hardly budged. He set the shotgun against the wall, and with the flashlight in one hand, began to climb up through the cave ceiling. He had just poked his head into the blackness when a dozen or more bats flew out the tight opening, almost causing Cole to lose his grip and fall backwards. He felt lucky that he hadn't lost his flashlight, but the bats had taken his breath away. After a couple of minutes, he regained his composure and entered the tight space.

The first step was difficult, but he could see where it would become more natural once he got used to it. This mineshaft, unlike the others, had shoring beams in several places and showed a lot of old mining activity. Cole reached up to a rusty lantern that hung from the ceiling off a grayed six-by-six beam, and brought it down to eye level for closer examination. It looked in pretty good shape, other than the rust.

Several dusty wooden boxes were carefully stacked in an area beside a support post, and against them leaned a large sledgehammer and drilling rod. Cole could see where the miners had worked numerous small shafts, until they apparently panned out. Whoever had built this shaft had spent a lot of time and effort here, and now all that remained were dusty tools and rubble. Cole spent the next two hours examining each shaft in turn, but there didn't seem to be any traces of gold. He walked over to a second stack of old boxes and began sifting through them. A small puff of dust worked its way into the air as he moved several chunks of wood that sat on a dusty pile of debris to gain access to one of the larger boxes. Inside, he found what was left of an old newspaper. Cole couldn't make out much from the yellowed paper, but the date was clearly visible in faded numbers: 1869. The time frame would have been about right for the Creager brothers to have been here.

He climbed down the ladder and picked up his gun and headed to the mine entrance where his fire had burnt down. Cole added a couple of well-placed sticks, and with several deep puffs of breath, the flames shot back to life. Opening his leather food bag, he got out some jerky, then took a long drink from his canteen. He felt a little stupid—he had risked his life to find this mine, but it seemed played out. He didn't look forward to talking to Wes, nor, for that matter, explaining to anyone about his decision to once more challenge this mountain and possibly run into the grizzly. He thought to himself that the only real thing he had gotten out of this whole effort was to challenge his own deep-seated fears. He had done nothing to help the ranch or Allen.

The trek was difficult and had taken more guts and nerve to return alone than anything he had ever done. The cold night woke Cole numerous times, and each time he worked to stoke the fire back to warm flames.

The next morning, he opened his eyes to the birds chirping outside the mine. He pulled his small coffee pot out of his backpack, filled it with creek water, and set it on a flat rock inside the fire ring. With a little wood and a dry bird's nest, the small fire snapped back to life. Cole reviewed the many things in his mind that didn't make sense. If there weren't any gold in this mine, why would Virgil Creager tell the woman who found him the story of the bayonet? He knew he was dying, so why would he have lied to her? Nothing made sense unless he was telling the truth. A lot of the legends of gold had been true, and Cole knew they had found a little gold. No, probably more than a little, or how did the Dunns rise from small homesteaders barely scratching out a living to owners of one of the biggest ranches in Nebraska, almost overnight?

And why would Virgil tell her about the mine if, during the robbery, the Dunns had gotten everything? Creager had told her about the mine trail, not the ranch they lived on or the wagon with the false bottom. If there had been gold in the wagon in the secret compartment, they were obviously smart enough to put the wagon back together. The Dunns must have known where at least some of the gold was or saw it being loaded. And with the wagon still at the Creager's ranch, they must have used mules to pack it cross-country over the mountain. If they had driven the wagon across McCabe's ranch on their way to town, who knows how many people would have noticed. Using the mules would have made for a secret and smart get away.

Cole was convinced that Virgil knew his brother was mortally wounded, and by telling people about the mine, they would be watching for someone to start spending gold. Virgil must not have known who the bandits were, but they did know that anyone with that much gold would draw attention. Cole thought it odd that no one connected the fact that the Dunns had abandoned their ranch within a year of the murder, especially after their bitter feelings for Gillis McCabe. If anyone had the answers, they were no longer alive to tell.

The water in the pot began to boil, so Cole took it aside and sat it on another rock barely out of the flame. He sprinkled some coffee grounds into the top and then added some cold water from the creek to sink the grounds. The hot coffee tasted great and Cole drank the whole cup before he stood up and went to his backpack for more jerky.

The Creagers were obviously skilled craftsmen. Their cabin and the trail were built well, well enough that almost everything was still in good shape seventy years later. They didn't seem to hurry anything, either. They had thought through the wagon and hiding the gold to avoid local attention. They had built the cabin to last, so they could comfortably live there while they worked the mine and perhaps return to it years later. Cole was convinced that at least some of the gold had to still be in the mine. They would probably have had a certain amount of lesser quality gold at the grading building near the cabin, maybe even as a decoy. Carrying all the high-grade ore and nuggets back to the cabin every night didn't make sense. It would have been heavy and awkward and exposed them more often.

If they found high grade nuggets, then why not hide them close to the mine, and then when they were ready, move them quietly down to the main ranch in one or two loads using mules? No, Cole thought, there had to be some gold left, but where? He knew the Creagers were smart, and he figured they would only mine after the snow had melted in the spring, so as not to leave any trail for someone to stumble on. Probably they had packed supplies in on rainy days to wash away any tracks. Then when they reached their cabin, they would shut the gate at the stone fence, unload their supplies, and let their stock graze until they needed them again. The line cabin wasn't built then, so they wouldn't have had to worry about a lone cowboy looking for cattle surprising them.

Cole finished the second cup of coffee, but instead of packing up, he got another pot of cold water and put it back on the fire. He needed more time to think. It almost made him tired. He was working through all the scenarios, as fire quietly crackled in front of him. Where would they have hidden the higher quality gold that they mined everyday? They had to have packed the rougher, low-grade ore down to the grading shed every night, but Cole was convinced the real good stuff was hidden somewhere by the mine.

The second pot of water began to boil, and Cole poured himself another cup of coffee. They wouldn't go outside day after day to hide things in the pouring rain and expose themselves to unseen eyes. Sooner or later they would have gotten careless, and the Creagers were all about being slow and thorough. That meant one thing—the gold had to be hidden in the mine. Cole got up and stepped into the stark cave passage. Overall, the cave walls were somewhat smooth, except where they had been hit with a pickaxe, and the silt floor was a combination of dirt, gravel, and broken rock. Cole knew that they could have hidden the gold deep down one of the many passages, and finding it could take a long time. He didn't believe it was too far back, because it would need to be reasonably convenient for their daily ritual of hiding it. If they hid it in an area they didn't work, they would leave tracks right to it. No, the gold had to be somewhere that, with reasonable effort, someone could get to it on a regular basis and not be noticed.

Cole walked to the ladder and climbed into the shaft in the cave ceiling. He knew he didn't have long before the second set of flashlight batteries gave out, and he had no more spares. He took the old shovel standing beside the pick and carefully began poking and examining the walls and ceilings, but he found nothing. They could have hidden it high in a wall or a ceiling, but sooner or later moving the ladder to that spot everyday wouldn't make sense. The more he thought about it, the more he didn't think it would be in a ceiling. Besides, that would be the first place someone would look. With that, Cole started moving debris on the ground and tapping the shovel handle on the floor, listening for unusual sounds. But it was rock solid.

Frustrated, he climbed down the ladder. He knew it would be up there somewhere, but he had checked everything, and now his flashlight was slowly dimming. Cole walked back to the fire, sat down, and threw a few more sticks on the small flames. If the gold were up there, then someone had figured out a hiding space that he just couldn't find. Cole sat there and poured himself another cup. He looked back up the shaft at the ladder that sat in the shadows. Where could they have hidden it?

He thought about the secret room at the house, and Allen's discussion of hiding things in plain sight. Was he missing something? For the next twenty minutes, he stared quietly down the cavern trying to determine what he had missed. Suddenly, he noticed movement by the ladder. In the shadows, he wasn't sure what it was, but he carefully walked toward it a few steps and stood perfectly still, allowing his eyes to adjust to the dark. After a couple of minutes, Cole thought the sound came from a mouse, no, it was larger, much larger. It was a pack rat.

The body was three inches across and the tail was at least twice that. Cole leaned against the wall of the cave and watched as the rat ran past him and hopped over to where some of his gear lay near the fire. The rat picked up a small piece of bread that Cole hadn't packed up from breakfast, turned, and scampered past him. Cole's first reaction was to throw a rock at it, but for some reason he let the rat hop past and disappear into a small pile of rubble six feet from the ladder. The pile was small, roughly eighteen inches square and three inches high, a comfortable hideout for a small mouse, but way too small for the large rat that just entered.

Until now, Cole hadn't paid any attention to the four inch high pile of small rocks, debris, and dirt near the ladder or to the other almost identical piles that were scattered around the cave floor. He had walked past all of them at least a dozen times examining the passages and old mining areas, but never did he give even a second look to these inconspicuous piles of dirt and dusty gravel.

Cole went back and grabbed the shovel he had taken from the ceiling shaft and began removing the rubble pile where the packrat had disappeared. There was a hole in the floor that was barely big enough for the rat to have disappeared through. He carefully took the handle of the shovel and poked the spot where the rubble had been moved. A hollow thumping filled the passage, the sound of wood hitting wood. Cole dropped to his knees and began pulling the remaining dirt and gravel away with his hands. He pushed and scraped the dirt away, until he had exposed what looked like a small wooden door. The door was built of thick planks, about sixteen inches square, slightly smaller than the pile that hid it. He wedged his shovel into the hole in its top and with one firm movement, the heavy planked door opened enough for him to wrap his fingers around an edge and pull it completely open.

It was dark, and a musty smell came from the hole. Cole jumped back as the rat skittered past him from the darkness, and in seconds it had made its way down the shaft and out the opening. Cole carefully shoved his hand into the darkness several inches and touched the rat's nest of leaves, twigs and a few faded pieces of paper. Then he reached a little further and felt something like small pieces of gravel. He carefully closed his hand around a couple of the pieces and, with a tight fist, pulled his hand from the hole. He got up and walked back over to the fire and slowly opened his fist.

He held three chunks of quartzite rock, each with several thick, rich, veins of gold running through them that sparkled in the light of the fire. A huge smile filled Cole's face, as he realized the legends of gold had been true. He had found Creager's mine. Cole sat down beside the fire and stared at the chunks of stone with their sparkling yellow veins of gold. He knew this would change his life and the lives of many others. It was hard to believe everything was real. Maybe he could buy back the ranch and cattle and then some, and have money left over to start developing the pastures. Julie would go nuts. It was a good day, a real good day.

Chapter 32

Cole sat beside the fire and stared at the gold nuggets, small chunks of rich ore that he had carefully placed beside the fire. He picked up a piece of gold the size of a marble and rolled its rough sides against his fingers, whispering, "I found it, Creager. I found your gold!" He thought about Julie and how much he loved her and the many things he could now change. He took a deep breath. He wondered about the well-being of Allen, how Dodge and Wilson had died trying to save the ranch, and how now he could at least make things right.

Finally, he reached for his pack and took out the two heavy cotton bags. He picked up one chunk at a time and put them in the bag. He then carried both bags and his pack back to the hole in the floor and began scooping out handfuls of ore and nuggets. He loaded thirty pounds of ore into each bag and tightly tied the tops with strings of deer hide. When he was done, one last time he reached into the hole. In the darkness, he felt hundreds of small ore pieces, even after filling two large bags. He withdrew his hand, closed the heavy plank lid and carefully began replacing all the small rock and silt back over the cover, until it looked as close to how he had found it as possible. Then he took his coat and dragged the ground to remove any sign of his footprints from the cave floor. When he was done, the floor looked as natural and aged as all the other areas of the mine, and Cole prayed it would keep his secret.

He placed his remaining gear in a neat pile in the corner created by a natural depression where the floor and wall met, next he placed small rocks and silt on top until it was well hidden. Carefully he placed the rope and jerky on top of the two sacks and closed his pack. His load would consist of sixty pounds of gold, his shotgun, and enough jerky, water and rope for the trip back. Before hoisting the pack, he used his coat to sweep away signs of his presence and threw the partially burned logs into the creek.

The pack was heavy, and sometimes he felt the rough ore pressing against the back of his coat. But it felt great to be carrying it down the steep canyon trail. The load was a little awkward, but thirty minutes later, he was at the bank of the creek. The rope that he had lassoed to a boulder was still where he had left it, and he used it to climb down to the creek bank. Once on the bank, he removed his pack and with branches and debris, covered his path up the slope the best he could. There was no way to remove the rope, so he did his best to cover it with branches. After putting his pack back on, he used a strong, bark less stick for balance as he crossed the slick mossy rocks back to the other side. Several times his foot slipped into the creek, soaking him to the knees.

Finally he reached the other side and sat down on a boulder just above the water. It had taken far more energy than he had thought to make it across, and he was tired. Removing his pack, he pulled a piece of jerky out and spent a few minutes eating and resting. He hadn't needed a rope to climb down the near bank, but he wasn't sure with the new heavy load if he could climb the steep bank without one. Cole covered his tracks as well as possible, then put his pack on and cautiously began climbing.

Struggling, he reached the top where he was filled with relief and comfort, for he knew the most dangerous stretch was behind him. He continued at a good pace down the trail, ever watchful for any sign of trouble, but with the exception of the birds and the raging creek, all was quiet. He passed the canyon trail that led to Red's camp but only gave it a glance and a smile. He had found the mine and gold, and that was all that mattered. As he walked down the main trail, he wondered if Red were busy with his "yellie." The thought made Cole laugh to himself. Red had saved his life and he was special, very special.

He made great time and only stopped at the meadow by Creager's cabin long enough for a drink. His shoulders ached, but he trudged along, and after a little less than two hours was close to the meadow where he had left Patch and Pumpkin. He was within a hundred yards of the clearing when he bent under a dead branch, his pack caught, and snapped with a loud pop. Everything had been so quiet up until then that he stopped for a moment and listened, but he heard only the normal sounds of the mountain. Finally, he arrived at the meadow. When he lifted the branch that hid the trail to the canyon, he saw Jay's handkerchief, and he thought about Jay and their friendship. Someday, he would go back and square things with that bear, and he vowed to help Suzie. Cole entered the gentle grade of the benched meadow, the warm sunshine again hitting his face. He was glad to be out of the dark timber.

Immediately, he noticed that Patch and Pumpkin were missing. From the looks of things it appeared that Patch had once again chewed through his picket rope. Cole had only scanned the clearing for a couple of seconds, when he noticed them both grazing peacefully on the next small ridge. He took a deep breath, because he needed those mules to get the gold out. He walked over to the spruce tree where he had hidden his gear, leaned his gun against it and removed the canvas manty. He was sorting through his stuff, when he remembered the old rusty bayonet. He turned and spotted it sticking in front of the huge dead Limber Pine where he had left it. He walked over and took a second to look at the huge monarch with its hundreds of thick dead limbs, before he reached down to pick up the bayonet. In the excitement, he sure didn't want to forget it, for it was the object of legends.

Cole was just bending down for the bayonet, when he heard several guns being cocked. "Well, Mr. Morgan, why don't you slowly turn around and put your hands up," said a firm gravelly voice that Cole immediately recognized as Prentice's.

Prentice had caught him flat footed. The giant tree and its multitude of massive limbs made it impossible to escape. He had let his guard down and left the shotgun against the spruce with the rest of the gear, and now all he had was the small pocketknife.

"I said turn around, Cole. I'd prefer not to shoot you in the back. But if I have to, that's fine by me," Prentice sneered.

Cole slowly turned around and faced Prentice, whose face was heavily bandaged on one side. Jake Prentice, John's cousin, was dragging his backpack into the meadow while another man that Cole recognized from the dance fight as a Dunn held another pistol on Cole.

"Well, Cole what do we have in the pack—gold, maybe?" Prentice laughed. Jake held out a handful of rich chunks of gold ore and nuggets for everyone to see.

"I've never hated or wanted to kill a man more than I want to kill you, Cole, but I've had to wait till you found our gold. You're one lucky son of a bitch. You've been able to figure out all the McCabe mysteries, and I knew sooner or later you'd figure out where the gold was. I also knew you'd make a mistake, sooner or later."

Cole knew he had to stall for time or Prentice would shoot him, so he asked, "Was it your family that died in the plane wreck?"

"I guess it doesn't hurt to tell you that it was my first cousins, Leroy and Thelma Dunn. You see, Cole, my mother was a Dunn, and we're a close family, maybe not the nicest family, but close." With that Jake and the other Dunn laughed.

"To tell you the truth, Cole, we would have loved to have gone hunting you yesterday, but we thought your trail was over there where your mules are. We were looking on the wrong ridge, but we found your gear just before you arrived. It was nice of you to break that branch back there to tell us you were coming."

For the first time, Prentice seemed to notice the rusty bayonet sticking in the ground. "Well, well, what do we have here? Could this be the legendary bayonet that shows the way? So it really does exist, and somehow you found it. Cole, why don't you take a few steps back so I won't have to shoot you yet?" Prentice spoke in a casual, authoritative voice. Cole inched back, and with his second step, he dove for the bayonet. He had just grabbed it when he heard and felt the shot. Pain sliced through his thigh, and he rolled on the ground, dropping the bayonet. "Now that was plain stupid for a smart young man like you. You almost made me kill you, and I haven't started having fun yet." Prentice picked up the bayonet, as Cole struggled to stop the bleeding. Prentice carefully examined the bayonet and then flung it into the middle of the tangled web of the snag's limbs, saying, "I guess we won't be needing this any more."

"It sure was nice of you to pack out all this gold for us. Tell you what, tell us where the rest is, and we'll just kill you, take the gold, and quietly disappear."

"What if I refuse?"

"Then we'll kill you and then go down and kill Julie and her whole family, that's all," replied Prentice. He looked back at the others and smiled. "One way or the other, you'll die."

Prentice suddenly stopped and raised his unarmed hand in the air for everyone to be quiet. "Did you hear that?"

"Yeah," Jake said. "It sounds like clicking."

Everyone listened as Prentice said, "There it is again, that clicking sound. It's coming from the woods."

A branch snapped and broke the silence as the three men looked at each other and then toward the forest where Cole had hidden his gear. Each man's face went white when a huge nine-hundred-pound, growling mass of brown fur burst through the dense trees into the meadow. The grizzly's massive mouth opened wide and grabbed Jake Prentice by the shoulder and shook him like a rag doll and threw his lifeless body to the ground. Prentice and Dunn opened fire with their pistols at close range, but it only intensified the bear's rage. With unbelievable speed, it turned and charged Dunn, who stood holding a smoking, empty gun. Dunn's horrible scream lasted only seconds before the huge paw ripped his chest open and threw his bloody body to the ground.

Prentice emptied his gun into the bear's body. The beast turned and began walking toward a cornered John Prentice. He froze for only a second, backing up as the bear charged. He smashed his empty gun into the bear's head with all his strength, to no avail. In one powerful motion, it knocked him backwards over Cole to the ground. Cole rolled sideways into the thick limbs of the fallen tree, as the bear let out a deafening roar. With one swipe of his huge paw, the bear ripped a large chunk of flesh from Prentice's thigh and then stepped on his chest. Prentice screamed, as the sound of his ribs breaking shook the woods. The ferocity of the attack and the speed with which the bear inflicted fatal wounds was incredible. Slowly, the killer turned and faced Cole, blood dripping from his mouth.

In a panic, Cole turned and frantically crawled into the maze of thick dead limbs. Maybe somehow the tree's heavy trunk and limbs might allow him an avenue of escape, or at least postpone the inevitable. His thigh screamed with pain as he pulled and twisted himself further away from Prentice's body and deeper into the thickest part of the huge, fallen monarch. Suddenly, he felt a tug on his boot, and then he felt himself being jerked backward. He turned to see the bear's claws imbedded in his boot. He smelled the bear's terrible odor and foul breath, and bright red blood oozed from the bear's thick coat. The bear held his boot, and Cole felt the pain of a claw digging into the meat of his heel as the bear tried to pull him out of the tangled branches. The grizzly raised his head and roared in anger. Cole pointed his foot as the bear yanked again, taking the cowboy boot and a bit of his flesh with it.

Everything was going so fast, but Cole's brain worked in slow motion. It was the same way he had felt when the bear had pushed him over the cliff, and he could remember how slow the fall seemed. The huge bear drooled at Cole through the thick limbs, slowly rocking from side to side, his teeth snapping as he made an intense, low growl. Cole turned and looked, then saw a small cavity near the trunk of the tree and scrambled toward it. He had nearly reached it, when he saw the rusty bayonet that Prentice had tossed into the tangled mess of limbs.

Behind him, the bear drew closer, breaking branch by branch with its massive front legs, as it pawed its way through the maze. Cole grabbed the bayonet handle and rolled under the branches, just as the bear broke through several more limbs, gnashing his teeth at where he'd just been. The bear was drooling red froth, and it opened its mouth in a terrifying roar. The sound was horrifying, and Cole knew that it would only be moments before the grizzly's head would break through the remaining limbs and finish the job. Trickles of salty sweat rolled down his face and into his eyes, and he knew he wouldn't survive the next surge. For a moment, the bear stopped and intently stared at Cole, slowly gnashing his teeth.

Cole readied himself with the handle of the old bayonet tightly gripped in his right hand. With a loud pop, the huge branch broke and the bear thrust its head further into the cavity. Cole gritted his teeth, screamed, and lunged forward at the same time with all his might. With every bit of strength he had, he thrust the bayonet at the eye of the bear. The bayonet buried itself deep in the socket, and the beast roared in pain and swung his huge paw at Cole. Twelve inches of old, rusted bayonet had buried itself totally into the massive head of the bear, but still Cole felt the smash of the bear's paw throw him backwards against the log. The enraged bear flailed its forelegs within the tight branches as he tried to move closer to Cole. The grizzly lunged one last time, trying to grab Cole with its massive paw. In one incredibly quick move, Cole threw himself further into the maze of limbs, kicking the bear's paw with his booted foot. The bear suddenly dropped on top of his foot and lay still.

Several seconds passed before Cole opened his eyes. He slid his foot out from under the bear, losing his last boot. He was hurt, his foot mangled, his thigh deeply gashed, and he had numerous cuts, but he was alive. The bear's huge body lay partially over the large branch that had protected him and pinned his foot. Cole heard guttural death groans coming from the bear, then a few seconds later the beast was silent.

Chapter 33

Cole crawled from the maze of limbs into the meadow. With pain, he rose to his feet and limped to the pack of supplies Jake Prentice had dragged from the woods. He noticed chunks of ore and nuggets of gold sprinkled over a small area from the open sack, their color reflecting in the sunlight. Cole sat down and first bandaged his thigh and then carefully dressed his foot. When finished, he dragged himself to the spilled bag of gold, and carefully returned each piece to the bag. He was exhausted and his head spun, so he lay back in the soft grass and warm sun and passed out.

He awoke to a gentle nudge by Patch, who was standing over him, blocking the sun. He sat up and quietly laughed. "So Patch, even with the smell of blood and a dead bear, you came over to see me, and am I glad to see you!" Pumpkin fidgeted around the dead grizzly and stayed back twenty feet, staring at the bear's body. Cole felt better and worked his way back over to the giant tree. With effort, he tried to retrieve the boot for his good foot but couldn't. His other foot was swollen enough that he didn't think he could get the boot on, even if he did find it. He had brought a spare pair of heavy wool socks, so he put them on both feet, and they helped keep the bandages in place.

It took over an hour, but Cole finally got Patch and Pumpkin saddled and loaded, and he painfully mounted up. Patch was a smooth ride and Cole appreciated this more now than ever before.

Three hours later, just at dark, the two mules and Cole rode into the line cabin. Cole was exhausted, and with all the effort he could muster unloaded and unsaddled the mules, then corralled them and shut the gate. He walked into the cabin and sat on the bed to rest for a moment, the next thing he knew the sun was shining and it was morning. Sometime in the night, he had pulled several blankets over himself, and the deep sleep had slightly revived him. However, the new injuries and blood loss left him weak as he struggled out the door to the creek to get some water.

He stopped to get his gun, then decided it wasn't necessary, and worked his way down to the creek with the bucket. It was difficult, but he filled the bucket and headed back to the cabin and drank, ate jerky, and painfully washed his wounds. The thigh wound was deep and four inches long. The bear had dug out almost three quarters of an inch of meat off the bottom of his heal, but somehow missed the tendon.

Several hours later, Cole was loaded and headed down the trail to the ranch house. It would be a hard ride, and every step Patch made, regardless of how smooth the mule was, hurt to some degree. Five hours later, he made it to the Canvas Creek trailhead, his foot was black and blue and badly swollen, and he wasn't sure he could make it to the ranch. His energy was almost gone, but not his determination.

* * *

There was a full moon, and after a hard day of moving, Julie had decided to relax on the porch by herself. Allen was recovering, and her dad was supervising the moving of the ranch. She thought about Cole almost every minute and wondered if she had done the right thing letting him go. Suddenly, she heard something on the main road below the house. Out of the darkness rode Cole, slumped over Patch's saddle, leading a tired Pumpkin.

Julie screamed and ran toward Cole, and people came out of the bunkhouse and the main house to see what was happening. Ballard took care of the mules, unloading and rubbing them down, while the others carried Cole into a spare bedroom in the main house.

The bloody bandages and Cole's pale color worried Julie as the men stripped him to his shorts, while Sally and Julie boiled water and made fresh bandages. Cole opened his eyes and smiled at Julie for a moment, then passed out while they changed the dressings.

A cold, wet washcloth flowed across Cole's forehead, and he opened his eyes. The bandaging was done, and Cole scanned the room. Everyone stood looking with concern at him. Julie saw his eyes open first. "Cole, how can you keep doing this to yourself, I have a mind . . ."

Cole put his finger to Julie's lips. "I found it. I found Creager's gold."

Everyone looked at Cole and then at each other. Then they heard Ballard's voice behind them. "Look what Cole brought back!" He poured one of the bags of gold onto the floor, and everyone gasped.

"By God, he did!" Wes said, stooping down to pick up several nuggets. "Cole did it"!

Cole took Julie's hand. "I missed you, oh how I missed you. How's Allen doing? Is he alive?"

"Yes, Allen is alive and doing much better. We hope to have him home from the hospital next week and I missed you too."

Cole smiled and closed his eyes. He needed more rest.

The next day, Cole awoke to see Doctor Knight cleaning his thigh wound and Julie standing behind him. "Damn Doc, what are you doing to me?"

"Son, you're the most unbelievable patient I ever had. You're lucky this infection hasn't taken off worse than it did, or you would have lost this leg. I hear you finally found it, old Creager's gold. Well it about killed you to do it. Would you mind doing both of us a favor and take it easy for a while? I'm getting tired of patching you up. I'll be done here in a few minutes, just hold still so I don't cut anything that I'm not intending to."

Julie turned her head and headed out of the room. Cole was still groggy and hadn't heard anything. About ten minutes later, Wes and Julie entered the room followed by Sheriff Burris, the attorney, George King, and another man sporting a badge on his chest. "How you doing, Cole? You look a lot better than you did last night. This is Sheriff Moore from Cody. I'll let George and the sheriff explain," Wes said.

George walked over to Cole's bed. "Cole, I just told Wes and Sally that my secretary, Miss Bright—I don't know that you ever met her, she had polio when she was young—anyway, the long and short is that she received five hundred dollars from Don Hamilton to tell him what we were doing about coming up with the money for the ranch. Well, when she found out that two men were killed and one more might die, she came into my office and cried like a baby and told me what happened. She's under arrest right now, and so is their bank's attorney, Don Hamilton. When I explained to the judge what happened, he put a stay of execution order on The Greybull's sale. Basically, that means everyone can stay put until the court sorts this thing out. I'm sure Prentice will have something to say and fight us in court, but at least we know what part the bank played in this deal."

Cole looked at George, in a soft voice he spoke, "Somehow, I don't think Prentice can bear to deal with this any more." He smiled and closed his eyes.

One Year Later

Julie and Cole had ridden for three hours up the valley, Cole on Patch and Julie on Gun Smoke. They were talking about how Suzie and her new husband, Matt Jones, were doing in Casper. The pastures were lush with new bunchgrass varieties, and cows with newborn calves dotted the rich landscape. The ranch had doubled its herd the past two years due to watering programs and range management changes and the huge old cross that marked Gillis McCabe's grave still towered over the valley.

The warm spring day was perfect for a ride. They carefully worked their mounts up the steep grade to the cross and tied them to an old tree, like so many times before. Cole carefully removed three stuffed socks from his saddlebags and set them on the ground beneath the cross. He removed the contents from two socks and Julie, the other. Inside were three Mason jars of strawberry jelly, Red's favorite. They waited on a large rock ten yards from the base of the cross. Shortly Red emerged from a stand of dense evergreens, where he had obviously been watching and waiting. He wore a dirty, bright red shirt that was even brighter than his gangly red hair, and he looked like the winter had been a little hard on him. He had lost another front tooth. He still tilted his head to one side, and when he smiled, his personality was as sharp as ever.

"Yellie?" Red asked.

Cole nodded. "Yellie."

Red quickly grabbed up the three jars and disappeared as quickly as he had arrived. On the way down the mountain, Cole began to laugh.

"What are you laughing about?" Julie demanded.

Cole looked back at her and said, "Did you notice he was wearing Ballard's new shirt?"

About The Author

Stephen Benson Smart is a Landscape Architect in Spokane, Washington. He has owned and operated a landscape construction firm and nursery for thirty-three years. Steve grew up on several ranger stations in Montana before moving around the country and finally settling in the Pacific Northwest where he graduated from Washington State University in 1975.

His hobbies are cartooning and packing, which he has done for over thirty years in Idaho, Montana, and Wyoming. While on a hunting trip to Wyoming, Steve fell in love with the country and history surrounding the small town of Meeteetse. *Whispers of The Greybull* was inspired by this town and the mountainous terrain bordering it.

I hope you have enjoyed reading this book and I look forward
to hearing what you think of this adventure/mystery.

Best wishes, *Stephen B. Smart*

For more on Stephen B. Smart and *Whispers of The Greybull,*
please visit:

www.authorstephenbsmart.com

Please email the author at:

authorstephenbsmart@yahoo.com

with any comments or feedback.